PRAISE FOR SIMON KERNICK

SIEGE

"Nonstop action. . . . A strong cast of supporting characters supplies a continuing stream of engaging subplots that play out within the larger takeover story. Kernick keeps all the balls in the air as he delivers an exciting performance."

—*Publishers Weekly*

"A fast-moving yarn with short chapters, tight writing, plenty of violence, and characters both flawed and believable. . . . Kernick is a first-rate storyteller."

—*Kirkus Reviews*

ULTIMATUM

"A fast-paced tale of terrorism, murder, cops, snitches, under-cover cops, and betrayal. . . . Lots of action."

—*Booklist*

"Bloodcurdling action and suspense. . . . A fast and satisfying read."

—*Kirkus Reviews*

ALSO BY SIMON KERNICK

THE LAST 10 SECONDS

A Thriller

SIMON KERNICK

ATRIA PAPERBACK

NEW YORK   LONDON   TORONTO   SYDNEY   NEW DELHI

ATRIA PAPERBACK
A Division of Simon & Schuster, Inc.
1230 Avenue of the Americas
New York, NY 10020

First Atria Paperback edition December 2014

ATRIA PAPERBACK and colophon are trademarks of Simon & Schuster, Inc.

For information about special discounts for bulk purchases, please contact Simon & Schuster Special Sales at 1-866-506-1949 or business@simonandschuster.com.

The Simon & Schuster Speakers Bureau can bring authors to your live event. For more information or to book an event, contact the Simon & Schuster Speakers Bureau at 1-866-248-3049 or visit our website at www.simonspeakers.com.

Designed by Kyoko Watanabe
Cover design by Jae Song
Cover image © Shutterstock

Manufactured in the United States of America

10 9 8 7 6 5 4 3 2 1

Library of Congress Cataloging-in-Publication Data

Kernick, Simon
    The last 10 seconds / by Simon Kernick.—First Atria Books Trade paperback edition.
        pages cm
    "Originally published in Great Britain by Transworld..."—T.p. verso. persons—Investigation—Fiction. I. Title. II. Title: Last ten seconds.
    PR6111.E76L37 2012
    823'.92—dc23

                          2012042600

ISBN: 978–1–4767–0620–7
ISBN: 978–1–4767–0622–1 (ebook)

THE
LAST
10
SECONDS

Today
8:05 A.M.

An empty shell of a building deep in the heart of the city. It's early, the first spears of bright sunlight advancing through the holes in the wall where the windows are meant to be, and here I am watching my blood form a visibly growing pool on the dusty concrete floor in front of me.

Propping myself further back against the wall, the gun still dangling precariously from my trigger finger, I concentrate on keeping my eyes open, forcing myself to focus on the carnage in this vast, empty room.

Three men dead. Two are lying sprawled on their fronts, arms outstretched theatrically, a dozen feet and hugely differing circumstances separating them. The third—a big man in a blood-drenched sky-blue polo shirt and jeans, younger than the others—is bound to a chair with flex, his head slumped forward, his thick, sandy-blond hair bisected by a huge hole where the bullet exited.

Outside in the distance, I can hear the faint, drifting buzz of traffic. But it all seems so far away, and as I listen it seems to grow fainter, consumed by the leaden silence inside the room—a silence that seems to rise up from the floor like some dark, malignant force, extinguishing all the life around it. It's going to extinguish me soon enough too. I'm bleeding to death, trapped on the third floor of this deserted place, a bullet in my gut, another in my right thigh, rendering the leg useless, a stiff coldness beginning to envelop me.

I've thought about death a great deal over the years, but always in a vague and abstract manner, never quite affording it the respect it deserves, even though I've skirted close to it on too many occasions.

But as I sit here, wounded and helpless, wondering how I've got myself into this terrible tomb-like place, I can hear death's steady, inevitable approach and I know there's no escape. That's the hardest thing to accept, the fact that my life is finally coming to an end, and I wonder briefly in these last few seconds, as the pain and the shock squeeze at my insides, whether there's anyone left to mourn my passing. Whether I'll even be remembered in ten years' time.

And then I hear it. A sound directly outside the door. The scrape of a foot on the floor.

Jesus. Is this nightmare still not over? Is there a final act to come?

I clench my teeth and slowly raise my gun arm, the effort almost too much to bear, thinking that I've fired five shots, so I should have one more left.

A shadow falls across the doorway and then, in an instant, a dark-haired woman in casual clothes is standing there, a warrant card in one outstretched hand and what looks like a can of pepper spray in the other. "Police!" she shouts, her voice tight with tension as it echoes through the room.

She opens her mouth to say something else, her eyes wide with shock as they take in the scene of slaughter in front of her, before finally her gaze comes to rest on me.

This is when she frowns in startled recognition. "Sean?"

Even in my weakened state, I manage to crack something close to a smile. "Hello, Tina."

"What the hell's happened?" she asks, taking a step forward, ignoring the fact that I'm still pointing my gun at her.

And that's when the shooting starts.

PART I

Thursday, 7:00 P.M.
37 Hours Ago

One

He was short, maybe five seven, with a build that was either slim or scrawny depending on how charitable you were feeling, and he was dressed in cheap gray slacks, a neatly ironed white shirt, and a dark tie with an unfashionably small knot. His hair, dead straight and surprisingly thick, was the only thing unconventional about him, falling down like a medieval helmet to his shoulders. Otherwise he looked like a perfectly ordinary, if slightly nerdish, young man. But then, in newly promoted Detective Inspector Tina Boyd's experience as a police officer, even the most brutal murderers tend to look just the same as everyone else.

As she watched from the back seat of the Kia Sorento, its blacked-out windows shielding her from the gaze of the outside world, thirty-two-year-old alarm engineer Andrew Kent walked by a pregnant woman, giving her the faintest of glances as he passed.

Andrew Kent. Even his name was ordinary.

He carried a small backpack slung casually over one shoulder, and Tina wondered if it contained the tools of his illicit trade. Ten years ago, the thought would have made her visibly shudder, but now she just watched him coldly as he turned the corner into the quiet residential street where he'd lived for the past four and a half years, heading for his front door thirty yards down, moving in a lazy shuffle reminiscent of a teenager. He looked like he didn't have a care in the world, and Tina smiled to herself, pleased that they'd finally got him after an investigation that, in one form or another, had lasted close to two years.

She picked up her radio, relishing the hugely deserved shock Kent was about to get. "Car three to all units, suspect approaching north along Wisbey Crescent. You should have the eyeball any time now."

"Car one to all units, we're ready," barked Tina's immediate boss, Detective Chief Inspector Dougie MacLeod, the head of Camden's Murder Investigation Team, or CMIT as most people preferred to call it.

Cars two, four, and five gave the same message, that they too were ready. They'd come mob-handed today: fifteen officers in all on Wisbey Crescent itself, all plainclothes, and a further two dozen uniforms at four different points in the streets around to cut off any escape. The Kent arrest was going to be high profile and the Met couldn't afford any mistakes.

But as Kent ambled down the street, now barely ten yards from the front door of the run-down townhouse that housed his first-floor flat, something happened. He began to slow down, then came to a stop, looking at one of the parked vehicles just up ahead. It was a white Ford Transit with "Renham & Son Carpentry" written in bold lettering on the side. Car three.

And in that moment, inexplicably, Andrew Kent seemed to realize that they'd come for him.

He swung around and started running, just as MacLeod's urgent shout came over the radio, "Go! Go! Go!" and the four cars full of detectives disgorged their loads onto the road in a cacophony of yells and commands designed to immediately cow their target.

The first out of the Transit was Detective Constable Dan Grier, all six foot four of him, the young blond graduate destined for the fast track, whose gangly legs ate up the distance between him and Kent within a couple of seconds. But as Grier flung out an arm to apprehend his quarry, Kent turned, swatted it out of the way with one hand, and launched the other upward into his neck in a clinically accurate chop. As Tina watched aghast, Grier went down like a collapsing pole of beans, while Kent, the shuffling five-foot-seven nerd, did a surprisingly nimble sidestep which completely wrong-footed Detective Constable Anji Rodriguez, who liked to bang on that she'd once represented England Under-16s at netball but who tripped like a rank amateur when she tried to grab hold of him. She tumbled over on her side and hit the tarmac with an audible smack, forming an immediate obstacle to the officers coming behind her, one of whom, Detective Sergeant Simon Tilley, lost his footing as he tried to hurdle over her rolling form, and went down as well.

The whole thing was surreal, like something out of the Keystone Kops. It would have been funny watching Kent take off in the direction he'd come, running down the middle of the road with more than a dozen cops scrambling over one another in hot pursuit, led by a panting, red-faced DCI Dougie MacLeod, if it hadn't been for the fact that this was a man far too dangerous to let escape.

Tina had wanted to be in on the actual arrest, had wanted to be one of the ones who put Andrew Kent in cuffs, but she was carrying a limp from a gunshot wound to the foot she'd received on a job the previous year and, much to her annoyance, the doctors had still not declared her fully fit for active duty, which meant she'd had to leave the arrest to her colleagues, something that now seemed grimly ironic as she watched Kent's rapid approach through the back window.

She was reluctantly impressed by his speed and coolness under pressure as she watched him get closer and closer, his angle changing as he made for the pavement on her side of the road, the expression on his face one of intense concentration.

Ten yards, eight yards, six yards . . .

She gripped the handle on the car door and placed her good foot against its base.

Four yards. She could hear his panting.

Two yards, and she kicked open the door in a single sudden movement, hoping she'd timed it right.

She had. Unable to stop himself, Kent sprinted into it just as it reached the limits of its hinges, the force of the collision sending him somersaulting over the top.

The adrenaline surged through Tina as she exploded out of the car, a pent-up ball of excitement and rage, half stumbling on her bad leg but righting herself through sheer force of will, a can of CS spray her only weapon.

Kent was clearly winded, but he was already rolling over onto his back, putting one hand down for support so he could jump back up, his eyes widening as he saw Tina bear down on him.

The laws governing arrests in the UK are some of the strictest in the world. Only the minimum force required to control a suspect should be used. But Tina had always treated the rules with flexibility, and she leaped onto Kent's stomach, knees first, putting all her weight into it, ignoring his gasp of pain as she positioned herself astride his chest and gave his open mouth and eyes a liberal shot of CS spray, leaning back so she wasn't affected herself.

He coughed, spluttered, and struggled under her, still showing reserves of fight she hadn't expected, and almost knocked her off, so she punched him in the face with all her strength. Once, twice, three times, feeling a terrifying exhilaration as her fist connected with the soft flesh of his cheek, the blows strong and angry enough to knock his head on the concrete each time they landed.

"Andrew Michael Kent," she snarled as he fought for breath, the resistance seeping out of him now as her colleagues began arriving in numbers, several of them pinning his limbs to the ground, "I'm arresting you on suspicion of murder. You do not have to say anything but it may harm your defense if you do not mention when questioned something which you later rely on in court. Anything you do say may be given in evidence."

"I'm innocent!" he howled, before breaking into a fit of coughing.

"You and every other one I've ever nicked," Tina grunted, getting to her feet and leaving her colleagues to finish off the arrest, unnerved but not surprised by how much she'd enjoyed hurting him.

Two

The media had dubbed him the Night Creeper. For a period of twenty-three months, he'd terrorized London, raping and murdering a total of five women in their own homes. The victims were, it seemed, all picked at random, but they also fit a broad profile. They were white, single, successful in their careers, and physically attractive. The youngest was aged just twenty-five, the oldest thirty-seven, and what had particularly focused media attention was that there was never any sign of forced entry to the victims' homes, even though all the properties were considered secure, and fitted with new alarm systems. This gave an almost mystical power to the Night Creeper—a man who could break in anywhere at will, making no sound and leaving no trace—and it had increased the fear among attractive and single London career women, and their families, no end.

When Tina had joined CMIT four months earlier, successfully applying for a vacant DI's position, the pressure on the police for an arrest had been intense. But leads had been scarce. The killer was forensically aware, leaving behind little in the way of clues, and no witnesses had ever reported seeing him.

In the end, it was that old classic "good old-fashioned police work" that finally led to the arrest, and the person who'd spotted the clue was Tina herself.

While interviewing a close friend of the last victim, Adrienne Menzies, Tina had discovered that the alarm system in Adrienne's apartment had only been installed a few weeks earlier and that the man who'd installed it had, in the words of the friend, "given Adrienne the shivers." Because of the length of time between the installation and the murder, and the vagueness of the friend's words, Tina hadn't initially been optimistic of a link, and the colleague who was with her at the interview, young, up-and-coming DC Dan Grier, had discounted it immediately. But when Tina thought about it more, it had struck her that one foolproof way of getting through alarms on buildings and residences was if you'd fitted them yourself, so she'd contacted the companies who'd installed the alarms at the other properties and asked them to supply the name of the engineer who'd carried out the work.

She would always remember that feeling she got, that utter exhilaration, when they all came back with the same name. Andrew Kent. Freelance engineer. Using his freelance status to keep one step ahead of the police, and his position to pick his victims at leisure. Their killer.

And now, thanks in large part to Tina, they'd finally got him.

She took a long drag on her cigarette and stubbed it underfoot, ignoring the sour expression on the face of a middle-aged woman among the throng of onlookers now gathering at the edge of the cordon that had been set up around Andrew Kent's building. It was dusk now and Kent himself had already been taken away to Holborn police station to have a DNA swab taken, await questioning, and, of course, get any medical treatment he needed as a result of Tina's enthusiastic arrest technique.

In the meantime, the team needed to search his flat for any evidence linking him to the crimes. They'd managed to get a warrant two days earlier, just as Kent emerged as their chief suspect, but the place was so heavily alarmed that they hadn't been able to bypass the security without potentially alerting him, even with the expertise they had available. Now, though, they had Kent's keys, and as Tina put on her plastic coveralls and walked past the assembled police vehicles toward his flat, ignoring the dull ache in her bad foot, she hoped it was going to give up something good. Because they still didn't have that much linking him with the crimes, other than the fact that he'd been inside all the victims' properties. This might be too much of a coincidence to explain away, but it was still nowhere near enough to secure a conviction for serial murder.

"How's the neck?" she asked Dan Grier as they ran into each other at the front door of the building.

"He caught me with a lucky shot," he answered, with just the faintest hint of belligerence in his tone, rubbing his throat through the material of the coverall. "I wasn't expecting it."

"No, I saw that. Quite a feisty little bugger, wasn't he?"

"He definitely had some kind of martial arts expertise. I think we should have researched his background better."

Tina smiled, thinking Grier was a pompous sod sometimes. They'd never really seen eye to eye, right from the word go. She thought him precious and over-serious; he clearly didn't think she should be his boss. Things had been even more strained since the interview with Adrienne Menzies's friend, when Grier had discounted her lead and Tina had followed it up on her own, and she had the feeling that he thought she'd deliberately set him up to look like an idiot, which she hadn't. It was just that generally she liked to work alone, relying on her own instincts. "Well, you know how it is, Dan," she said to him. "You live and learn. And at least we've got him now." She put out a hand. "After you."

Grier didn't reply, just walked inside in silence.

As Tina went to follow, someone called her name. She turned and saw DCI MacLeod walking toward her, his phone in one hand, his coveralls in the other. His face was still red from his earlier exertions, even though by Tina's calculations he'd only run the best part of thirty yards, and there were obvious sweat stains on the underarms of his shirt. With his middle-aged spread spreading way too quickly and an unhealthy pallor that matched the gray in his hair, he looked like a heart attack waiting to happen.

"Sir?" She hadn't spoken to him since the arrest—he'd been on the phone nonstop ever since—and she wondered what he wanted to say.

"Well done on stopping Kent," he said as he reached her. "It could have been embarrassing if he'd got away."

She liked that about him. The fact that, unlike many of the senior officers she'd dealt with over the years, he was honest, and said what he was thinking. "No problem. It's nice to have had the chance to get involved."

MacLeod frowned. "You know I'd have you back on active duty like a shot if I could, Tina. But it's the bloody regulations. You know how it is. They swamp us."

"If there's anything you can do, it'd be a help. I didn't join up to watch other people do the glory jobs."

"I'll have a word." He breathed in deeply, and Tina could tell he hadn't just come over to congratulate her. "I don't suppose there'll be any complaints from Kent about any inappropriate use of force . . ."

"I should imagine right now that's the least of his problems."

"But you're going to have to be careful, Tina," he continued, leaning in closer, clearly choosing his words carefully. "Sometimes you can let your enthusiasm for stopping a suspect get the better of you. You laid into Kent pretty hard back there."

"He needed to be stopped."

"I know that, and quite frankly, on a personal level I think he deserves everything he gets, and plenty more besides. But you're a high-profile officer."

She started to argue but he held up a hand. "I know it's not your fault that people know who you are, but like it or not, you're just going to have to accept it. And you're going to have to remember that your actions get noticed. You step out of line, people are going to come down hard on you. I'm only saying this because you're one of my people, and I want to protect you. I also think you're an extremely good police officer. It was you who got the break with Kent, you who should get the credit. Don't ruin it by kicking the hell out of our suspect in the middle of the street in broad daylight."

Tina felt defensive, and her first instinct was to fight back, to say that she'd only used the minimum amount of force necessary, and if people couldn't handle that then frankly that was their lookout. But she didn't. She had no desire to have a run-in with her boss, and, if she was honest with herself, he was right. "Thanks, sir. I'll bear that in mind. Is that everything?"

He smiled. "Yeah, that's everything. Lecture over. And well done again."

She turned away and went inside, making her way up the threadbare staircase to the first floor, conscious that her foot was acting up again. It was the second time she'd been shot in the space of five years. Add to that the fact that she'd killed a man and that two of her colleagues, one a lover, had been murdered, and it was hardly a wonder she had such a high profile.

The Black Widow, they'd called her at one time. Perhaps they still did, she wasn't entirely sure. Either way, people tended to keep their distance from her, as if she was some kind of jinx, and because of this she'd become something of a loner. She was a nomad too, unable to settle fully in any one job. She'd already left the force once before coming back a year later and joining SOCA, the Serious Organized Crime Agency, where she'd lasted a year before returning to where she'd first been a wet-behind-the-ears DC, at Islington CID. But regular detective work hadn't lived up to her expectations either, so when a slot on CMIT had come up with a chance for promotion, she'd jumped at it. Perhaps her profile hadn't done her as much harm as she'd thought, because she'd got the job, and was making a pretty decent go of it too, although she preferred detective work to the management of others.

The reinforced door to Andrew Kent's flat had been propped open with a telephone directory and there was a vague smell of stale sweat coming from inside, mixed with cheap air freshener. It was a cramped little one-bed place with a narrow corridor connecting the rooms, and it was already busy with members of the team, working two and three to a room, meticulously going through Kent's possessions. They would take this place apart piece by piece over the next few days until they'd searched every last inch of it. A man who'd brutally murdered five women was always going to keep some kind of trophy from his experiences—a means of helping him to relive them—and however well he might have hidden it, they'd find it. Because now that they had him in custody, time was on their side.

Tina made her way down the corridor, flicking on the light as she did so, and stopped at Kent's bedroom.

It was surprisingly spacious, with ancient-looking wardrobes rising up on either side of an unmade double bed with sheets that were badly in need of a wash. A framed Van Gogh print of a night scene hung, slightly crooked, above the bed and there was a stack of paperback books on the bedside table, one of which was *Nicholas Nickleby*.

DCs Anji Rodriguez and Grier were already in there. Rodriguez was going through one of the wardrobes, patting down various items of Kent's clothing with the kind of ferocity that suggested she was imagining he was still in them, before chucking each item onto a pile next to her. She looked in a bad mood, courtesy no doubt of being made to look like a fool during the arrest, and she didn't look around as Tina came in. Grier, meanwhile, was on his hands and knees pulling open the bedside table drawers, and sifting through Kent's underwear. He gave her a brief nod and went back to his work while she stood in the doorway thinking that it was hard to come to terms with what made murderers tick. To all intents and purposes, they lived just like anyone else. Watching soap operas, eating takeaways, reading Charles Dickens novels. Yet they could carry out crimes so horrific that it was almost impossible for a normal human being to comprehend them. And Andrew Kent's crimes were about as bad as they got. Tina had seen what his victims had looked like after he'd finished with them. Tied helpless to their beds and beaten so savagely that they were rendered utterly unrecognizable. Mutilated both before and after death in ways that had made some of the officers on the scene physically sick. It was the main reason Tina had taken so much pleasure in spraying the bastard with the gas and hitting him with all her strength as he'd lain incapacitated in front of her.

"What's this, then?" said Grier, his voice interrupting her thoughts. He was tugging at something behind the bedside table. A second later there was the sound of tape being torn away from the woodwork, then Grier slowly got to his feet with his back to Tina and Rodriguez, who both stared at him, waiting.

And then, as he turned to them, a wide smile on his face beneath the coveralls, Tina saw what he was holding in his hand.

She tensed, her mouth suddenly dry, experiencing a curious mixture of elation and nausea.

It was the evidence they were looking for.

PART II

Yesterday

Three

All my life I wanted to be a police officer. To protect the weak and the vulnerable and take on the bad guys. As far back as I can remember, I had this burning desire for justice. At school I confronted bullies if I saw them picking on smaller kids. If they didn't back down, I'd fight them. In the early days I lost more times than I won, so I took up boxing, and the ratio quickly changed. My dad always said I should join the army, which is what my brother John ended up doing. He said I was too aggressive for the police, and maybe I was, because my first three years in uniform were an exercise in boredom and gradual disillusionment. I could never quite get over the fact that the public could abuse and assault me at will, with little fear of prosecution, whereas I couldn't do the same back to them. So I decided to become a detective, only to find that life in CID is ninety percent paperwork, nine percent detective work, and one percent excitement, and that's if you're lucky. Not exactly *Dirty Harry*.

My boss at the time, and the man who, with the possible exception of my dad, I've always respected most in the world, saw my frustration and told me that maybe I should try undercover work.

DCI Dougie MacLeod—he taught me one hell of a lot,

including the art of patience, which was something I thought I'd never pick up. Right up till yesterday, I always thought his greatest service to me was that particular suggestion, because for the past nine years of my life I've been working with CO10, Scotland Yard's elite (their word, not mine) undercover unit. Working undercover, I've finally found the excitement I was looking for, and I've also put away some extremely nasty characters, many of whom still want me dead. And as I stood in the windowless back room of a grimy Soho nightclub that morning, I had the feeling that there weren't many much nastier than the two men sitting across the table opposite me.

"I hear you're looking for work," said the one on the right. He was in his mid-forties, with closely cropped silver hair, a noticeable squint in one eye, and features that were long, sharp, and unforgiving, as if they'd been hand-carved from hardwood, and dominated by a nose skewed by a long-ago breakage and missing a lump at the bridge. He was wearing a faded Lonsdale T-shirt that showed off wiry, muscular arms peppered with faded tattoos, and his good eye homed in on me now, hunting for weaknesses. His name was Tyrone Wolfe, and he was suspected of involvement in at least five murders.

The man sitting next to him was called Clarence Haddock. It was, speaking frankly, a ridiculous name, and one that simply didn't do justice to the huge, terrifying-looking thug with the beard and dreadlocks who for the past five years had been Tyrone Wolfe's closest associate. More than a dozen gold labret studs peppered his face, including one that went horizontally straight through his fat, splayed nose, giving him the appearance of an angry bull preparing to charge. He sat with his trunk-like forearms on the table, glaring up at me in silence, the barely suppressed rage he'd become legendary for seeming to emanate from him in short, brutal waves. It was said that Clarence Haddock had once cut a man's throat with such force that he'd decapitated him with a single pull of the knife, and looking at him now I could picture him feeding on the still-twitching corpse afterward. I knew all about him, of course, but even so, standing a few feet away from him in a claustrophobic room reminded me of the first time I'd seen a great white shark in real life while on a cage-diving trip off Gansbaii in South Africa. A mixture of primeval fear and sheer awe.

I held both their gazes, ignoring the drop of sweat running down my temple. "Yeah, I could be. What have you got?"

Wolfe turned to the third man in the room, a big middle-aged guy with long, graying blond hair and a face with more lines than the Bible, who was leaning against the wall. This was Tommy Allen, another of Wolfe's close associates, and the man I'd spent the last three months getting to know. He was the one who'd brought me to this nightclub at ten thirty in the morning to make the introductions.

"Yeah, he's clean," said Tommy confidently, his voice a cockney, cigarette-fueled growl. "I had the RF detector on in the car and it didn't pick up anything. I've searched him too." He winked at me. "I think he enjoyed that part."

Wolfe didn't smile. "Watch?"

"I've taken his watch, his mobile, everything. Even his shoes. It's all outside."

These guys were very thorough, and totally surveillance aware, knowing all the tricks of the trade. Never using the same phones for too long, regularly sweeping their meeting places for bugs, always checking for tails. I'd been hoping to record this meeting using the microscopic recording device in my watch, but now they'd scuppered that, which was going to make my job even harder than it was already. But then, when you were armed robbers turned drug smugglers, running nightclubs staffed by illegal immigrants who were little more than sex slaves, it paid to be careful, which was why I was here.

Because conventional methods for putting these guys away weren't working.

"I once heard of an undercover copper who wore a listening device up his arse," said Wolfe, speaking slowly, almost languidly, enunciating every word in a strong east London accent. "It was on a smack deal. Apparently, it picked up every word. Two people went down for twelve years apiece."

I didn't like the sound of this. One, because not surprisingly I didn't much fancy the idea of a detailed rectal examination, and two, and more importantly, because the undercover copper in question had been me. And yes, it had been bloody uncomfortable, although, as Wolfe pointed out, it had also been successful, which had pleased the bosses no end. There was no way Wolfe could have known my identity since he'd had nothing to do with the dealers I'd put down, but I still felt a twinge of anxiety.

Criminals are just like hyenas, or the playground bullies I used to fight: they sniff out fear immediately, and go straight for whoever's exhibiting it. I'd been in the game long enough to stand my ground, so I glared contemptuously at Wolfe. "I'm not a copper," I told him firmly, "and no one's feeling my arsehole from the inside, either. Understand that? If you've got something for me, tell me now. I haven't got all day."

"He sat down pretty easily in the car, boss," Tommy chuckled throatily, "so I don't think he's wearing anything up there."

"Don't worry, no one's going to search your arsehole," said Wolfe as if he was doing me some massive favor. "But I need to be sure about you."

"And I need to be sure about you, too," I said, knowing I couldn't take these kinds of liberties lying down. "I mean, how do I know you're not coppers?"

"I'm no fucking copper," growled Haddock, speaking for the first time, fixing me with his big dark eyes. His voice was higher-pitched than I'd been expecting, with the faintest sign of a lisp. It was, however, no less menacing for that, and I could feel the atmosphere in this shitty little room darkening.

At this point, Tommy peeled himself off the wall and came over to the table. "Listen, Sean," he said, addressing me, "I can vouch for these two men. I've known them years, and you know I'm kosher, so I wouldn't be messing you about."

This was true enough. In the three months since I'd met Tommy in a well-known villains' pub in Stepney, we'd not only spent a lot of time together shooting the breeze in various drinking holes, I'd also done work for him on his sideline operations. This had involved delivering quantities of coke to some of his wholesale customers, as well as going with him to collect a debt from a dealer who owed him money. I'd had to hold the guy's legs while Tommy lifted him off the floor and repeatedly dunked his head down the toilet. I hadn't wanted to do it but knew I had to prove myself to my new boss, and thankfully the dealer had coughed up the money before any real pain was inflicted on him.

I nodded slowly, appearing satisfied. "I trust you, Tommy, so if you vouch for them, that's OK with me."

His face cracked an almost paternalistic smile, even though he was only a dozen years my senior. "Good lad."

He turned to Wolfe. "I can vouch for Sean as well, Ty. He's reliable."

"I don't like the look of him," Haddock grunted.

"I don't like the look of you, either," I snapped back, "but I'm not complaining, am I?"

Haddock's eyes narrowed and he glowered at me with an almost theatrical rage, but the other two laughed. "Lighten up, Clarence," said Wolfe, standing up. "Come on, Sean," he said. "Why don't you, me, and Clarence take a walk?"

I could think of any number of reasons why not, but I knew that unless I went with them, this op was dead before it had even begun. I glanced over at Tommy and he gave me a nod in return to tell me it would be OK. He might have been a thug and a career criminal, but there was something about Tommy I implicitly trusted (maybe it was this paternal air he had), so when he let me know that it would be OK, I believed him.

Wolfe led the way out of the door, and I followed him, conscious of Haddock's looming form falling into place behind me, so close that I could hear his low breathing. I tensed, not liking the fact that I was vulnerable, but knowing better than to act scared.

We walked through a narrow corridor and then out into the nightclub proper—a dimly lit, windowless space of low balconies, cluttered with tables and chairs, surrounding a dance floor and stage. The decor was cheap and tired, the two gleaming poles in the middle of the stage the only things looking less than twenty years old.

"You ever been married, Sean?" asked Wolfe without looking back as we slowly circumnavigated the room in single file.

"No."

"You ever served time?"

"Yeah."

"How long?"

"Seven years."

"Where did you serve it?"

"Parkhurst. Then Ford."

The questions came thick and fast as we did slow laps of the club, but always delivered in a casual manner, as if he wasn't too worried about the answers. What wing was I in at Parkhurst? Who did I know in Ford? Did I have kids? When did I get out? Did I know such-and-such the armed robber? Where did I grow up?

Wolfe was testing my legend, hoping to trip me into a mistake, but I'd learned my part perfectly, every last detail. Because if you don't, you're dead. You have to go through this rigamarole on every op you do, and the higher up the food chain the target, the more detailed the interrogation. I answered everything. Without complaint. And, more importantly, without a pause.

I was using an old alias I'd first used several years earlier when I was seconded to SOCA, that of Sean Tatelli, an ex-con from Coventry who'd served a seven-year stretch in the 1990s for supplying class A drugs, firearms offenses, and the attempted murder of a police officer during the course of his arrest. Anyone making detailed inquiries would find that Sean Tatelli had indeed served seven years, first at Parkhurst Prison, then at Ford Open, and that his partner in crime was a Midlands-based gangster called Alan "Hocus" Pocus, who'd ended up serving five years for drugs offenses.

It was all bullshit, of course. My details had simply been made up by SOCA and put on all the relevant databases, including the PNC, with flags in place so that if anyone accessed them looking for information, SOCA would know. And Hocus might be a kosher criminal who had actually served his time, but he was also now a police informant who'd been drilled to give me a glowing reference.

Finally, Wolfe stopped at the top of a flight of steps leading down to the stage and turned to face me, his hard, narrow features lit up bizarrely in the pink fluorescent glow of an overhead light. "You ever shot someone, Sean?" he asked, fixing me with his squint.

I was beginning to feel extremely uncomfortable. The room was quiet and I was boxed in, with railings on one side, a cluster of tables and chairs on the other, and Haddock looming up behind me. But the trick when you're cornered is to do the same as they do in the animal world: make yourself big, not small. So straight away I went on the offensive. "Hold on here. You're getting a little bit personal for someone I don't even know. Now why don't you help me out here and tell me who the hell you are and why I should be answering your questions. Because right now you haven't exactly made it clear." At the same time, I turned around and faced down Haddock. "And why don't you give me some space as well, instead of breathing down my neck like something out of the fucking *Munsters*?"

To my surprise, he took a step backward, while Tyrone actually apologized and immediately introduced himself and Haddock. "The reason you're here," he explained, "is because I've got a vacancy in my firm for the right person and Tommy tells me you're a decent bloke who might fit the bill. So, consider this a job interview."

"What sort of work do you do?"

"A bit of this," he answered, with the beginnings of an unpleasant smile, "a bit of that. Not all of it strictly legal."

"Well, let me tell you something. I've been out of jail eight months. No one wants to hire me for legit work. I've done some jobs for Tommy but I've still got debts up to my eyeballs, and I need something now. Not minimum-wage shit, or flipping burgers in McDonald's. Real work, that pays real money. You know my background—I know you've checked me out, otherwise I wouldn't be standing here now—so you know I'm not afraid to handle a gun, and you know I'm no hotheaded kid who pulls the trigger and asks questions later. I'm reliable, so if you've got something you want to talk about, talk about it now. Otherwise I'm out of here. Your choice. But do me a favor and make it now."

I knew that whole spiel back to front. I must have delivered it a thousand times in front of my mirror, probably another twenty out in the field in situations like this one, occasionally substituting the odd word and phrase, but always with the utter conviction of a man at ease with his conscience. To work in undercover as long as I have, you've got to be the consummate method actor, a copper's Robert De Niro, immersing yourself in the part, working with an ever-changing script, which means you've got to ad lib on demand and be able to bullshit your way out of every tight corner. Let me tell you something else, too. That spiel never fails. It's always the one that breaks the ice and gets me in.

Wolfe and Haddock exchanged glances, Wolfe's expression questioning, as if he was deferring to his immense colleague.

Haddock nodded once, and Wolfe turned back my way. "I've got one day's work," he said quietly. "Short notice, definitely in the next few days, but the date's not finalized yet. The pay's a straight hundred thousand cash. Interested?"

Of course I was interested. I hadn't been expecting much

from the initial meeting, but already I had Wolfe offering me an armed job. I didn't show too much enthusiasm, though, because that kind of thing sets people's alarm bells ringing as well. Instead, I shrugged and said, "Depends what it is."

"It's a job against an unarmed vehicle in transit."

"I'd prefer a share of the proceeds."

Wolfe shook his head. "It's not that kind of job. The cargo's human. One man."

"Who?"

"I can't tell you that. Not yet. But I can tell you that it's thirty grand up front. Seventy on completion."

I acted like I was thinking about it. I wanted to find out more because that way I could finish the job pretty much on the spot, but knew better than to push things at this early stage. "I like the sound of thirty grand, but I'll need to know more before I commit."

"I'll tell you everything, but first I want you to do a little job."

"What kind of job?"

It was Haddock who answered, leaning down so his mouth was uncomfortably close to my ear, his words delivered in that strangely effeminate voice. "The kind that'll prove to us beyond a doubt that you're not a copper."

Four

It was hot and stuffy in the interview room and DI Tina Boyd was longing for a cigarette. "If you're innocent of all charges, why did you run away from us, violently assaulting two police officers in the process?" she asked.

"Why do you think?" demanded Andrew Kent, wearing the same panic-stricken expression he'd been wearing since Tina and her boss, DCI MacLeod, had begun questioning him in the interview room almost two hours earlier. "I was on my way home from work and suddenly all these people came out of nowhere screaming and shouting. I panicked and made a run for it."

"But they clearly identified themselves as police officers," Tina persisted.

"I didn't hear them, OK?" protested Kent, in tones not far short of hysteria. "I just ran, and when they grabbed me, I thought they were trying to mug me or something, so I fought back. I'm sorry I hurt those officers, but it wasn't my fault."

His lawyer—a young, studious-looking duty lawyer wearing big glasses with the Nike emblem on the frames, and reeking of ambition—put a reassuring hand on his shoulder. "It's all right, Andrew," he said soothingly. "You can answer in your own time."

Kent nodded.

Across the table, he looked even smaller and more harmless than he had when Tina watched him walking home the previous evening, just before his arrest. His whole demeanor was one of submissive fear, his pale eyes awash with confusion. But Tina had seen the way he'd fought the arresting officers, the cold determination he'd shown, and she wasn't fooled, although she had to give him full marks for his acting abilities.

"For a terrified civilian, you gave a pretty good account of yourself, Mr. Kent," she continued. "Both officers needed medical treatment, and I had to use CS spray to subdue you."

"I'm a black belt in karate," said Kent with a sigh. "I've been mugged twice in the past so I wanted to make sure I was able to defend myself when it happened again. I've been going to classes for the past six years, and I'm not going to make any apologies for it."

"It doesn't make my client guilty of anything either," put in his lawyer, whose name was Jacobs.

Tina ignored him. "So you're still protesting your innocence about these murders?" she asked Kent.

"Of course I am. I've never killed anyone, and I don't understand why you think—"

"How do you explain your DNA being at the properties of every one of the five victims, then?"

"Because I fitted the alarms at all the different properties. I've already told you this."

"Not very good systems, then, were they, Mr. Kent, if the killer managed to bypass every one of them?" said DCI MacLeod.

"I thought they were."

"My client's not being questioned about his skills as an

engineer, now is he?" Jacobs looked at MacLeod over his half-rimmed glasses with the gravitas of a man twice his age.

MacLeod wasn't deterred. "Don't you think it's a bit of a coincidence that every one of our five victims had their brand-new alarms fitted by you? What do you reckon the odds of that are?"

"Look, I've fitted thousands of alarms over the years. I'm a hard worker. I can do two or three clients in one day, so the odds probably aren't that great."

"What about the odds of the killer being able to bypass every one of your alarms?"

Again Kent protested his innocence, and again Jacobs intervened with the same objection—that it wasn't his client's work-related capabilities that he'd been arrested for.

"So, how come your DNA was found in four of the victims' bedrooms if you were only fitting the alarms?" Tina asked, keen to move the interview on.

"I had to have access to the whole of each property while I was doing the work, because I needed to fit sensors in different rooms."

"But you didn't fit sensors in any of the victims' bedrooms. We checked. Nor did any of your employers think you should have been in them. So what was your DNA doing in there?"

"I don't know," answered Kent. "Maybe it got carried in there somehow from other places in the house. Is that kind of thing possible?"

Technically, it was within the realms of possibility, but only just. When Tina pointed this out to him, Kent gave an exaggerated shrug and said he couldn't understand it.

"Our understanding is that the victims were subjected to violent sexual assaults before being murdered in a brutal fashion. Were any of the DNA samples from the bedrooms that you say match that of my client found on the bodies themselves?" Jacobs asked, his tone carrying just the right mix of weariness and skepticism.

Tina and MacLeod exchanged glances. This was their big problem. The killer had cleaned up the bodies scrupulously, using bleach, and so far they'd given up no DNA evidence at all.

"No," MacLeod admitted reluctantly, "but that doesn't mean a thing."

"Well it does, DCI MacLeod, because my client's already provided a perfectly adequate explanation as to why his DNA might have been in the bedrooms of some of the victims. Now, if you have no further evidence, then I'm asking that you release him immediately."

Tina fixed Kent with a cold stare. "Tell us about the hammer," she said baldly.

Kent's eyes widened. "What hammer? What are you talking about?"

"The hammer we found in your bedroom, Mr. Kent. The one covered in blood and brain matter, which we've just been told belonged to your last victim, Adrienne Menzies. Your DNA was also on the handle."

Kent shook his head. "No. No way."

"Yes. The lab did the tests twice, just to make sure."

"I . . . I don't know anything about a hammer," he stuttered. "I really don't. Jesus, this can't be happening." He looked desperately at Jacobs, who also seemed caught out by this revelation, then back at Tina and MacLeod. "I'm innocent, I promise you. Someone must be setting me up."

He resembled a frightened child, sitting there barely as tall as Tina and with a skinnier build, seeming to shrink in the chair as the evidence was steadily laid out against him. For the first time, Tina began to doubt that they had the right man. All the evidence seemed to point to him, but it was the way he was reacting. He came across like an innocent man. Most of the people she faced didn't. Most of them were guilty and tended to limit their answers to a monotonous refrain of "no comment," but Andrew Kent was acting like an ordinary man caught up in a terrifying situation over which he had no control.

"Who do you think set you up?" demanded MacLeod, his voice laden with skepticism.

"I told you, I don't know. I honestly don't. If I was ever going to do something like this, why would I keep the murder weapon in my room? That would be madness . . ."

The words died in his throat as he saw the looks on his interrogators' faces.

Tina was just about to respond when MacLeod tapped her arm and shook his head. "OK, you probably need some time with your client, Mr. Jacobs, so you can discuss this latest piece of evidence. Interview suspended at eleven forty-six A.M." He got to his feet, motioning for Tina to follow him out the door.

"We had him on the rack there. Why did we stop?" Tina asked when they were out in the corridor.

"There's been a development. DC Grier just called through on the earpiece. Apparently, there's something we need to see."

"Any details?"

"No," he said, looking at her seriously, "but I don't like the sound of it."

Five

The incident room on the fourth floor of Holborn station, where CMIT had been carrying out the Night Creeper murder inquiry, was absolutely silent as Tina and MacLeod entered.

Half a dozen officers, all members of Andrew Kent's arrest team, were gathered in a loose circle around a widescreen Apple Mac laptop on a desk in the middle of the room. DC Grier stood closest to the desk, his features pale and drawn, his prominent Adam's apple, still bruised from its encounter with Kent's hand, visibly pulsating, as if he was trying to keep something down. The expressions on the faces of the other officers present—a grim mixture of nauseated, depressed, tense, and stoical—told the same story. Whatever they'd just witnessed had affected every one of them, and the eyes of DC Rodriguez were wet with tears.

"What have we got, then?" asked DCI MacLeod, his soft Edinburgh burr somehow easing the tension in the air. There was a quiet decency about MacLeod that naturally drew people to him, as did his air of calm unflappability, that made you look beyond the beer belly, the thinning gray hair and unfashionable mustache, and see only a natural leader. Once again, Tina was glad she worked for him.

"We've found stuff on here," sighed Grier, running a hand

roughly across his face as if he were trying to remove the memory of whatever it was. "Films."

"What kind?" asked Tina, feeling a twitch of morbid excitement.

"Footage of the murder of two of the victims. It looks like he filmed it himself." Grier paused. "It's extremely graphic."

"It's more than that," said DS Simon Tilley, normally an exuberant copper with a big personality and a laugh like a bass drum, but who was also the father of two young children. "It's the worst thing I've ever seen."

MacLeod took a deep breath. A father himself, he clearly had little appetite for the task ahead but was far too professional to let that stop him. "We'd better take a look, then."

He turned to Tina, his expression suggesting she didn't have to watch if she didn't want to. She noticed some of the others looking at her, including Grier and Rodriguez, and had this feeling they were willing her to back out of it.

"Don't worry," she told MacLeod bluntly without looking at them. "I can take it."

"I can't," said Grier, getting to his feet. "Not again. Just press the play button when you're ready to begin."

There were murmurs of agreement from the other officers and they moved away from the desk. Although they remained in the incident room, it seemed to Tina as though they were keeping as far away from the laptop as possible, as if whatever was on it was somehow infectious.

MacLeod leaned forward and pressed the button on the screen. Then he and Tina stood side by side as the screen lit up to reveal a lengthwise shot of a young woman lying on a bed. Tina immediately recognized her as the final victim, Adrienne Menzies, a thirty-three-year-old accountant from Highgate with hair the same dark color and style as her own, and whose DNA was on the hammer found at Kent's apartment. She remembered the bed's expensive yet old-fashioned teak headboard, which she later found out had been handmade by Adrienne's father. It was always the little details that stayed with you, even amid the horror. And the horror here was unrelenting.

Adrienne was naked and bound to the bed with black PVC bondage straps of the kind Kent had used in all but one of his murders, and her mouth was gagged with duct tape. The picture quality was very good and Tina could make out the bruises and scratches on her thighs and around her breasts. The camera moved in slow, jerky movements more akin to a homemade film as the person holding it walked carefully around the edge of the bed, filming Adrienne's vain struggle to free herself from the bonds that kept her firmly in place. Beneath the gag, her muffled cries of fear grew steadily more desperate and her eyes widened and bulged as if the fear in them was a living thing trying to squeeze its way out.

The cameraman stopped moving and focused in on her face so that it filled the screen entirely with a pleading expression Tina found hard to bear because she knew exactly what was about to happen to this pretty young woman who, until a few hours before this, had lived a generally happy, ordinary life with family and friends who cared for her. Tina had been at the murder scene. She had stood in that bedroom, looking down at the unrecognizable face in a mask of coagulated blood; the thick splatters on the bed linen and the walls; the long smear only just visible on the teak headboard . . .

The camera panned out and the screen suddenly went black. Tina's mouth was dry and she was conscious that she was rubbing her hands together with such force that it was almost painful. She needed a drink. More than she'd needed one in ages. A bottle of good Rioja with a couple of vodka chasers. Anything just to forget about all this.

The screen lit up again, and this time the camera had been placed in a fixed position about three feet away from Adrienne's head, and slightly above it—most likely on a bedside table. Tina couldn't remember if Adrienne had had a bedside table or not. Her head swung from side to side, the moans loud beneath the gag. There was music playing in the background. "Beautiful Day" by U2. Only just audible. Tina would never be able to listen to that song again without being reminded of Adrienne Menzies's bloody murder.

The hammer came out of nowhere, striking Adrienne full in the face, only the head and the top of the handle visible.

Tina flinched and turned away. She'd seen some terrible things in her career, including a young woman being shot dead in front of her, but this was somehow worse, because it felt sickeningly voyeuristic, almost as if she was giving the killer her tacit support by watching.

She could hear the crunching sound of the hammer as it struck Adrienne again and again, but it wasn't that sound that Tina would remember. It was the rasping, gurgling wail of pain and terror that Adrienne made in time with her tortured but surprisingly deep breathing as she lay dying.

Tina forced herself to turn back, knowing that it was part of her job to view the evidence. She kept her eyes rigidly on the screen, her world reduced to this laptop and the savagery being played out on it.

It seemed to last for an interminably long time, although she found out later that the film was only seven minutes and twenty seconds long, and it involved the killer doing other things to his victim, terrible sexual things that she recalled from the autopsy reports. And throughout it all there was not a single glimpse of him, not even a gloved hand at the end of the hammer. Even in the midst of his bloodlust he was being careful and controlled in his actions, and when he'd finished, and what was left of Adrienne Menzies was no longer moving, the camera shut off abruptly. Just like that.

Tina swallowed hard, and for a number of seconds continued to stare at the blank screen, conscious of how hard and fast her heart was beating—a thought that made her feel ashamed. Beside her, she could hear DCI MacLeod's labored breathing. Then he stepped forward and shut the laptop's lid, as if by doing so he could shut out the horror they'd just witnessed.

"Good God," he said quietly. "What drives some people?"

There was no answer to this. All Tina knew for sure was that she'd met far too many of them in her police career, and the crimes they committed never got any easier to handle. More than once in recent months, her parents and brother, still reeling from the fact that she'd killed a man in the line of duty, and even more horrified that she'd joined the team tasked with tracking down a serial killer, had suggested that her job was doing her more harm than good. They were almost certainly right, yet Tina was capable neither of leaving the career that she seemed to love and loathe in equal measure, nor of coping with its constant pressures.

"The hammer looked like the one we found at Kent's place, didn't it?" she said at last.

"Impossible to tell for sure, and that's exactly what a defense lawyer would say in court. There must be plenty of hammers like that one in existence."

"It'll be a lot harder for him to argue about the fact that Adrienne's DNA was on it, and that there's a video of the murder on his laptop." She shook her head, annoyed with herself for doubting even for a moment that Kent was the Night Creeper. He was just one of the better actors she'd come across in the interview room, and she should have remembered that that was exactly what true psychopaths were. Consummate actors who liked nothing more than pulling the wool over the eyes of those around them.

MacLeod gave her a sympathetic smile. "I'm sorry you had to watch that, Tina. I hope it doesn't bring back any memories."

She guessed he was referring to when she'd been kidnapped and shot the previous year, but if so, he was wrong, because the memories had never gone away, and as far as Tina was concerned they were her business and no one else's. "I'm sorry you had to watch it too, sir," she told him. "And don't worry, it didn't."

"Good," he said simply, then turned to face DC Grier, who was approaching the two of them almost gingerly. He still looked pale, and Tina felt a renewed respect for him. At least he wasn't trying to be all macho about it, pretending that it hadn't affected him.

"There's another film on there along the same lines," he said. "It captures Diane Woodward's murder." Diane was the third victim, and at thirty-seven, the oldest. She'd died ten months earlier in very similar circumstances.

"Any clues as to the identity of the perpetrator on that one?" asked MacLeod.

Grier shook his head. "It was all handheld stuff similar to the one you've just seen. There's also a lot of further footage of the victims taken while they were still alive, but before he broke in to kill them."

"What do you mean?"

"I mean he must have put hidden cameras in the apartments when he was fitting the alarms because it shows the victims going about their daily lives. It's clear he's edited it down a lot because it's mainly of an intimate nature. Them getting changed, walking around naked. In one case having sex. That sort of thing. I suppose it made it more fun for him. Stalking them like that but without running any risk of getting caught."

"And is there footage like this of all of the victims?"

"Three that we've found so far."

MacLeod ran a hand across his brow. "Good God."

"Is there any way it could have been planted on his laptop?" Tina asked.

Grier looked at her like she was mad, and she remembered immediately why she didn't like him. "No way. There's so much of it for a start, and the dates the footage was first added to the system tie in with the dates of the murders. This stuff's been put on there over a long period of time. It's authentic, and it belongs to that computer."

"Were the files well hidden?"

"They were in a folder within a folder within a folder, squirreled away among a lot of other files in the My Documents section, all with bland, irrelevant names. It was quite a trawl to locate them."

"They weren't that well hidden though, were they? They didn't have password protection or an encryption system like some of the pedophile networks put on their PCs to stop us accessing the hard drive?"

Grier looked defensive. "Are you suggesting they were easy to find, ma'am?" he asked her.

"I don't think Tina's saying that at all, Dan," put in MacLeod hastily.

"No, I'm not. I'm just checking the facts. That's all, Dan. OK?"

"I'm sorry," he said. "I didn't mean to sound disrespectful, it's just I've been here with that laptop for most of the last twelve hours trawling through reams of crap until I finally found them."

"We've all had a bit of a traumatic few minutes," said DCI MacLeod, "so let's just concentrate on the most important task, which is keeping the evidence safe and secure. Download all the relevant files to a memory stick, Dan, then get the laptop bagged up and sent over to the lab. I want it tested for Kent's DNA, fingerprints, the lot. I don't want him trying to deny it belongs to him."

Grier looked surprised. "He won't do that, will he, sir?"

"He's denied everything so far. We need to keep building up the case until it doesn't make a blind bit of difference how good an actor he is, because the jury'll have no choice but to find him guilty."

When Grier had gone with the laptop, MacLeod turned to Tina. "All right, are you ready to finish this bastard off?"

She nodded firmly. "Never readier."

"Let's see how he responds to the fact that we've found all his home videos." He put a hand on her arm. "You had a big part in bringing him in, Tina. When we're ready, do you want to be the one who charges him?"

But had it all been too easy? Andrew Kent had been delivered to them on a plate with the murder weapon in his bedroom and his laptop full of hugely incriminating video evidence. But even as this nagged at her, Tina pushed it aside, knowing that she was just ignoring the obvious explanation, which was that Kent was like all the other cold-blooded killers who'd begun to believe the hype of their invincibility and had become too complacent.

"Definitely," she said. "I want to watch him squirm."

Six

The job Tyrone Wolfe wanted me to carry out was to buy some guns from an underworld dealer based in Canning Town. Although he'd told Tommy to drive me to the destination, he'd made it clear that I was to go in and make the purchase alone. His rationale was simple: if I bought the guns, I was committing a serious crime and therefore couldn't be a copper. But the rationale was flawed, because by sending me on my way with Tommy driving they'd put me in a position where I had no choice but to commit it, since failure to do so would have blown my cover. I wasn't sure whether my handler at CO10 would see it quite like that, of course. DI Robin Samuel-Smith, or Captain Bob as he was universally known behind his back, liked to play things by the book. But I'd worry about that one later.

Wolfe had given me an envelope containing five grand in cash—payment for two automatic shotguns and a handgun—handed me back the rest of my possessions, including my recording watch, and told me that I was expected at the dealer's place half an hour ago, and that he'd see me with the goods later.

We were now in Tommy's car en route. In the back seat, sitting up with his tongue lolling out, was Tommy's dog,

Tommy Junior, an unhealthy-looking mongrel with a mangled ear who always smelled of old raincoats. The story went that Tommy had rescued him from a gang of teenage thugs who'd tied his front and back paws together and were about to dump him in the murky waters of Regent's Canal. Tommy had thrown in one of the thugs instead, and when a second pulled a knife on him, he'd produced an extendable baton and broken his nose with it before sending him in with his mate. The others had done the sensible thing and fled.

Tommy Junior loved his master and, perhaps unsurprisingly, distrusted everyone else. He seemed to have taken a particular dislike to me because in the last three months I'd become something of a regular in the front seat, which was the one he liked to occupy.

It had taken me a month of hanging around the periphery of the north London underworld, drinking in grimy little backstreet pubs with small-time crims and putting my name about as Sean Tatelli, an ex-con on the lookout for decent work, before I got introduced to Tommy. That was three months ago now, and we'd spent a lot of time together since. For a while that had involved nothing more than going out drinking and shooting the breeze. Like a lot of criminals, Tommy was good company, with a wealth of amusing stories to tell. Slowly, though, he'd begun to take me into his confidence, giving me bits and pieces of work to do, always suggesting that something bigger would come along, until finally, today, he'd pulled up outside the flat I used for my undercover ops and told me that he had work for me. Real work this time.

"Who's it we're meant to be snatching?" I asked Tommy, keen to have something to go back to Captain Bob with.

"I don't know," he said, fixing me with deep-set eyes that

always had a melancholy expression in them, even when he was telling a good story. "I don't work with Wolfe as much as I used to these days. But you said he offered you a hundred grand. Well, he offered me one fifty, so I'm thinking him and Haddock must be making at least two apiece, maybe more, which means whoever it is we're after's worth a lot of money to someone. All I know is it's one man, and his escort's not going to be armed. That's it. I don't even know the location."

"Do you know how Wolfe got to hear of the job?"

He shook his head. "He's keeping everything close to his chest, and he's even more jumpy than usual about it. That's why he's being all cloak and dagger with you. He doesn't like using people from outside the crew for work, but he needed a fourth man, and seeing as you and me are mates, and you need the work . . ."

"Thanks for thinking of me," I said, feeling an unusual twinge of guilt that I was going to betray him. Tommy Allen was a violent criminal, but I'd grown closer to him than I'd have liked. At forty-five, he was only twelve years older than me, but sometimes he acted as if I was the son he'd never had.

The car fell silent, and he lit a cigarette.

I looked at it longingly. I only allow myself two cigarettes per day, one after lunch, one after supper. It's my routine, and I stick to it. But I was sorely tempted to make an exception now, knowing that I was heading out of the frying pan and possibly straight into the fire.

I stared out of the car window, trying hard to ignore the pounding of my heart as the hotels, theaters, and pavement cafés of the West End gave way to the grand Victorian buildings of Lincoln's Inn Fields and the legal quarter, and then the steel-and-glass highrises of the City. Finally, the wealth slipped away and we were into the poorer tenements and terraced housing that was the sprawling East End. This area of London had suffered most under the bombardment of the Luftwaffe in the Second World War, and it showed in the slapdash nature of much of the architecture: Victorian tenements, 1950s terraces, 1960s tower blocks, all running into one another to the cheerful beats of Tommy's *Best of Level 42* CD.

Tommy, I'd found out in the time I'd known him, was a big fan of 1980s music, and particularly Level 42. He'd been singing along pretty much nonstop to the tracks throughout the journey, occasionally accompanied by Tommy Junior howling from the backseat, creating an out-of-tune cacophony that would have made me gouge out my own eyes if I hadn't been so preoccupied. Finally, as one of the band's lesser hits, "Microkid," came on, Tommy seemed to notice for the first time that I wasn't saying much.

He turned down the music. "Listen, Sean, you're not scared, are you?"

"No, I've just been struck dumb by the quality of your and Tommy Junior's singing."

He chuckled. "'Lessons in Love' is Tommy Junior's favorite. He really catches the high notes on that one." He turned to me, his face growing serious again. "I can vouch for these blokes, you know. The ones you're buying off. I've done stuff with them myself before. They're reliable."

Which was a refrain I'd heard plenty of times before about criminals. They're reliable. The problem was, for the most part, they weren't. They tended to be paranoid, highly strung, violent, and often drugged up, which was a pretty lethal combination. In the course of my career I've had two guns pulled on me, four knives, an ax, a tire iron, baseball bats, even a fake medieval ball and chain. I've been held down by a gang of crazed thugs, flying on a diet of vodka and crack, who doused me in petrol and threatened to burn me alive unless I gave them the drugs I was supposed to be carrying (I didn't, and they didn't), and many's the time I've woken up in the morning wondering when my luck's going to run out.

But in spite of all that, I knew I could never give up the job. I was too much of a believer in the old adage: evil triumphs when good men do nothing. Evil was doing pretty well as it was these days, and there was no shortage of those doing nothing. When I was a young kid, I went to sleep at night thinking that there was a copper standing guard on the street outside my window, there to protect me from all the creatures who haunt the nightmares of children, and it always comforted me to believe he was there. Now I was that copper, and there were plenty of people out there relying on me.

It was just after one P.M. when Tommy pulled into a decrepit-looking street of prewar terraced housing north of the Barking Road. One end of the terrace ended suddenly where part of the last house had collapsed into a pile of rubble, and was then replaced by a strip of uneven wasteland on which a burned-out car sat, missing its wheels. Forlorn pieces of litter scattered and drifted across the tarmac in the dusty breeze, and in the distance, red and blue tower cranes rose like mantises above the crumbling skyline. Facing the wasteland on the other side of the road was a line of cheap, windswept shops, the majority of which were either boarded up or had the shutters down.

"There's the place," said Tommy, parking up and motioning toward a takeaway restaurant called Zafiah's Fine Jamaican Cuisine, which sat hunched and uninviting next to an empty unit with scorch marks up its front, like it had been petrol-bombed. A couple of kids in hoodies, their faces hidden, sat on mountain bikes outside, sharing what looked like a joint.

"It looks closed," I said.

"It is, but they're expecting us. Just go around to the side door and ask for Mitchell. And check the guns work before you give him any money. I'll wait here for you."

I stared at him. "You're really not coming in with me?"

He gave me a regretful, hangdog look that made his fleshy jowls hang down. "I can't, mate. Wolfe wants you to do this alone. It's his orders. That way he knows he can definitely trust you."

"But Wolfe's not here, Tommy. I don't even know these guys. You've got to help me out here."

"There'll be no problem, Sean. Honest. You'll be all right."

It was then that I realized Tommy didn't trust me entirely either. That I was doing this to prove myself to him as well as to Wolfe. I was well and truly on my own.

"Do me a favor," I said, opening the door. "If I'm not out in ten minutes, come and get me."

He gave me a reassuring smile, said sure, no problem, there was nothing to worry about. But in my game there always is.

It had already been a bad morning, and I had to force myself to get out of the car. At that moment I felt like jacking the whole thing in and applying for desk duties at Scotland Yard, far away from all this crap. The envelope containing the five grand was tucked into the front of my jeans, with my shirt covering it, and even though it was out of sight, I knew I was still vulnerable.

I crossed the road and walked past the kids in their hoodies, ignoring their stares and keeping my pace casual, before passing by the front of the takeaway. The interior was dark and empty, and as I rounded the corner and moved into the alleyway leading down to the side door I pondered calling Captain Bob to let him know my current status, maybe even get some emergency backup in case things didn't run as smoothly as Tommy was claiming they would. But Bob would never have authorized me to go inside alone. I was just going to have to hope this deal went OK, then I could pass on the information about the gun dealer, and in a few days' or weeks' time, when the memory of my visit had faded, the dealer could be arrested without fuss or hassle. That was the good thing about undercover work. The domino effect. Infiltrate one gang and you soon get leads on another. The underworld, like the legitimate one, is all about people doing business together.

The alleyway was narrow and dotted with black rubbish sacks, several of which had been split open to reveal decaying household detritus. Graffiti—gang signs, teenage boasts—took up most of the space on the whitewashed walls on either side, and there was a smell of animal fat in the air. I picked my way through the mess until I came to a heavy wooden fire door that had been painted sky blue about a hundred years ago. The smell of fat was stronger here, and a pile of black bin bags had been fashioned into an unwieldy pyramid balanced against the wall opposite.

I took a deep breath and knocked hard on the door.

There was a long pause—twenty, maybe thirty seconds—and I was just about to try again when it was opened a few inches on a thick chain and a pair of cartoon-wide bloodshot eyes stared out at me from the gloom.

"I'm here to see Mitchell. I'm expected. My name's Sean."

The eyes stared at me for a couple of seconds longer, then the chain was released and the door opened.

A tall, slim black man of about forty stood appraising me with a slow, disjointed gaze, and a contented smile that was vaguely disconcerting. He was wearing jeans and a loose-fitting red T-shirt with the name of the takeaway emblazoned across it. Behind him thin wisps of dope smoke floated out the door. "Who sent you, mon?" he asked in a soft Jamaican accent.

"Tyrone Wolfe," I answered firmly. "Are you Mitchell?" I knew he was, of course. He might have been stoned, but he had an air of seniority about him which I've learned to spot a mile off.

"That's me," he said languidly. "You'd better come in, mon."

As I stepped inside, he let go of the door and it shut automatically with a series of loud clicks, locking me away from the outside world.

He led me through a narrow corridor and into a cavernous kitchen, with high ceilings and no windows, that smelled of meat and dope, and walked over to a table and chairs in the middle of the room. He picked up a half-finished joint from the ashtray and took a big hit.

"So, Sean, you got my money?"

If I said yes straight away, he might decide to rip me off rather than go through with the deal. Criminals can be very short-term like that, even supposedly reliable ones. On the other hand, if I said no, he might just tell me to get lost. In my experience, these kinds of negotiations rarely took a simple and direct route. In the end, I compromised. "Sure," I answered casually, much as I might have done if the guy had asked if I liked the color of the paint on the walls. "Have you got what I came for?"

"How come Wolfe and Haddock don't come 'round here

no more? They getting too high and mighty to deal with a bwoy like me?"

"They're busy today," I answered, hearing a movement behind me. I turned and saw a black guy of about twenty leaning against the kitchen door and blocking my exit. He was dressed in a gaudy track suit and New York Yankees baseball cap and wore Ray-Bans even though the room was dark. He also had his right hand behind his back, which was never a good sign. Trying to remain as unfazed as possible, I turned back to Mitchell. "I'm in a bit of a hurry, so if you can get the stuff I'd appreciate it."

Mitchell nodded slowly, never taking his big bloodshot eyes off me, then shouted something over his shoulder in a rapid Jamaican patois that I didn't quite catch. "How long you worked for Wolfe, mon?"

"I don't work for anyone. I work with people."

"Yeah, well, how long you worked with him, then?"

I shrugged. "A few months maybe. What does it matter?"

"I like to know who I'm dealing with, that's all."

"Someone who wants to buy some guns, then get the hell out of here."

We stood glaring at each other for a few moments, the atmosphere souring fast. I could hear my heart pounding and the guy behind me shuffling from foot to foot as he stood guard with his hand behind his back—a hand that was almost certainly holding a gun. A bead of sweat ran down my forehead, and I was suddenly conscious of how hot it was in here, and how vulnerable I was.

A door at the other end of the kitchen opened and a big guy in a dirty apron and chef's overalls came in with a huge leg of lamb over one shoulder and an Adidas tote bag in his free hand. He dropped the tote bag on the table between

Mitchell and me, then threw the lamb down on one of the work surfaces, took a wicked-looking cleaver from the knife rack, and began systematically chopping it up.

"There are the guns, mon. All there for you."

I opened the tote bag and looked down at the weaponry inside: two compact semi-automatic Remington shotguns and a black Sig P226 pistol. I rummaged around inside, quickly locating a box of shotgun shells and another of 9mm ammunition, both of which were still in their wrapping and, like the guns, looked brand spanking new. The UK has some of the strictest gun laws in the world, and we've had some major successes breaking up arms importation networks, so this was an unusually high-quality haul.

I took out one of the Remingtons, admiring its finish. It was a black Model 870, a lightweight weapon with a short eighteen-inch barrel, often favored by American law enforcement officers and criminals because it was compact, easy to use, and deadly. I knew the 870 well enough from my police firearms training, and I flicked on the safety, then pumped the hand grip to check that it was unloaded.

"All dese guns are completely clean, mon," said Mitchell. "Never been fired. Never been hired. Fresh to your crew. Now, you got me da money?"

I pulled the envelope from my jeans and handed it to him. "Five grand. It's all there."

He opened it up, pulled out the wad of cash, and started counting.

Which was the moment when the far door opened again, and every undercover cop's worst nightmare walked in.

Seven

Weyman Grimes was wearing ill-fitting chef's overalls and carrying a sack of onions as he loped over to one of the worktops, his long, horse-like face wearing its familiar dour expression.

Five years ago he was a mid-range coke dealer working an estate in Dalston when I'd turned up posing as a customer with lots of money to spend and, along with a dozen colleagues, busted him for possession of fifty wraps of ultra-low-grade gear cut with worming powder. But it was my face he'd remember because it was me who'd stood in front of him discussing prices and haggling for a bulk buy deal; me who'd told him he was under arrest; me who'd grabbed him as he tried to make a bolt for it and slammed him face first into the stairwell wall where we'd been doing our deal; me who'd been the subject of his (unsuccessful) claim of police brutality; and, finally, me who'd stood in the courtroom smiling at him as he was led away to begin a four-year sentence for intent to supply.

A wave of cold fear, the type that makes your heart lurch, hit me head-on. But I'm a quick thinker by nature and I took a pack of cigarettes from my shirt pocket and pulled out a smoke, deciding to break my after-meal-only rule on the basis that it might well save my life. I kept my head down, pretending I couldn't light it, fighting the urge to turn and run for it.

Mitchell was taking his time counting, going through the notes one by one, and I was conscious that I couldn't keep standing like this without looking conspicuous, so I lit the tip and took a long drag, turning my head as casually as possible in the direction of the far wall so Grimes couldn't see my face. Willing Mitchell just to hurry up so I could get the hell out of this airless place.

Finally, he stopped counting and grinned. "All there, mon. Good doing business with you."

I nodded curtly, not wanting to speak in case my voice was recognized. Out of the corner of my eye I could see Grimes turning around and looking at me. Beginning to stare. I couldn't see whether or not there was recognition in his gaze, but I wasn't going to wait to find out, so I picked up the tote bag and turned for the door, still keeping my face away from him.

Five more seconds and I'd be back on the street and out of danger. But I'd barely taken a step when the words I'd been dreading broke the silence, delivered in Grimes's peculiarly whiny tones that I suddenly remembered all too well.

"Hey, I know you. Mitch, man, I know this fucker. He's a cop."

Immediately, the young guy standing at the door, the one with the cap and the hand behind his back, tensed.

I hesitated, unsure whether just to keep going or turn and front this out.

The decision was made for me when Mitch barked an order and the guy on the door brought the hand around to reveal a pistol that looked too big for his grip, which he pointed directly at my head, coming forward, so the end of the barrel was only a couple of feet away.

At the same time, the big guy in the apron stopped chopping the lamb and slowly turned around, the bloodstained cleaver still in his hand.

I turned on Grimes. "What are you talking about? I've never seen you before in my life. Get back to cutting your vegetables, and don't poke your nose into shit that doesn't concern you." My voice resonated with confidence and anger, just like it had to if I was going to get out of here in one piece, and for a tantalizing half-second Weyman Grimes wavered, taken in by the act. I'm a pretty ordinary guy—medium height, medium build, no stand-out features—and I looked a lot different from how I had when I'd nicked Grimes all those years back.

But then his features hardened. "No way, man, you're a fucking cop. You put me away years ago!" He turned to his boss. "He's undercover, Mitch. He was the one who nicked me for that old coke deal back in Dalston. I never forget a face."

"Don't insult me, you piece of shit, or I'll take you apart. Understand?" I took a step forward and he backed away instinctively, looking pleasingly nervous.

Mitchell looked confused, but the problem was that Grimes wasn't letting it go. "He's a fucking copper, Mitch, I tell you. I swear it. Seriously, I wouldn't bullshit you about something like this. We should do the bastard."

I took another step forward, which was when the big chef raised his cleaver to let me know it wouldn't be a good idea to go for Grimes.

"Fuck you," I said, waving a hand dismissively and turning away. "I'm out of here. You've got your money."

"You ain't going nowhere, blood," whispered Mitch, pulling a switchblade from his jeans and clicking open the blade, the fifth time now one had been pulled on me. "Not till we find out exactly who you are."

"He's a pig," crowed Grimes, a smile on his face now as he saw an opportunity for revenge. "Let's gut him." He grabbed a large chopping knife from the worktop and held it up.

I was surrounded. Standing alone in a stinking room with four violent thugs. Three of them with knives. The fourth holding a gun only three feet from my head. The sweat poured down into my eyes, making me blink, and the adrenaline pumped through me as I hunted for a way out, telling myself that there had to be some way of extricating myself from this situation.

"J-Boy, bring him over here," barked Mitchell, and the gunman grabbed me by the arm, pushing the barrel of the gun into my face.

"Drop the bag, pussy," he hissed, showing teeth, a sadistic glint in his eyes, reveling in his moment of power.

I did as I was told, thinking that this guy had seen too many films because he'd made a huge mistake by standing so close to me with the gun against my face. I'd been told once by an ex-SAS guy that all you have to do when a gun's pointed to your head is knock the arm holding it out of the way, and by the time the gunman's pulled the trigger, it'll be pointed elsewhere. Then all you had to do was deliver a gut punch, twist his wrist around until he let go of the weapon, and bang, you were sorted.

It had sounded easy when he said it over a few beers one night. A lot less so when you can feel the cool, bare metal of the barrel against your skin.

But I didn't have much choice, because these guys weren't going to let me go—not until they'd torn me into way too many pieces. So, as he gave me a shove, I made my move, knocking his elbow with my forearm and punching him in the gut at the same time.

Just as my SAS man had predicted, I caught him completely by surprise. The gun went off with a tremendous bang in the confines of the room, deafening us all as the bullet ricocheted off the ceiling and the floor. The gunman grunted in pain and the other three instinctively hit the floor, buying me a couple of seconds. I grabbed his gun hand at the wrist, keeping the barrel pointed away, then butted him in the face, two, maybe three times, twisting his wrist at the same time. But this guy wasn't going to give up easily and his grip on the gun remained strong as the two of us struggled around the floor together in a tight, awkward waltz, with him trying to bring the gun around so he could take me out with a shot, and me trying desperately to keep it pointed just about anyplace else.

The others were getting to their feet now, and the one with the cleaver came striding forward with it raised high above his head, his mouth opened in a roar I couldn't hear and an expression of pure murder on his face. Behind him, Weyman Grimes followed, knife outstretched, while Mitchell jumped up like a jack-in-the-box from behind the table, a weird grin on his face, his bloodshot eyes bugging out like they were on stalks.

The gun went off a second time, almost taking off the top of Mitchell's head before hitting the far wall. Mitchell went down fast, disappearing beneath the table like he'd been grabbed from underneath. Cleaver Man and Grimes froze like kids in a game of statues as they recovered from the blast.

That was when I used the palm of my hand to smack the gunman on the underside of his nose in a classic martial arts move, and as he stumbled backward I kneed the bastard hard in the balls.

Finally, he let go of the gun and fell to his knees, but Cleaver Man had recovered and was now almost on me, and I had to dive backward to get out of his way, landing hard on my shoulder blades. But I had the gun and, turning it around in my hands, I pointed it up at him, holding it two-handed, my finger tensed on the trigger.

He kept coming, raising the cleaver, moving almost in slow motion.

My reaction was a reflex. I didn't make a conscious decision to pull the trigger. I just did it. Three times in rapid succession, the retorts muffled by the intense buzzing in my ears.

One round struck him in the thigh, taking out a chunk of flesh as it exited and spinning him around wildly so that the next round struck him in the arse. I didn't see where the third went, but I thought I saw Grimes go down in a heap, just before Cleaver Man dropped his cleaver, which landed blade-first in the filthy linoleum flooring. He then grabbed at his wounded leg with two huge hands and let out an animal howl so loud that it roared through my deafness. He stumbled forward, toward me, and I fired again, a last shot that took him just above the knee in the other leg, and this time he fell hard to the floor.

"No one move!" I shouted, swinging the gun from left to right.

Grimes was down and clutching his belly, so I guessed he'd taken a hit there; Cleaver Man was pawing at his legs; and the young guy in the cap, who'd now lost his cap, had one hand on his balls, the other stretched out in front of him in a gesture of surrender, his face crumpled in pain.

I turned the gun on Mitchell, who'd once again reappeared, but this time with his hands in the air, a very sober expression on his face, and his knife nowhere to be seen. "OK, mon, OK. Take it easy now."

Still panting, I stood up, moving the gun around so that it kept everyone covered, my heart hammering in my chest as I began to come to terms with what I'd just done. I'd never fired a gun in anger in my life, but now I'd crossed a line, and there was no going back.

"I'm not a copper, all right?" I told Mitchell. "I'm not a fucking copper. Do you understand?"

"Sure, mon. OK. No problem."

I picked up the tote bag. "I'm going to walk out of here, and I want that to be the end of it. You've got your money, and I've got my guns, so we're both happy. OK?"

"Sure, mon, sure."

"He's a cop," hissed Grimes through gritted teeth, the agony on his long face almost making me feel sorry for him.

"Shut the fuck up, arsehole!" yelled Mitchell, who'd clearly had enough of this particular strand of conversation.

Still keeping the gun trained on all of them, I backed out of the room, then as soon as I was out of sight I stuffed the gun in my jeans and ran for it, unlocking the door and feeling a desperate relief as I got back out on the street.

I sprinted all the way back to the car, checking my watch as I did so. Eight minutes. That was how long the whole thing had taken, and now my life had changed dramatically and irreversibly.

"What's happened?" demanded Tommy as I jumped in the passenger side and threw the tote bag in the back, narrowly missing Tommy Junior.

"Just drive. Now."

The engine was already running and he pulled away in a screech of tires. "Talk to me, Sean," he said as we turned onto the Barking Road, heading back into town. "What happened in there?"

"We had a disagreement," I said at last, the adrenaline still pumping through me. "I got the guns but one of them accused me of being an undercover copper, things got a bit heated, so I shot him. And one of his mates." As I spoke the words, the whole thing seemed utterly surreal. I still couldn't believe I'd done it.

Tommy's eyes widened. "Not Mitchell. Tell me you didn't shoot that loon Mitchell."

"No, he's still standing. Don't worry."

"And the blokes you shot. Are they dead?"

I shook my head. "They'll need patching up, though."

For a couple of seconds Tommy didn't say anything, and I wondered if I'd blown it. But then he hit the steering wheel and burst into a fit of loud, throaty laughter. "Christ, Sean, you're like some sort of ice man! I can't believe you popped two of Mitchell's people. Wolfe'll be tearing his hair out!"

He clapped me on the shoulder, staring at me with an expression that looked dangerously close to admiration. And I knew then that, although it might have cost me my career, at least now I was one of them.

Eight

It was at exactly 1:15 P.M., and with the images of the Night Creeper's brutal murders still fresh in her mind, that Tina took her seat in the interview room with DCI MacLeod to begin the final stage of Andrew Kent's questioning.

Kent clearly sensed that something was wrong because he looked nervously from one officer to the other and kept licking his lips. Jacobs, his lawyer, just looked impatient.

Tina made the necessary introductions for the camera, then stared hard at Kent, wondering what it was like to have such a base disregard for human life. He'd inflicted unquantifiable levels of pain and misery, not only on his victims but on their families and friends too. She hated him then. Hated every single fiber of his being because, sitting there acting innocent, he reminded her of everything that had gone wrong in her own life as a result of someone like him.

Steadying herself, and conscious of MacLeod waiting for her to begin, she finally spoke. "We've found a number of home videos on your computer, Mr. Kent, that depict the murder of several of the Night Creeper's victims."

Kent looked stunned. "What are you talking about? I don't have anything like that on my computer."

"As your lawyer, I'm advising you not to say anything else,

Mr. Kent," said Jacobs, who also looked shocked. "Not until we've spoken about this." He turned to Tina. "I need a few moments alone with my client, officers."

But Kent didn't seem to be listening. He was staring at Tina and MacLeod. "I don't know what you're talking about. Honestly. I don't have any graphic videos on my laptop. Did you find this stuff on a computer in my flat?"

"I think we need time alone," said Jacobs firmly, putting a hand on his arm.

Kent pulled away and leaned across the desk, getting close enough to Tina that she could smell the sourness of his sweat. "Someone's setting me up," he pleaded, getting louder. "They've got to be. I don't know why, but someone's setting me up."

"Calm down, Mr. Kent," said MacLeod, speaking for the first time.

"What computer did you find? Just tell me that. Because I've got a Dell Inspiron. That's my one. I promise."

MacLeod told him it was an Apple Mac, and Kent continued with his frenzied denials: he'd never even owned an Apple Mac, let alone put graphic videos on one.

Tina sat back and watched him. She'd seen no end to training courses over the years on body language, in which she'd been taught to spot the telltale signs of a liar: lack of hand movements, defensive posture, failure to make eye contact. But Kent was exhibiting none of these.

Tina forced down the shred of doubt she was feeling. He was obviously just an incredible actor, as were a small but not insignificant minority of criminals. With a quick glance at MacLeod, who gave her a barely perceptible nod, she looked her suspect right in the eye and charged him with murder.

Kent leaped to his feet and shouted that he was innocent,

his face stretched into an expression of dismay and righteous anger. "Can't you understand that? I'm innocent!"

"Sit down," demanded Jacobs, grabbing him by the arm.

Kent angrily swatted his hand aside and stared again at Tina, his eyes wide in the kind of little-boy-lost impression that might have worked before she knew what type of man he was. "Please . . ." he whispered.

"Do what your lawyer says and sit down, Mr. Kent," she told him. "You'll get your opportunity to put your side of the story in court."

She noticed he was shaking and, concerned that he was about to lash out, maybe even make a break for it, she tensed, placing a hand on her CS spray under the table, remembering all too well how fast he could move when he wanted to, and how dangerous he could be.

But he didn't, and it took Tina a second to realize there were tears running down his cheeks. Then, finally, he fell back into his seat, and as Tina continued to charge him with each of the five murders, he put his head in his hands and sobbed quietly, Jacobs looking down at him with an expression of distaste. Once she'd finished, Tina stood, and she and MacLeod left the room, but as she did so she glanced back at Kent and felt that twinge of doubt reappear.

Could it possibly be that he was telling the truth?

Nine

It had just turned three o'clock, and I was still buzzing with the after-effects of the adrenaline when we pulled into a deserted pay-and-display parking lot just west of the Brent Cross shopping center, where we were going to be rendezvousing with Wolfe and Haddock. Tommy had already called Wolfe to say that, although we had the goods and they seemed in order, there'd been a problem. He hadn't elaborated, being cunning enough never to say too much on the phone, but I'd heard Wolfe's distinctive growl down the other end, the volume notched up a few levels, and it was clear he wasn't happy.

"Don't worry, Sean," said Tommy as he found a spot in the corner of the parking lot, near a couple of anemic-looking trees that were the only greenery I'd seen in the last ten minutes. "Wolfe'll smooth things over with Mitchell and his people. The relationship we've got with them's good, and Wolfe's got enough clout to make sure there are no come-backs. Know what I'm saying?"

"Sure," I answered, still finding it hard to come to terms with what I'd done.

I've come close to the edge before. One time, not long after I'd started out in undercover, I infiltrated a gang of West

Ham football hooligans to try to gather evidence against some of their top guys, who were suspected of involvement in drug dealing and gunrunning. The assignment lasted four months, and during that time I had to prove myself by joining in the clashes with rival fans. This meant hand-to-hand fighting. Hitting people in the face; kicking them when they were on the ground; chucking chairs through pub windows (I did that twice). I'd like to say that I tried to do as little damage to people as possible, but that's not entirely true. Several times I found myself caught up in the thrill of the moment—it's difficult not to when the war cries break out and the adrenaline's pumping through you. You're surrounded by your mates, guys you know will always watch your back, and it was the nearest thing to going into battle that I've ever experienced. It was wrong, I always knew that, but I justified it by telling myself that joining in was the only way I was going to keep my cover intact. And anyway, the men I was fighting against were football hooligans too, and knew the score when they got involved.

Then, during a mass brawl on the Seven Sisters Road with Spurs fans, I was one of ten people caught on CCTV throwing punches and kicks. Stills of the footage were shown on *Crimestoppers,* and though it was thankfully pretty grainy (this being the early days of CCTV), I was still recognized by both my bosses at the time, Dougie MacLeod and Captain Bob, as well as several colleagues. Not surprisingly, this caused huge embarrassment among the Met's brass who, desperate to avoid a scandal, got *Crimestoppers* to remove my mug from their website, stopped any further broadcasts, and told Captain Bob to pull me off the job immediately.

The grim irony in all this was that my guest appearance on *Crimestoppers* improved my credibility within the Firm no end. On the day I was told it was all over, I got a call from the Firm's head honcho and our main target, saying that he wanted a meet. But it was too late. I tried to persuade Captain Bob that it had to be worth carrying on now that I was finally in with the people we were after, but he wasn't having any of it. Sometimes as an undercover copper you've got to commit crimes to prevent other, bigger ones from happening further down the line. The key is not to get caught. I did, and it cost me a black mark on my record.

What I'd just done was different, though, because I'd deliberately shot two men. The fact that it was self-defense, and that they'd almost certainly survive if they received medical treatment, wasn't making me feel better either. There was always the chance that they were seriously wounded, or that they wouldn't get help in time, and then I'd have one, maybe even two deaths on my conscience. And if they did get help, it was also possible that one of them might talk to the cops. I was pretty sure that the big guy I'd taken in the legs wasn't the sort to blab, but Weyman Grimes was a small-time scrote, and he could get me into a whole shedload of trouble. And not the slap-on-the-wrist kind either. A shooting meant I was looking at an attempted murder charge, regardless of the circumstances. Even if I got off, I'd lose my job and my pension and end up on the scrap heap at the age of only thirty-three. And if I was found guilty I was looking at the next ten years of my life at least inside, cooped up with the pedophiles and rapists for my own safety.

I don't usually worry about things. You can't in my job, otherwise you'd end up with a coronary. But it was difficult to get over the enormity of what I'd just done, and on the journey over I'd been contemplating the idea of coming clean. Getting Tommy to stop the car, making my excuses and walking free, then calling Captain Bob to let him know what I'd done.

But in the end, I decided not to. I'd worked for too long now to infiltrate Tyrone Wolfe's crew simply to walk away as soon as the going got tough. I wanted to bring these guys down—Wolfe, Haddock, even Tommy—and I wasn't going to let anything get in the way of that.

I still had the gun. Unloaded now and pushed down the back of my jeans. I'd break it up and get rid of it later, so it wouldn't be found. In the meantime, pressed against my coccyx, it was just serving as a constant and uncomfortable reminder of my recklessness. The device in my watch had also recorded the whole thing, as well as my conversation with Tommy on the way over there, and now I was going to have to bin the recording in the name of self-preservation.

Tommy picked up the tote bag containing the guns from the back seat, gave a couple of dog treats to Tommy Junior, telling him we'd be back soon, and we got out of the car. I followed him along a dirt path to the anemic trees, then down an alleyway until we came to the back entrance of a shabby-looking 1930s townhouse. A flight of bird-crap-infested steps led down to a derelict-looking basement flat with filthy windows and a set of ancient net curtains that made seeing inside impossible. I crowded in behind Tommy, ducking my head as he knocked hard three times on the door, which rattled under the force of his blows.

It opened almost immediately, and Clarence Haddock's huge dreadlocked head appeared looking none too happy, as seemed to be the usual case with him.

I followed Tommy inside, still feeling pumped up and not in the mood for shit. Although I'd just put my job and my liberty on the line that day, it was still amazing what shooting your way out of a life-threatening situation could do for your confidence. Haddock slipped into place behind me, but I ignored him.

The room we entered was dark, dusty, and devoid of furniture, and smelled strongly of damp. Tyrone Wolfe stood off in one corner squinting at us angrily.

"Nice place you've got here," I told him, feeling bizarrely relaxed. "I was hoping your line of work paid better than this."

"Don't take the piss, Sean," he snapped. "I don't like it when people take the piss out of me. Understand?"

I shrugged, unfazed. "Sure."

He came off the wall and took the tote bag from Tommy, briefly looking inside before setting it down. "Now, what the fuck happened?" he snapped. "You said there was a problem."

He looked at Tommy when he said this but it was me who answered. "Yeah, there was a problem. One of Mitchell's little runts accused me of being an undercover cop, and they all went for me. I had to take evasive action."

"What kind of evasive action?"

"One of them had a gun. I got it off him, there was a struggle, and I shot a couple of them."

"But not Mitchell," put in Tommy hurriedly. "He's fine."

"Are they dead?" demanded Wolfe, clearly working hard to keep his voice down.

I shook my head. "I took one of them with leg shots. The other got hit in the gut with a ricochet, but they'll both live."

"I don't believe this. Mitchell's a reliable source. Nothing like this has ever happened before."

"I don't like being insulted, no matter who the hell it is. And being called an undercover cop is an insult in my book."

I became conscious of Haddock standing very close to

me. "Why's he accusing you of being a cop if you ain't one?" he said quietly, bringing his immense head close to my ear. "Why'd he bother saying that, uh?"

I'd taken a big risk by admitting to them that I'd been accused by one of Mitchell's people of being a cop, but in my experience, it's always best to confront these sorts of issues head-on. Keeping up my aggrieved act, I turned and looked Haddock in the eye. "Because he made a mistake, that's why."

A low growl came from deep inside him, and he began to sniff, his nose going up and down with exaggerated movements.

"What's your problem, friend? You got hay fever or something?"

He stopped, glaring at me with slit-thin eyes. "You think you're funny, boy, but you ain't."

I knew then that I'd made an enemy of Clarence Haddock, but I also had no choice but to act the way I did. So much of criminal life is macho posturing, using your personality, your reputation, your size as a means of intimidating those around you. To back down in a confrontation is a sign of weakness, and if you want to be taken seriously by the big boys like Tyrone Wolfe, you just don't do it.

"He can't be an undercover cop, Clarence," said Tommy. "He shot two blokes. Coppers don't do that."

"It's a good point, Clarence," put in Wolfe, seeming to appreciate this pretty obvious point for the first time. "But I'm going to need to speak to Mitchell and iron this shit out. Either of you two got a clean mobile?"

"I got one," Haddock answered, still staring at me, although he'd moved his face back a little now so we were no longer quite so intimate. He pulled a phone out of one of the dozen or so pockets of his knee-length black shorts and chucked it over. "I got my eye on you," he said, pointing a stubby finger at me as Wolfe went through a door at the end of the room to make the call.

Deciding to bin my two-a-day habit for now, I lit a much-needed cigarette.

It wasn't long before Wolfe was back in the room. "Mitchell ain't happy, Sean," he told me, shaking his head.

I was prepared for this and had already thought of my retort. "Neither am I, Wolfe. You think I want to have to go off shooting people? It's risky and it's bad for business. I'm no nutter. I'm just an ordinary bloke looking for a decent job, that's all. Now, you send me out on a delivery to pick up your guns, and I don't complain, I just do it. And then some toerag who needs his eyes tested, a poxy little chef who was probably stoned up to the eyeballs, reckons I'm a copper who nicked him years back, and then suddenly the guns are out and it's looking like I'm a dead man if I don't do something, when all I was guilty of was doing you a favor. It's not even as if you were paying me for it, for Christ's sake."

"All right, all right," said Wolfe, lifting his hands in a conciliatory gesture. "I get the picture, and I've sorted stuff now. Mitchell's pissed off about his boys, but he knows you weren't to blame."

"Are his boys OK?"

He nodded. "They're getting treatment and they won't talk, so there's going to be no repercussions, although I don't think Mitchell's going to want to deal with us again for a while."

His words relieved me, but I didn't show it. "I'm not saying sorry. I did what I had to do." I took a drag of the cigarette. It was time to move things along. "So, you've got the guns. Now, are you going to tell me who we're supposed to be grabbing and how it's going to work, so I can decide whether I'm in or not?"

Wolfe looked over at Haddock, who nodded. He might not have liked me much, but apparently that wasn't going to stop us from working together.

There was a long silence in the room before Wolfe finally spoke again. "I can't tell you who we're snatching until the last minute. That's the client's orders, all right? You're going to have to trust us on this."

In the past, Tyrone Wolfe had always planned his own operations, and the whole idea of a client paying someone like him to carry out a kidnapping was pretty much unheard of. Even the term "client" seemed weird coming out of his mouth. But if there was one, then I needed to find out who he was. So I asked him.

"I can't tell you that, either," he answered. "He wants to stay anonymous."

I sighed. "Look, you spend all day giving me the tenth degree, saying you can't trust me because I might be an undercover cop, then you go and expect me to trust a man I've never met, and whose name I don't even know. I mean, how the hell do I know that *he's* not a cop?"

"Because I've known him for a long time, and more importantly, he's got the money. All you've got to do is a little bit of crowd control and cover our backs while we snatch the target. Do that, and you'll be a hundred grand richer. Guaranteed."

I frowned, still confused as to exactly what I was getting involved in. "So, it's a hit?"

Wolfe shook his head. "No. We just hold up the guards and retrieve the guy. The client takes it from there."

"And what's the client going to do with him?"

Wolfe shrugged. "I don't know. He hasn't told me, and I haven't asked. It's not my business. And it shouldn't be yours, either. Are you in?"

Of course I was in, but I was surprised they were giving me the choice now that they'd told me the details. Then I realized that the reason they were was because, having shot two men, I could hardly go to the police and report them myself. I was going to have to think very carefully about how I got around this.

In the meantime, I was still playing the part of an unemployed thug in need of some quick cash. Which meant demanding that advance on the hundred grand, because failure to do so would just look suspicious. "You said it's thirty grand up front."

"That's right."

"Well, you get me that, and I'm in."

For the first time in my presence, Tyrone Wolfe grinned. Even Haddock seemed to relax. And Tommy was beaming from ear to ear. He came over and clapped me hard on the back. "You're part of the crew now, Sean."

"Welcome aboard," said Wolfe. "You won't regret it."

And then the man who'd murdered my brother put an arm around my shoulder and pulled me to him. And I had to make myself smile back at him, knowing that finally I had the opportunity for revenge I'd been waiting almost fifteen years for.

Ten

My brother John was the kind of guy everyone liked. He had a big grin and an infectious personality. He was always helping people out—friends, family, neighbors, everyone. He used to do the shopping for the old lady who lived down the road, and when she died, just after his sixteenth birthday, she left him five thousand pounds in her will. And do you know what he did? He gave a thousand of it to the local army cadet corps where he was a member so they could buy some new equipment, and another fifteen hundred to my mum and dad to put toward a family holiday for us all. That was John for you. Generous to a fault.

He was six years older than me and, growing up, I'm not ashamed to say I worshipped him. He'd always take time to play football with me or take me fishing, and knowing he was always there as a protective influence was one of the reasons I was confident enough to take on, and make enemies of, the playground bullies.

While I always wanted to be a police officer, John's burning ambition was to join the army, and after his A-levels, that was exactly what he did. I'll always remember the day of his passing-out parade at Sandhurst to celebrate the end of his officer training. The pride on the faces of my mum and dad as he marched past us; the excitement I felt as a thirteen-year-old boy, waving my Union Jack flag and seeing the Queen for the first time as she inspected the parade; the family photos of the four of us together afterward, with John pristine in his uniform—photos that would grace the walls and mantelpieces of our home for years afterward.

We were all scared when he did his tour of Northern Ireland. At that time, in the tail-end of the 1980s, it was still a very dangerous place for British troops, with bomb attacks a regular occurrence. But he came back unscathed with tales to tell of street riots, tense patrols in the bandit country of South Armagh, and hours of mind-numbing boredom stuck on base waiting for something to happen.

And then, in August 1990, Saddam Hussein's forces invaded Kuwait and the Gulf War began. John was one of forty-five thousand British troops sent out to help liberate the country, along with half a million others from a wide coalition of countries, and I remember him being excited at the prospect of finally seeing some real action. My mum was worried about him. She didn't want him to go, but on his last visit home before he went he'd put a big protective arm around her and told her not to worry. He'd then shaken hands with my dad and me, and headed out the door with a final wave goodbye.

When the ground war broke out at last in February 1991, it was one of the biggest mismatches in history. The Iraqi army was routed and Allied casualties were minimal. Unfortunately, they included members of John's unit, whose armored personnel carrier was targeted by mistake by an American A10 war plane. John survived the attack, unlike six of his colleagues, but he suffered serious burns to his face and body, and lost three of the fingers on his left hand. He spent two months in hospital, and when they first removed his bandages, Mum fainted. He was unrecognizable, his face a cruel tangle of scar tissue. Even I flinched, and had to fight back tears.

At twenty-one, John was invalided out of the army. Extensive plastic surgery and skin grafts helped to improve his appearance, but the mental scars proved harder to heal. He became withdrawn and depressed, suffering from post-traumatic stress disorder, a condition I don't think was even recognized at the time. He argued constantly with Mum and Dad, and ended up moving to a small flat in north London where he lived alone, preferring not to venture out so he couldn't be seen.

But the thing about John was that he was a fighter, and, though it took a long time and a number of setbacks, including an arrest for drunk and disorderly and assault after a row in a pub when someone made a disparaging comment about his face, he slowly began to come out of his shell and get his life back together. He even got himself a job in a secondhand bookshop, which he was really enjoying. I'd just joined the Met as a trainee based out of Holborn, and had moved down from the family home in Herefordshire, so I often used to visit him. We'd go for drinks together in the pubs near his flat, and I was impressed at how he was turning his life around. He was even talking about running the London Marathon to raise money for an ex-services charity.

But he never got the chance, because a few weeks later he was dead.

It happened one lunchtime. John had just finished his morning shift at the bookshop and was walking down the high street to pick up a sandwich when he walked straight into an armed robbery. Two masked men armed with shotguns were holding up a cash delivery van outside a NatWest Bank branch. As they forced the two security guards to their knees, and ran to their getaway car, where a driver was waiting with the engine running, John sprang into action and gave chase, rugby-tackling one of them.

It was a crazy move, but just the kind of one John would make. He was like me in that respect. He never liked to see the bad guys get away with their crimes. And he'd always been recklessly brave, even more so, I suspect, since his injuries, because now he had a point to prove, and this was just the opportunity for the glory he'd always craved, yet had never quite attained.

Unfortunately, he'd picked on the wrong bad guys. According to one of the dozens of witnesses at the scene, the robber John had rugby-tackled was powerfully built and had managed to throw him off. At this point, the second robber strode over, shouted the words "Oi, freak!" and as John, down on one knee and presenting no threat, raised his hands in surrender, the gunman had shot him once in the head from a distance of no more than five feet, killing him almost instantly. They'd then escaped with their haul intact.

Forty-six thousand three hundred and twenty pounds—the price of my only brother's life.

Oi, freak! I'll always remember those words. They still sting now. Not only did they murder someone who was a hundred times the man either of them would ever be, but his executioner had even seen fit to mock him for the injuries he'd suffered in the service of his country.

There was a huge public outcry at the killing. No one likes it when an innocent man's killed standing up to thugs, especially when that man is a wounded war hero. But unfortunately an outcry on its own is not enough. Although there was huge pressure to find and prosecute the gang, who were believed to be responsible for a further five armed raids over a two-year period, they'd left behind very little evidence for the investigating team to work with.

That wasn't to say that the police didn't know who they were. Three names were quickly in the frame: Tyrone Wolfe, Clarence Haddock, and Thomas Allen, career criminals from Hackney with at least twenty convictions between them. They were all arrested and taken to separate police stations for questioning, but none of them gave up a thing, and searches of their homes unearthed no evidence linking them to the crimes. So no charges were brought, and although they were put under surveillance for a while, eventually they fell off the radar.

It was a different story for my family. First the bomb and John's injuries, then him being killed, ripped my parents apart. My father never recovered from it. He'd always had a strong exterior, but he was more brittle inside than he'd ever let on, and he was gone within two years. My mother hung on for another seven—I think, because of me—but she was never the same, and in her last years, as she aged and withered and fell apart, we saw each other less and less. She couldn't stand the idea of me risking my life as a cop, not after what had happened to John, and didn't see why I couldn't just get a normal job, as an accountant or a lawyer or something equally boring. She would nag, I'd get sick of it and shout at her, she'd cry, I'd apologize. And our own small domestic tragedy played out the same way again and again like a broken tape, until finally I buried her, five years back now.

But I never forgot about the men who killed my brother, and throughout my career I kept pushing my various bosses to investigate them. And there were investigations. Wolfe and

Haddock later went down for three years apiece for supplying cocaine and heroin, while Tommy Allen did eighteen months for tax evasion, but it wasn't enough, and when they came out they went back to drug importation, as well as running brothels and people smuggling, except this time they were a lot more careful. I kept pushing. I kept following their progress. I kept looking for chinks in their armor.

Then, six months ago, while I was on another job, I finally got my breakthrough. An informant of mine told me that he'd heard Tyrone Wolfe bragging that he was the man who'd shot my brother, and I decided then and there that I had to infiltrate his crew. Although they were a tightly knit unit, they did use other people in the commission of their crimes, particularly on the brothel and people-smuggling sides of the business, and I was convinced that if I could just get close enough I could get Wolfe to admit on tape that he'd killed my brother, and then we'd have them all bang to rights.

But when I went to see Captain Bob in his office at the CO10 HQ in Brixton to get the authorization to go ahead, he turned me down flat.

Captain Bob's a bald, cadaverous ex-public-schoolboy in his late fifties with a plummy accent who's been my boss at CO10 for more than ten years. He sits on his arse and supplies the jobs. I go out and do them. He gets paid twice what I do (I sneaked a look at one of his pay slips once) and I take all the risks, which seems to encompass perfectly how the world of work works.

I've always been able to tolerate that because generally he's not been a bad boss and doesn't interfere too much, but the day when he sat behind his immense tinted-glass desk in his expensive suit and told me there were other bigger and more important targets than Tyrone Wolfe, I blew my top.

"Not to me there aren't," I'd said coldly, leaning over the desk, getting in far too close to him. "That bastard killed my brother, and now he's walking round scot-free, boasting about it, and still making his living from crime. What does he need to do to get you interested? Assassinate the fucking Queen?"

As unflappable as always, Captain Bob had told me to calm down and sit down. "I will pass on your information to the powers-that-be, but it's precisely because this is so personal to you that I can't authorize it. Look at you, Sean. It's almost fifteen years since your brother died, and you're still full of rage. You'll never be able to approach the situation objectively and gather evidence without blowing your cover."

"I will. Just give me the chance."

"No. I can't." There was a finality to his words, and I knew he wasn't going to budge.

"Will you use someone else, then? I've got evidence that he's still heavily into the drug trade."

"How have you got evidence?" he demanded, looking pissed off.

"How do you think?" I countered. "Because I take an interest."

"I'll see what I can do, but I'm telling you this, Sean." He pointed a long, bony finger at me. "I don't want you spying on Tyrone Wolfe or any of his associates any more. If I hear that you are, I'll have you up on it. I promise you that. I don't want your personal life interfering with the job."

There was nothing else I could do at the time. But when, three months later, there was still no infiltration job authorized against the Wolfe crew, I knew I was going to have to do it myself, and do it alone.

And that, unfortunately, is exactly what I did.

Eleven

It should have been a good afternoon for Tina Boyd. The arrest and charging of Andrew Kent, not to mention the evidence that had been discovered as a result of the search of his apartment and laptop, were a massive result for the team, and there was an atmosphere of excitement bordering on euphoria in the incident room as the necessary paperwork was completed and the first stage of the case against him closed off.

But Tina wasn't sharing in it. Instead, she felt a heavy, black gloom descending on her as she sat in her shoebox-sized office in the far corner of the incident room, listening to the noise and banter outside the door, feeling like the perpetual outsider she was. It wasn't that she thought Kent was innocent. She didn't. She'd felt the odd twinge of doubt during the course of the interviews, but that was more down to what she was now convinced were his Oscar-winning acting abilities. Only once in all her years as a copper had Tina ever seen someone play the part of an innocent man as effectively as Andrew Kent. That was a guy they'd arrested on suspicion of murder during her first stint in Islington CID, after his wife had gone missing following a series of violent arguments, and he'd turned out to be telling the truth.

Tina, though, had concluded that there was too much

evidence against Kent to suggest he was innocent. It was humanly possible, of course, that the hammer and the laptop containing footage of the murders could have been planted, but only by the murderer himself, or someone working with him, and how would he have even known who Kent was? Only the members of the inquiry team knew Kent's identity, and they'd only discovered it in the past few days. In that time he'd been under almost constant surveillance, making planting evidence both risky and difficult.

It was too far-fetched a theory to waste time on. And it wasn't what was making Tina unhappy. What was depressing her was the fact that a seemingly ordinary man like Andrew Kent—someone who'd never been in trouble before, who'd had no known psychiatric illnesses, who looked like he wouldn't harm a fly—could commit such utterly inhuman and barbaric crimes. Earlier that afternoon she'd called the managers of three of the companies who'd used his services in the past year to tell them that Kent had been arrested and charged with murder, and that officers would be coming around to take statements from them, and all three had expressed total shock. One of them had even commented on what a nice guy Kent was, describing him as friendly, polite, a great worker. None had used the classic "serial killer" sobriquets of "quiet" or "withdrawn." They'd liked him. It had shown in every one of their voices.

Yet somehow he'd felt the urge to take a ball-peen hammer and smash it into the face of his victims again and again until there was nothing left but pulp, and then rape them as they lay dying.

It was this that was tearing Tina apart. The fact that people could be so terribly and inexplicably evil, and that every time she, as a police officer, helped to bring one to justice, another popped up, hydra-like, to take his place—except this time Kent had raised the bar still further, almost as if he was trying to outdo all those who'd gone before.

He'd filmed his victims dying. For his own pleasure. So that he could watch their death throes afterward in the comfort of his own home.

Like a masochist taking pleasure in her own pain, she replayed the film in her head, listened once again to the choking, desperate sounds of Adrienne Menzies dying, until finally she shook her head violently to try to force the images out.

She needed a drink. Badly. More than she'd needed one for a while. She never normally drank at work, preferring to wait until the end of the day, when she could finally let herself go and enjoy peaceful oblivion. She'd always been able to keep her habit under control in that respect, which was why none of her colleagues had ever suspected she had a problem. But occasionally, when things were tough, as they were now, the urge came hard and unforgiving, like an arrest team in the night, and the more she resisted, the stronger it became until there was no choice but to succumb. Like now.

She pulled a single key from the back pocket of her jeans and unlocked the bottom drawer of her desk, rummaging around beneath the files of paperwork until she found what she was looking for: a quarter bottle of Smirnoff Red Vodka and an open packet of Sharp's Extra Strong Mints. Slipping them into one of the inner pockets of her suit jacket so the booze at least wasn't visible, she got to her feet and walked through the incident room, throwing out the occasional instruction to members of her team as she passed, knowing she was taking a big risk but already excited at the prospect of a quick, much-needed fix.

The ladies' toilets were empty and she took the cubicle furthest from the door, unscrewing the lid even before she'd locked the door.

She sat down, and it was then, surprisingly, with the bottle barely an inch from her lips, that she hesitated for a long moment, taking the opportunity to ask herself what the hell she thought she was doing. She didn't want to be like this. Reliant on something that would eventually destroy every facet of her life. All it would take was one on-the-spot test and she'd be sacked immediately, and everything she'd worked so hard for would be lost. All over one quick drink, the pleasure of which would be long-forgotten by tomorrow.

There'd been a time, a long time back now, when she'd had a boyfriend she cared about, maybe even loved, when she hadn't needed to do this. She couldn't bring back John—he was gone forever now—but she could start again. Kick the booze, make a fresh start, maybe even a new job . . .

I'll stop, she told herself. I'll stop soon. When things have calmed down a little and I've got the chance to get my head together.

She took a decent-sized gulp, a double's worth at least, flinching as it burned its way down her throat and into her bloodstream. She paused, disciplined enough to know she couldn't overdo it and draw attention to herself, before drinking again, a bigger gulp this time, already telling herself that it was going to be the last.

She leaned back against the wall and sighed, waiting for that first hit of lightheadedness. Wondering whether to risk having another slug or call it a day and go outside for a smoke before returning to her desk smelling of mints.

She was still considering this when the door to the ladies' room opened and someone came inside. She froze like a naughty schoolkid, then relaxed as she realized that nobody could see her, so they wouldn't have a clue what she was doing.

"Ma'am?" came a female voice, sounding uncertain and vaguely embarrassed. "Are you in here?"

It was Anji Rodriguez.

Realizing it must be urgent, Tina slipped the vodka bottle back inside her jacket and took a deep breath. "I'm in here," she called out, enunciating her words carefully to hide any sign of inebriation. "What is it?"

"It's Andrew Kent. He's asked to see you. I've got no idea what he wants, but he says it's urgent and he'll only talk to you." Rodriguez's tone was hostile, but then Rodriguez didn't like her, having never made any secret of the fact that she thought Tina was too much of a celebrity for her own good.

In preparation for his court appearance the following morning, Kent was being held in the cells of Holborn station, after which he'd be remanded in custody in one of the capital's maximum-security prisons. Although UK law states the police aren't allowed to question a suspect after he's been charged, they're still allowed to talk to him if he requests it. Usually, it means they want to confess.

"OK," she said, relieved that she sounded perfectly sober. "I'll be down as soon as I've finished."

As the main door closed and Rodriguez left, Tina slowly got to her feet, wondering what it was Andrew Kent had to say that was suddenly so important.

Twelve

Andrew Kent, all five feet seven inches of him, was sitting on his cot at the far end of the cell when Tina looked through the inspection hatch, his head in his hands, his feet dangling. It was the classic pose of an innocent man, straight out of TV central casting.

"Will you be all right in there with him?" asked the custody sergeant, an overweight Welshman with an appalling side parting, whose name she could never remember but who seemed to have a soft spot for her. "I know you're a bit of an action woman, but you've got to be careful." He winked to show that he was only yanking her chain.

"I'll be fine, thanks," she answered, trying not to breathe on him. He'd be the sort who could smell it. And who'd report her like a shot. Soft spot or not.

As the door clanked open and she went inside, Kent took his head out of his hands and looked up at her, brushing a thick lock of hair away from his face. His eyes were red and blotchy where he'd been crying, and he looked about seventeen. "Thanks for coming," he said, managing a tight, respectful smile.

She stood in the middle of the room, feeling disgust rather than fear. "No problem. What can I do for you?"

"I'm innocent, DI Boyd."

"I don't want to rain on your parade, Mr. Kent, but I've got to tell you, most people I arrest say that, and most of the time they're lying. Right now it's up to a jury of your peers to establish whether you're telling the truth or not, but in my humble opinion, with the evidence stacked up against you, I'd have to say that you haven't got a hope in hell of getting off. Now if you've got nothing else to say—"

"I can prove it."

He delivered the words calmly, looking her right in the eye.

"How?"

"I remember one of the victims. Her name was Róisin O'Neill. She was really friendly to me when I was putting in the alarm system—not in a come-on kind of way," he added hastily, as if Tina might disapprove, "just nice, do you know what I mean? Interested in me as a person rather than just some workman doing a job. We chatted a fair bit while I was working and I remember her telling me that the name Róisin meant 'blooming rose' in Gaelic."

"Get to the point, Mr. Kent."

"Because of that, I remember her murder more than the others. I can still recall how shocked I felt when I first read about it in the papers and saw it on the news." He shook his head wearily and Tina had to resist the urge to tell him to knock off the dramatics. She was getting tired of his acting, however good it was. "And I don't know why I didn't remember it before. I think perhaps it was the shock of being arrested and interrogated for something I didn't do. But now I've had some time on my own to think properly, I've remembered something very important." He paused, staring at her. "Can I ask you a question?"

"What?"

"How long after Róisin died did you discover her body?"

Tina was beginning to feel a little spaced out as the vodka kicked in, and it took her a couple of seconds to remember. Róisin was the fourth victim, a very attractive blond-haired girl in her late twenties—not one of the ones, thank God, that Kent had filmed himself killing. "I think it was the day afterward. The cleaner let herself into the flat and found her."

"So, you should have had a fairly precise time of death, yes?" There was an eager, expectant look on Kent's face.

"Precise enough. Now, tell me where you're going with this."

He took a deep breath. "At the time of Róisin's murder, I'd had a family tragedy of my own. My father died, and I'd just come back from his funeral when I heard what happened to her. I know it was the day after I got back that they named her, and I think that was the day after her body was discovered. Which means, by my calculations, I was attending the funeral on the day she died."

Tina looked at Kent sharply, uneasy suddenly. "And?"

"The funeral was in Inverness, where my father had been living for the past twenty years since he divorced my mother. I flew there and back on Easyjet. I was there for three days in all and there are at least fifty witnesses who can put me in the church at the time I'm meant to have been murdering someone six hundred miles away in London. Where I'm going with this, DI Boyd," he said, "is letting you know that I've got an alibi for Róisin O'Neill's murder." His face broke into an expression of relief and elation. "I've got an alibi."

Thirteen

The stark fact was this. I'd shot and seriously wounded two men while working on an unofficial job. It might have been self-defense but that wouldn't save my career, or my liberty. Or my conscience, either. I'd taken the law into my own hands, ignoring the fact that I was paid to uphold it, and now matters had spiraled out of control.

I thought through what would happen next. Usually, in infiltration jobs, the path to an arrest follows a pattern. Once I've gained the trust of my targets, I use my recording devices to gather evidence of the targets' planned wrongdoing. If I can gather enough in this manner, I call in my colleagues, and while I'm safely off the scene they come in and make the arrests. If, however, more's needed, we tend to allow them to carry out the crime they're planning—usually with me accompanying them—and then move in and catch them red-handed on my signal. These are the best ops from my perspective, because I tend to get nicked along with the bad guys, and we don't have to use any of the taped evidence we've got, which means my cover doesn't get blown.

However, allowing the targets to carry out their crimes and taking them down mid-act can be a dangerous business, especially if there are guns involved and one of the gunmen is an undercover cop. So I knew damn well that the bosses would never sanction it with Wolfe and his crew, which meant I was going to have to wait until I knew exactly where and when the snatch was going to happen and then let Captain Bob know. It was hardly the ideal plan of action, but right then it was the best I had.

After the meeting with Wolfe and Haddock was over, Tommy drove me home. On the way, I again tried pumping him for information on the job, but he wasn't giving anything away.

It was an unusual situation, because what intelligence there was on Tyrone Wolfe stated that he was the boss of his tight-knit and very small crew, which effectively consisted of him, Haddock, and Tommy, and that he masterminded the business himself, rather than doing work for other people, which usually tends to be a surefire way of getting caught. It meant that they had to know a lot more about this op than they were telling. I studied Tommy's face but, like Wolfe, he was good at keeping his cards close to his chest.

It had just turned five o'clock when we pulled up outside the postwar terrace containing the flat I'd rented in the name of Sean Tatelli. I was officially on long-term sick leave from CO10 suffering from stress, having convinced the police psychiatrist I saw once a month that I was having a nervous breakdown, which had given me the time to focus entirely on the job at hand. Surprisingly, even after everything else, it was this deceit I felt most guilty about. I didn't like going sick, and until then my attendance record had been one of the best in the unit.

"Fancy a pint tonight after I've taken Tommy Junior for a walk?" asked Tommy, trying to get out of the way as the dog jumped on him at the mention of his daily exercise. "Not a big one, cos this job's going to come up pretty soon. Maybe even tomorrow. Just a celebration drink to welcome you to the team."

Normally I'd have said yes. I never liked to miss an opportunity to get closer to a target. But I needed to think. "Thanks, Tom, but I'm going to turn in early."

"You're all right, though, yeah?" He looked genuinely concerned.

I wondered irrationally if he could read my mind. "I'm fine. Why shouldn't I be?"

"Cos you shot two blokes today. It's not the kind of thing you do on an everyday basis."

"They asked for it," I said, with a defiance I wasn't feeling. "I was just defending myself."

He grinned, showing teeth that could have done with some investment, and gave my shoulder a meaty squeeze—an expression of affection that he'd given me on more than one occasion. "You're all right, Sean, do you know that? I trusted you from the beginning. I knew you'd work out. You're like us. You're a pro."

I thanked him once again for getting me the work, before watching him drive off with conflicting feelings. This was the man who'd driven my brother's killers away from the scene of their brutal crime and who'd gone on to commit numerous others. For years I'd built him up as a monster who'd not lost a moment's sleep over what had happened to John. And maybe he hadn't. I don't know because I was always careful never to raise the subject with him, but in the three months I'd spent getting to know him, he'd become far more human in my eyes. A flawed character, certainly, an uneducated thug unafraid to use violence when he considered it necessary, but a funny, generous guy as well, who was popular in the pubs we drank in, who doted on his dog, and who genuinely seemed to like me.

Usually, I was good at compartmentalizing the different lives I led. I looked at my undercover one as a fantasy, a risky role-playing game where the people I worked with were little more than fleshed-out characters. A game which came to an end only to be replaced by a new scenario with new characters. But it was different with Tommy. A part of me hated his guts for what he'd done to me and my family, but like some deluded victim suffering from a form of Stockholm Syndrome, another part of me genuinely liked him. Either way, I knew that getting him arrested would give me a lot less satisfaction than I'd been expecting when I first started out on this job.

As I turned away and walked up to my front door, Tommy's words rang out in my ears: "You're a pro." But I wasn't. I was an amateur who'd let his emotions get the better of him, and because of that I was about to put everything I'd ever worked for at risk.

Fourteen

"I can't believe this," said DCI MacLeod as Tina sat opposite him across the desk in his office. "We question him on and off for the best part of twenty-four hours and then, while he's twiddling his thumbs in his cell, he suddenly remembers that he's got an alibi." His tone was more confused than angry, and he was pulling on one end of his mustache, which was a habit of his when stress was getting the better of him.

Tina nodded. "He said the anxiety of the arrest made him forget about it. Also, we're charging him with five murders so he's not going to remember immediately that he had an alibi for one."

"You don't believe him, though, do you?"

She threw up her hands in frustration. "I honestly don't know. The fact is, he's got what might be a cast-iron alibi for one of our five murders, and as far as I remember, this particular murder had exactly the same MO as the others. So, if he didn't do one . . ."

"We don't know he didn't do it. He could just be messing us about." The way MacLeod said it suggested he was clutching at straws.

"I don't think he is, sir. He seemed adamant. I've had to give him permission to call his lawyer."

MacLeod sighed. "Fair enough, I suppose. You know, Tina, I've been doing this job for getting on for twenty-five years—"

"You look too young for that, sir," she said, spurred on by the vodka.

He gave her a strange look, clearly not expecting a flippant comment like this from his normally serious DI, particularly in the midst of a serious conversation, and Tina cursed herself for being stupid enough to drink on duty.

"Anyway," he continued, "in all my years, I can't remember the last case I came across where the suspect's guilt was so bloody cut and dried. He has to be guilty, Tina. He just has to be."

She was about to say she agreed when his phone rang. MacLeod looked at the handset, clearly pondering whether it was worth picking up or not, before deciding it was.

He was on the line for about two minutes, during which time he hardly spoke as he listened to the person at the other end. Finally, he said that he'd get back to the caller and hung up, banging down the receiver hard enough to startle Tina.

"That was Jacobs," he said wearily, referring to Kent's lawyer. "He's just been speaking to Kent's mother and grandmother. According to them, the funeral did indeed take place on the day the pathologist said Róisin O'Neill died, and Kent was in attendance. Easyjet has also confirmed that he was on the flight going up to Inverness the day before the funeral and on the flight coming back to Luton two days later. Jacobs says he's going to collect more witness statements testifying to Kent's presence, and in the meantime he wants the charges dropped since it's obvious he can't have killed Ms. O'Neill. Ergo, he can't have killed any of them."

"What are you going to do?"

"What do you expect me to do?" he said, raising his voice. "We've got the murder weapon by his bed, with his DNA and the DNA of at least two of his victims on it, as well as the graphic footage on his computer. I can't very well let him go, can I? Whatever his lawyer might like me to do."

"No, I understand that, sir."

"Sorry, Tina, I know you do." He wiped a hand across his brow. "But this has really thrown things off kilter. Has Kent come up with alibis for any of the other murders?"

She shook her head. "No. Just Róisin O'Neill's."

"So we've got enough evidence to hold him."

"But we've still got the problem of explaining his alibi to a jury. If it really does turn out that he couldn't have killed Róisin, then our whole case is up the creek. The MO was the same for Róisin as it was for all the others, wasn't it? I thought it was, but I didn't join the team until after her murder."

MacLeod nodded slowly. "It was."

He sat back in his seat and tugged hard on the edge of his mustache, as if he was making a strong effort to pull it off completely. He looked red-faced and unwell, the stress of the case clearly getting to him. It was known that he liked a drink, and Tina wondered if she might end up looking like him one day, burnt out by the job, an early grave beckoning.

"Andrew Kent committed the murder," he said firmly. "I don't know how he's worked this alibi, but it's bullshit, and one way or another we'll be able to prove it. In the meantime, we've got more than enough evidence for the magistrates to remand him in custody tomorrow. So I think the whole team deserves a celebration drink. Including you." He made a valiant effort to smile. "Are you going to grace us with your presence tonight?"

His tone suggested he was just ribbing her, but there was

also an underlying issue wrapped up in it. Tina rarely social-
ized with the members of her team. These days, she preferred
to finish up at work and head home to the flat where she lived
alone, make a bite to eat, and then get slowly and steadily
pissed alone in front of the TV, unseen by her colleagues,
and unbothered by the problems of the outside world. But
she was also aware of her responsibilities now that she was a
DI and in charge of people, and she knew she was going to
have to at least show she was willing. "Sure, I'll come along
for a while."

"Good. It'll be nice to see you let your hair down."

Tina doubted that. When she hit the bottle, she tended
to hit it hard, and it wasn't a pretty sight. But she didn't say
anything.

"And let's not spoil it by going on too much about Kent's
alibi in front of the others," he continued. "It's just a last-
ditch attempt by a man who's been caught near enough red-
handed to pull the wool over our eyes."

She nodded. "OK. You've convinced me."

But the problem was, he hadn't.

Fifteen

One of the nastiest people I ever had to deal with was an up-and-coming Essex-based gangster by the name of Jason Slade. Slade owned a security company that ran the door on nightclubs across Kent and Essex and controlled all the illegal drugs being sold in them. He also ran a team of thieves who stole and rebadged luxury cars, before exporting them for sale in Russia and the Middle East, which was a hugely lucrative business, estimated at the time by the National Crime Squad to be worth several million in profits per year, making him extremely rich for a twenty-eight-year-old without a qualification to his name.

Like Tyrone Wolfe, Slade was surveillance-aware and very careful in his dealings. He was also a sadist, who took particular pleasure in torturing the people who got on the wrong side of him—something which was worryingly easy to do. There was a story doing the rounds that he'd once gouged out a love rival's eye with a teaspoon handle, while the girl whose attentions they'd both been vying for (and who hadn't chosen Slade) was forced to watch. Whether this story was true or not (and I've always thought it was), it cemented Slade's reputation both as a man not to be crossed and as one who was going to be very difficult to bring to justice, since everyone seemed to be so damn scared of him.

Then one of his gang was stopped in a stolen Porsche 911 Turbo with a kilo of cannabis and a hundred one-gram wraps of coke in a bag on the backseat. The guy, a good-looking chancer named Tony Boyle, who was still on parole for earlier drugs offenses and therefore facing a minimum seven-year stretch for his crimes, decided to cut a deal with the law.

Now we had a way of getting to Slade. Boyle's testimony alone wasn't enough to convict him, so it was decided that Boyle would have to set him up. Apparently, Slade was having difficulty getting a reliable wholesale supply of cocaine for dealing in his clubs and was having to get it from London gangsters at high prices—including, incidentally, one Tyrone Wolfe—so the plan was for Boyle to introduce me and another undercover officer as coke importers who would be able to solve Slade's problems.

It took weeks of wrangling, as these things often do, before a meeting was set up in a cheap motel room just off the A127 near Southend. It was a good few years back and recording devices weren't as advanced as they are today, so it was just an intro meeting and we weren't wired up. Our plan was to get Slade interested, arrange a test purchase of the contraband, then take him down red-handed as he handed over the money.

Slade had agreed to see us without Boyle present, and was alone when we knocked on the motel room door and went inside, fifteen minutes early. He was sitting at a crappy little desk wedged in between the wardrobe and the window. It was 10:15 P.M. and dark outside.

"Thanks for coming, gents," he said, getting up and shaking our hands in turn. He wasn't a big guy, no more than five nine, but he had the wiry build of a featherweight boxer, and he projected an aura of menace that comes naturally to the more serious criminals.

He offered us a seat on the bed, but we preferred to remain standing.

The guy I was working with was a veteran copper called Colin (I can never remember his last name), a short, stubby cockney with silver, slicked-back hair and a face that looked like it had been whacked with a spade. "I hear you want to buy some high-quality chang," he grunted, while I stood next to him, hands crossed in front of me, acting the part of his bodyguard.

"I hear you've got some to sell," answered Slade cleverly, refusing to be drawn, knowing that if we were undercover police officers then it would be illegal for us to encourage him to commit a crime by offering to sell a product he hadn't specifically asked for. All annoying semantics, you might think, but we had to be very careful how we operated if we wanted a case to stand up to a judge's scrutiny.

And that was the theme of the meeting. In the ten minutes we were in there, Slade was the one asking the questions—about our background, credentials, the size of the product we could deliver—but, at the same time, we couldn't get him to admit that he actually wanted anything.

In the end, Colin lost his rag with him. "Are you in the fucking market for some gear or not?" he demanded. "Or are we just wasting our time with the hired help?" His words were designed to provoke an angry reaction, to get Slade to start boasting about his seniority (as criminals will often do when their reputation's called into question), and I remember thinking that, given Slade's reputation for violence, Colin was taking a bit of a risk.

But Slade just smiled. "Ask around about me, and you'll

see I'm in a position to do business, big business, but I'm careful who I deal with. Maybe we'll talk again soon." And with that he turned his back, signifying that the meeting was over.

"Do you think he sussed us?" I asked as we got back to the car.

"No reason why he should," grunted Colin, opening the door. "Our legend's good. We'll get him soon enough. He's greedy. I could see it in his eyes."

The smell hit me as soon as I sat down. Overcooked meat.

I frowned, exchanging glances with Colin. He'd smelled it too. Then we heard the sizzling. Like bacon frying in a pan. Followed by a desperate, muffled mewing, a sound that instantly reminded me of an injured dog. And it was coming from inside the car.

We both turned around.

Tony Boyle was sitting in the back seat, although it took several seconds to work out that it was him, because his face was melting in front of us as the acid did its work, smoke rising from the dying flesh in thin, stinking coils. Only his head was moving, swinging frantically from side to side, because he was strapped like a mummy from mouth to ankles with brown parcel tape, rendering him helpless as he burned.

Instinctively, Colin reached out to pull what was left of the masking tape away from Boyle's mouth, and jumped back as the acid burned his fingers.

Yelping in pain, Colin called for an ambulance while I used the Swiss Army knife I was carrying to cut the tape from Boyle's body. I kept telling him it would be all right, that help was on its way, but I couldn't bring myself to look at the damage being wreaked on his face, or stop myself from choking at the toxic stench that was filling the car.

Finally, I managed to cut off all the tape, but when I

tried to pull him from his seat so we could get him outside to throw water on the wounds, I found he was stuck fast. It was only when I looked down through the smoke that I saw the reason why.

The bastards had nailed his feet to the floor.

The whole meeting had been a set-up. Slade had known we were cops all along, and this was his way of teaching us a lesson. We had nothing on him, either. He hadn't incriminated himself, and we had not a scrap of evidence to connect him to the attack on Boyle. In fact, like all good gangsters, he had the perfect alibi, having been in the presence of two undercover police officers while the crime went down.

Although he remained a target of the NCS, intelligence on him began to dry up. Nobody would talk, and it was considered far too dangerous to instigate another undercover op. The net result was that Jason Slade became even more well-established on the Essex underworld scene.

As a police officer, you have to get used to the fact that for every success you have there will always be at least one failure, and usually a fair few more. You learn to move on when you take a hit, not taking it personally, hoping for better luck next time. That was exactly what I did. I was traumatized by what I'd witnessed, but not so much that I couldn't do my job.

And then, just under a year later, I read about the tragic case of the father who'd been found dead in his car in Epping Forest, along with his six-year-old daughter. Tony Boyle, whose facial injuries had been so bad that his wife had asked for a divorce, and whose daughter had grown terrified of him, had simply not been able to carry on and had decided to take his only child with him.

I felt rage then. Real anger, the kind I'd experienced when I heard about the way Wolfe had murdered my brother. At that time, only a few years had passed since John's death, and the wounds were still raw. Jason Slade reminded me of all the injustices in the world. As far as I was concerned he was directly responsible for the deaths of Boyle and his daughter, yet he was at large and still untouchable.

But Slade had a weakness. Although he lived with a long-term partner, he also had a mistress whom he visited most Wednesday nights after he'd been out with his cronies. We'd known about her at the time of the undercover op, and had even bugged her flat at one point, but to no avail. It was a stupid move on Slade's part to keep to such a specific and obvious routine, especially as he traveled there alone, but it served my purposes, because one Wednesday night I waited in the driveway of the mistress's block of flats to meet Slade when he arrived there.

I'd been building myself up to it for several weeks, knowing that I was stepping way over the line, but for once letting the rage guide me in my actions.

Sure enough, at about half past midnight one fine, balmy summer's evening, Slade's Jag pulled into the driveway, and as he got out of it, looking more than a little worse for wear, and walked toward the main door, fiddling in his pocket for keys, I launched myself out of the shadows, a balaclava over my head and an image of Tony Boyle's burning face in my mind.

At the last second he saw me coming but wasn't fast enough to get out of the way. I had three two-pound coins wedged between my fingers, acting like an improvised but less lethal knuckleduster, and I bunched my fist as tightly as possible and unleashed a flurry of punches to his face, opening up a number of nasty little cuts as I sent him sprawling over the bonnet of the Jag, a feeling of real catharsis flowing through me.

Before he could recover, I was on him again, dealing blow after blow to his head and body, not giving him a chance to fight back as I beat him to the ground. I knew, like me, he'd been a boxer in his youth, and that he might also be armed, so it was essential I incapacitate him as quickly as possible. He was bleeding badly from his nose and cheek, and even in the darkness I could see his face beginning to swell, which pleased me no end. I wanted to humiliate this bastard and make him pay for some of the suffering he'd inflicted on his victims.

He landed on his back on the gravel, but as I grabbed him by the collar of his black leather jacket and dragged him to his feet, he threw a whip-like punch that hit me in the side of the head, catching me completely by surprise.

I let go of his jacket and retreated a couple of steps, shaking my head to clear it, but Slade was clearly nothing like as incapacitated as I'd thought and he was on his feet like a shot, coming at me in a classic protective boxer's stance before launching a well-aimed three-punch combination that sent me reeling before I could muster a decent defense.

My nose was bleeding under the balaclava, and I began to panic. I couldn't believe how stupid I'd been to go after him like this. Either I should have brought a real weapon, something that would have shifted the balance in my favor, or better still, taken the sensible option and not come at all. Instead, I'd compromised, and now I was going to pay for it.

I was wobbling precariously, partly stunned, as Slade came in close, grabbing me by the throat with one hand, a look of pure rage on his battered face, and yanking off my balaclava with the other.

It might have been a year but I could see the spark of recognition in his face, the realization that he knew me from somewhere. Then the surprise as he remembered exactly where.

Which was when I came to my senses and drove my knee right up into his groin with all the strength I could muster, managing to gather enough to lift him bodily from the ground. He let out a single, tortured gasp, and as I delivered a quick uppercut to his jaw, he went down like a sack of potatoes.

That was it. Given a chance of escape, all the anger and aggression seeped out of me and I turned and made a run for it, wondering what the hell was going to happen now that I'd made an enemy of the gangster some had taken to calling "the acid man."

For a while, nothing did happen. I kept my head down, hoping that he'd forget about it, and got on with my work. In those days, like a lot of undercover officers, I only worked part-time for CO10, and I was back on my day job at Camden CID, a good few miles from Jason Slade's stomping ground, when one day, about two weeks later, my boss, Dougie MacLeod, took me aside and asked me if there was anything I wanted to tell him.

Dougie was the kind of guy you didn't try to bullshit. Like all the best coppers, he could smell it from a mile off, and as he sat behind his desk waiting for me to speak, I realized that he knew something. So I told him everything, throwing myself on his mercy, and saying I didn't know what had come over me.

When I'd finished, he told me that Jason Slade had found out exactly who I was, as well as where I was based, and had put a contract out on my head. "He wants you dead for what you did to him, Sean. It made him look bad and it's done a lot of damage to his reputation. Damage he's very keen to repair."

I couldn't help but feel a small amount of satisfaction on hearing that, but unfortunately it was somewhat overshadowed by the fact that he was also willing to pay money to have me killed. There aren't that many contract killers operating in southeast England, but there are more than enough to take Slade up on his offer.

"How much is the contract for?" I'd asked.

He gave me a dirty look, but I could tell that behind it he was amused. "Twenty grand. At least double what you're worth."

The thing was, he could have lectured me about how stupid I'd been. He could also have recommended me for disciplinary action. He could even have said he'd washed his hands of me and that I was going to have to sort it out myself. It was only a couple of years after my football hooligan infiltration op, which had all gone so badly wrong, so he'd have been justified if he had. But Dougie MacLeod wasn't like that. He cared for his people and he was pragmatic enough to know how tough it could be being an undercover operative.

Instead, he left me to sweat (which I duly did), then a week later he took me aside again and told me that the whole thing had been sorted, and that the contract was now rescinded. He also told me that he'd enrolled me in a course of specialist sessions with a psychiatric counselor in an effort to sort out my problems and that if I ever crossed the line again, that would be it. He'd make sure I was drummed out of the force.

It was years before I found out what had actually happened. Apparently, Dougie had talked to my boss at CO10, Captain Bob, who'd initially wanted to sack me but who'd eventually been persuaded by Dougie to give me a second chance. The two of them had then put the word out among

London's bigger underworld players that if the contract was carried out there'd be serious repercussions from the police, not only against Slade himself, but against all the capital's organized criminals. It was all bluster, of course, but it must have done the trick because there was never any comeback from Jason Slade or any of his cronies, although the last I heard Slade was still running the Essex drug scene, and giving the finger to the authorities.

But the relationship between Dougie and me became strained after the Slade case, and although I worked hard to pay my debt to him by attending all my counseling sessions and keeping as much on the straight and narrow as possible (and being largely successful at it too), eventually I came to accept that it was never going to be the same again, which was one of the reasons I ended up moving full-time to CO10.

I still missed Dougie and the old crowd at Holborn station, though, and now and again, particularly when things weren't going well in my life, I turned up at the Fox and Hounds, the pub around the corner where we used to drink. I needed some of the old camaraderie that night, so, after spending way too much time sitting at home trying to work out how I was going to get out of this latest situation, I took a round-about walk to the Fox and Hounds, stopping only to throw the gun I'd used that day—now dismantled and disinfected, missing the firing pin, and wrapped in several layers of cloth—in an overflowing Dumpster on the way.

It was just after half past six when I stepped inside my old haunt for the first time in far too long. The pub was busy, but I recognized a few familiar faces in the crowd gathered around the bar, although fewer than I'd been hoping for. Dougie was there, of course, but then he'd always enjoyed a drink. He was talking to a group of about half a dozen people, and I was pleased to see that it included Simon Tilley, who'd joined Holborn CID in the same year as me and who was one of the few people I'd stayed in touch with. They were all laughing and joking, and there was that feeling of camaraderie that I'd been missing for most of the last few years.

The problem with working undercover is you don't get much of an opportunity to build relationships, either with colleagues or socially. You spend so much time living a lie that you begin to forget who you really are and what makes you tick. It was close to a year since I'd had a girlfriend, nearer five since there'd been anyone serious. Sometimes I thought about quitting undercover work and going back into CID, or maybe putting in to join Dougie MacLeod's murder investigation team. But I knew I'd get bored if I did, because I'd miss the buzz that undercover work provided.

I reminded myself of that as I bought a drink at the bar and sauntered over toward the group of coppers.

Simon spotted me straight away, coming over pint in hand and putting a friendly arm on my shoulder. "Hello, mate, haven't seen you in a while. What brings you here?"

I told him I was just passing through, and he pulled me over to the main group. I caught Dougie's eye and he smiled, with just a hint of awkwardness, and put out a hand. "Sean. How's life at CO10?"

I told him things were OK and that we'd had a few decent results recently, pleased he hadn't heard I was on long-term sick leave.

He nodded, looking distracted. "Well, it's good to see you," he said, and I knew then, with real disappointment, that he was bullshitting, that he didn't think it was good to see me. I wanted to tell him that I'd done all right in the end, even though the events of that day were still at the forefront of my mind, but there didn't seem to be much point if he wasn't listening, and anyway, Simon was already introducing me to several of his more recent colleagues.

I did the usual glad-handing thing as Simon explained to them I was now a big-time CO10 operative bringing down organized crime's Mr. Bigs. He then told me that they'd had a bit of a result themselves, catching the killer known as the Night Creeper. I was familiar enough with the case. It had had plenty of coverage in the media, and I knew that Dougie's team had been heavily involved in the hunt for him because Simon had told me about it the last time we'd seen each other for a drink.

I talked about it with Simon and his colleagues for a few minutes, and it was clear they were all pretty elated that they'd nicked such a high-profile suspect and that there seemed to be enough evidence to secure a conviction, which is always the hard part. I was pleased for them, but I also couldn't avoid the feeling that I was an impostor. This was their result, not mine. Their celebration. Simon might have been making an effort to make me feel welcome, but it wasn't really working, and I found myself quickly growing bored. And with the boredom came the reminder that I was a man potentially in a lot of trouble.

It was then that I saw her, standing on the edge of another group of people I didn't know, looking a little like me—someone who didn't belong. I recognized her instantly, of course. Tina Boyd was one of the most high-profile police officers around, having had the kind of career that made mine look uneventful. Kidnapped. Shot on two separate occasions. And last year, she'd run down and killed a fleeing suspect who later turned out to be responsible for a string of killings and a major terrorist plot. I'd heard that she'd joined Dougie MacLeod's team, and I remember Simon admitting grudgingly that she was a good detective, although she was also a bit up herself.

I watched her as she walked toward the pub's exit, reaching into the pocket of her suit for a pack of cigarettes. She was an attractive woman with classic Celtic features of dark hair and pale skin, but there was also something serious about her, as if she neither smiled that much nor suffered fools gladly. She was frowning as she left the pub, walking purposefully, and people instinctively moved out of her way.

I've never been the kind of guy to go for the right woman, so I moved effortlessly away from the conversation, pulling out my own cigarettes. I could no longer see Dougie, and Simon didn't notice me go. He was too busy talking to a young Spanish-looking woman at the bar, and getting in way too close to her.

When I got outside, Tina Boyd was leaning against a wall, smoking and looking deep in thought.

"Hi," I said, lighting a cigarette and walking over. "I don't think we've met. My name's Sean Egan," I told her, using my real name for the first time in what felt like weeks. "I used to work with Dougie MacLeod in CID."

She turned to me and I noticed she had eyes the color of mahogany. "I know," she said with the hint of a smile, putting out a hand. "I'm Tina."

"How do you know I used to work with Dougie?" I asked as we shook.

"He told me."

I was pleased. It meant she'd been asking about me. "Is that right?"

"He said I should keep away from you. He said you were trouble." Her expression had turned serious, but I got the feeling that she didn't care whether I was or not.

I thought about that one for a moment. "I wouldn't say I'm trouble," I concluded, "but I have to admit I quite enjoy looking for it."

"What do you do now?"

"I'm with CO10. Undercover work."

"Must be pretty stressful."

"It has its moments," I said, recalling my brush with death earlier that day. "But no more stressful than some of the things that have happened to you."

She shrugged, and I got the feeling that she didn't want to talk about it, which was fair enough. Usually, I'd have left things at that. Had my smoke and gone back inside. But there was something about her that made me want to persist with the conversation. I had the impression she was an outsider like me; someone I could relate to if only I could get past the hard shell.

I took a long pull on the cigarette, looking out toward the steady stream of passing traffic. "It's a thankless life we lead sometimes, don't you think? Chasing all these arseholes, just for more of them to pop up. You know, occasionally I feel like chucking it all in and doing something completely different. Running an organic farm or a surf school." As I spoke the words, I realized with something of a shock that I genuinely believed what I was saying.

"You'd be bored out of your mind within a week."

"You reckon?"

She smiled, wider this time. "I'm sure of it. Perhaps you just need a holiday."

I thought about that one. I hadn't had a holiday for years. The last time was a two-week trip to Antigua with a girl called Britt, who wasn't even Scandinavian. It had rained a lot and we'd fallen out by about day three.

I was about to tell Tina about this last trip, throwing in a couple of amusing anecdotes before asking her if she fancied a drink, because I had a feeling I was getting through to her, when the mobile I'd been using for the past few weeks to talk to Tommy jolted me from my thoughts. The ringtone was a bone-rattling, old-fashioned car horn I'd put on there so that I would never forget which phone it was. I thought about not answering, just forgetting about Wolfe, Haddock, Tommy, all of them for one night, but the world doesn't work like that. When you're undercover, there's no such thing as time off.

"That's a horrible ringtone," said Tina.

"It's designed to make me answer," I told her ruefully as I pulled it from my pocket. Once again it was a number I didn't recognize. "Excuse me for a moment. I need to take this."

I walked rapidly up the street, putting a good twenty yards between us before answering.

"Where are you?" demanded Tyrone Wolfe, and I knew immediately it was serious.

"Out for a drink with an old mate."

"Where?"

"Holborn. Just down the road from where I live. Why?"

"Because the job's on, Seany boy."

I froze. "What do you mean it's on? When?"

"Now," he growled. "Right now."

Sixteen

I kept walking, the phone pressed to my ear and my mind racing. "But I told you I wanted thirty K up front."

"And I've got it for you here. Things have moved on quicker than we thought they would. How much have you had to drink?"

"Only a pint. I'm fine."

"And what's your exact location?"

"I'll be at the junction of High Holborn and Grays Inn Road in two minutes. Where are you?"

"Not far away," said Wolfe ominously, and I suddenly had this horrible idea that he'd been following me. In which case he'd know I'd been drinking in a coppers' pub full of coppers.

I told myself to stop being paranoid and to get details of the job so I could feed the information to Captain Bob, who'd blow a gasket when he found out what I was up to, but was also professional enough to act on the information. "You're going to have to tell me more first."

"All in good time, Seany boy. You just get yourself to that junction and wait for us. Then you get your advance and we can talk."

"And you've got the guns?"

"Watch what you're saying over the phone," he hissed, and cut the connection without another word.

I wondered then if I'd overstepped the mark, but I had to find out if we'd be armed so that I could feed this to Captain Bob as well. He could then use the signal from my mobile phone to track my movements, while at the same time organizing an arrest team of armed officers who could intercept us before we carried out the kidnapping. If Wolfe had the guns with him, he could be nicked on a host of charges, and it would be job done. I'd be in all kinds of shit, of course, but that was something to worry about later.

The problem was, until I knew for certain they had guns, there was no point trying to get them nicked, because I didn't have a shred of concrete evidence against them.

I was still trying to figure out my best move as I walked along the quiet, tree-lined thoroughfare of Doughty Street, once home to Charles Dickens, when a dark vehicle with tinted windows and bearing more than a passing resemblance to the old *A-Team* van, pulled up beside me, the power-sliding side door opening automatically. There was no one in the back but I could see the figures of Wolfe and Haddock in the front.

"Get in," called Wolfe, and as I stepped inside I realized my decision had been made for me.

Seventeen

"What are you thinking of, talking about guns over the phone?" snarled Wolfe as he pulled away from the curb. "Are you some sort of rank amateur?"

"I told you we couldn't trust him," grunted Haddock, turning around and giving me a cold glare.

The atmosphere in the car was tense, and both men seemed agitated and jumpy, which told me, if I hadn't known it already, that the job was imminent.

"All right, all right, calm down," I said, putting up my hands in a defensive gesture. "You caught me off guard, that's all. When you said the job was soon, I didn't think you meant tonight." I made a play of looking at my watch, at the same time flicking the switch to turn on the recorder.

"We only just found out ourselves," said Wolfe.

"That's the problem with doing stuff for other people," grunted Haddock, who didn't seem too pleased about the way things were going, either.

I got the feeling then that I wasn't the only person who didn't know who the client was: Haddock didn't either. This surprised me. I'd always been under the impression that he and Wolfe were as thick as the thieves they were.

"I haven't even told you I'll do it yet," I protested. "And where the hell's Tommy?"

"Tommy's nearby. Don't worry about that."

But I was worried. Tommy was my only ally in the group, and I wanted him around while this was going down, just in case Wolfe and Haddock decided to get rid of me afterward.

"You said you'd do the job if we gave you thirty grand up front," continued Wolfe. He turned to Haddock. "Clarence, can you do the honors?"

Haddock produced a white jiffy bag and handed it to me, eyeing me carefully as he did so. "You got a phone on you?" he demanded as I took the bag and tore it open to reveal three phonebook-thick wads of used twenties.

"Yeah."

"Give it to me. Now."

"Fuck you."

Haddock's piggy eyes narrowed to angry slits and I saw that he was clenching his massive fists. But I stood my ground. I needed that damn phone so that I could text Bob and get him to track my location.

"Do me a favor, Sean, and give him the phone," said Wolfe, his tone conciliatory. "We're just going to turn it off and keep it while we do the job. It's more secure that way. You ought to know that. Mobiles are a copper's best friend."

Reluctantly, I pulled the mobile—the only one I was carrying—from my pocket and switched it off before handing it over. "I want it back afterward," I told them both angrily, but inside I was growing increasingly nervous because it looked like I was going to have to carry out the job with them, which was against every rule and regulation in the book.

Wolfe was watching me in the rearview mirror. "So," he said, "are you in?"

"This is a kidnapping, right? Not a killing. I'm not killing anyone. Not even for a hundred grand."

"That's right. We spring him from his escort and deliver him to the client. That's all."

"But what's the client going to do with him?" I asked, knowing that if I could get enough information on the recorder, I might get the evidence I needed to convict them later.

"The less you know about that the better," Wolfe answered with an air of finality.

"At least tell me the name of the person we're kidnapping."

Wolfe nodded to himself, seeming to come to a decision. "He's a real piece of shit," he answered. "The sort who rapes and murders defenseless women."

And even before he said it, I knew it was going to be the man my former colleagues had arrested only twenty-four hours earlier, the man whose name was known to no one outside the Metropolitan Police.

Andrew Kent.

Eighteen

Tina watched Sean Egan walk off down the street. On a different night she might have been interested in talking to him. The fact that Dougie MacLeod had called him trouble intrigued her, and he was a good-looking guy, who looked like he might be good company. But right now she was preoccupied with the Night Creeper case, and more specifically, with Andrew Kent's alibi.

Before leaving the station to come to the pub she'd run a check on the General Register Office database and found that Kent's father had indeed died just before the murder of Róisin O'Neill. She'd then called the vicar of the church in Inverness where his funeral had taken place and they had buried him on the day the coroner claimed Róisin had died. What was more, the vicar remembered meeting Kent before the service when he'd greeted the deceased's immediate family. When the vicar had asked the reason for Tina's call, she'd replied that it was in connection with a routine inquiry, and asked that he not mention it to anyone else. She had no desire to give him the full details of the case, even though she knew that Kent's lawyer Jacobs would be contacting him to do just that soon enough.

By the time she'd got off the phone, the rest of the team

had already gone to the pub, and when she'd walked in fifteen minutes later and seen them clicking glasses in celebration of catching the man who'd been terrorizing London's young women for the past two years, she hadn't had the heart to say anything about Kent's alibi. But she hadn't had the heart to join in the celebrations, either, and had forced herself to drink orange juice rather than a real drink because she needed to think.

All the available evidence suggested Kent was their killer, yet his alibi seemed cast-iron, and he was screaming his innocence from the rooftops. She felt the familiar stirring of excitement at the prospect of working alone to solve a puzzle that no one else seemed interested in.

Now that she'd done her bit and shown her face at the pub, her plan was to go back to the station and look through Róisin O'Neill's file to see if she could find any clues. Róisin was the fourth victim, murdered only a few months before Tina joined the team. Perhaps the coroner had made a mistake with the timing of the death? That kind of thing occasionally happened, and right now it seemed like the obvious alternative. Or that, at least, was what she was hoping as she stubbed her cigarette underfoot.

She noticed that Sean had disappeared and thought fleetingly that it was a pity they'd not said goodbye. She wondered if she'd have given him her number if he'd asked for it and concluded that she probably would have.

As she turned to walk back to the station, Dan Grier hurried out of the pub door, and she asked him if he was heading home.

He nodded. "What about you?"

"I'm heading back to the station. I've got some more work to do."

"What kind of work?" he asked as they fell into step. "I thought we'd solved the case."

"We have," she answered, "but there are a few ends that need tying up."

"Anything I can help with?"

"You were on the team when Róisin O'Neill was murdered, weren't you? Do you remember if anything stood out about her case? That made it different from the others?"

"I heard talk that Kent's claiming he's got an alibi for the O'Neill murder." Grier looked at her. "Is that right?"

She and MacLeod had agreed to keep Kent's alibi quiet, but it was always going to get out and she saw no reason not to say anything about it now. "It looks like he has, yes. That's why I wanted to go back and have a look at the file. Róisin's murder was before my time, so I need to read up on it."

Grier was silent for a few seconds. "There was no footage on Kent's laptop relating to it. And it was the only one for which there wasn't, which I suppose in the light of his alibi seems a bit strange."

"This whole thing seems bloody strange. Try to think, Dan—was the MO exactly the same as the others?"

"Jesus."

She put a hand on his arm. "What?"

"The MO was the same, but . . ." He screwed up his face in concentration. "But not exactly. There were minor differences."

"What kind of differences?"

"The hammer blows. Róisin had her face pummeled in like the others, but if I remember rightly, the actual cause of death was strangulation. He laid into her with the hammer, like he did with all the others, but the difference was he did it after she was already dead."

They stood in the middle of the pavement stock-still as the full ramifications of what Grier was saying washed over them both.

"His alibi's watertight," said Tina at last.

"But if he didn't kill Róisin O'Neill, then who did? And what about the other four girls? Did he kill them, or didn't he?"

Tina sighed. "I don't know. But that's exactly what we need to find out."

Nineteen

"You don't have to help me, Dan," Tina told him as they headed back up to the incident room. "I know you've put in the hours, and I don't mind doing this myself." In truth, she preferred the idea of working alone, especially in an empty office. It meant she could sneak a quick drink if she needed one without arousing suspicion.

"If there are problems with the case, then I'd like to help," he answered coolly. "I'm in no hurry to get home. Melinda's not expecting me until late anyway."

Melinda was Grier's wife. They'd met at university, and had been together ever since. Tina had never been introduced to her, but she'd noted that whenever Grier spoke about her it was with an obvious fondness in his voice, which was very different from the rest of the married men on the team when they spoke about their wives. It should have made her like him more. Instead it made her jealous.

Tina split the task of trawling through the Róisin O'Neill file into two, Grier concentrating on Róisin's background while she looked into the mechanics of the murder itself.

The first thing Tina noticed was that Róisin fit the profile of one of the Night Creeper's victims perfectly. A successful brand manager for a pharmaceutical company, she was physically attractive and, at twenty-nine, right in his age range. She also lived alone and was apparently single. Most importantly, she'd ordered a new alarm system for her West End apartment three months before her death, and it had been installed by Andrew Kent.

The similarities didn't end there. As Tina read through the file, she was confronted by a series of graphic photographs from the crime scene itself. Róisin had been found in exactly the same way as the other four victims, lying naked and face-up on her bed, her long blond hair standing out against the sky-blue sheets. Her ankles and wrists were tied with rope so that she was spread-eagled, and her face had been smashed to a pulp, rendering it utterly unrecognizable. It looked just like all the other crime scenes, except there was far less blood, and when Tina examined the close-up shots of Róisin's upper body, she could see extensive bruising on the neck, which hadn't been present on the other victims.

The pathologist's report confirmed Grier's revelation that the cause of death had been manual strangulation, and that the blows to her face had been delivered postmortem using a blunt object, most likely a hammer. He hadn't been able to give an accurate estimate as to how long after her death these injuries had occurred, but what he could say, with accuracy, was that, given the state of decomposition of the victim when she was discovered (and he went into a lot of detail on this), Róisin had definitely died at some point between six P.M. and midnight the previous evening—the day of Kent's father's funeral. The time of the funeral was two P.M., so it was humanly possible that Kent could have stolen or hired a car, driven back to London—a distance of 456 miles according to the AA website—and committed the murder before driving back to Inverness by breakfast time the following day. But it was also extremely unlikely, and, for the moment at least, Tina didn't think it was worth inquiring about stolen or hired cars in the Inverness area.

Instead, she concentrated on other differences between Róisin's murder and the others. Two stood out particularly.

The first was the lack of any traces of chloroform at the Róisin crime scene. Part of the Night Creeper's MO was to use chloroform to subdue his victims after he'd broken into their homes, which allowed him to bind and gag them at leisure, before moving on to the next stage of his assault. Traces of it had been present at the other four murders. Whoever Róisin's killer had been, and Tina was pretty certain now it wasn't Andrew Kent, he'd used some other means to overpower Róisin and bind her.

The second was the absence of any physical signs of a violent sexual assault. The Night Creeper liked to be rough with his victims, even though they were unable to offer any physical resistance, and typically he'd inflicted sexual injuries, mainly in the form of lacerations. But not on Róisin. As a consequence, the pathologist was unable to conclude whether, in her case, a sexual assault had even taken place.

What he could say definitively, however, was that Róisin had had sex at some point in the twelve hours prior to her death, because traces of sperm had been recovered from inside her vagina. DNA tests on the sperm had already proved that it was not a match with Kent's. Nor was it a match for any of the two million other people held on the government's central DNA database.

Tina sat back in her seat and stretched, looking across at Grier who was hunched over his desk, making studious notes as he read from the open file. The clock on the wall above his head said it was ten past eight. They'd been back at their desks for an hour or so, and in that time they'd hardly spoken.

"Is there anything in the witness statements about Róisín having a boyfriend, Dan?" she asked him, breaking the silence. "Or a lover of some description. I know she was meant to be single, but according to the pathologist's report she had sex with someone, other than her killer, on the day she died."

He shook his head. "There was no boyfriend—at least not according to her friends and family. And because we were hunting a serial killer by then rather than someone known to her, we didn't pursue it. Why? Do you think whoever she had sex with had something to do with it?"

"I don't know, but I'd like to find out who it was. Just so we can eliminate him from the inquiry."

"I'm taking it from that that Kent's alibi's still looking good."

"It's looking perfect," she answered wearily, and she told him what she'd found out.

Grier wiped a hand across his brow. "Then we've got a problem."

"Why?"

"Well, there's something I don't understand, either. I've been trawling through all the witness statements, from friends, family, neighbors, everyone who knew her, and it seems she was a nice, ordinary girl with no enemies. In fact, only one thing stands out. I don't know if you remember, but Róisín lived in an old four-story house in Pimlico that had been converted into luxury flats."

"I didn't, but go on."

"Each floor had its own apartment, and they were linked by a communal staircase, with Róisín's on the top floor. About a week before her murder, and three months after Kent had fitted the alarm, one of the neighbors ran into someone she didn't recognize coming down the staircase from the direction of Róisin's apartment. Her statement said . . ." He paused while he checked his notes. "He was, and I quote, 'a very suspicious-looking character, a young man with long hair, quite short, who didn't want to meet my eye.'"

"Did she challenge him as to who he was?"

"No, she didn't say anything. She probably didn't want a confrontation. She said he left through the front door and that was it. I remember at the time we didn't take it that seriously."

"Why not?"

"Well, mainly because the sighting was a week before the murder, rather than the day it happened. Also, the neighbor was a bit of a busybody, in her seventies, and when we tried to do an e-fit based on her description, it just didn't work. Every attempt turned out to look nothing like him, according to her. We did go back to Róisin's friends to ask if she knew someone who fit the guy's basic description, but, unsurprisingly, none of them did. Which was why it ended up going to the bottom of the pile."

Tina had never heard about this sighting, although given the size and scale of the inquiry, and the number of detectives involved, this wasn't that surprising. "So, what makes it stand out now?" she asked.

"Because the description might be basic—short, long hair, moles on cheek—but it's possible that it fits Kent."

Tina recalled the two very small dark moles an inch apart on Kent's left cheek. "It's more than possible. It does fit him."

"Listen, ma'am, it wasn't my fault," said Grier defensively. "How was anyone to know at the time that he could have been our killer?"

"Have you got a number for this witness?" she asked, not wanting to get into a debate about past mistakes. When he nodded, she told him to call her straight away. "Arrange to get a photo of Kent across to her, see if she recognizes it."

Two minutes later, Grier was on the phone to seventy-six-year-old Beatrice Glover, reminding her of the case and asking if he could come around with a photo to show her. "Oh, you've got email," she heard him say, unable to hide the surprise in his voice. Ageist sod, thought Tina, and typical of an arrogant young guy like Grier to make rash and thoughtless generalizations. She wondered if that was why he'd been so dismissive of her testimony in the first place.

She waited as he emailed Beatrice Glover the mug shot that had been taken of Kent after his arrest the previous night. Grier stayed on the line while she opened up the file to view it.

When he came off the phone, he looked utterly confused. "She's not a hundred percent sure—she says it's been a long time—but she's pretty confident the man in the photo is the man she saw on the staircase the week before Róisin's murder." He sighed. "But if Kent didn't kill her then what on earth was he doing hanging around her place when he had no reason to?"

Tina had been thinking about that for the last five minutes, and there was only one conclusion she kept coming up with. "I really hope it isn't the case," she said quietly, "but it's possible that Andrew Kent wasn't working alone."

Twenty

Grier shook his head disbelievingly. "My God, two of them? No one's even mentioned that as a possibility in the whole time I've been on the case."

"I'm not surprised," said Tina. "Two serial killers working together is a real rarity. I can only think of one case like that in the UK in the past thirty years."

"The Railway Killers, Duffy and Mulcahy," he said, confirming that he knew exactly who Tina was talking about. "Do you think there could be an innocent explanation for his presence there?" he asked. "Maybe she called him back to service the alarm or something?"

Tina shook her head. "We'll check with the alarm company, but as far as I'm concerned, Kent may not have been the killer, but he knows a lot more than he's letting on."

Tina was annoyed with herself. She'd been taken in more than once by Kent. At times, even with all the evidence against him, she'd thought it possible he'd somehow been framed. Now she knew he was nothing more than a cunning and manipulative sociopath who could potentially get himself acquitted over the Róisín O'Neill case, even though he had to have had something to do with it.

"I'm going down to see him," she announced, getting to her feet.

Grier looked surprised. "Are you allowed to? He hasn't actually given us permission to talk to him."

"He gave me permission earlier," she said, walking past him, unsure exactly what she was going to say when she got down there. "That'll do me. I'll be back in a few minutes."

On the way down to the cells, she thought about what they'd found out. Most murder cases are fairly straight-forward and throw up obvious suspects, which is why the clearance rate's so high. Even serial killer cases aren't usually complicated. The killer kills until the police have gathered enough evidence to identify him. Then, bang, they make an arrest, and it's the end of the problem.

But this case was different. It was turning into a complex puzzle with no obvious solution. Kent had installed Róisin O'Neill's alarm system, and it was now almost certain that he had been stalking her, but he hadn't actually killed her, even though it was highly likely he'd killed the other four women. Whoever had murdered Róisin, though, had also been able to break into her apartment on a winter's night without trip-ping the alarm, and knew enough about the Night Creeper's MO to carry out a copycat crime which, though not perfect, had thrown the investigating officers off the scent. But there was no obvious motive for Róisin's murder. There'd been no sexual assault, and in keeping with the Creeper's MO, no robbery either. Yet the killer had added the hammer blows because he'd wanted to make the police think it was the work of the Creeper.

But why? That was what she simply couldn't work out.

Andrew Kent could supply the answer, she was sure of that. He hadn't been forthcoming so far, but she was determined to at least try to get him to talk before they lost him the following day when he was remanded into the custody of the Prison Service.

The Welsh custody sergeant, the one whose name she could never remember, was still on duty when she arrived at the front desk. He was sitting down with a cup of tea and a copy of the *Daily Express*. "You're working late," he said, looking up from the paper and giving her a smile that was only just short of lecherous.

"The fight against crime never stops," she told him with mock seriousness, and they exchanged a few pleasantries before Tina told him as casually as possible that she needed a quick word with Kent.

The custody sergeant looked unsure. "He hasn't asked to see you again, Tina."

"It's just something to do with what he wanted to talk to me about earlier." She flashed her best smile. "Come on, it's nothing major, and it's off the record."

Bloody jobsworth, she thought, as he finally got to his feet and led her slowly through to the cells.

"How does he seem?" she asked him. A suspect's guilt or innocence could often be guessed at by how he or she acted in the cells. Anger tended to point to guilt, as did indifference. Resignation or tears tended to point the other way.

He gave a bored shrug. "He's been fine. A lot politer than most we get. I just looked in on him a few minutes ago, and gave him a drink of water." He stopped at the cell door and lifted the flap. "You've got a visitor," he bellowed, peering inside. "Christ, where's he got to? Mr. Kent? Visitor."

That was when Tina heard it. A tight, rasping sound coming from inside the cell. The custody sergeant heard it too, and reached for the keys.

"Open up quickly!" she snapped, and as soon as he'd turned the key in the lock, she pushed past him and rushed inside, reaching for the CS spray in her belt in case it was a trap.

But there was no trap. Andrew Kent was lying on his back on the floor of the cell, writhing in agony, his eyes bulging out of his head as he stared up at Tina. His face was beginning to go purple and he was clutching his throat. Beside him on the floor was an upturned plastic cup.

"Jesus Christ!" Tina turned to the custody sergeant, who was standing stock-still, seemingly unsure what to do. "Call an ambulance, quickly! Now!"

He disappeared at a run, and Tina crouched down beside Kent.

But before she could do anything, he lurched over onto his side, facing away from her. His legs kicked wildly as he vomited noisily on the floor. She jumped out of the way as his whole body bucked and jerked in a violent seizure, then he swung back around, immediately unleashing another projectile of vomit that only just missed her as it splattered across the floor. Finally, he rolled back onto his back and was still. His face was still a deep red, but even so, he looked a lot better than he had only moments earlier.

"Oh God," he groaned, clutching his stomach.

"What happened?" Tina asked him, unable to stop herself from retching at the stench and mess around her.

"They tried to kill me," he whispered.

"Who?" she demanded.

"Get me to a hospital."

"Who tried to kill you, Mr. Kent?"

He screwed his face into a pained grimace. "Jesus, it hurts."

"An ambulance is on the way. You're going to be OK. But you need to tell me what happened."

"The water," he hissed, looking up at her. "It was something in the water."

The custody sergeant reappeared at the door, looking flustered. "The ambulance'll be here any minute."

She grabbed the empty plastic cup and threw it toward him. "Where the hell did that water come from?"

"F-from the tap," he stammered nervously. "I didn't do a thing to it, honestly."

"Get it in an evidence bag. It's going to need to be analyzed." She dismissed him with an angry wave of the hand and turned back to Kent.

"They don't want me to talk," he said, his voice an angry croak.

"Who's 'they'?"

He swallowed hard, and grabbed her by the hand, his grip surprisingly strong. "Get me to a hospital and I'll tell you everything. I swear it. I'll tell you everything."

Twenty-one

It was 8:25 P.M., and I was sitting in the back of the people carrier. We were parked up on a backstreet only a few hundred yards from the place where Wolfe and Haddock had picked me up over an hour earlier, except now I was wearing gloves and a boiler suit, and holding one of the Remington shotguns I'd got in the ill-fated gun deal earlier across my knees. The car's engine was off, the air was muggy and warm, and there was a leaden silence in the car as we waited to go to work, and all the time I was wondering how on earth I'd managed to get myself into the current situation and, more importantly, how I was going to get out of it.

After I'd got into the car earlier, Wolfe had driven us to a lock-up just up the road in Islington where the guns were stored, along with the change of clothes. We'd changed, and then each of us loaded his own gun. I'd told Wolfe once again that I wasn't going to pull the trigger for any reason, and once again he'd reiterated that this was a straight "snatch" job and no shots would be fired. "But there's no way we're walking into a job unloaded," he added. "That'd just be stupid. Never be unprepared, Sean."

Once we were kitted up and back in the people carrier,

we'd driven around while Wolfe gave me the lowdown on the job itself.

The first surprise was that there were five of us involved. As well as the three of us and Tommy, Wolfe's girlfriend, a Thai girl called Lee he'd been seeing for the past couple of months, and who Tommy said reminded him of a dirty-looking cage fighter, was acting as a spotter. She was currently stationed at a pavement café fifty yards from my old station, Holborn. Within an hour Andrew Kent, our target, was going to be leaving through the front gates in an ambulance with flashing lights, and as soon as he did so she would let us know using the shortwave VHF radio she was carrying.

It was about a minute's drive tops to where we were now, and as soon as the ambulance passed, we would pull out and follow it. Tommy was parked in a Bedford van a further hundred yards up the road, also armed with a VHF radio set to the same frequency, and when we gave the signal he would pull out and block the ambulance's path, forcing it to a halt. We'd then be out of the people carrier, in Wolfe's words like shit off a greasy stick, with Wolfe taking the front of the ambulance and making the driver open the doors at the back. Then Haddock would pull out our quarry while I provided cover. Tommy would join us in the people carrier, and we'd be out of there in the space of thirty seconds. Any police escort would, Wolfe assured us, be unarmed, since there'd have been no time to organize an ARV to accompany the ambulance, and as such they'd be helpless when confronted with our weapons.

What frightened me was the level of information these guys had. They just knew too much, which meant that they had to be privy to some kind of inside information. I'd spent more than seven years working out of Holborn station, and I liked to think that the coppers there were decent, honorable people, not the kind who'd sell information to a scumbag like Tyrone Wolfe, or to his client, whoever that person was. But it seemed someone had. There was no other way they could know that Kent would be traveling in an ambulance, or the time he'd be leaving. The problem was, including civilian workers and the various uniforms, it could be any one of more than two hundred people.

I sat back in my seat, conscious that I was sweating. Knowing that if this plan backfired, and shots ended up being fired, then that would be it. My life as I knew it would be over.

But I could still get out of it, I told myself, if I could get these guys nicked. Maybe not now, but later, when we had Kent in our grasp. That way we could also get to the person behind this, the client, and bring him down with them, thereby wrapping things up perfectly. I doubted if I'd ever get my job back, but it might keep me out of prison.

"Listen," I said, breaking the heavy silence in the car, "I know you can't tell me who it is we're working for, but at least give me an idea what he wants with this guy."

Wolfe sighed loudly. It was obvious he was getting tired of my questions. "If I tell you, will you shut up afterward?"

"What you telling him for?" grunted Haddock. "He don't need to know nothing. He's just hired help."

"Because I'm sick of being kept in the dark," I snapped.

Wolfe turned around in his seat, fixing me with his good eye. "I told you the bloke's been charged with the rape and murder of five women, didn't I? Well, the client's a relative of one of them, and he wants justice. He doesn't think the law'll give it to him. That's why we're involved."

"How does he know that Kent's going to be leaving

Holborn station in an ambulance in the next hour?" I asked, thinking it was somewhat ironic that an arch-criminal like Tyrone Wolfe was suddenly turning vigilante to make up for the inadequacies of the British legal system.

"I didn't ask him," he replied. "Unlike you, I know when to keep my mouth shut."

I was pleased. Wolfe's answer would help us identify his client, because there couldn't be that many of the victims' relatives with the influence needed to get information on Kent's movements. But it also left me with another problem.

"The client's going to kill him, isn't he?"

"I thought you said you'd stop asking questions if I told you why he wanted him."

"But he is. There's no other reason why he'd want him."

Haddock shifted his huge bulk in the front seat, and the car seemed to move a little. "What do you care?" he hissed, in his weirdly effeminate tones. "You're getting paid, and it's just a nonce who's going to die."

"I told you both before, I don't want to get involved in murder."

Wolfe sighed loudly. "You're not getting involved in murder, Sean. The client is. We're just pulling the guy. Then it's up to him what he does with him, but he assures me that once he's finished with Kent, he'll disappear off the face of the earth and that'll be that. No one'll care that much, because this is the Night Creeper we're talking about, a piece-of-shit sex killer who murders defenseless women in their homes. And the coppers won't be looking that hard for the people who took him. They'll just want everyone to forget the fact that they had one of their prisoners snatched from under their noses."

I thought Wolfe was being unduly naive, but that was his

lookout. Mine was to stop his client from getting his hands on Kent. He might be a piece-of-shit sex killer but it was still my job to protect him from the person or persons plotting his murder.

I was still working out how I was going to do that when Wolfe's radio crackled into life. It was Lee, his girlfriend.

"Cargo on move," she snapped in quick, accented staccato. "With you in one minute."

I felt a burst of adrenaline surge through me.

It was on.

Twenty-two

Andrew Kent's face was deathly pale beneath the oxygen mask as the paramedics rushed him out of the custody area on a stretcher, with Tina following.

She hadn't been able to get anything further out of him about what had happened. He'd vomited twice since she'd first discovered him writhing on the cell floor, and he was clearly still very sick. The cup he'd been drinking from was already on its way to forensics for testing, although the custody sergeant remained adamant no one had interfered with the drink between him pouring it and it reaching Kent's mouth.

It was possible that it was a suicide attempt. Although suspects are given a full body search when they're placed in custody, Kent might still have been able to store a potentially poisonous substance in his mouth that was missed in the search. But it was unlikely, particularly given his cryptic comments about people wishing to silence him. It was also possible he was faking it. The paramedics had only given him a cursory checkover before putting him on oxygen and getting him onto the stretcher, and were unsure as to what substance he might have ingested, preferring to get him to hospital for tests. But if he was faking it, he was doing a damn good job.

Either way, Tina knew that Kent was still an extremely

dangerous man. She'd experienced a dangerous offender escaping from an ambulance before, so she'd arranged for two uniformed officers to travel in the back with him and a squad car to travel behind on the route to the hospital, just in case he made a rapid recovery.

As Kent and the paramedics disappeared out of the station's front doors, Tina pulled out her mobile and called Grier, giving him a ten-second précis of what had just happened before telling him to get straight down to the reception area. "We need to get to the hospital fast. I want to find out exactly what Kent has to say."

Less than a minute later, Grier was running alongside her to the station's parking lot. "I'll drive," she told him, unlocking her battered Ford Focus and jumping in while Grier struggled to fit his gangly legs into the passenger seat. "Sorry about the squeeze," she added, pulling out of the parking spot before he was fully inside. "The last person I had in there was my mother, and she's five foot two."

"What's the hurry?" he asked, finally shutting the door as the Focus turned onto the street, heading in the direction of University College Hospital. "He's not going to speak to us for a while yet."

"Because I don't like having him out of my sight. He said he wants to tell me something, and I want to make sure we find out what it is."

"Have you called MacLeod yet?"

"No." She pulled out her mobile and, ignoring the fact that she was breaking the law, speed-dialed his number.

But before he had a chance to answer, she turned into Doughty Street and immediately slammed on the brakes as she was confronted by a scene of flashing lights and chaos that made her drop the phone involuntarily.

Twenty-three

The ambulance came roaring past in a blur of blue lights followed immediately by a marked patrol car. As I pulled on my balaclava with slippery hands and we drove out onto the road behind them, I saw through the gathering darkness Tommy's white Bedford van reverse out of a turning up ahead and block its path.

The driver hit the brakes, but he was too late to prevent a collision, and he lost control in a shriek of tires before slamming into the back of the van with a loud smash, shunting it sideways but failing to knock it out of the way. Smoke rose from its ruined bonnet.

Meanwhile, the patrol car's driver also hit the brakes, but his reactions were better and he came to a halt ten feet behind the ambulance, siren blaring. Before either he or his passenger could get out, though, we came hurtling up behind them in the people carrier.

This whole op was about speed, surprise, and overwhelming force. As a cop with fifteen years on the job, I knew that if you catch people completely off guard, they tend to acquiesce immediately.

And we hit these guys hard. "Ramming speed!" whooped

Wolfe as we careered into the back of the patrol car, knocking it forward several feet.

For a few seconds, I was caught up in the drama of the whole thing. The adrenaline rush was incredible, the most intense I'd experienced for years, as I threw open the door and leaped out, wielding the shotgun in front of me, finger instinctively placed on the trigger.

While Wolfe rushed over to the ambulance to intimidate the crew into opening the back doors, Haddock went straight for the patrol car. For a man of his bulk, he moved extremely fast, and as the driver made the stupid mistake of opening his door, Haddock grabbed it with one hand and slammed it against his head, knocking him back inside. A second later he was looming over the front of the car like some kind of avenging demon, legs apart as he pointed his shotgun through the window at the two unarmed officers, bellowing at them not to move or he'd blow them away. Just to emphasize the point, he lowered the barrel with a sudden jerk and shot out the front near-side tire with a deafening blast that made my heart lurch and brought me right back to reality.

I caught a glimpse of the two cops as I passed. The driver, who was holding the injured side of his head with both hands, was unfamiliar, but I recognized his passenger: Ryan James, a cheery forty-something uniform who'd become a copper after fifteen years as a secondary school physics teacher, and who'd once lent me fifty quid when I was short before payday. I'd always liked him, and seeing his face now, pale and terrified, caught my conscience.

But this was necessary. It had to happen like this. And if he stayed stock-still, he was going to be OK.

A second blast echoed around the quiet street as Haddock

blew out the other front tire. His whole body seemed to be shaking with excitement as he moved the Remington in a tight arc, reveling in his power. "Get your fucking hands in the air! Both of you! I'll fucking blow your heads off if you try anything! Understand? Under-fucking-stand?" Then he turned my way. "Cover those bastards, and watch me as well," he snarled, before charging over to the back of the ambulance where the rear doors were already opening.

It was no easy task, keeping my eyes on two sets of people at once, but I did what I could. The good thing was, neither of the two cops I was covering looked like he was capable of trying anything, and Ryan James looked like he was going to have a heart attack as he stared at the barrel of my gun, hands thrust rigidly in the air.

I risked glancing backward at the ambulance, where Haddock had joined Wolfe. The doors were fully open now and I saw two uniforms—a man and a woman, both young and fresh-faced—in the back, on either side of the gurney, while a female paramedic in green coveralls stood over it, her hands out in front of her in a gesture of submission.

Wolfe leaped in the back and told the paramedic to unstrap her patient.

"You can't take him," I heard her say. "Please. He's sick."

"Shut up and do what I say! Now!"

The two uniforms in the back of the ambulance remained frozen in their seats, with Haddock moving his gun from one to the other, covering them and hissing murderous threats, his whole demeanor radiating the kind of controlled rage that made crossing him suicidal, and I remember praying that nobody was stupid enough to make a move.

But the female paramedic wasn't playing the game. "You're not taking him," she shouted, following it with another "please," although she must have known that Wolfe was going to do exactly that.

With a sudden movement, he grabbed her by her hair and shoved the barrel into her face. "Do it!" he screamed, dragging her back toward the gurney.

I winced at his violence, feeling my finger tighten on the trigger as I remembered what he'd done to my brother all those years ago, wishing I could do the same to him but knowing that I had to bide my time and hope that this snatch was going to be concluded fast, because with every second that passed we came closer to being rumbled by police reinforcements which right now, with Wolfe and Haddock pumped up on adrenaline and violence, would mean a bloodbath.

Finally, the paramedic got to work on one of the straps with shaking hands while Wolfe undid the other, all the while pointing his gun in her face.

And then, as Wolfe shoved her aside and tore the oxygen mask from his face, I finally saw our target for the first time. Andrew Kent, the so-called Night Creeper. The man my former colleagues were sure was responsible for the rape and murder of five young women. He was small and thin, with the gray pallor of the sick, but he was also conscious, and looked just as terrified as the people who'd been protecting him, because he must have known that whatever we had planned for him, it was not going to be nice.

He looked more like a computer geek than a killer, and even though I knew what he was supposed to have done, and that killers never look like killers—they all look just like you and me when they're vulnerable—I still felt sick as Wolfe dragged him out of the ambulance, with the gun shoved hard into the hollow of his cheek.

Which was the moment when it all went horribly wrong.

The male cop lunged forward, jumped out of the back of the ambulance, and grabbed Wolfe's gun hand, trying to wrestle the weapon from his control. Why he decided to do it was anyone's guess—maybe it was the need to be hailed as a hero—but one thing that's drummed into all police officers is never take on a gunman when you're unarmed, because it can turn a dramatic situation into a disastrous one. As it did now.

Clearly sensing an opportunity for escape, Kent struggled free of Wolfe's now tenuous grip and made a bolt for it.

I was barely ten feet away and moved fast to intercept him, holding my shotgun like a club. There was no way I could let a serial killer escape from custody on top of everything else I was involved in.

But for a sick man, Kent's reactions were surprisingly quick, and he leaped at me, launching an improvised karate kick at my stomach. I tried to get out of the way but his foot caught me and I stumbled backward, colliding with the corner of the cop car's bonnet.

I'm no slouch myself, however, and though I was winded, I bounced back off the car, and as he scrambled past me, I slammed the stock of the shotgun into the side of his head. It was a good shot, and he went sprawling onto the tarmac in a heap, a deep cut already forming along his hairline. He wasn't moving either, and for a moment I thought I might have killed him.

It was then that I saw Wolfe break free of the cop who'd made a grab for him and shove him backward so that, for the first time, there was distance between them. "No!" I heard myself shout as Haddock swung his shotgun around from where it had been covering the female cop and pointed it directly at her foolish colleague, while Wolfe raised his own gun, holding it two-handed.

Everything suddenly seemed to move in slow motion as the male cop—twenty-five at most, probably younger—raised his hands in surrender, his dreams of being a hero evaporating across his face as the fear took over.

I wanted to react. To turn my gun on Wolfe and Haddock and tell them to drop theirs because I was the police, maybe even open fire and rid the world of my brother's killers forever. But then Haddock calmly pulled the Remington's trigger.

The cop was lifted off his feet by the force of the blast and he literally flew backward through the air, hands down by his side like a toy soldier, before landing hard on his back.

"Out of here, now!" roared Wolfe, looking at me. "And grab Kent!"

Even through the intense ringing in my ears I could hear the panicked shouts coming from Ryan James and the other cop in the car behind me as they reacted to the sight of one of their own being shot in front of them. This was my worst nightmare. Getting in too deep on a job and seeing it all go pear-shaped in front of my eyes. The wounded cop was still moving, thank God, and had rolled over onto his side, but without medical help he'd be finished. And with the ambulance on the scene a wreck and the paramedics traumatized, I wasn't at all sure he was going to get it.

Hating myself, I ran forward and hauled the injured Kent to his feet, half strangling him as I dragged him over to the people carrier, helped by Wolfe, while Haddock kept everyone else covered.

Incredibly, only about thirty seconds had passed since the whole thing had begun, and no traffic had appeared on the street. However, the first pedestrians were now appearing from up and down the street, staring at the scene unfolding in front of them from behind rows of parked cars, and making me feel strangely like an actor in a cheap, contemporary street play.

Wolfe opened the side door and I threw Kent inside, stuffing the shotgun into his spine and forcing him into the aisle between the back seats, before jumping in behind him, while Haddock leaped in the other side.

Wolfe backed up in a screech of tires, then drove around the ambulance as Tommy reversed the Bedford van into a parked car to create a gap we could drive through. As we passed, Wolfe slowed and Tommy jumped in the open door, yanking it shut behind him.

We were on our way.

Twenty-four

For a good three seconds, Tina sat there trying to take in what she was seeing through the glare of the flashing lights and the gloom fifty yards down the street. At first she just thought there'd been a bad accident involving the ambulance carrying Kent and a van that must have reversed out of one of the side streets; but then she saw men in balaclavas wrestling another man through the side door of a black people carrier, and she realized what was happening. Kent was being sprung from his escort and, more worryingly, the people doing it were armed: she could see one holding a shotgun and, farther away, a uniformed police officer, recognizable by his white shirt and black stab-proof vest, was lying injured on the ground.

"My God," said Grier disbelievingly. "Is this some kind of hijack?"

"Call back-up," Tina snapped as the people carrier suddenly backed up and drove around the ambulance. She shoved the Focus into first.

"What are you doing?"

"What do you think? I'm not letting Kent get away."

Wishing she had a better pursuit vehicle, Tina accelerated away after the people carrier, telling Grier to stick the emergency halogen light she kept in the glove box on the dashboard so that their quarry would know the police were after them.

Another balaclava-clad figure jumped in the back of the people carrier, then it drove through the small gap between the crashed vehicles and the parked ones lining one side of the road before picking up speed as it continued down Doughty Street toward Theobalds Road.

Tina followed it through the gap, clipping a parked car in the process. She couldn't read the people carrier's license plate as it was driving without lights, so she slammed her foot hard on the floor in an effort to catch up.

The driver must have realized he was being followed because he speeded up as well and hurtled straight across the junction without stopping, narrowly missing a man on a bike who had to mount the pavement to avoid being hit, before doing a hard right, tires wailing, and accelerating in the direction of Bloomsbury.

Tina knew she had to do the same. She couldn't lose them. Not when they were carrying a cargo as valuable as Andrew Kent. Clenching her teeth and ignoring Grier's protests, she shot across the junction, yanking the wheel and only just managing to straighten up in time to avoid hitting a taxi that was dropping someone off on the other side of the road.

Only twenty yards separated the Focus and the people carrier, and Tina felt a burst of delirious excitement that would have shocked her if she'd had time to think about it.

Her quarry overtook a bus on the wrong side of the road, squeezing between oncoming traffic, hitting speeds of fifty miles an hour and getting faster all the time, and Tina followed suit, keeping tight to him.

"Christ, be careful!" yelled Grier as they swerved to avoid an approaching car. "You'll get us killed!"

"Get on the phone and tell them his plate number. We're not losing this thing!"

The people carrier weaved in the road and overtook another car, but it couldn't shake Tina off. Now only fifteen yards separated them and she could just make out the numbers and letters on the plate.

Then, without warning, one of the balaclava-clad figures leaned halfway out of the window and pointed a shotgun at them, looking very much as if he was taking aim. Grier yelled something unintelligible and Tina instinctively slammed her foot on the brakes and spun the wheel. She just had time to duck her head before the windscreen exploded, showering her with glass. The car spun around as she lost control and left the road, the suspension jarring angrily as she mounted the pavement and smashed sideways into an empty shopfront, scattering the diners at a next-door pavement café but managing to avoid hitting any of them, before finally coming to a halt.

Tina's breathing came in short, rapid bursts as she sat back up in the seat, letting shards of glass fall off her. The car had turned around completely now, but she could see the people carrier disappearing around the corner in her rearview mirror.

She quickly checked herself but couldn't see any sign of injury, then looked over at Grier, fearful that he might have been hurt, which would have been her fault. But he looked OK, shaken but uninjured. She felt an immediate relief. She'd already lost two colleagues in her career. She couldn't face losing another.

In fact he was still talking on the phone to the 999 operator, describing what had just happened, before adding that he hadn't got a chance to take the registration number of the suspect vehicle. "We're going to secure the scene now," he said, and rang off.

Tina sighed. "Are you all right?"

He glared at her, and she could see he was trying to keep calm, knowing that, whatever might be going through his head, she was still his superior—although for how much longer was anyone's guess. Tina had always been considered something of a loose cannon, a copper who attracted trouble, even if that trouble wasn't usually her fault. People who worked with her got killed; she'd even killed someone herself the previous year, while officially off duty, and though no blame had been attached to her for that, it was still seen by some as a blot on an already badly bloodstained copy book. Crashing a car into a shop during a high-speed chase and narrowly missing a dozen terrified pedestrians was another, especially when she'd been drinking.

Tina sighed and rubbed her eyes. There was bound to be a breath test, and she was hugely relieved that she hadn't drunk anything in the pub earlier, and that the two hits of vodka she'd sneaked in the toilet were long enough ago now to keep her under the limit.

Even so, pretty soon her luck was going to run out.

"I'm OK," Grier said quietly, his voice trembling with emotion, "but why did you do that, ma'am? You could have killed us both."

Grier was one of the new breed of cops, a desk man who didn't like taking big risks, and although he'd held himself together enough to finish the phone call to the 999 operator, Tina felt a wave of contempt for him. "I had to make a split-second decision," she answered firmly. "I didn't want to lose them."

"Well, you did lose them, ma'am," he said slowly, and she noticed that his hands were shaking. "You did bloody lose them."

And she had. She'd failed. She should have made sure Kent went to the hospital with an armed escort.

Not only had she misread the situation, she also knew with a terrible lurch of certainty that if she'd held back rather than sped after the carrier like a teenage boy who'd just passed his test she would have stood a better chance of following them.

She groaned. Whichever way she looked at it, the whole thing had been a set-up. And she'd fallen for it hook, line, and sinker.

Twenty-five

"What did you shoot him for? You told me there was going to be no need for violence, and then your buddy here blows away a copper at point-blank range. Why?"

We were now in the second getaway vehicle, a clapped-out minibus that had been stolen the day before from an old people's home—a typically callous move from Tyrone Wolfe. He and Haddock were again in the front, with me sitting directly behind them, my shotgun resting on the back of Andrew Kent, who was lying lengthwise along the narrow aisle separating the seats, face down and not speaking, eyes tightly shut. He was clearly desperate not to see any of our faces now that we'd removed our balaclavas, since to do so would effectively sentence him to death. Blood was still dribbling out of his head where I'd hit him earlier, and one side of his face was covered in a network of dark rivulets. Behind me sat Tommy, smoking a cigarette and not saying a great deal.

The people carrier had been dumped in a deserted parking lot behind a block of flats on the massive Barnsbury Estate in Islington, barely a mile from the snatch point, and set on fire to destroy any forensic evidence linking any of us to it. According to Wolfe, the area wasn't covered by CCTV cameras, and no one had seen us change vehicles, so the minibus we'd been in for the last fifteen minutes as we drove northwest across London, mingling naturally with the other traffic, was clean.

During that time I'd sat in brooding silence, shocked at what had just occurred. I was also thinking furiously about what I had to do to bring this situation under control. I knew I needed to gather as much information as possible about our next movements so I could lead police reinforcements to wherever we were going. First, though, I wanted to vent my spleen at the men who'd just gunned down a fellow police officer and, for the benefit of my recording device, get them to admit what they'd done, so there'd be no way they'd see the outside of a prison cell again.

Wolfe was in the passenger seat now, Haddock doing the driving, and he swung around in the seat, the sharp, unforgiving features of his face pinched into an angry glare, the squint even more obvious than usual. "He got shot because he went for me, all right?"

"But you got the guy off you," I snapped back. "At that point he wasn't offering any resistance, so you could have just left it at that. Or if you were that worried, given him a whack with the butt of your gun. But no. Instead, this prick"—I pointed at Haddock's huge bulk—"shoots him, and now we're going to have every copper for a hundred miles after us, not just for kidnapping but murder as well. Maybe more than one, after the way you shot up the unmarked car that was following."

"Who are you calling a prick?" demanded Haddock, glaring at me in the rearview mirror and slowing the van as he did so. "You apologize, or I'll cut your fucking head off."

Wolfe told him to keep driving. "We don't want to attract any attention. And you," he said, pointing at me, "apologize to him. Now."

I faced him down, no longer bothered about angering either of these two psychopaths, and finding it close to impossible to keep a lid on my emotions. More than anything right then I wanted to turn the shotgun on them, tell them who I was, and remind them of what they did to my brother. Then pull the trigger. Instead, I shook my head angrily. "Fuck you. Fuck you both. You've landed me in all kinds of shit."

"Come on, boys, calm down," said Tommy from behind me. "What's done is done."

He'd already expressed his displeasure at the fact that a cop had been shot. But typical Tommy, after what could be described as a bit of a moan, he'd accepted it as an occupational hazard and was now clearly trying to return everything to some sort of status quo. Like most violent criminals I've come across over the years, he rarely wasted time worrying about the plight of his victims, particularly those who wore a uniform, and I wondered if he used the same words to summarize what had happened to my brother. What's done is done. Then just carried on with a big shrug of his shoulders, unworried by the havoc he'd caused in my family.

"Well put, Tommy," said Wolfe. "What's done is done. And I did what I had to do. If I'd tried to give him a slap and he'd grabbed the gun again, the whole thing could have been a complete fuck-up. There were four cops there as well as paramedics. We had to send a warning. That's all there is to it. It was either put a hole in that copper, or run the risk of getting caught and spending ten years apiece inside." He sighed. "No one wants to shoot a copper—"

"I do," said Haddock. "I hope the bastard's dead. And I still want an apology from this dog."

"Leave it, Clarence," said Wolfe, before turning back to me and putting on a conciliatory expression. "What I'm trying to say, Sean, is that I don't like hitting cops either, it's always way too much hassle. But the fact is we've done what we were paid to do, which is get hold of this little fuck." He motioned toward Kent, who remained stock-still with his eyes shut. Instinctively, I pushed the barrel of my shotgun against the small of his back. After every other mistake I'd made with this investigation, I wasn't going to let a dangerous and deranged sex killer escape.

I sighed, wiping sweat from my brow with a gloved hand. The minibus had no air-conditioning and the night was muggy and warm. "I want the rest of my money," I said, knowing I had enough evidence now to bag both Wolfe and Haddock and finally avenge my brother. "Then I'm gone."

"You'll get it when I've spoken to my client."

I wondered how the client was going to take the news that his plan for revenge had led to the death of at least one innocent person. If he was that interested in obtaining real justice, he was going to be very unhappy.

"Speak to him now," I said.

"Don't order me around, Sean. I'll speak to him at the rendezvous."

"And where's that?"

"It's a nice, quiet spot, a long way from any nosy neighbors. About half an hour's drive away."

"Who does it belong to?"

"What do you need to know that for?"

"Because I want to make sure there's no paper trail that'll lead the police to your client and then back to me. That's why."

"There's no paper trail attached to this place. It's been abandoned for years."

"How do you know that?"

"The client told me, all right?" Wolfe was sounding exasperated. "Now stop asking me questions. You'll get the rest of your money later, and that'll be the end of it."

I fell silent, knowing I was going to have to keep my wits about me for the next few hours because one thing was certain: no one in this van could be trusted. I'd had an uneasy feeling about this job from the beginning, but now, sitting here in the stifling heat, a trickle of fear ran down my spine.

It was a feeling that grew a whole lot worse when Andrew Kent opened his eyes, looked up at me—his eyes full of the same kind of fear I'd seen in the uniformed cop in the moments just before he was shot—and said something very strange indeed.

Twenty-six

"You're not one of them, are you?"

Kent spoke the words in a high-pitched, effeminate voice that fit perfectly with the soft, boyish features of his face—features that I knew to my cost were dangerously deceptive. He'd almost escaped earlier, and my stomach still ached from where he'd caught me with what had been a particularly deft karate kick.

I tensed. Surely he couldn't know my true identity. I'd never seen him in my life before tonight.

"What do you mean?" I asked him.

Wolfe shot around in his seat. "Shut the fuck up, you little runt! No one's interested in what you've got to say. Tommy, gag this bastard."

"I'm innocent," said Kent desperately, staring up at me. "I swear it. You know that. They're never going to pay you."

"I told you, shut it or I'll kill you myself!" roared Wolfe, pointing his Sig down at Kent's face.

But Kent didn't back down, and when he spoke again there was a new defiance in his voice and a glint in his eye. "But you can't, can you? Because you need what I know. Don't you?"

A flicker of doubt crossed Wolfe's face, then disappeared.

"I can still put one in your kneecap easily enough. And I'll do it with pleasure too. Cos I've got no truck with filthy little sex cases. Tommy, get that gag on him."

Tommy bit off a length of extra-thick parcel tape from a roll he had on him and grabbed Kent by the hair, lifting him off the floor.

But I used my foot to push him back down so that Tommy had to let go. "I want to hear what he's got to say. I thought we were here on a vigilante job."

"You don't know anything," said Kent to me, gabbling out the words. "This is nothing to do with a vigilante job. It's much bigger. I've got information they need and once they've got it they'll kill all of us. You, too."

"Shut your mouth now!" Wolfe's words reverberated around the minibus's interior. Ripping off his safety belt, he lurched snake-like between the front seats, grabbing Kent by the throat with one hand and shoving the barrel of the pistol right into his face. "One more word," he whispered, "just one more word, and we'll have a dead nonce in here."

As he lay there, unable to speak, the pressure of the gun contorting his features, Kent met my eyes and mouthed two words: "Help me."

I suddenly felt terribly sorry for him, lying helpless on the floor of a filthy van. He might have been a murdering rapist, but there was no excuse for treating him like this. It was sadistic. If I was going to have any future outside prison walls, then I was going to have to behave like a cop and do my best to protect him. And if he had information that might have a bearing on this op and the identity of the client, I needed to hear it.

"I want to know what he's got to say," I repeated firmly.

"Well you can't," snapped Wolfe, glaring at me from

barely two feet away now. "You're just the hired help, remember?"

That's when a part of me just snapped. Being spoken to like that by the man who'd murdered my brother made the red mist come hurtling down, and before I could even think about it I'd lifted my shotgun and pointed it at Wolfe, so that the end of the barrel was barely six inches from his chest. "Don't talk to me like that. You've messed me around enough. I'm entitled to know what this piece of shit's talking about, so do me a favor and drop your gun. Now."

But Wolfe made no move to pull his pistol away from Kent's face. "What the fuck do you think you're doing?"

To be honest, I wasn't at all sure, but now that I'd made the move I was going to have to see it through. "I don't like the way this whole thing's gone down," I said, keeping the shotgun trained on him, my finger steady on the trigger. "I want to know why we've sprung this guy, who your client is, and where exactly we're going. And I want to know it now."

"Come on, boys," said Tommy uncertainly from behind me. "Let's all calm down and do what we're meant to do. Sean, stop pointing that thing at Ty."

"I'm being bullshitted, Tommy," I said over my shoulder, "and I don't like it. I want to know what this guy's got to say."

"You'd better drop it now," hissed Wolfe, his whole body tensing.

"I told you we shouldn't trust this dog," Haddock rumbled from the driver's seat.

I could hear my heart thumping in my chest, and I knew I'd made a bad move, because now I'd made an enemy of both the men in the front of this vehicle, and there was going to be no coming back from that. But there was also something badly wrong here. This wasn't a vigilante job. It never had been, which I guess I should have known all along. But what did Wolfe want with a suspected serial killer like Kent? From what little I could gather, Kent had information that made him confident Wolfe couldn't kill him. I had no idea what it was, but if it had something to do with Wolfe's client, I needed to hear it. I already had enough evidence on the recording device to convict Wolfe and Haddock. If I got out now with Kent, I could find out what he knew, deliver him to the authorities, and take my chances with the inquiry that was sure to come later.

But first I had to get out.

I stared at Wolfe. He stared right back.

My whole world had been reduced to the interior of a tiny van that smelled of age and sweat.

"Drop the gun," I repeated, trying to keep the fear out of my voice.

Wolfe kept it pressed in Kent's cheek. "Or what? You'll pull the trigger? I don't think you've got the balls, son. Cos I'm looking in your eyes, and I can tell you won't do it."

I swallowed, conscious of a bead of sweat running down into the corner of my eye, forcing me to blink.

That was when I felt something cold against the back of my head. "I think it'd be better if you dropped yours, Sean," said Tommy. "I'm sorry, mate, but it's better this way."

I hadn't expected this from Tommy, but maybe I should have. After all, his first loyalty was always going to be the crew. Even so, I still felt a sense of relief as I lowered the shotgun, which lasted as long as it took Wolfe to jerk it from my hand, turn it around, and shove the barrel between my legs while at the same time placing the pistol right between my eyes. For the first time in my life I was on the wrong end of three different firearms.

"Cover Kent," Wolfe snapped at Tommy. "And put that gag on him. Tie his hands behind his back too. I don't want that bastard moving an inch." Then he turned to me, his face a screwed-up ball of pure hate.

I didn't speak. I couldn't, because I knew with absolute certainty that the man holding the gun against my head was the cold-blooded murderer who'd shot my brother all those years before, and that now it was my turn. I've been close to getting killed before. Jesus, I'd been close enough earlier that day. But not like this. I could feel the coldness of the barrel pressing into my skin, and see the dark contempt in Wolfe's good eye. I couldn't even repeat the trick I'd used earlier and swat the gun away, not when there were three of them trained on me.

Wolfe clicked off the Sig's safety catch, his lips curling upward in a sadistic sneer, and I saw his index finger tightening on the trigger. "Not so nice now, is it, Seany boy? Having someone point a piece at you."

I swallowed hard, my heart hammering in my chest, as possibly the last ten seconds of my life ebbed away, and wondered whether John had experienced the gut-wrenching terror I was feeling now as I sat there waiting to die, knowing there was nothing I could do to prevent the bullet from coming. I was helpless, and everyone in that stinking van knew it.

"Don't do it, Ty," I heard Tommy say. I could see him out of the corner of my eye, holding a small snub-nosed revolver against Kent's neck while he put the tape over his mouth. "We're all pretty emotional after what happened. Sean shouldn't have done what he did, no question, but we've all done stupid things in the heat of the moment, and we don't want any more complications right now, do we? So come on. Let's all put the guns down, get to the rendezvous, and sort it out there."

"What do you reckon, Clarence?" said Wolfe, not taking his eyes off me.

"Blow his fucking head off. He's a liability, and we don't need him no more."

The minibus fell silent. It was decision time. Life or death.

Wolfe nodded slowly as if he'd come to a decision. "The next time you point a gun at me," he said, speaking slowly and carefully enunciating every word, "I will kill you without a second's thought. Do you understand that?" Pause. "Do you?"

"Yeah," I answered, experiencing a sense of relief so powerful I almost vomited.

"Good," he said, removing the gun and replacing it in his waistband before taking the shotgun out from between my legs.

Then, without warning, he slammed the butt into my face and my whole world exploded in searing pain.

Twenty-seven

Tina dragged hard on her cigarette and wished she could have a drink. It was now ten to ten, more than an hour since she'd written off her Focus, and the gentrified quiet of Doughty Street where she was standing now had been transformed into a major crime scene. Police vehicles blocked access at both ends while SOCO swarmed over the three vehicles—the ambulance, the patrol car, and the Bedford van—which were all that remained of the audacious operation to spring Andrew Kent from custody.

Details of what exactly had happened were still sketchy, but according to all the eyewitnesses, most of whom were police officers, it had been a well-planned and professional assault involving four men, most or all of whom had been armed. They'd been ruthless too, shooting one of the officers guarding Kent when he attempted to intervene. Twenty-seven-year-old Gary Hancock was currently in intensive care at University College Hospital, the same place Kent had been on his way to, and his condition was unknown. Tina knew him to say hello to and remembered that he was a nice guy who'd recently got engaged to a WPC based out of Camden station.

And now the perpetrators had disappeared into thin air. A burnt-out car, thought to have been their getaway vehicle, had been found up in Islington, and a full-scale manhunt involving helicopters and strategically placed roadblocks at points all over north London was now under way. But they no longer knew what car they had to look for, and Tina knew from experience that with this much time gone, it was highly unlikely they'd get a result that day.

The thought angered her. The gunmen had tried to kill her, and had almost succeeded too. If she and Grier hadn't ducked at the right time it could have been them in intensive care like Gary Hancock. Or worse.

She'd get them, though. She swore it to herself. And Kent. Although for the first time, she wondered if he was still alive. Someone had gone to a lot of trouble to break him out. It was possible, of course, that he'd faked his poisoning, knowing that he was going to be rescued, but she didn't buy it. He'd said to her that he'd tell her everything when she got him to a hospital, but everything about what? He had to be the Night Creeper, there was still too much evidence against him to suggest otherwise. And yet . . . and yet there was a gap in this jigsaw puzzle. Something missing.

Tina took another drag on her cigarette, determined to find out what it was, even if it meant working solidly for the next week.

Out of the corner of her eye she saw Grier giving his statement to two detectives from Scotland Yard's Serious and Organized Crime Agency, who didn't look any older than he did, and doubtless telling them what a reckless fool his boss was. It was funny how at the age of only thirty-one, Tina saw herself as a veteran when it wasn't really that long ago—five, perhaps six years—that she was a wet-behind-the-ears DC like Grier, a graduate herself with all these big ideas, and more than her fair share of ideals (even though she never liked to admit it). She hadn't supported the death penalty in those days either. How life had changed, and not for the better. She'd been through so much that sometimes the thought of all the terrible things that had happened both to her and to the people close to her made her want to lock herself away from the whole world, shut her eyes, and never wake up.

And then there were the other times, when she was filled with a terrible homicidal rage that made her kick the wall of her bedroom, smash crockery, scream at the top of her voice, as she imagined herself beating thugs into submission, or torturing the man she held responsible for so much of the wreckage of her life, a short, balding businessman called Paul Wise. The man she desperately wanted to bring down—to kill, if she was honest with herself—and the one person against whom she was utterly powerless.

Tina knew she was beginning to deteriorate mentally. Her neighbors on both sides tended to give her a wide berth these days whereas once they'd exchanged pleasantries, and one of them—she didn't know which—had even called the police when a night of red wine and tequila slammers in the front room had led to her methodically smashing every mirror in the flat. It was the one in the hallway that had caused the problem. It was a two-foot-by-four-foot in pine trimming from Ikea that faced the bedroom, and she'd taken it out with a chair. It had made such an explosive noise that she'd jumped back with fright, tripped over and hit her bookcase. She'd lain there, confused yet strangely sated, as half a dozen paperbacks and an old hardback Jackie Collins she'd bought as a teenager landed one after another on her head. She'd somehow convinced the two uniforms who turned up that it was all a fuss about nothing, and, recognizing who she was, they'd let her off with a friendly word of warning.

She'd given up the booze after that (at least for a couple of weeks), but the moods hadn't gone away, and it had crossed her mind more than once to ask at work to be referred to a psychiatrist, or simply take a period of absence for stress, but she'd rejected both alternatives. The job was the only thing that gave her life a semblance of balance and, in spite of everything, she was still damn good at it.

But now she'd gone and messed things up by taking a dramatic risk, not only with her own life, which she could accept, but with Grier's as well. He'd hardly spoken to her since, and she could understand why. Her behavior was erratic and undisciplined, and people like that were best avoided, particularly by someone who wanted to keep his copy book pristine.

She saw DCI MacLeod emerge from one of the police vans at the edge of the cordon. He looked pale and tense, but she could hardly blame him for that. What had started off as a happy evening in the pub to celebrate the successful conclusion of a long-running case had turned into a violent tragedy, with the suspect they'd spent so many man-hours hunting down having disappeared into thin air. Already news helicopters were whirring steadily overhead, and film crews from the various stations jockeyed for position with curious members of the public behind the scene-of-crime tape.

MacLeod saw her and came over, asking if she was OK.

"I've been better," she said, stubbing out her cigarette and trying to maintain a cool reserve, although in truth she was quite badly shaken up. What had happened to her that night reminded her of too many incidents in her past.

He gave her the kind of look a father gives an errant daughter. Kindly and caring but with more than a hint of worry crinkling his features. "Your luck's going to run out one day, you know. Be careful, Tina."

She was touched by his words, but typically didn't show it. "I had no choice but to follow them, sir. I couldn't let Kent go without a fight, could I?"

He shook his head, and Tina was struck by how stressed, and how old, he looked. "I wish I knew what was going on here."

Tina exhaled, thinking she might as well tell him what was on her mind. "You don't get a gang of four men springing a prisoner like that without a very serious motive. I don't think we know the half of it yet, sir."

MacLeod looked at her sharply. "You think someone inside the station helped them?"

"Don't you?"

"But why? And why are all these people willing to shoot police officers to get their hands on a man who's just a particularly nasty sex killer?"

"I don't know," said Tina, "but I think I might have a lead." She explained briefly about the differences in the Róisin O'Neill murder compared to the other four. "We definitely need to look into it further. Talk to some of her friends and family and see if that turns up anything?"

But MacLeod didn't look convinced. He sighed, his face looking redder than ever, clearly thinking about something else.

"I may have to hire a car," she continued. "My Focus is a write-off."

"Do what you have to do," he told her, suddenly dismissive. "Put it on expenses. I need to get going. I've got to go and explain myself to the DCS." Tina knew he was referring to DCS Frank Mendelson, the head of Homicide and Serious

Crime Command, the body to which all London's murder investigation teams belonged. He told her to take care, then with a small, forced smile he strode off in the direction of the station.

She watched him go, thinking that could be her in ten years' time—unhealthy, unfit, and burnt out by a job which, when it was stripped down to the bare bones, was not and could never be anything more than a continual stream of failures.

Having finished giving his statement, Grier walked over to her, his suit jacket tucked over one arm. He looked a lot calmer than he had earlier, although Tina wondered how long that would last. She knew from experience that the shock often came hours, even days, later.

"My God, what a night," he said, thrusting his hands into his trouser pockets and looking around at the crime scene.

Tina thought about saying sorry for earlier, almost got the first words out, but stopped herself. Saying sorry would be an admission that she'd been wrong, a sign of weakness, and something an ambitious young man like Grier could use against her.

Instead it was Grier who made the first move. "You know, about earlier. I know I got angry. It's because I was shocked after getting shot at. You're probably used to it, you know, the number of times it's happened to you. But I think it was the right thing to do for us to give chase, and that's what I told those guys."

He smiled at her, and she smiled back, feeling guilty. "Thanks. I appreciate it."

"How did your statement go? They're not going to put the blame on you for anything, are they?"

She shook her head. "I don't think so. We had just cause

to give chase, and I managed to pass the breathalyzer. Just."

"I didn't think you were drinking in the pub earlier," Grier said, looking puzzled.

"I just had a couple," she answered, thinking he was far more observant than she'd given him credit for. "Listen, Dan, you can go home now if you want. It's been a long day."

"And what are you going to do?" He paused. "You're going to carry on, aren't you?"

"We've spent months hunting down Kent, and now someone's snatched him from right under our noses, shot one of our people, and tried to kill us as well. It's only natural that I want to find out who they are and why they did it."

"And where are you going to start?"

"With Róisin O'Neill, of course. She's the only break in Andrew Kent's pattern."

Like MacLeod, Grier didn't look convinced. "But she was just a normal girl. What could she have had to do with what's going on now?"

In Tina's experience, even the most ordinary people could find themselves caught up in the most terrifying crimes. "I want to speak to her close friends and family, see if they can shed any light on her personal life that might throw up some leads."

"But we've just told them that we've arrested and charged the man who murdered their daughter."

"I know. And pretty soon they're going to find out that he's been broken out of custody, and they're not going to like that much, either. But we've got to work with the facts in front of us, and right now they're telling me that there's something wrong."

"I'm still convinced Kent had something to do with her murder, though. He was seen at her place, remember?"

"I do remember. But someone else was also involved—they had to have been. And that person might have been known to Róisin, which is why I want to talk to the people who knew her well."

He nodded. "I'd like to help, then," he told her.

"Sure you don't need to go home?" she asked, immediately regretting the vaguely mocking tone in her voice.

"No," he said firmly, "I don't. Do you want my help or not?"

Tina often liked to work alone, which was a bad trait for any DI and was one of the reasons she never felt comfortable in the role. But she was also pragmatic enough to know that in a case like this, where time wasn't on their side, she needed all the help she could get, and she was also beginning to realize that she hadn't appreciated quite how savvy Grier was. "That'd be good," she said. "I want to start by talking to Róisin's parents."

"I remember dealing with her dad. He took it very hard. His wife died when Róisin was still a child. She and her sister were all he had." He took out his iPhone. "I've still got his number on here somewhere. He lives in Rickmansworth."

"Can you call him? Apologize for the time, but tell him we'll be coming by in the next hour or so."

Grier walked off to dial the number while Tina called directory assistance and got a number for the nearest branch of Hertz. She was just about to call them to hire a replacement car when Grier came striding back, the phone no longer to his ear, his face etched with a potent mixture of concern and confusion.

"What is it?" she asked warily.

"When I called Róisin's dad's home number, his daughter answered—the other one, Derval." He paused.

"And?"

"And she told me that Kevin O'Neill died of a heart attack."

"When?"

"Last night."

Twenty-eight

I'd been dazed by the blow from the shotgun butt, but not fully knocked out, and although my nose had bled profusely, I didn't think it was broken.

In the half hour since then, I'd kept my mouth shut, my eyes down, and as low a profile as I was able to muster under the circumstances, while I tried to plan my next move. It had crossed my mind several times simply to jump out of the van and make a bolt for it, but what held me back was the fact that Haddock and Wolfe, or even Tommy, might use it as an excuse to put a bullet in me.

But I knew I couldn't hang around, not after what had happened. Wolfe had come very close to killing me earlier. It was eminently possible that he still would as soon as a more convenient opportunity presented itself, and as we pulled off the main road somewhere near the Hertfordshire/Bedfordshire border and drove down a long, winding road that was little more than a track, I began to wonder if that moment might soon arrive.

It was around ten when we finally reached the rendezvous, an abandoned two-story building tucked away among woodland and fields that loomed up in the darkness. It was a bizarre-looking place. The central section was at least a hundred years old and built from cobbled stone, but the rustic, traditionalist look was ruined by the two distinctly modern, cheap-looking extensions on each side, which didn't fit with the ambience at all. There were several wooden outbuildings dotted about, making me think it must once have been an old farm which some budding entrepreneur, whose budget didn't match his ambition, had tried to turn into a hotel. By the look of the ivy that had swarmed across the front, it had been shut down a good few years before, yet it still had electricity because there were lights on inside, on the ground floor.

A flimsy chainlink fence surrounded the plot with a Keep Out sign on the unlocked and open gate, and an estate agent's For Sale sign next to it.

"Looks like Lee's already here," said Haddock as he drove through the gate and up what was left of the gravel driveway before pulling up outside the front door. "Right," he growled, turning around in his seat, "let's get this filthy scumbag out of here."

He and Wolfe jumped out and strode around opposite sides of the van, pulled open the double doors at the back and dragged a struggling Kent out by his ankles, helped by Tommy, who was still holding the gun he'd put against my head, a cheap-looking snub-nosed revolver.

As I watched, Wolfe yanked Kent to his feet by his hair and punched him hard in the gut. He fell backward into Haddock, who delivered a short sharp kidney punch that sent him collapsing to his knees with a muffled shriek of pain from behind the gag. With his hands taped behind his back, the poor bastard could offer no resistance as Wolfe kicked him in the solar plexus, a malevolent glare in his eyes, the force of the blow knocking Kent sideways so that he temporarily disappeared from view.

What I was seeing sickened me. It was nothing more than bullying. Whatever someone's done, you don't hit them when they're helpless and can't fight back, as Wolfe was doing. And enjoying it too, by the look of things.

Then he turned to me. "Get out of the van, you, and make yourself useful. Help get this piece of shit inside."

As I clambered out of the back of the van, wiping congealing blood from my face with my shirtsleeve, Wolfe pulled Kent back up and shoved him in my direction. He was already collapsing again, and as I took his full weight I was surprised at how light he was.

"Tommy, you introduced this bastard to the team," Wolfe continued, squinting angrily at me. "You can help him with Kent."

Tommy grabbed one of Kent's arms while I held on to the other, and together we hauled him toward the front door, while he dragged his feet and made terrified moaning noises beneath the gag.

A second later, the door opened, and a wiry-looking, dark-skinned Thai girl dressed in jeans, a white T-shirt with a garish pink butterfly on it, and a pair of killer stilettos appeared. She was attractive but in a hard, showy way, with false breasts that sprang out aggressively, elaborate tattoos covering both arms from elbow to shoulder, and the kind of stony expression that suggested she'd had to fight tooth and nail for everything she'd ever got in life. This was Wolfe's girlfriend, Lee, and she fit Tommy's description of "a dirty-looking cage fighter" perfectly.

She was also blocking our way, forcing us to stop.

"Hey, Lee, baby," I heard Wolfe call from behind me. "You got the power on, then?"

"Sure I did," she answered in heavily accented English.

"It's not hard." Then, seeing Kent for the first time, and clearly knowing his history and the crimes he was accused of, her eyes darkened. "Is this him?"

"Don't hurt him, baby," said Wolfe with a chuckle. "The client wants him in one piece."

"He's a dirty cocksucker," she said, leaning forward and spitting full in his face, before grabbing him by the crotch and giving his balls a vicious twist.

Kent made the kind of noise any of us would have made in similar circumstances, and he struggled in our grip as she cursed him in Thai. Finally, she let go, cursed him one more time, then strode casually past us and into the arms of her lover, letting out a squeal of delight that was about as natural as her bust.

Kent slumped in our arms, saliva running down his face, and once again I found myself feeling sorry for him.

"Take him in there," snapped Haddock, looming up beside me.

Together, Tommy and I maneuvered Kent through the door and into a surprisingly large foyer, with doors going off on three sides and a dilapidated wooden staircase at the end. There was an old pine reception desk with an anarchy sign daubed in black paint on the front, along with more garbled graffiti. A couple of psychedelic posters covered the walls, making me think that this place had been a squat for a while. The carpet, dark and stained, was rotting in places, and cobwebs had formed, net-like, across the corners of the ceiling. The place reminded me of the vampires' lair in the classic 1980s movie *The Lost Boys,* and the smell of damp, earthy decay stuck in my nostrils. If you were going to torture and kill someone, you'd be hard pushed to find a better place to do it in.

Haddock moved in ahead of us, holding his shotgun one-handed, and strode over to the far door, pushing it open and motioning for us to follow. It led through to a large empty room with more graffiti on the walls.

"Down here," he said, unbolting another door in one corner, and switching on a light.

A flight of concrete steps led down to a dank-looking cellar that smelled of urine and decay, and as we reached the top of them, Kent started struggling and moaning. He must have known that when he went down those steps he'd never be coming up them again.

Without a word, Haddock moved around behind him and drove a heavy boot into the small of his back, sending him flying forward. He cracked his head on the overhead beam, then rolled down the steps in a tangle of legs before landing on his back at the bottom. He looked in pain but was still conscious and didn't seem to have broken anything, but I hated the way he gazed up at us, with that terrified expression in his eyes.

He knew what was coming. That's what got me. He knew.

Haddock waved to Tommy, who started down the steps after Kent, then turned to me. "Get out of my sight, we don't need you anymore," he said, before adding ominously, "We'll talk later."

He followed Tommy down the steps, closing the door behind him.

According to Wolfe, no one was meant to hurt Kent, but since I couldn't see what else they'd be going down there for, I put my ear to the door and listened.

"What do you think you're doing?"

Wolfe had come into the room and was right behind me, the Sig stuffed in the front of his waistband with just the handle showing.

One thing I've learned in life is, when you're caught red-handed always go on the offensive. "I wanted to hear if they were torturing him or not," I said, walking past him. "Now, if you've got the rest of my money, I won't hang around any longer."

"You'll get it when the client arrives," he answered, following me back into the foyer.

Lee was standing by the old reception desk, smoking a cigarette and looking nervous. She gave me only the barest of glances.

I turned to face him. "And when's that going to be?"

For the first time, I saw that his expression was uncertain. "I don't know. He should be here by now."

"Why don't you phone him?"

It was Lee who answered, her voice annoyed. "Because there's no mobile phone reception here, that's why. No reception. No nothing. I want my money too, you know."

"Are you sure none of them can get a signal?" I said. "Why don't you let me try mine?"

"I have tried it. And both of mine. It's totally dead on all of them."

"How did you leave things with your client?" I asked, lighting a cigarette of my own and taking a much-needed drag.

"That he'd be here tonight. Before midnight."

"And is he reliable?"

"'Course he is," he said, but something in his voice suggested he wasn't totally sure.

This was when I realized that maybe Wolfe didn't know his client all that well, which surprised me, given his reputation for being so careful about whom he dealt with.

I could hear Haddock and Tommy talking as they came

out of the cellar and decided that now was the right time to make a break for it and raise the alarm. I didn't think they'd panic and disappear with Kent if I suddenly took off, because they were still waiting for their money.

"I need a piss," I said with an irritated sigh, and turned away from Wolfe, starting for the front door.

"Sure," he answered, and I was so busy making for the exit and freedom that I never even saw him take the gun from his waistband.

The first I knew about it was when I felt the sudden, explosive pain as the butt of the Sig caught me in the back of my head. My vision blurred and I felt my legs give way, then I was hitting the filthy carpet with a painful bang, only just managing to get out a hand to break my fall.

"I think we've got some unfinished business, Seany boy," I heard him say, his voice sounding far away. "Don't you?"

Then another voice came from somewhere behind him, and that's when I knew I was in real trouble.

"I want this dog's head," said Clarence Haddock.

Twenty-nine

My head spun, and I could feel the blood leaking out from the wound where I'd been struck, but luckily I still had the presence of mind to roll myself into a tight ball and put my hands over my head as the kicks rained in on me.

I couldn't see who was doing the kicking. All I could hear was heavy breathing as they worked on trying to cause me the maximum injury possible. There was no pain—there never is when you're in a fight, even one as one-sided and brutal as this. The huge surge of adrenaline puts paid to that. All I felt was a series of jarring shocks as I was knocked about the floor. One of them—I think it was that bastard Haddock—was aiming his blows at my kidneys, but they weren't that accurate, and I was fairly certain that neither of them had done me any permanent damage yet.

But I knew that this was only the beginning. I'd managed to make both Wolfe and Haddock lose face, which was some achievement considering I'd only known them roughly twelve hours, and hugely stupid given their history of violence. The only thing counting in my favor was that the other two people in the room were trying to calm them down.

"Ty! Stop! Stop!" Lee was crying in a voice so shrill it could have shattered glass. "What are you doing?"

Tommy was also telling them to leave me alone, that what they were doing was madness, but the tone of his voice was hopeful rather than confident, and he wasn't making any move to intervene.

The kicking continued. Fast and furious, carried out largely in silence.

Then, just as quickly, it stopped, as they finally grew bored.

At least that's what I thought, but as I lay there unmoving, the pain finally beginning to make its presence felt, I heard Haddock snarl and rumble out a low, angry curse. The next second Lee screamed, and I opened my eyes and saw him standing over me, legs apart, the Remington raised above his head like a club, the butt aimed directly at my face. There was a glint of madness in his eyes as he stood there stock-still, and then, with a roar that temporarily drowned out everything else in the room, he brought it flying down.

Instinctively, I rolled over and it bounced off my shoulder and smashed into the carpet with such force that the stock broke in two, sending a piece flying across the room in a cloud of dust. If it had made contact with my head, as it was meant to do, it would almost certainly have killed me, and I felt a rush of relief even as he lifted what was left of it above his head again, to have another go.

"I'm going to have you, you dog," he snarled, and lunged forward, smashing it down again.

This time I rolled into him and he missed completely.

Seeing my chance, I grabbed one of his legs with both hands, hoping to knock him off balance, but it was like trying to uproot a tree trunk, and he shook me off easily, catching me in the midriff with a frustrated final whack of the battered Remington, the angle too low to do any real harm.

"All right, Clarence!" barked Wolfe, still panting after his exertions. "Leave it. He's had enough."

I rolled over onto my back, every movement seeming stiff and painful. It felt like I might have a couple of cracked ribs. "I haven't done anything," I whispered, the very act of speaking hurting me. "All I did was ask you what we were doing here."

"You pointed a fucking gun at me," said Wolfe.

"And you pointed one at me. So now we're even."

"I don't see why we don't just get rid of him," muttered Haddock. "We don't need him, and we can take his share of the cash."

"Hey, boys, come on," said Tommy. "Let's be careful what we say here."

Haddock shook his head. "I don't trust him. All he does is ask questions."

"All I want to know is why the hell we kidnapped Kent. I still do."

"Because he's a dirty rapist," put in Lee, striding over, her heels clacking on the moldy floor.

"Look," I said desperately, trying to appeal to anyone who might listen, "there's something wrong with this whole thing." I turned toward Wolfe. "I mean, if your client's a relative of one of Kent's victims, then how did he manage to set all this up so fast? Kent was only arrested yesterday. When did you get hired? Because if it was before then, then this whole vigilante story's bullshit."

Lee looked at Wolfe. "Is this right?"

"The client's a relative," Wolfe replied defensively. "Maybe he had some inside knowledge. Who else would want a nonce like Kent?"

"We can't let this dog leave here," said Haddock, prodding

me with the barrel of the ruined Remington. "He knows too much. And we don't know nothing about him."

"I vouched for him," said Tommy, "and I still do." But there was something half-hearted in his tone, as if he himself wasn't sure of me anymore.

This confirmed for me, if I hadn't known it already, that I was now arguing for my life. And that if I failed, I was dead. It was as simple as that. "Listen," I said, clutching my injured ribs, "you've had your fun with me. You've given me a kicking, and you've made your point. You can keep the rest of your money. In fact, keep the stuff you gave me if you want," I added, remembering that I'd left it in the minibus. "I just want out."

"He put a gun in your face, Ty man," snapped Haddock, interrupting my flow. "What the hell will it do for your rep if you let him walk out of here?"

I caught Lee's eye, remembering how Wolfe had eased up when she'd started shouting, and knowing she was my best chance of getting him to let me go.

She looked away quickly, then turned to Wolfe. "Don't kill him, Ty. It's not worth it."

A troubled look crossed Wolfe's face, and I thought he was wavering, but then he saw the way Haddock was staring at him, and his expression darkened. "Shut the fuck up! This bastard wanted to kill me earlier."

I started to protest, but he gave me a kick to the gut that I wasn't expecting, and I doubled up, trying to catch my breath.

He pulled the Sig out of his waistband and yanked me to my feet by the shirt collar. "Right, let's get him upstairs."

Lee put a hand on his shoulder. "Don't kill him, Ty. Please. You're no killer."

He brushed it aside, then swung me around and shoved the gun into my side while Haddock twisted my right arm behind my back with such force it made me cry out involuntarily.

I looked toward Tommy, my eyes watering with the pain, but he'd already turned his back to me, as had Lee, and I realized with a grim finality that I was on my own as Wolfe and Haddock marched me over to the staircase and began pushing me toward the darkness above.

Thirty

I craned my neck and asked Wolfe not to kill me, even though I hated myself for begging to the man who'd murdered my brother. But that's what the instinct for self-preservation does to you. You'll say most things to stay alive. But he said nothing in return, and Haddock yanked my arm upward again, and this time I almost passed out with the pain.

Somehow the arm didn't break as I was manhandled up the last of the stairs and down a dark corridor, the floor creaking precariously beneath my feet.

"In here," said Wolfe, stopping at a door about halfway along. "It's got a bolt." He pulled it open and together they threw me inside.

I stumbled forward in the darkness, realizing I was in some sort of cramped, windowless store cupboard, then deliberately fell to the floor, wanting to show them I was being as passive and unthreatening as possible. Every part of my body ached, my ribs were killing me, and the back of my head and my nose were still bleeding from where I'd been hit earlier with the two different guns. In short, I was a mess. Probably the most battered I'd ever been in my life.

The two of them stood in the doorway, silhouettes in the gloom, looking down at me. Then the door shut and I heard a bolt being pulled across, followed by hushed words from out in the corridor.

"He's got to go, Ty," I heard Haddock say in a whisper that was so loud it had to be deliberate. "But my gun's fucked. You're going to need to do him."

"I need something to muffle the sound," was Wolfe's response, quieter but still audible.

I heard footsteps moving away from the door. Then silence.

It's difficult to describe what I was feeling at that point. It wasn't fear exactly. I was too bruised and exhausted for that. It was closer to resignation. A knowledge that I'd tried to go it alone, for the best of reasons, but that ultimately my plan had been found wanting, and I'd failed.

And now I was the last one of us left, and my life too was about to end, with the grim irony that it was going to be at the hands of the man who'd set in motion so many of the events that had destroyed the Egan family.

The footsteps return, and I took a deep breath that made me wince. I couldn't die like a coward. Not after all the effort I'd put into bringing Tyrone Wolfe to justice. Maybe somewhere up there they were all watching, willing me to at least go down fighting. I had to do something to make them proud.

I pictured John then, as he was just before he went off to join the army. A big smile on his face. Full of jokes, as always. My dad clapping him on the back, the pride in his eyes. The three of us having a last game of football in the garden. John letting me score through his legs.

Jesus, John, I miss you. I miss you so fucking much.

The door opened and I felt a surge of anger as I saw Wolfe standing there with the Sig in one hand and a filthy-looking pillow in the other, the looming, demonic figure of Haddock at his shoulder. I could hear him breathing and his whole body was shaking with adrenaline as he psyched himself up for the kill.

I tensed, moving into a position where I could spring up at him and make a grab for the gun.

But I was too late. Wolfe lunged at me suddenly, dropping his knee into my stomach and driving the wind right out of me. As I tried to recover, he sat astride me, pinning my arms by my side, then everything turned to darkness as he pushed the pillow against my face, and I felt the metal of the gun barrel hard against my cheek.

Clenching my teeth against the impact of the bullet I knew was coming at any second, I struggled beneath him. But it was useless. He was a strong guy with all the momentum, and I was still battered and dazed.

"Go on, Ty, take him," I heard Haddock hiss in the darkness.

Oh God. This was it.

All over.

"Jesus," Wolfe cursed.

"What is it?"

"The gun. The fucking thing's jammed."

"Are you sure?"

"'Course I'm sure."

I felt the pressure lift on my face and the pillow slipped sideways. The next second, Wolfe was getting to his feet.

"Are you just going to leave him?" Haddock growled.

"I'm not putting a knife in him. You don't do that in business. Don't worry, he's not getting out of here."

The door closed and I heard the bolt being moved across, then their voices faded as they moved away.

For a good few seconds I didn't move. I was too shocked. To have come so close to death and then be spared was almost more than my already shredded nerves could bear.

But it wasn't that that was occupying my mind as I lay on the hard wooden floor. It was the fact that Tyrone Wolfe had deliberately spared my life. He might have told Haddock that the gun was jammed but there was no way he could have known for sure.

Because he hadn't tried to pull the trigger.

Thirty-one

Kevin O'Neill had been a self-made man. One of seven children from a village in County Cork, he'd left school at sixteen and come to England to make his fortune, building up a construction and property development company from nothing. He hadn't been immensely rich, according to what Grier had told Tina, but he'd made enough to send his children to private school and live in a big detached house on a secluded private road in the northwest London suburb of Rickmansworth.

It was ten past eleven and starting to spit with warm summer rain when the two police officers pulled up outside the security gates at the front of the property. Tina waited while Grier got out and pressed the buzzer, noticing the CCTV camera attached to the gatepost above his head. It wasn't uncommon to have this level of security in London, even out here in the suburbs, but Tina knew that, although it might have acted as a deterrent against opportunistic burglars, the more determined and organized intruders would always get through, simply by bypassing the gate and going over the eight-foot-high wooden fence that bordered the grounds.

Although she wasn't convinced that someone had killed Kevin O'Neill, the timing of his death was worryingly coincidental, given that his daughter's murder was the only one of the five supposedly committed by the Night Creeper that stood out.

Grier had been less enthusiastic about coming, telling her as they'd driven through the dark, silent streets that he thought O'Neill's death was exactly what it looked like, a coincidence. He'd also given her some compelling reasons, the most important of which was the lack of any obvious motive. On the night O'Neill died, Róisin had already been dead eight months, so why would anyone choose to murder him then?

It was a question Tina couldn't answer.

The gates opened automatically as Grier got back in the car, and they drove down the short driveway that led to the main house, an imposing whitewashed building done in a faux Georgian style.

Derval O'Neill, Róisin's sister, was at the door when they pulled up outside, dressed in jeans and a halter top, her feet bare. She was a physically striking woman in her early thirties, tall and willowy, with long auburn hair and narrow, delicate features. Grier had told Tina that the name Derval meant "true desire" in Celtic, and even in grief, it was a description that fitted her easily.

"Thank you for seeing us at such short notice, Miss O'Neill," said Tina, after Grier had introduced her. "We're both very sorry for your loss."

Derval's expression seemed to wobble. Her eyes were puffy and red from crying, her face pale, and close up she looked thin rather than willowy. "He never got over Róisin's death," she said quietly, fixing Tina with a look of surprising intensity. "It finished him. So now that bastard's got himself another victim." She sighed. "Come inside. Would you like a drink of something?"

Tina fought down the urge to ask for a glass of decent red wine and requested water, as did Grier.

They followed Derval through a spacious hallway and into a tastefully furnished lounge with floor-to-ceiling windows that looked out onto the back garden. Tina and Grier sat down at opposite ends of a three-person sofa and waited while Derval went to get their drinks.

"This was where we interviewed her dad," said Grier quietly, gazing slowly around the room. "He sat on that sofa opposite, this huge guy with massive hands, and he was just sobbing quietly with his head down. He couldn't even look us in the eye. All he wanted to know was whether Róisin had suffered or not." Grier sighed deeply, looking at Tina with a troubled expression on his face. "We had to tell him the truth. We couldn't lie to him—he'd only have found out the truth from the media. So we had to tell him that his daughter had been raped and beaten to death with a blunt instrument. It was the hardest thing I've ever had to do. That's why I don't even want to begin to think that we arrested the wrong man for it."

"I know," she said. "Neither do I." But the problem was, she knew they had.

Derval returned with their drinks and took a seat opposite them. Tina saw that she had a full glass of white wine. She tried not to stare at it as Derval took a large gulp before running a finger delicately over her lips.

"I was just here sorting out Dad's affairs before the funeral," she told them, as if her presence at the house needed explaining. "It's set for next Thursday. It's going to be at home in Cork. That was Dad's request."

Tina felt a twinge of regret. If any evidence of foul play did emerge, then there was no way her father's body would be released for burial. And if it wasn't, her own actions would be prolonging the grief and pain this family was having to bear.

"Are you managing OK?" asked Grier, leaning forward in his seat. "Do you have any other relatives who can help?"

"I'm doing fine," Derval answered, her expression wobbling once again. "But why have you both come here at this time of night? Has something happened with the man you've arrested for Róisin's murder? The liaison officer said his name was Andrew Kent."

"That's right. And yes, it has," answered Tina. She told Derval about Kent's abduction. "There's a major manhunt under way now, but so far we haven't located him."

Derval looked shocked. "Oh my God. How did that happen? Who took him?"

"We don't know yet."

"Well, whoever it is, I hope they kill him. He's destroyed my whole family. He killed my father, just like he killed my sister. He deserves everything he gets." She stared at the two police officers defiantly, as if daring them to disagree.

Tina knew exactly how she felt. "Was your father here in this house when he died?" she asked.

Derval nodded. "Yes. It must have been sometime last night. The cleaner found him this morning when she came. He was in his study at the desk. She said he looked very peaceful."

Tina managed a small, reassuring smile. "That's one blessing at least. And the cleaner called the doctor, did she?"

"Yes. He was certified dead at the scene. The doctor said it was a massive heart attack."

"Did he have any history of heart trouble?" asked Grier.

The implication of his question was obvious, and Derval

picked up on it straight away. "He had a triple heart bypass six years ago, but since then he'd given up smoking and started exercising and watching what he ate. He was looking the fittest I'd ever seen him in the months before Róisin was murdered. But what's my dad's death got to do with any of this?"

"Nothing," answered Grier, glancing at Tina as if to say, *See? He had a history of heart trouble. It's just a coincidence. What the hell are we here for?*

Tina suddenly felt very tired. It had been a long day and she was desperate to finish it by unwinding with a drink. Maybe she was simply seeing conspiracies where none existed. "Were you very close to Róisin?" she asked, knowing she was going to have to tread carefully.

"What does any of this, or my dad, have to do with what's happened to Andrew Kent?" Derval's voice was suddenly laced with suspicion.

"It's just routine, Miss O'Neill," put in Grier. "It helps us to build up a picture in advance of the trial."

Grier's explanation sounded utterly lame, and Tina knew she was going to have to be honest with Derval. "There've been some developments in your sister's case," she said firmly. "The evidence still points to Andrew Kent as being the killer but, strictly off the record, there are one or two areas of doubt, and we need to look at them again."

"You're saying Kent may not have murdered my sister?" Derval looked utterly shocked. "My God, I didn't think things could get any worse."

"It's almost certain he did," said Grier soothingly, which Tina knew was bullshit since Kent had a cast-iron alibi. "We just want to make sure, that's all."

Derval took another generous gulp of the wine and flicked

back her long hair. "Yes, I was close to Róisin. I lived on the other side of London from her but we still got together now and again for drinks in the West End. Not as often as I'd have liked . . . you know how busy everything gets in London. But yeah, we were friends."

Tina had a theory. It was vague and full of holes, but it was all she had to go on. "I understand from the interviews with friends and family that Róisin was single when she died, but had she been in any serious relationships at any time in the immediate run-up to her death?"

"The only serious boyfriend Róisin had since university was Max." The way Derval spoke his name suggested she hadn't entirely approved of him. "She went out with him for a long time—three, four years, something like that."

"And when did it finish?"

"About a year ago. He was seeing an Australian girl on the side and they ended up disappearing off to Oz. As far as I know, that's where they still are. He didn't even bother making contact after Róisin's murder." She sighed. "I never liked him, but I can't help thinking that if they were still together, she'd still be alive."

Tina sighed. Her theory of the killer being a boyfriend with inside knowledge of the police investigation was looking pretty dead in the water. "Róisin was a very attractive woman. Was she seeing anyone else? Having any flings in those last few months?"

"What are you trying to imply? That some irate ex-boyfriend killed her? Andrew Kent was the man who fitted the alarm in her apartment, the same as with the other victims. If he didn't kill Róisin, then presumably he didn't kill the other girls either. Is that what you're trying to tell me? That Kent's innocent? That there is no Night Creeper?" She was slurring her words slightly, and Tina realized this wasn't her first glass of wine of the evening.

"I'm just trying to make sure we've got the right man, that's all. Now I know how you must be suffering, Derval—"

"No you don't. You don't have a fucking clue. Has anyone you know ever been murdered?"

"Yes." The word came out louder than Tina had intended. "I know exactly what it feels like. I think about it every day."

Derval looked stricken. "I'm sorry," she said quietly. "I didn't mean to shout."

"It's OK," said Tina, feeling a wave of compassion for the woman in front of her. She got to her feet, went over, and sat beside her, putting her arms round Derval's shoulders, hugging her to her chest.

As she held her, her eyes met Grier's and he mouthed the words *What do you think you're doing?* before turning away, an expression of disgust on his face.

A few seconds passed, then Derval gently pulled away and wiped her eyes with a well-used tissue, while Tina returned to her seat.

Derval picked up her wine and drank most of the remainder, letting out a long, satisfied sigh that was utterly familiar to Tina.

"There was someone else."

Tina snapped back to reality, the urge for a drink temporarily forgotten.

Derval stared into space as she spoke. "Róisin never actually came out and said she was seeing someone, but I knew she was. We went out a couple of times, and she'd just give off telltale signs. It was the way she smiled over her texts and disappeared off to make phone calls. I asked her about it, but she just said it was friends." She looked at Tina. "But I knew.

And I'm guessing he must have been married. She would have known that I wouldn't have approved. I had an affair once myself and got my fingers burned very badly, and Dad . . . Well, he'd have hated it."

"So you have no idea who it might have been?"

Derval shook her head. "No, but I'm absolutely certain there was someone."

"Are you sure Róisin wouldn't have talked to your father about it?"

"I suppose it's possible," Derval answered cautiously. "They were close, after all." She frowned. "You don't honestly think that someone killed Dad to protect a secret lover of Róisin's, do you? That's just unbelievable."

That was the problem. It was. But then so much of what had happened that day had been unbelievable, and that hadn't stopped it from happening. "We're just following up every avenue of inquiry," said Tina, aware how hollow her answer sounded.

Derval looked at them both in turn. "I want some closure here. I want to know that justice is being done for my sister and my father, and I want to know, most of all, that the right man has been arrested for the crime and that you're going to get him back."

"We're doing everything we can," said Grier.

"You keep saying that. But are you? Look, I'm suffering enough as it is without you talking in riddles." Her voice was getting louder, and she looked like she might burst into tears at any moment.

Out of the corner of her eye, Tina saw Grier getting to his feet. She rose too, walked over to Derval, and put a steadying hand on her shoulder. "I promise you justice will be done, Derval. I will personally keep you informed of everything that happens with regard to Andrew Kent and this whole inquiry. You have my word on that."

"Do you suspect that my father's death was suspicious?"

"Yes, that's a possibility," she said reluctantly.

Derval's expression tightened, giving her cheeks a sunken, hollow look. "Oh God. After everything else . . ."

"It might not be, Derval, remember that. It's just we're keeping an open mind. Now, I need to see the CCTV tapes from the camera at the front of the property. I don't suppose they'll give us anything, but we need to take a look."

Derval nodded, and led them through to her father's study where she booted up his PC and located the camera's digital footage for the previous day. But Tina was right. The footage didn't show anything suspicious, although that was to be expected. If anyone had killed Kevin O'Neill in his own home, they wouldn't have allowed themselves to be caught on camera.

Unfortunately, it also left them with nothing. They thanked Derval for her time, Tina reiterating her promise to keep her informed of developments, as well as taking the number of the doctor who'd certified her father's death.

As they drove out of the gates of the O'Neill property, Grier asked if they were finished for the night.

"Soon."

He raised his eyebrows. "Really? What else are we going to do?"

"First of all, I want to call the doctor. We need a time of death for Kevin O'Neill. Then we'll have something to work with."

As they reached the bottom of the road, where it joined the A404 heading back into London, Tina stopped the car. She was feeling frustrated. They were still fumbling about in the dark, and she knew that Grier was rapidly losing interest in her theories, if he'd ever had any at all.

"Where are you going now?" he asked as she opened the car door.

She pointed up to a CCTV camera on top of a metal pole, partially obscured by one of the oak trees that lined both sides of the road, which she'd spotted on the way in. It covered the entrance to the cul-de-sac, and any vehicle that came in or out of it would have to pass under its gaze. Beneath the camera was a sign advertising the twenty-four-hour security company that operated it. "Maybe the operator saw something," she said, walking over to take down the company's number.

The drizzling rain had stopped now and the night was warm.

"Listen, ma'am." Grier had also got out of the car, and walked up beside her. "I think we could be wasting time here."

She pulled out a cigarette. "I know. You've made that clear."

"O'Neill died of a heart attack. Not a bullet to the head. He was a big guy in his late fifties who'd had heart trouble before, and who'd been under a lot of pressure since his daughter's death. This could just be the culmination of it."

"His daughter died eight months ago."

"I think you're becoming a conspiracy theorist."

Tina felt a punch of anger. "And I can't believe you can't see what's happening. Kent's been snatched for a reason. There are a lot of people involved, and now, when we look more closely at the one victim where the MO's not like the others, we find that her father, who hasn't had any recent health problems, has suddenly dropped dead. There is a conspiracy, and there's no theory about it. It's real."

"But even if Róisin's murder is different, and wasn't committed by Kent, why would the person who did it kill her father? And why, then, would they also snatch Kent? It just doesn't make sense."

Ignoring the rain, Tina lit the cigarette, noticing that Grier was giving her a look that might be construed as pitying. She'd received a fair number like that over the years from people who professed to admire her determination and tenacity, and her excellent record for helping solve high-profile cases, but who also wondered how someone who'd lost several colleagues in the line of duty and who'd been kidnapped herself, not to mention shot twice, could genuinely be "all there." In truth, she should never have been a DI, since she was a far better detective than a manager, but the reason she'd been promoted was because she didn't give up.

"Maybe you're right. Maybe I am barking up the wrong tree. But it's better than barking up no tree at all."

Grier made a play of looking at his watch. "There's nothing else we can realistically do tonight, ma'am. It's not long till midnight, we've been on duty for fifteen hours, and phoning doctors or security companies, or whoever else, isn't going to help us find Andrew Kent. But a good night's sleep might."

Tina was beginning to realize she didn't like being called ma'am. It suggested she had a responsibility toward the people reporting to her that she wasn't sure she could handle. After all, today she'd almost got Grier killed. "Do me a favor, Dan. For tonight at least, call me Tina."

He sighed. "OK, Tina. Just for one night, why don't you take a step back, relax a little, and get a decent night's sleep?"

She wanted to say, *Because this job, and the fact that I'm good at it, is all I've got.* Instead, she turned and walked back to the car, wondering how long she had left before she finally burned out.

Thirty-two

I lay in the darkness for a long time, wondering why Wolfe hadn't killed me when he'd had the opportunity, but without coming to any conclusions. All I knew was that I had to try to get out of there.

But when I finally felt ready to get to my feet and try the door, I found it was stuck fast, and it wasn't budging, however hard I pushed. So I sat back down and waited for Wolfe and Haddock to come back and finish off what they'd started, trying to recover as much as possible from the beating in the meantime so that I'd be ready to make a break when the opportunity arose. My injuries, though painful—especially the ribs, one of which was definitely fractured—were tolerable and wouldn't stop me from making my move.

But it was hard being trapped in there, unarmed and waiting to die, trying to ignore a growing feeling of claustrophobia. I could hear occasional noises coming from downstairs—mainly banging about, no voices—and at some point I thought I heard the sound of a car driving away.

This was followed by silence, and I wondered whether the others had left the building. At first, the thought filled me with a delirious hope—if they'd left me here, it meant they weren't going to kill me—but the realization quickly dawned that I was also imprisoned in an abandoned building miles from anywhere and would almost certainly starve to death before I was discovered.

So I got back up and repeatedly shoulder-barged the door, no longer concerned about drawing attention to myself, until finally, my shoulder sore with trying, I gave up and sat back down again. Waiting. Although for what, I wasn't sure.

I wondered if Kent was still here, if he was even still alive. More than that, though, I wondered why he'd been snatched in the first place. He'd claimed to know something, and Wolfe had been extremely keen to shut him up before he said any more. What could he have known that was so important that it was worthwhile for someone to pay for him to be broken out at gunpoint? And what did it have to do with the killings he'd been accused of?

I was in the process of cursing myself for ever getting involved in such a terrible mess when something happened. All the lights in the building went out. I could tell this because even though I was in a tiny windowless room, there'd been a thin orange glow in the crack beneath the door. Now, suddenly, it was gone.

I got up and listened at the door.

For several minutes there was nothing, then I heard the sound of footsteps, quiet yet unmistakable, coming up the staircase, accompanied by the creaking of old wood.

I clenched my fists, took a deep breath, and waited.

The footsteps came closer, slow and cautious.

I could hear my heart beating. This was it.

"Hello?" The footsteps stopped. "Hello?"

The voice was female and heavily accented. It was Lee, Wolfe's girlfriend, and she sounded worried.

Straight away I decided it couldn't be a trick. "I'm in

here," I called out, rapping on the door. "It's bolted from the outside."

I heard the bolt being pulled across, and stepped back as the door opened.

Lee stood in the doorway, only just visible in the gloom. "Are you OK?" she asked, then, as she stepped forward to get a better look at me, she gasped as her question was answered. "You are hurt badly." She touched my face in a strangely erotic gesture, running her fingers along the bruising.

"I'm OK," I said, removing the hand and stepping out into the darkened hallway. "But what's going on?"

"I don't know. Ty had to go off and bury the guns some-where."

"Do you know where?" I asked, thinking once again about gathering evidence.

She shook her head. "No, but he promised he wouldn't be long. He told Clarence to look after me, but Clarence . . . him and me, we're not friends. He goes off to another room, leaves me in kitchen, and then, ten minutes ago, boom, all the lights go out. Now I can't find Clarence anywhere. I call out his name, he doesn't answer."

"What about Tommy? Where's he?"

"The other one? He was around earlier but I haven't seen him for a long time now."

"And has the client turned up?"

"No. No one's come here."

I frowned. Had Haddock and Tommy abandoned the place while Wolfe was gone? From the silence in the house, I had to assume they had, but I couldn't understand why, particularly if the client hadn't arrived.

"How long's Wolfe been gone?"

"Half an hour. Maybe longer."

"Was he on foot?"

She nodded. "Yes."

So he was burying the guns somewhere near the building, which meant it probably wouldn't be long until he got back.

"What's your name?" she asked suddenly.

"Sean."

"I'm Lee." She moved closer to me. "I'm scared, Sean."

"We need to get out of here."

I moved past her in the direction of the stairs, listening for the sound of anyone else but not hearing anything.

"What about Ty?" she asked, following.

"You can do a lot better than Ty, Lee."

"He says he'll kill me if I leave him."

I put a finger to my lips and we moved as quietly as we could down the staircase. But it still creaked angrily under our combined weight, sounding like it was going to give way at any moment. The silence in the gloom was loud in my ears, and I could hear my heart beating hard as I felt the first stirrings of hope. After coming so close to death, it actually looked like I might get out of here in one piece after all. I had Lee to thank for this, which was why I was taking her with me. I was going to do her a major favor by getting Tyrone Wolfe out of her life.

The door was unlocked and the air cool as I stepped outside. Woodland surrounded us on all sides, and aside from the faint orange glow of London in the distance, there was just more silence. The night was clear and starry, and I felt the first yearning for freedom. The minibus we'd come here in was still in the driveway where Wolfe had parked it earlier, which puzzled me, because it meant that if Haddock and Tommy had left, they'd used some other form of transport.

I turned to Lee. "How did you get here tonight?"

"I came on a motorbike."

"Where is it?"

"'Round the side of the house."

"Have you still got the keys?"

She nodded, feeling in her pocket. "Yes."

"Good. We're leaving on that, then. I just need to collect something."

I went up to the minibus window and peered inside, looking for the jiffy bag containing the thirty grand that Haddock had given me, and wasn't surprised to see that it was gone, doubtless removed by one of them earlier.

But as I turned away, keen to get going as quickly as possible, I saw something that stopped me dead.

It was the tires on the minibus. There were deep, uneven gashes in them.

"What is it?" asked Lee uncertainly.

I didn't say anything, wondering who could have done this. And why. Then I went 'round the other side. It was the same.

"Someone's slashed the tires."

"Who?"

"I've no idea."

I looked out into the trees, scanning them for any sign of life. But there was nothing, no movement at all, and I experienced a growing dread.

I grabbed her by the hand and we hurried around the side of the building, with me leading, just in case whoever had sabotaged the minibus was waiting for us.

But they weren't.

There was only a 125 motorbike, leaning up against the exterior wall. I looked down at the tires and my worst fears were confirmed. They too had been slashed.

"What's going on here, Sean? Who's doing this?"

"God knows," I whispered, looking around in the silence, wondering if whoever had done this was watching us now.

Finally, I turned back to Lee. She suddenly looked more like a terrified girl than the confident über-bitch who'd greeted us at the door earlier. "This place is abandoned. How did you get the lights on earlier?"

"Generator," she said, pointing to a brick outbuilding a few yards away. "But I shut the door when I got it working."

The door was now wide open.

So, whoever had slashed the tires had gone to work on the generator as well.

I approached the door slowly, hoping there might be some tools in there we could use for basic weapons, but wary too of going inside. Lee stayed a few yards back as I slowly entered the doorway and stared into the gloom. Boxes, most of them empty, were piled up untidily on both sides of the room, while the generator itself—a clapped-out old thing that had probably been put in when the place was still a farm—took up most of the opposite wall.

The place looked deserted and there didn't seem to be anywhere to hide so I went inside, making my way slowly over to the generator itself, conscious of my own breathing. Reaching into my pocket, I pulled out my lighter and flicked it on, glancing around nervously.

As I'd expected, the flap to the electrics box was open and a bundle of severed wires poked out.

Trying hard to ignore the fear running up my spine, I started to turn away.

And jumped back in shock as the lighter picked up the figure in the shadows.

It was Haddock. He was standing in the corner, watching me.

Except he wasn't moving, and the expression in his wide, staring eyes was blank and sightless.

I took a step forward, holding up the lighter. And that was when I saw the hunting knife embedded to the hilt in his chest, impaling him against the wall, and the huge bloody gash across his throat where it had been cut from ear to ear.

Clarence Haddock, the six-foot-three, 270-pound killer—said, I recall, by one police officer to be the most frightening man he'd ever met—had been butchered like a stuck pig.

Thirty-three

It had just turned one A.M. when Tina finally walked in her front door, physically exhausted but mentally wide awake. The first thing she did was open a bottle of Rioja, pour a third of it into a giant tumbler, and take a long, deep gulp, savoring the strong, rich taste. Keeping the glass tight to her lips, she took several more, feeling herself relaxing, then refilled the glass and carried it with her into the apartment's shoebox-sized lounge, collapsing onto the sofa and lighting a cigarette.

During the drive back home, she'd called the local GP who had certified Kevin O'Neill dead. He hadn't been best pleased to hear from her, since the call had got him out of bed, but Tina was used to receiving less-than-warm welcomes and she'd brushed aside his complaints by telling him foul play was suspected, which had quickly galvanized him into action. He'd been able to say with some certainty that O'Neill had died between six P.M. and midnight the previous night.

Tina wasn't a hundred percent sure what "some certainty" meant. Either you were certain, or you weren't.

However, it had given her enough information to go on for her second call, to the security company operating the CCTV cameras covering the entrance to O'Neill's cul-de-sac. After about ten minutes of being shunted around among those staff members still working at that time of night, none of whom seemed to be of any use to her, and being put on hold more than once, she'd finally been put through to someone who was willing to help her. His name was Jim, and he was a retired copper who liked to talk a lot.

But at least he didn't faint when she told him what she needed, which was for him to go through all the footage taken by a particular camera from four P.M. to midnight the previous night, making a list of the plates of all vehicles captured that didn't belong to residents of the road in question, and to get the results back to her as soon as possible.

While Tina remained on the line, Jim had looked up the account in question and told her that the footage from Thursday night was still there, and it should be possible to find her the information she needed, since the company kept a database of all the residents' vehicles. "Will it help solve a case?" he'd asked her, sounding excited at the prospect that he might be a part of something important once again.

In truth, though, it was the longest of long shots. There was, as Grier had pointed out several times, no evidence that O'Neill had been murdered, and even if he had been, it didn't necessarily mean that the killer had driven up to his house. But that wasn't what Tina had told Jim. Instead, she'd said that she genuinely hoped so.

"You don't give up, do you?" Grier had said with a mixture of admiration and exasperation when she finally got off the phone.

"Someone once said there was a solution to every problem."

"Do you believe that?"

She'd thought about her alcoholism, about the way her life had turned out, a long battle that never seemed close to completion, let alone victory. "No." She'd managed a smile. "But I always live in hope."

When she'd dropped him off at home a little while later, he'd given her a strange look, as if he wanted to say something. But then the look had gone, and he'd got out of the car, asking if he was going to be needed tomorrow.

"I'll let you know," she'd said, and watched as he let himself into his attractive redbrick townhouse where his wife, a successful corporate lawyer, was waiting.

Now, sitting in her poky little living room with her cigarette and her booze, Tina concentrated on the case, because she knew that as soon as she stopped thinking about it she'd slip into the inevitable self-pity. And there was plenty to think about. This case was one of the most puzzling she'd ever been involved in. On the one hand, they had a man against whom the evidence seemed overwhelming. There was the murder weapon in his flat, incriminating footage showing a number of the murders on his computer, and he had a direct link with every one of the victims. Yet, at the same time, they also had a murder that was different from the others, and for which their suspect had a cast-iron alibi. Added to the mix was Kent's claim to have important information, something which he thought was worth killing him for. Whether or not he'd faked his poisoning in the cell back at the station, the fact remained that an armed gang had been prepared to break him free from police custody at gunpoint. Which meant that one way or another he was important to someone.

But who? And why?

She took another gulp of the Rioja. Booze wasn't usually that helpful where intensive thinking was concerned, but she was hoping now that it might give her a new angle on things.

Because she knew she was missing something. Everything

happened for a reason. The solution was in there somewhere, it was simply a matter of finding it, and the way to do that was to follow the Sherlock Holmes route of removing every scenario that was impossible until you were left with one that fit. And that would be the truth.

Kent did not murder Róisín O'Neill. Someone else did. That person had strangled her, although there were no obvious signs of sexual assault. But the killer had known the Night Creeper's MO, even though the information wasn't available to the public, and had tried to make her death look like one of his, in order to cover up his own guilt. But what did that killer then need from Andrew Kent?

Think . . . Think . . .

And then she slammed her glass down on the coffee table as the answer came to her in a mad rush. She didn't even notice the wine spilling and dripping down onto the carpet. She was too excited for that because for the first time she was sure she knew what had happened, and why Kent had been targeted.

Now they just had to find him.

Thirty-four

I was out of that outbuilding fast, and the shock on my face must have been obvious, because Lee put a hand to her mouth.

I took her arm and moved her away from the door. "There's a body in there."

"It's not Ty, is it? Please not Ty."

It was then that I realized she must have genuinely cared for him, although God alone knew why. "No, it's Haddock, and he's been murdered."

"Haddock? But he's so big."

"They must have been waiting in there for him and caught him by surprise."

I walked slowly around to the front of the main building, with Lee following. I had no idea who'd killed Haddock, but whoever it was had known what they were doing. And if they could take out an immense brute like him, they could just as easily take out Lee and me.

I thought I caught a flash of movement from somewhere inside the treeline. I squinted, watching the area like a hawk, but saw nothing more, making me wonder whether I'd imagined it. The night was dark and I was feeling hugely jumpy.

"We need to go," I told Lee, "but we're going to need some weapons."

"What about Ty?"

"Have you got a phone? You can call him and get him to meet us somewhere."

"I tried. There's still no signal."

"Shit."

"Do you think whoever killed Haddock is still here?" Lee looked around fearfully in the darkness.

"No, there'd be no point." But the truth was, I had no idea. I only knew that I didn't want to hang around, and I wasn't going to walk through those woods without some kind of weapon. There hadn't been anything I could use in the outbuilding, which left only one alternative. "We need to go back in the house."

"There were knives in the kitchen," said Lee. "I saw some earlier, in one of the drawers."

"That'll do," I said, and started walking, hoping they were still there and wondering if I was making a very stupid decision by going back in.

But as I stepped inside the front door and back into the dusty old foyer, no one tried to attack me. Instead, the place remained as eerily silent as it had been before. I waited a couple of seconds, listening hard for any out-of-place sound, but all I could hear was Lee's quiet breathing coming from behind me. I asked her where the kitchen was.

"Over there," she whispered, pointing to a door to the right of the staircase, her actions making it quite clear that she expected me to lead the way.

I went over and gave the door a kick so that it flew back on its hinges with a loud crack that shattered the stillness of the building and made Lee jump.

"What did you do that for?" she hissed.

"Because I'm not taking chances," I answered, walking inside and looking around.

It was a big room, with a breakfast island in the middle, more graffiti on the walls, and an odor of grease. It also looked empty.

Lee pointed to the drawer where she'd seen the knives and, moving fast, I pulled it open, rifling through the cheap cutlery until I found a blunt, rusty-looking carving knife and a small kitchen knife with a four-inch blade. I handed the smaller weapon to her and took the carving knife.

I couldn't imagine ever stabbing someone. I'd seen enough stabbing victims in the past to make me realize what a terrible thing it was to do to a person, and I knew I wouldn't have the mental strength to shove the blade into human flesh, even if the person was trying to kill me. Still, I was relieved to have a means of defending myself at last, even if it was just a deterrent.

"Can we go now?" Lee asked.

I could see the fear etched on her features in the gloom, and I nodded, starting back toward the front door.

Then I stopped. "Wait."

I was looking at the door through which we'd dragged Kent earlier. Kent. In my desperation to escape I'd completely forgotten about him. Had he been freed by the mysterious client? Was he still trapped down in the basement? Was he even still alive? I had to find out. Because if he was, I had a duty to take him out of there and get him back into police custody.

I told Lee what I planned to do, and she looked at me like I was some kind of madman. "Don't go down there," she pleaded. "Let's just leave."

I shook my head, then kicked open the door in the same way I'd done earlier. This time Lee let out a high-pitched shriek that would have woken the dead.

"Just being cautious," I said, before stepping inside the empty, cavernous room and flicking on my lighter.

Shadows danced through the gloom, revealing the graffiti on the walls but nothing else.

Then, as Lee came in behind me, I saw it.

The door to the basement was ever so slightly ajar, its bolt pulled back. Wolfe and Haddock wouldn't have left it like that, not with their prize—the man they'd shot a police officer to get hold of—down there. And I couldn't see how Kent would have been able to escape on his own, not when the door had been bolted from the outside.

I walked over, conscious of the sound my footfalls were making on the creaking floorboards. I stopped two feet away, listened. Hearing nothing once again, I used the carving knife to pull the door further open and stared down into the darkness, the flame from the lighter doing little to illuminate it.

"I don't want to go down there," whispered Lee.

I put a reassuring hand on her shoulder. "You stay here by the door. I'll be back up in a moment."

She asked me again not to go, and a huge part of me felt like agreeing with her. But I had to know what had happened to Kent.

The metal on the lighter cap was burning my fingers so I let the flame go out, then with the knife out in front of me I moved slowly down the stone steps, every sense attuned to my surroundings as I tried to pick out any unnatural noise within the silent blackness.

When I reached the bottom, I leaned back against the

cold stone wall, tightened my grip on the knife, and flicked the lighter back on.

The basement was large and windowless, full of empty cobweb-strewn shelves. In the middle of the room on its own was a brand-new, heavy office chair with its wheels removed. It had thick rolls of duct tape wound around both arms and two of the legs. One of the rolls carried what looked in the near-darkness like a bloodstain.

But it wasn't that which caught my attention. It was the fact that the chair was empty.

Where the hell was Andrew Kent?

Then I spotted something in the far corner beyond the chair. I slowly walked toward it, keeping the lighter raised high.

Jesus.

It was a body, lying curled up in a fetal ball, in the blue boiler suit he'd been in earlier. His face might have been caked in blood, but I recognized him straight away. It was the shock of dirty blond hair, Tommy's pride and joy.

As I looked down at him, I saw a drop of blood run to the edge of his chin before dripping onto the stone floor, which was the moment when I realized he'd only died very recently. Probably in the last few minutes. Possibly even since we'd been back in the building.

And then I heard the noise behind me.

Thirty-five

I turned just in time to see a dark, silhouetted figure leaping at me through the darkness. I saw a glint of metal in the dim glow of the lighter flame, but then the lighter flew out of my hand, plunging the basement into near total blackness, as my attacker slammed me bodily against the far wall and twisted the wrist of my knife hand in an effort to get me to drop it.

My ribs felt like they were going to explode with the pain, but adrenaline and the survival instinct took over and I lashed out with my free hand, trying to intercept his blade. I managed to get hold of his wrist, but he was strong and I felt the blade nip at the skin of my belly as he tried to push it into me. At the same time he increased the pressure on my knife hand, and it took every ounce of willpower to hold on to my knife.

I was once told by a football thug and ex-boxer that in close-quarters combat, when you're struggling hand to hand, your best weapon is your head. Remembering that now, I launched mine into the blackness, hoping to catch him with a strong enough blow to knock him off balance. Unfortunately, he'd also had the same idea, and our foreheads met somewhere in the middle with a loud, agonizing crack that shocked both of us.

For a moment, he loosened his grip on me and I managed to launch myself off the wall, pushing him backward. But he kept his balance and remained tight to me as we wrestled frantically across the floor, with him trying to land another headbutt on me.

I dodged two of the blows but banged into the office chair, lost my footing and stumbled, only just managing to stay upright. At the same time, he drove his knife hand upward in a sudden movement until the blade was so close to my face that I could actually see it. Using his momentum, he charged me back into a set of shelves, pushing the knife even further into my field of vision, so close to me now that the tip of the blade was barely an inch from my left eye.

I could see nothing in the gloom, bar the blade and the darkness. But I could hear his labored breathing, smell the stale odor of his breath.

"For Christ's sake, help me!" I roared, willing Lee to come down. "Help!"

My arm was shaking with the effort of holding his wrist and keeping the knife from plunging right through my eye and into my brain. It was a trial of strength but one I was always going to lose because my attacker had all the momentum and the physical strength, and all I had was desperation. Just the smallest slackening of my grip would mean certain death, and I couldn't have that. Couldn't. Not before I'd found out what was going on here.

I let out an angry howl, and with my last remaining strength I drove my knee up into my attacker's groin, knocking him backward. Seeing my chance, I twisted my own knife hand free and lashed out into the darkness with the blade. The only thing I stabbed was air, though, and a second later his own blade came flashing out of the darkness in a vicious, scything arc. Instinctively, I dived out of the way, lost my footing completely this time, and fell to the ground, twisting so that I landed on my back with the knife outstretched.

"Help me!" I screamed again, but this time my assailant didn't continue his attack. Instead, I heard him racing up the steps.

Exhausted, I got to my feet and scrambled in the direction of the steps, starting up them myself, just as his silhouette reached the top. I was five steps behind him by the time he slammed the door shut, two steps by the time he threw the bolt across and left me once again in total blackness.

With a scream of frustration, I shoulder-barged the door with every ounce of strength I had, but bounced uselessly off it and toppled down a couple of the steps. Panicking now, knowing that Lee was out there somewhere and that I'd betrayed her by not leaving with her when we had the chance, I kept hitting it, making as much noise as possible, feeling a rising sense of panic, claustrophobia, and anger at myself. Having just been released from forced captivity, I'd got myself back into exactly the same situation only minutes later because I'd broken the first rule of undercover work: when things go tits up, get out fast and let the cavalry mop up the mess.

I paused for a few seconds, panting as I waited to get my breath back, the questions racing through my mind. Was it Kent who'd just attacked me? If so, how had he managed to break free from his bonds, and how did he manage to kill Clarence Haddock fifty yards away? Why, too, had he come back to the cellar in which he'd been incarcerated when he'd had the chance to make a break for it? And if it wasn't Kent who'd attacked me, then, with both Haddock and Tommy already dead, who the hell was it?

THE LAST 10 SECONDS

One obvious name sprang out at me, and pretty much as soon as it did I heard the sound of cautious footfalls coming from the room outside.

"Hello?" Tyrone Wolfe called out, his voice echoing around the emptiness of the building. "Where is everybody? Clarence? Lee?" His voice carried a ring of uncertainty as if he'd just walked in the front door and was surprised to find the place dark and deserted.

My first thought was that this was some kind of trick Wolfe was pulling. But if he was the guy who'd just attacked me, then he had me trapped anyway, so he wouldn't need to play any kind of trick. Stuck in the darkness, I had little choice but to give him the benefit of the doubt.

I rapped hard on the door. "Tyrone. It's me, Sean. Let me out of here."

The footfalls came closer. "What are you doing in there?" he demanded.

So I told him the truth. About Lee freeing me; the discovery of Haddock's corpse; then Tommy's; and finally Kent's empty chair and the attack on me.

"Where's Lee?" he snapped, the tension in his voice clearly audible.

"I don't know. I left her where you are now. Isn't she there?"

"No, she isn't. No one is."

"She was there two minutes ago, I promise."

"How do I know you're telling the truth?"

"Because I didn't lock myself in here, did I? And if you don't believe me about Haddock, go and check. He's in the outbuilding around the side."

"And he's definitely dead?" Wolfe sounded incredulous, which I could understand. It was difficult to believe someone as huge and menacing as Haddock could be brought low by anyone.

"As a doornail," I told him. "And Tommy."

There was a long, heavy silence as he took stock of what I'd just told him—that his crew was no more, having been wiped out in the time it took him to bury a couple of guns, and that his girlfriend was missing, possibly dead. Possibly even involved, since right now pretty much anything was possible. One thing was clear, however, and that was that Tyrone Wolfe was as much in the dark as me, which was about the only thing that gave me some hope.

Finally, I heard the bolt being slid across and I took a step back, holding on to the staircase rail as the door opened. Wolfe stood there pointing his gun at me. By the dim moonlight coming through the windows, I could see his forehead glinting with sweat.

He spotted my knife and told me to drop it.

"No way. Someone's just tried to kill me, and they're still around here somewhere. In fact, I'm still not a hundred percent sure it's not you. I mean, you look a bit out of breath."

"I've just been digging a bloody great hole. Of course I look out of breath."

"But you kept your gun I see."

"It didn't get fired so there's no need to be rid of it."

"And as you can see, my knife hasn't been used either. But I'm like you. I need something to protect myself with."

He licked his lips and nodded. "Fair enough, but we need to find Lee."

"And Kent. He's the man the client wants, isn't he?"

He nodded again, but more uncertainly this time.

"Who's the client, Tyrone?"

"I can't tell you."

"That might have worked before everyone started dying on us, but it doesn't anymore. I want to know who it is we're up against."

He looked around nervously. "OK. But first I want to find my girl. Understand? She's got to be in here somewhere."

"How do you know she's not behind all this?" I asked him.

His expression darkened, and he brought his face close to mine. "You know something, Sean? She loves me. She always has, and she always will. Now, if you want to stay on the right side of me, you won't say nothing like that again. Understand?"

I stared him down, making sure he knew I was no longer intimidated by his tough-guy routine. Tyrone Wolfe was definitely not a man to cross, but for the first time I wondered if his bark was actually worse than his bite. I wasn't convinced about Lee, either. In my admittedly limited experience of Thai working girls, they're nothing if not ruthless, and most of the Western men who fall for them are naively oblivious to that. Wolfe, I was pretty certain, fell slap-bang into this category. But I wasn't going to get into an argument about it.

"Sure," I answered. "Lead the way."

He glared at me for a moment, his nostrils flaring, then turned back toward the door.

Which was when I grabbed him by the collar of his boiler suit, dragged him back, and, in one swift movement, put the carving knife to his throat. "Don't move," I whispered in his ear. He tried to turn his gun arm around so that the barrel was pointing in my general direction, but the angle was too difficult and I was in too close to him. "I don't want to hurt you, I just want to know who I'm dealing with here. So if you tell me who the client is, I'll remove the knife and we can talk calmly."

"Fuck you," he spat, but there was a tremor in his voice.

I increased the pressure on the knife, not wanting to draw blood, but prepared to do so if I had to. After all, this was the man who'd killed my brother.

"I'll kill you for this," he whispered.

"Just tell me."

And that was when he dropped his final bombshell: "I don't know."

Thirty-six

"What the hell do you mean?" I asked incredulously, still pressing the knife against his throat.

"Exactly what I say. I don't know the name of the guy who's paying us to do this. I just know him as Alpha. Now, can you please remove the blade from my throat?"

I thought about demanding he give me the gun but concluded that he almost certainly wouldn't comply. "As long as you promise not to put a bullet in me, and to answer my questions."

"All right, but I've got to find Lee. She's out there on her own."

"And I'm prepared to help you, but first we need to get a few things clear." I moved the knife away from his throat, but kept it close, and didn't release my grip on him. "First off, I want to know how you know this guy Alpha."

Wolfe took a deep breath and started talking. "He works on behalf of some people we've been importing coke and smack from. We get calls from him now and again, giving us instructions on when and where the transactions are going to take place. He also gives us tip-offs if he thinks we're being watched."

"Is he a cop?"

"To be honest, I don't know anything about him. We've only ever spoken on the phone. But he's always got good information, and he's reliable. So when he phoned up last week and told me he wanted someone busted out of police custody, and was willing to pay a load of money to make sure it was done, I didn't think there'd be a problem."

"And this was when last week?"

"Friday, I think."

"But Andrew Kent was only nicked last night."

He craned his neck, looking at me with an angry glint of suspicion in his eyes. "How do you know? I never told you that."

"Tommy did," I lied. "And don't ask me how he knew because I haven't got a clue. But the point is, what was Alpha doing hiring you to break someone out of custody who wasn't even in custody at that point? That's completely illogical."

"That's what happened. And he was paying us big time as well. Half a million for the job. I couldn't believe it, but he sent me the key to a deposit box and there was a hundred grand in it. He called it a 'golden hello,' something to seal the deal. Clarence wasn't sure about getting involved, because we'd never done anything like that with him before, but I wanted to go for it."

"I can't believe this. And you're meant to be a careful operator."

"I thought it was kosher. And you try and turn down that much money when it's there in front of you. It ain't easy. Anyway, Alpha told us all the details, except the name of the prisoner. He said we'd get that later. In the meantime, he wanted us to set everything up."

"Who organized this place?"

"He did. The instructions were to bring Kent back here,

get him down into the basement, and make sure he wasn't roughed up too much. Then wait for him to turn up. We were going to meet him for the first time when he gave us the rest of the money."

"Did you ask what he wanted Kent for?"

"He told me I didn't need to know."

"So all that stuff about us doing it on behalf of a relative of the victim was bullshit?"

He nodded.

"And you weren't suspicious it was a set-up?"

"Why should I be? We did what we were paid to do. There was no reason why he wouldn't give us the rest of the money."

I sighed. Wolfe was right. The problem was, it was clear he wasn't going to. Instead, he seemed to want to make sure that everyone involved in the Kent snatch ended up dead.

Feeling confused and exhausted, I relinquished my grip on Wolfe and took a step back. He turned to face me, making a great play of rubbing his throat, an angry look on his face. "When we get out of here . . ." he growled.

"When we get out of here, Wolfe, we're quits. But first we've got to make it out."

"With Lee."

I nodded, knowing that I was going to have to give her the benefit of the doubt, since if she was innocent, I owed her big time. "With Lee."

"Come on," he ordered. "And watch my back this time."

I followed him as he moved back out into the darkened foyer and stopped, looking around anxiously. "She can't have got far," he whispered, before calling her name, his voice reverberating through the silence of the house.

There was no answer.

"Maybe she's outside somewhere," I said. "She could have made a run for it."

"You should have stayed with her, you arsehole."

I felt like arguing the point, but didn't bother. It didn't matter what Wolfe thought. As soon as we were out of here, I was going to get him nicked, using the evidence I'd got on the recording device in my watch. And I was going to make sure he knew who'd done it as well.

The bump was faint but audible, and it came from somewhere up on the next floor.

We both stopped and listened. It came again, sounding like movement. Then it stopped.

Wolfe called Lee's name for a second time. For a second time, there was no answer.

"You know the layout upstairs, don't you?" I said quietly.

He nodded. "Yeah. Me and Clarence came here a few days ago to check the place out. There are about a dozen empty rooms up there, but the floor's pretty flimsy in places so you've got to be careful where you tread. Do you think it's Lee making the noise?"

He suddenly seemed vulnerable and, in spite of myself, I found myself feeling sorry for him, just like I'd felt sorry for Kent earlier when he was being kicked and beaten all the way down into that claustrophobic basement, and I had to remind myself what he'd done to my brother.

"I'm guessing as soon as she heard me fighting in the basement, she made a run for it. She's probably halfway to London by now."

"I'd try her on her mobile but there's no bloody reception here."

"It's probably why the place was picked."

"What do you mean?"

"So that we couldn't call for help."

Wolfe shook his head. "No way. You're getting paranoid."

"Look, two men are dead in here, the man we abducted is missing, and someone—and I've got no idea who it was—just tried to kill me as well. And for what it's worth, I don't think Lee's up there. I think she ran."

"But what if she is? What if the bloke who just tried to kill you's got her and she can't answer?" He paused. "I'm going up. Are you coming?"

I looked up into the darkness. "OK," I said at last. "You've got the gun. Lead the way."

Our progress up the staircase was slow and comparatively noisy, each step creaking precariously underfoot. Wolfe stopped at the top and looked both ways. To our right were two doors, both closed. To our left, a long corridor stretched the length of the building with a number of doors, all closed, on either side—including the one that had been used to imprison me—and a large window at the end.

Wolfe started to turn right. Then he stopped. He'd heard something. Coming from down the corridor to the left.

I'd heard it too. A terrible rasping sound that sounded like someone trying desperately to breathe while their mouth, nose, and throat steadily filled up with liquid.

Wolfe looked at me, the fear in his eyes obvious, because he knew, just like I knew, that it was the sound of a person dying.

Thirty-seven

Wolfe ran down the corridor, shouting Lee's name, losing all sense of danger as he tried to locate her.

"For Christ's sake, stop!" I called after him, but he wasn't listening.

He paused by a door about halfway along and, without hesitation, flung it open.

"Oh God! Lee, baby!" His words came out in a tortured wail as he ran inside.

I was five yards behind him, moving far more cautiously, but as he disappeared from view, I ran forward, knowing I needed to cover his back. Knowing too that if Lee was the victim then it was almost certain the killer was still up here because he wouldn't have had a chance to leave.

My fears were confirmed before I reached the door. Wolfe let out a sharp grunt of pain, then stumbled backward into view, putting out his free hand to support himself on the opposite door, the hilt of a knife jutting out of his ribcage, a thick dark stain already visible against the blue of the boiler suit. He stared at me, his eyes wide with fear and confusion, as if he couldn't accept what was happening to him, and the Sig fell from his hand and clattered onto the floor. He took another step back, trying in vain to steady himself, before falling slowly to one knee, his eyes still locked on mine, mouth silently opening and closing as if he was trying desperately to say something.

He was two yards away from me. The gun was lying on the floor just outside the room from where that terrible rasping sound, much louder now, was coming.

Instinctively I went for it, reaching down to pull it up from the floor.

But I never made it. A shadow appeared in the doorway and a hand shot out and grabbed me by the material of the boiler suit, yanking me upward with worrying strength. At the same time, out of the corner of my eye I saw a figure beyond my attacker, lying with its head propped up against the far wall. I couldn't see the face because it was a black mask of blood, but the pink butterfly on the T-shirt told me immediately it was Lee.

I was still holding the knife and I lashed out with it, but my attacker was already pulling me away from the gun and with the momentum I already had I went flying forward without making contact. I tripped over Wolfe and went down on my side, rolling over several times and losing my grip on the knife. Ignoring the pain in my ribs, I scrambled to my feet, unable to resist a glance back.

My attacker was standing facing me in the corridor, while Wolfe lay sprawled on his back at his feet. He had a claw hammer in one hand and Wolfe's Sig in the other. The hammer was stained dark with blood, and as I watched, a drop formed on one edge of the claw before dripping onto the floor. Even in the dim light, I could see who it was. He might have had cuts to his face and head, including what looked like a deep gash in his cheek, but there was still no doubt that it was Andrew Kent. Except this time he no longer looked like the baby-faced young man we'd taken earlier, who'd pleaded his innocence in the back of the van. Now he struck a confident pose, legs apart, the gun pointed toward me, the bloodstained hammer tapping idly against one of his legs, an expression of cold indifference in his eyes.

He pulled the trigger before I had a chance to move, and the corridor exploded with noise. But he was also a little too casual and misjudged the gun's recoil, so that when it kicked in his hand, the bullet went wide.

This was my cue. I ran straight at the nearest door and, keeping as low as possible, yanked the handle before diving inside as a second bullet whistled past close to my head.

My ears rang from the noise but I could still hear his footfalls behind me. I was back up in an instant, racing across the empty room in the direction of a newish-looking double-glazed window with a handle-opening system, praying it wasn't locked, because there was no sign of a key. But when I pulled the handle, it didn't budge. I was trapped.

Desperate times call for desperate measures, but only if you've got the nerve, and thankfully I had. I turned and charged back at the door as he came into view, keeping low and bellowing like a bull, hoping to catch him off guard.

It worked. He wasn't quite fast enough, and by the time the gun went off a third time I'd already slammed into him with all my strength and knocked his gun hand wide, managing to grab it by the wrist. My momentum sent us both flying back across the corridor and straight through the door into the room opposite. I felt the hammer strike me in the small of the back but he couldn't get enough behind the blow to do me any real damage. The gun went off again as I continued to drive backward toward the opposite wall, but once again the shot was wide.

Then somehow he managed to pull his gun hand free and dig his heels into the floor, bringing me to a halt. I felt him bring the gun around so it was pointed at my side, but I knocked it away again before he could pull the trigger and, with a final push, tried to knock him off balance.

We took a step back together in a tight, vicious dance, which was when there was a loud crack beneath our feet and, without warning, the floor gave way, sending us flailing through the air.

We hit the floor beneath with a loud thud in a cloud of dust. I landed on top of Kent, the force of the impact sending me flying back off him so that we ended up lying next to each other among pieces of ceiling plaster. Kent wasn't moving, although the claw hammer still hung loosely from his hand. I could see bits of torn flesh sticking to it, and knew they belonged to the woman I was supposed to be protecting. But there was no time to think about that now. More important was the fact that Kent was no longer holding the gun.

I clambered to my feet and looked around desperately for it in the darkness. It was only a few feet away, but just as I stepped forward to get it there was a roar from behind me and Kent rose from the floor and drove the hammer down at my foot.

I managed to jump out of the way just in time but tripped on a piece of plaster. I fell to my knees but jerked myself around so I was facing him as he leaped on me, a maniacal grin on his savage little baby face, the hammer raised above his head.

He knocked me onto my back and sat astride me, pinning my right arm with his leg as he tried to get into the optimum position for landing a hammer blow. "Gonna die now, fuck!" he hissed, his eyes widening with a sadistic joy.

But I could still move my left arm enough to grab a palm-sized piece of plaster, and before he could bring the hammer down, I threw it in his face.

He reeled back, and I saw that he'd got dust in one of his eyes. Seizing my opportunity, I thrashed around under him with enough force to knock him half off me, then scrambled toward the gun, grabbing it by the barrel just as he righted himself and raised the hammer again.

In one movement, I smashed the butt into his cheek with a loud crack, just as he caught me across the chin with a glancing blow from the hammer.

He fell off me and rolled over, howling in pain. "Bastard!" he screamed, the word sounding stilted, as if he was trying to shout it through pursed lips.

And then, as I stood up and turned the gun on him, he got onto his hands and knees, and the maniacal look disappeared, replaced by a look of injured innocence that was almost angelic. "Please don't hurt me," he whispered, the words clearer now. "Please. Not in cold blood. I need help for what I've done. I can't help it."

I was a police officer. How could I kill a man in cold blood? How would I be able to live with myself afterward? Those were the questions racing through my head as I stood looking down at him, holding the Sig two-handed.

There was a long silence. He looked at me imploringly. I looked back at him. Intensely. Thinking.

And then he sprang at me like an animal, the hammer still in hand, and I pulled the trigger. Again and again, sending him dancing backward through the gloom, until finally the gun was empty, and Andrew Kent, the Night Creeper, lay dead at my feet.

I stood looking down at him, feeling no satisfaction,

simply a sense of relief that it was all over, before letting the empty gun fall from my fingers.

There was one thing still left to do, so I walked over to the staircase and climbed it for the third time that night.

Tyrone Wolfe was lying on his back where I'd last seen him. A large pool of blood had formed beneath his torso where the knife was buried up to the hilt, and his face was pale, almost luminescent in the darkness. But his eyes were open and he was still breathing.

"Lee. Help her, Sean. Please."

I forced myself to walk inside the room where Kent had assaulted her, and the first thing I noticed was that her breathing had stopped. My jaw tightened as I looked down at her torn and ruined face. Only a true savage could have inflicted those kinds of injuries on a defenseless woman, and a savage was exactly what the Night Creeper had been. Standing in that filthy room with only the smell of blood and death and grime for company, I felt no satisfaction for killing Kent. I just felt numb, and even though I knew it would be no good, I bent down and checked Lee's wrist for a pulse, almost relieved that there was nothing there.

When I walked back out, Wolfe lifted his head up with what was clearly a huge effort and asked me if she was all right.

"I'm sorry," I told him, meaning it. "She's dead."

His face contorted into a mask of complete despair, and he whispered her name again and again, as if by doing so he could somehow undo the terrible damage inflicted that night. Then his body started to shake. "I'm so cold," he said. "I think I'm dying."

He was, and I didn't have much time left to say what I needed to say. "Why didn't you shoot me when you had the chance?" I asked him.

"Because," he answered, "I'm not like that. I can't kill someone in cold blood. Whoever it is."

"But you killed my brother."

A look of surprise flickered across his face. "What?"

"Highgate High Street. Thursday the second of November 1995. A man tried to stop you robbing a security van. His name was John Egan. He had facial scarring because he'd been injured in the Gulf War. You called him a freak just before you shot him. Remember?" I leaned in closer, staring right into his eyes. "He was my brother."

"That guy?" He looked confused. "Your brother?"

"That's right. My brother. And I'm no lowlife thief and killer like you. I'm an undercover copper. Got that? I infiltrated your crew so I could bring you down. And now I have. You're all finished."

"Oh Jesus, you don't understand . . ." He shook his head slowly from side to side.

I leaned in even closer, my face only inches from his. Wanting to hear his excuses. "What do you mean?"

"It wasn't me."

"But I heard it from a reliable source that you were bragging about it."

"That's all it was," he whispered. "Bragging." He made a huge effort to look me right in the eye. "I never killed your brother, Sean."

And then, as I stood back up, reeling from this piece of news, I smelled it. Coming from downstairs.

Petrol.

Thirty-eight

The next second there was a loud roar, and the corridor was suddenly completely lit up. I turned around as a wave of heat rushed over me and saw flames leaping up the staircase.

Who the hell had set the fire? Everyone I'd come here with was dead. But I didn't have time to worry about that because the first of the cloying black smoke was billowing down toward me.

"Who killed my brother?" I yelled down at Wolfe, grabbing him by the collar of his boiler suit, desperate to know.

But his eyes had closed and he went limp in my grasp, and even as I shook him with an angry frustration, the smoke wafted thickly about me and I started to choke.

I turned and ran for the window at the end of the corridor. It was older than the one I'd tried getting out of earlier, and though double-glazed, the glass was thin, with a crack running diagonally up one side, and its frame looked loose and unwieldy. But there was also no sign of a handle to open it.

The smoke was really getting thick now, and, though exhausted, adrenaline born of total desperation was coursing through me. I slammed into it hard. The frame rattled, but didn't budge. I did it again. Four times in all. But nothing was happening, except that my ribs were screaming and I was having trouble breathing. Forcing myself to keep calm, I took five steps back and charged it shoulder-first. This time I heard it splinter and loosen. Coughing, and with the roar of the flames getting louder in my ears, I took another five steps back, wincing as the heat began to burn my back. Then, shutting my eyes in an effort to stop them stinging so much, I charged the window again, only this time I actually dived into it.

The whole thing, glass and frame, toppled down to the ground, and I only just stopped myself from going down with it. Desperately, I breathed in the fresher air as the smoke billowed all around me, then swung myself out of the gap I'd created so that I was hanging by my fingertips. The drop to ground level was probably ten feet but I had to get out of this place as fast as possible, so I swung out my legs, let go, and landed hard, jarring my ankles and rolling across broken glass.

I was almost opposite the outbuilding where I'd discovered Haddock's body. Ten yards beyond it was the first of the trees, and relative safety.

Ignoring the pain in my ankles—Jesus, everywhere—I started running for it. But as I did so, I heard the heavy click of a shotgun being cocked only yards behind me. I turned, caught the faintest glimpse of a man in a boiler suit like the ones we'd all been wearing, and a balaclava. He was aiming the shotgun at me.

I zigzagged, keeping low, and as the shotgun blasted into life I dived behind the outbuilding wall, temporarily out of sight, before scrambling back to my feet again and running for my life.

I hit the trees at a pace I didn't think I was capable of at the best of times, let alone after everything that had happened to me, and tore through the undergrowth. There was another blast from the shotgun, which passed quite close, but I kept on going, through bushes and foliage, leaping over dips, covering as much ground as I possibly could before finally stumbling and falling to the ground.

I couldn't hear any sounds of pursuit behind me so I slid under a holly bush and stayed where I was, my breathing coming in low pants that I found hard to keep quiet. The whole forest was lit up by the flames coming from the building as they danced high into the night sky, and I looked around cautiously, trying to make myself as small and inconspicuous as possible.

Two minutes passed. My breathing became more regular and gradually I started to think that maybe the worst was over.

Then I heard the sound of a twig breaking close by.

I froze. From my position lying in the dirt, I saw a pair of boots moving slowly and purposefully through the undergrowth straight toward me. Five yards, four yards, three. I had no energy left. None at all. I'd been through hell these past few hours, and every part of me burned and ached. I still had enough of my wits about me to stay silent and hope, but if it came to it, and I ended up looking down the barrel of the shotgun, I'd take what was coming to me.

The boots stopped a yard away from my face. Could my pursuer see me? My body tensed, waiting for that final shot that would end every experience and every emotion I'd ever felt.

But it never came. A siren wailed in the distance, followed moments later by another, and the man who was hunting me turned and walked away.

I lay there for a long time, listening to the sirens getting closer, and, although I was almost too exhausted to think straight, two questions kept running through my head. The first was, why had the man with the shotgun tried to kill me, and then taken a risk by trying to hunt me down in the forest? I could only assume he was the client we were working for, yet he must have known that I couldn't ID him.

But it was the second question that was really bothering me. If Tyrone Wolfe hadn't killed my brother, then who the hell had?

Thirty-nine

Despite the hour, Tina was wide awake. She had a theory. It was basic, and far from watertight, but it fit the facts.

She finished her glass of wine, drank some water to clear her head, and logged on to the CMIT database where the details from the Night Creeper inquiry were kept electronically. Working as fast as was possible when you'd done a sixteen-hour day and just polished off most of a bottle of wine, she found the witness statements pertaining to the Róisin O'Neill case and began skim-reading them. As with any major inquiry, the police were obliged to take detailed statements from as many people as possible to minimize the chances of missing something. In this case, though, because they already suspected Róisin's death to be the work of a serial killer who had no prior connection with his victim, and whose motive was clearly established, the background questioning of friends and family was less detailed. Instead, more effort had been aimed at Róisin's neighbors and anyone who'd been in the area around the time of her death. It was these individuals Tina concentrated on now.

Even so, this involved sixty-three different people, and it was twenty minutes before she found what she was looking for. It was a single sentence from a woman who lived in one of the flats overlooking Róisin's apartment building, a throw-away comment that at the time would never have aroused any interest but which now added another, albeit tenuous, layer of support to Tina's theory.

Five minutes later she found something else. Another comment, this time from Beatrice Glover, the woman who lived in the flat below, whom Dan Grier had spoken to earlier about her separate sighting of Andrew Kent on the staircase. Again it was insignificant when put against the background of a major serial killer inquiry, and something that would never have been linked to the statement made by the woman across the road, but now it made Tina's heart race.

She was on the right track.

Next, she hunted down Róisin's mobile phone records. It was standard practice in any murder inquiry to check the phone records of the victim, although as far as she remembered, in Róisin's case they'd been used primarily to give a more accurate time of death. That was the beauty of the plan hatched by whoever had killed her: he'd known that her murder would be lumped in with the others committed by the Night Creeper, so all the police resources would be pushed at trying to locate, identify, and gather evidence against the Night Creeper himself. None of the people involved in the inquiry at the time had assumed for one moment that Róisin wasn't his fourth victim, because it seemed inconceivable.

Róisin's phone records had been scanned onto an electronic file after being thoroughly checked by the investigating officers, so there were handwritten notes next to the phone numbers listed, identifying to whom the numbers belonged. This made Tina's task a lot easier. Róisin had clearly been a popular girl. The numbers of calls she made and received averaged some thirty a day. Most of them were to friends and family members. She was in regular contact with her father and Derval. There were work calls in there as well.

But one particular number stood out. A mobile from which she'd received eight calls in the four weeks before her death, and made a total of sixteen calls to, eleven of which had gone to voicemail. Someone she was obviously very interested in talking to but who wasn't always interested in talking to her. Their calls were sometimes brief, but other times they were a lot longer. One she'd received had lasted for ninety-seven minutes. But what really interested Tina was the handwritten word next to the number, made by whichever officer had checked the records.

Dead.

She tried the number again now and was given the automatic message that it was out of service. No one had followed this up at the time, but again, there'd been no reason to. Róisin was the victim of the Night Creeper. End of story.

But she hadn't been. Someone else had killed her.

Tina sat back on the sofa and lit a cigarette, wondering to whom that number belonged, and how she was going to find out.

Her own mobile rang. She picked it up and frowned. It was a blocked call.

"Miss Boyd?" came an uncertain-sounding voice as Tina picked up.

She recognized it instantly. It was the guy from the security company whose cameras covered Kevin O'Neill's road. "Hello, Jim. Thanks for getting back to me."

"I haven't woken you up, have I? You did say call back whatever the time."

"Don't worry, I'm still working."

"God, at this time? You must be keen."

Keen or obsessed, she wasn't sure which. "What have you got for me?" she asked, trying not to sound impatient but wanting to get him off the phone nevertheless, now that she had a new lead to follow up.

"You asked me to check through the Mayflower Lane footage from Thursday night, and give you a list of all the nonresidents' cars that went in and out. I've got it."

"Is it long?"

"No. Just three cars."

She took down the numbers and the times they'd passed by the camera, and thanked him for his efforts.

"It must be pretty important if you're still working on it at this time," he said.

"I promise I'll let you know what it is the minute I can," she told him, and hung up.

Tina didn't have particularly high hopes that Jim's information would provide another lead, but since there were only three cars on the list, she logged on to the PNC and ran a check to see if any of them were stolen, hitting gold with the very first one, a silver Honda Accord sedan. The plates were false and had been removed from a silver Honda Accord coupe in Islington four days earlier.

She sat back and rubbed her eyes. It was the killer's car. It had to be.

She finished the cigarette and stubbed it in an ashtray that was close to overflowing, resisting the urge to have another drink. She was getting somewhere now, narrowing things down, getting closer to the truth. But she also needed help.

She looked at her watch. It was 1:30 A.M. She knew whom she had to call.

Forty

Mike Bolt had been Tina Boyd's boss at SOCA, the Serious Organized Crime Agency, for more than a year, but that was only
telling a small part of the story. He'd recruited her when Tina
was at a low ebb, and had done a lot to get her back on her
feet. During that time, a close friendship had developed between them, which had almost ended in a love affair, and was
the main reason she'd left SOCA and returned to the Met.
But the feelings she'd had for him, and which she knew he'd
had for her, had never gone away, and they were solidified a
year later when he risked his own life to save hers after she'd
been kidnapped by a psychotic thug in a case that had thrown
them both into the limelight.

It was that incident that had left Tina with the gunshot
injury to the foot. She'd also managed to kill the thug in question, and for weeks afterward she'd retreated into her shell
while on sick leave, ignoring all offers of help, including those
from Mike Bolt. It was only after she'd returned to work and
made the transfer to CMIT that she'd felt confident enough
to contact him again. She'd spent a long time musing over
whether she should finally make her feelings known, before
finally deciding that she should, and after plucking up the
courage and pushing down her doubts, she'd made the call.

He'd sounded genuinely pleased to hear from her and they'd talked for a good five minutes before he dropped the bombshell. He had a new girlfriend. Her name was Claire and it was going well. He hadn't elaborated—he'd always been careful not to hurt other people's feelings—but she'd known the truth. He was happy with someone else.

They'd kept talking for another ten minutes, during which time she did a solid job of keeping the sinking feeling she had in her gut out of her voice. As the conversation wound up, he said that they would have to catch up over a drink sometime, but his tone was vague and noncommittal, and she knew he didn't mean it.

When she got off the phone that time, she'd cried her eyes out, before getting hideously drunk in the poky little lounge where she sat now, ruing her self-destructiveness and all the opportunities she'd deliberately missed over the years.

And now she had to call him at 1:30 on a Saturday morning, having drunk three-quarters of a bottle of Rioja. It wasn't a thought she relished, but it needed to be done. Mike Bolt was one of the best detectives she'd ever worked with. More importantly, he was a high-flyer with excellent contacts within both SOCA and the Met.

"God knows what his girlfriend's going to think," she said aloud as she dialed his number. But she knew he, at least, would understand.

He answered on the fourth ring, sounding tired. "Tina?"

So he hadn't removed her number from his phone. "Hi, Mike. Sorry to bother you at this time of night, but I need your help urgently," she said, hoping she wasn't slurring her words. As far as she knew, he didn't know anything about her drinking.

He yawned. "That's OK. I was only half asleep anyway, and Claire's away. What's the problem?"

"Have you been watching the news tonight?"

"Are you talking about the Night Creeper snatch from outside my old jail? They've got wall-to-wall coverage on every news channel going. That's your case, isn't it?"

"That's right."

"I thought it was. I was actually going to phone you about it tomorrow. I thought you'd be too busy tonight. Any news on how the hunt for him's going?"

"Nothing yet," she answered, realizing that she should be talking to Dougie MacLeod about this. Yet she felt more comfortable talking it through with Mike, who she knew would be more receptive to her theories. In spite of herself, she was also glad that he'd been thinking about phoning her to discuss the case. It wasn't much, but it was something.

"Kent and his abductors could be anywhere by now. But they're incredible circumstances. What's the story behind it?"

She told him everything that had happened since Kent's arrest, starting with the initial interviews and his passionate denials; and then the huge reams of evidence against him, his ironclad alibi for Róisin O'Neill's murder, the attempted poisoning in the cell, the highly professional snatch, and, finally, Róisin's father's suspicious death. "I've got a car with false plates that was spotted driving into Kevin O'Neill's cul-de-sac on the night he died that doesn't belong to anyone living there. I need a check on the ANPR to see where it is now."

"Can't you get your boss to authorize that?"

"Right now, no one's interested in looking for weaknesses in our case against Kent. They're just interested in finding him."

"Which I can understand."

"So can I, but there are plenty of other people out there looking for him. I need to find out why it happened. And in my opinion, the key's Róisin."

"But how? You said yourself, there's a huge amount of evidence against Andrew Kent."

"There is, and I'm sure he killed the other four women. But he didn't kill Róisin. He couldn't have."

She heard Mike yawning down the end of the line again. "Blimey, Tina, this is quite hard to get my head around at half past one in the morning. Let me get up. I need a drink of water."

She waited a couple of minutes, lighting her last cigarette of the night while she listened to him moving about in his flat.

"OK," he said at last. "It's clear you've got a theory. What is it?"

She suddenly felt uncharacteristically nervous about discussing it, just in case he dismissed it out of hand, although she knew in her heart he wouldn't. He was one of the few people on the force who'd always believed in her. He thought she was good, and she needed that reassurance now. "I told you we found a lot of film footage of his crimes on Kent's computer. Well, he didn't just like to film himself killing the victims, he liked to film them in the days running up to the actual act itself. It was a form of cyber-stalking. He'd break into their homes, bypassing the alarm systems he'd installed, which was no problem for him to do, then set up hidden cameras so that he could watch them going about their daily lives, knowing he was going to snuff them out. It must have been quite a power trip for him."

"And there was film of Róisin on his laptop, was there?"

"No. There was no footage at all of Róisin. But I think that was deliberate."

"What do you mean?"

"The way I see it, Kent had every intention of killing Róisin. He'd installed her alarm system, just like he had with all his other victims, and I believe he also broke into her apartment in the days before she was murdered, to set up hidden cameras. We have a witness who lived in the same block of flats who saw a man coming down the stairs from her apartment a couple of days earlier, and when we showed her Kent's photo she thought that it might well be him."

"But not a definite ID?"

"It's been a long time, Mike, but she was sure enough for me. And it fits. I think he set up the camera, then before he had a chance to carry out his crime, his father died in Scotland and he had to go up there for the funeral. Except by the time he came back, Róisin was already dead. So someone else killed her."

"I still don't quite get it, Tina. If the Night Creeper didn't kill her, then who did?"

"I don't know," she said. "But Andrew Kent knows."

"How?"

"Because he filmed it. Don't you see? The footage must have been on the camera he'd already installed."

Forty-one

Mike Bolt exhaled loudly. "That's some theory."

"It fits the facts, Mike. And right now, it's the only one that does."

"But you said there was no footage on Kent's laptop."

This was where Tina knew her theory became tenuous. "I think he must have removed it for some reason."

"Why would he do that?" asked Mike. "It's not as if he was expecting to be caught. There'd be no point removing it."

But she'd thought about that. "There was if he was black-mailing someone. Let's say Kent filmed the murder and managed to find out who the murderer was. He then makes contact and demands money. At the same time he removes the footage from his laptop and keeps it safe somewhere. Think about it, Mike," she continued. "It would explain why he was broken out of prison. The person he was blackmail-ing would know that Kent possessed explosive knowledge about him, so he set up the abduction. And now he's got Kent somewhere. He can find out where the incriminating evidence is, get rid of it, and then get rid of Kent. End of threat. End of story."

Bolt was silent down the other end of the phone for what seemed like a long time. "But that means that the person he was blackmailing has to be someone with some major clout."

"We both know there are people out there who could have done it."

"There aren't many of them though, are there? Have you got any idea who it might be?"

"Not yet, but from Róisin's phone records it looks like she had a lover, and two neighbors reported seeing an older man with silver hair leaving her flat. It's possible he killed her."

"It's possible, Tina," said Bolt after a long pause. "But if her lover killed her, how did he know to cover up the murder to look like the work of the Night Creeper? The Creeper's MO was never public knowledge, was it?"

"No, it wasn't. But Róisin's murder was a definite cover-up. She was the only victim to be strangled; the hammer blows were delivered to her face postmortem. I don't know how the real murderer knew about the Creeper's MO, but the fact is he did. At the moment, the most important thing is for us to find out who he is. Once we've done that, we can find Kent, although I've got a feeling he's no longer alive."

"How can I help with that?"

"I've got a mobile number that I think belongs to the killer. It's a pay-as-you-go, and I'm pretty certain it's been dead since Róisin's murder, but if there's any way we can find out who it belonged to . . ."

"That's not going to be easy."

"The phone company'll be able to triangulate the old calls made from it though, won't they?"

"Maybe, but that's more your area of expertise."

"You've got the contacts though, Mike. Can you get it checked out? Urgently."

"You don't ask for much, do you, Tina?"

"It'll help solve a major crime," she persisted, knowing that Bolt would help her.

He sighed again. "Well, I'm awake now. I'll see what I can do."

She thanked him, promising to make it up to him as soon as she could.

"You always say that, but we only seem to talk when you need something. Other times, I don't hear from you for months on end."

He sounded genuinely hurt, and she felt a sudden rush of relief. So he still had feelings for her after all. "I'm sorry," she said quietly. "I would have called, but things have been . . . difficult."

"I know. You've been through a lot, but you've also got to let go and move on. It's the only way."

"I know."

"Is everything OK with you at the moment?" he asked. "Life-wise, I mean?"

The question made her uncomfortable, because the true answer was a resounding no, and it was one she could never give. "It's fine," she answered. "I'm enjoying CMIT. The work's a lot more satisfying than CID. Or SOCA, to be honest. And you?"

"It's good. Busy as always."

"And Paul Wise?" she said, referring to the man who still haunted her, and who, more than anyone else, was preventing her from moving on. "Any developments on his case?" Even as she asked, she regretted bringing it up, knowing full well what the answer was going to be.

"There's still an ongoing inquiry, but I'm less involved on that side now. But they're not going to give up on him, Tina. He's too big a target for that."

"I'm pleased to hear it, but I've got to say, the speed you guys are going, he'll be dead by the time you get any evidence against him."

"It takes time, Tina," Bolt said evenly. "You know that. Particularly with someone as savvy as Wise."

"Yes," she conceded, "I guess I do." She stood up and looked around the living room. "It's late and I should go. But if there's anything you can do on that car reg and the phone number, it would be hugely appreciated."

Bolt said again he'd do what he could and rang off, leaving her staring at the phone, feeling tired and curiously depleted, knowing that for the moment there was nothing more she could do.

Ten minutes later she was lying in bed, trying not to think about Paul Wise. It was hard, because Wise was a classic case of justice not being done. A ruthless thug and suspected pedophile, he was also a hugely successful businessman who'd built an empire which encompassed everything from property development to large-scale drug smuggling. Although suspected of organizing dozens of murders, including that of Tina's former partner, in his twin pursuits of financial gain and avoiding prison, he was currently living scot-free and out of reach in Turkish Cyprus. Mike was right, she needed to dust herself down and move on with her life, but it was hard to do that knowing that the man who'd ruined it was giving the finger to the law, and at her personally.

She shut her eyes, afraid of what she might dream of, wondering what psychopaths like Andrew Kent and Paul Wise dreamed of. Wondering if they too ever had nightmares.

She hoped so.

Forty-two

I suppose I must have slept, because when I next opened my eyes and saw the darkness of the woodland all around me, with the orange glow beyond it, I wasn't entirely sure where I was.

Then it all came back to me in a huge, terrifying rush. The abduction. The beating. The murders. The escape. And finally the knowledge that I was in real trouble.

The flames from the burning building no longer danced across the night sky, but they still threw up a deep glow that mingled with the flashing blue lights from the emergency vehicles. I could hear a lot of shouting coming from the firefighters in the distance as they fought to bring the blaze under control, and by the sound of their voices it was still some way from being put out. The treeline was some fifty yards distant and I could make out figures moving in the flickering light.

I slid out from underneath the bush and stood up. It was a slow procedure. Every part of my body ached, but my ribs, particularly, were agony. My face still hurt, and I had a raging thirst, having not had a drink of anything since I was in the second getaway van, hours ago now.

I looked at my watch, wanting to know how much time had passed, which was when I got a nasty shock. It wasn't there. I cursed, crouching down and looking under the bush.

It wasn't there either. I tried to remember when I'd last had it. I thought it was when I'd been locked away in the room upstairs in the house, but couldn't say for sure. So much had been happening that knowing the time had been the least of my concerns. But now I had a real problem. All the evidence I had against Wolfe and Haddock was stored on the listening device within that watch. I hadn't had time to download any of it onto another disk. Without copies I had nothing. Wolfe and his whole team might be dead, but now there was nothing to back up my story that I was only involved in Kent's abduction because I'd had no choice. In other words, to all intents and purposes I was a criminal who'd taken part in a kidnapping during which a police officer had been shot, and possibly killed.

I exhaled loudly. I had to get away from here as soon as possible. It wouldn't be long before the first bodies were discovered, and then this whole area would be declared a major crime scene. I was confident any evidence of my own involvement left behind in there would have been extinguished by the flames, but unfortunately at least one person other than me was still alive—the man who'd tried to kill me earlier, and who presumably had started the fire. And it was possible he knew who I was.

It also begged an intriguing question. If no one knew his identity—and I was pretty certain no one did—then why did we all have to die? It would have been just as easy to keep to the original plan. Get us to deliver Kent to the house. Leave the remainder of the money there for us to collect, then wait until we'd gone before going in and doing whatever he'd wanted to do to Kent. But he hadn't done that, and I wanted to know why.

It was difficult to gauge what time it was, but the sky

above me was still black through the trees so I guessed it was maybe two or three A.M. Taking a deep breath, I began walking.

I didn't dare double back and take the driveway back to the road. It would have been far too dangerous, given that I could still hear vehicles arriving. Instead, I kept moving in the opposite direction, crossing several fields and moving through more woodland before coming to a winding, tree-lined B-road. I had to stop for a couple of minutes to get my breath back, then turned left, again trying to put as much distance as possible between myself and the fire. I moved quickly, knowing that if I got spotted by a passing police car in my current state—smoke-blackened, with torn clothing, and doubtless looking like death—I was finished.

I must have walked about a quarter of a mile, and was beginning to think I couldn't carry on much longer, when a driveway appeared on my right. It led down to an ugly-looking 1960s bungalow with lawn frontage and two cars parked outside. One was a BMW wagon that was either new or recently cleaned. The other was smaller and looked like a Ford Fiesta. This would be the far easier one to steal.

I crept up the driveway, moving off the gravel and onto the lawn at the first opportunity to mask the sound of my approach, and I was within five yards of the cars when an intruder light came on at the front of the house. I ducked down behind an apple tree and waited. The curtains inside didn't move. I imagined they got a lot of animals around here that set the lights off, so would sleep through it. With the light still on, I reached the Fiesta and looked inside, hoping rather optimistically to see a box of the kind of tools I was going to need. Not surprisingly, it was empty.

Taking my shoes off, I crept across the gravel and around

the side of the house where I spotted a water butt attached to the drainpipe. Such was my thirst, I had to stop myself from yanking off the lid and throwing it aside. Instead, I removed it carefully, placed it on the ground, scooped up the water with my hands, and drank it down as quietly as possible.

When I'd finished, I replaced the lid and continued into the back garden. There was a garden shed at the far end of the lawn, but I didn't go there straight away, preferring to wait a few minutes so that if I set off another intruder light it wouldn't worry the occupants either. When I'd concluded enough time had passed, I crossed the lawn and was still in darkness at the end, surprised that they didn't have a light at the back as well as the front. The shed door wasn't locked either, which was stupid, since it contained everything I needed to commit any number of crimes. Maybe it's because I've spent too long in the company of criminals, but I can never understand how people can be so complacent. Thieves are like scavengers. Leave something out for them and they'll have it just like that.

I gathered up the things I needed before returning to the front of the house, stopping again for a few minutes by the water butt en route. The security light went on again and I hid behind the Fiesta. Once again, no lights were switched on and nothing moved.

By my calculations, the light would stay on for about two minutes, which meant moving fast. Like any good copper, I know the tricks of the thief's trade, and getting into an old car like a Fiesta is easy. All it requires is a length of garden wire and about a minute's effort. The light turned off a few seconds after I'd got inside, but the sensor couldn't pick up my movements inside the car, giving me the opportunity to use a screwdriver to break the steering lock at leisure. The locks on older cars are far easier to break, but though I know what I'm doing, I'm no expert, and it took me a while to get the wheel turning. I counted slowly to five hundred, desperate to get going but knowing that it was also better to be patient, then released the handbrake and slowly maneuvered the car down the drive. When I was at the bottom, I used the screwdriver, and the car started with an angry sputter.

The drive back to London was uneventful, although it took me a long time to find the main road. It was 4:57 according to the clock's dashboard when I finally pulled up on a backstreet in Colindale, half a mile down the road from the two-bed 1930s terrace that was my real home. I felt bad about stealing the car, and even toyed with digging out the owner's number and calling him to say where he could find it. But I quickly thought better of it. After what I'd done to it, the damned thing was ruined, so he might as well collect the insurance money.

Ten minutes later, and as the first gray light of dawn flickered over the tower blocks on the horizon, I finally stepped inside my front door, having avoided being spotted by anyone on the way. I was shattered and desperately needed to sleep, so allowed myself an hour's power nap before the alarm clock woke me up. Then I cleaned up, had a shower, and made myself a strong mug of coffee.

The thing was, I couldn't leave matters as they were. As soon as the fire brigade realized their fire had been lit deliberately and that the building contained the remains of five people, including a dangerous fugitive and his likely kidnappers, there'd be a huge hunt for whoever was behind it. It was going to be hard to trace the client, given his lack of direct involvement, but there was a possibility that my name could end up in the frame. My undercover op to become one of

Wolfe's gang might have been unofficial, but Captain Bob, for one, knew I'd been lobbying to infiltrate them for years. Someone might also have seen me getting into Wolfe's car in Doughty Street earlier that evening. My image might have been caught on CCTV.

If I kept quiet and my name ended up in the frame, my silence would count against me hugely. But if I came forward and admitted everything, there was still no guarantee that I'd be believed. I knew I couldn't count on Captain Bob for support. He was a career man first and foremost, and would drop me like a stone if he thought I was liable to become an embarrassment to him.

But there was one person who could help me. It had been a long time, but I trusted him, which was hugely important because I was going to need to tell him the whole truth. The time for operating on my own was over.

I pulled out a mobile, then stopped. This was going to have to be done face to face. It would be too dangerous otherwise.

I was going to have to turn up at his door.

Forty-three

Tina Boyd was in a deep, dreamless sleep when the constant ringing of her mobile dragged her back to reality. The alarm clock read 5:35 as she fumbled for the phone on the bedside table.

It was Mike. "Sorry to wake you," he said, sounding surprisingly perky. "I've got some news."

She sat up in the bed, rubbing her eyes. "Don't apologize. You're the one doing me a favor."

"You've stumbled on something big, Tina," he continued. "I don't know how you do it."

She grabbed the notebook and pen she always kept by the bed, feeling the familiar thrill of a lead coming to something. "What have you got?"

"The anonymous mobile number that showed up on your victim's phone records is definitely a pay-as-you-go, and it hasn't been used since November the twenty-second last year."

"That was the day before Róisin was murdered."

"That doesn't necessarily make the person who used it the murderer, though. It could just be that he was a lover who didn't want to get sucked into the police inquiry. In fact, that's far more likely than your theory."

"Someone killed her, Mike, and it wasn't the Night Creeper. It still had to be someone who could get past the alarm system, though. Someone who knew her. So a lover's as likely a scenario as any. Is it possible you can find out the locations where the mobile was used before it was abandoned?"

"I've done it. We've also managed to triangulate the location where it was switched off, which is also the location it was used from on a number of occasions. It's a residential address."

Tina felt her excitement rising. She'd woken up completely now. "Whose?"

"This is big, Tina. Very big."

"Tell me his name. It is a 'he,' isn't it?"

"Yes, it's a 'he,' and his name's Anthony Gore."

She frowned. "Not *the* Anthony Gore?"

"Yes," he answered grimly. "Anthony Gore. The Minister for Home Affairs."

Forty-four

Light was breaking, and Tina could just hear birdsong above the distant rumble of traffic as she picked up the phone.

"I'm sorry to bother you this early in the morning, Mrs. Glover," she said when Beatrice Glover answered, "but it's the police again. My name's DI Boyd and you spoke to my colleague DC Grier last night."

"Don't worry, I've been up for half an hour," said Mrs. Glover brightly. "At my time of life you make the best use of your time because you never know when it's going to run out. And yes, I did speak to your colleague. He wanted me to look at a photo of a young man I saw in our apartment block last year. I hope I was of some help."

"Yes you were. A great help. But I'm afraid I have another question for you. You saw a gray-haired man leaving your building on more than one occasion, didn't you? According to your statement, he was in his fifties, gray hair, quite tall."

"That's right. I met him on the stairs once with Róisin. She didn't introduce him and I had the feeling he didn't want to be seen that much either, because he didn't really look at me. You don't think he had anything to do with her death, do you? He didn't seem the type."

THE LAST 10 SECONDS

"No," lied Tina, "but we need to trace him."

"I saw him again, too, leaving through the front door when I was on my way back in with the shopping. That was a couple of weeks afterward, I think. Not that long before the murder. He held the door open for me, and he seemed to be in a hurry. I think he was her boyfriend, you know," she added in conspiratorial tones. "And I think he was married too, which was why he didn't want to be seen."

Tina smiled to herself. "I think you're right, Mrs. Glover. That's very perceptive of you."

Beatrice Glover chuckled infectiously. "I may be old but I'm not senile. Róisín was a lovely girl, you know. Always smiling. She could have done so much better than a married man. Those kinds of affairs never end happily, do they?"

"No, they don't," said Tina, remembering the only one she'd had many years before when she was in her early twenties and new to the force. He was a businessman, sixteen years older and, as she'd found out three months in, married with two children. It had been a painful learning experience, and one she'd never repeated. "I understand you've got access to a computer and the internet, Mrs. Glover. Could you do me a favor and look something up on it for me?"

"Yes, of course. Just let me go and turn it on."

Tina waited patiently while she got her computer booted up, listening to her say how worried she'd become as a result of the murder and asking what the world had come to when you could be murdered in your bed.

"Murder's far rarer than people think, Mrs. Glover, and lightning doesn't usually strike twice, so I'm sure you have nothing to worry about," Tina explained, although she was only too aware that lightning had struck far too many times around her.

"All right, Miss Boyd, I'm all booted up and ready. What do you need me to look up?"

"The name Anthony Gore. Can you Google it, and add the words 'Minister of Home Affairs'? It should come up with some image results. I want you to look at them."

Beatrice Glover slowly repeated the words out loud, then Tina heard her click a key at the other end.

Five seconds passed.

"Can you see a photograph of him yet?" Tina asked, trying not to sound impatient.

"My goodness. It's him. That's the man I saw with Róisin. I thought he looked familiar."

"Thank you, Mrs. Glover, that's all I need to know," said Tina, and after instructing her not to say anything to anyone about their conversation, she said her goodbyes before the old lady could ask any more questions.

She took a deep breath and lit her first cigarette of the morning, wincing as the smoke tore down her throat. So Anthony Gore had definitely been Róisin O'Neill's lover. Of course, as Mike had pointed out, that might be all he was, but Tina wasn't so sure. She'd Googled Gore herself before phoning Beatrice Glover. A fifty-six-year-old former trial lawyer, married with two adult children, he had a reputation for being combative in the courtroom, and for getting results. He'd become an MP after the 2001 general election and had risen steadily through the government ranks, even though in 2003 he'd become embroiled in controversy when a story appeared in a Sunday tabloid accusing him of having a relationship with a prostitute. Gore had issued a spirited denial and taken legal action against the paper. The prostitute later retracted her story, claiming that all Gore had been guilty of was offering her free legal advice, which was why he was at her flat, and the paper ended up having to pay him 120,000 pounds in libel damages. Tina noted wryly that he'd made a big point of donating 10,000 pounds to charity but had kept the rest of the cash himself.

And that was Tina's problem with Anthony Gore. Maybe she was reading too much between the lines, but there was something about him that left a bad taste in the mouth. In the photographs, there was an arrogance in his bearing, a vague glint of contempt in his eyes, and Tina didn't like the way the prostitute had changed her story. The new one smacked of bullshit and suggested that she'd been persuaded to do it. Either by Gore himself, or perhaps he had some powerful friends to do it for him. There was no obvious evidence of wrongdoing in any of the basic research she'd done on Gore in the past half an hour, but that might have been because he was careful. Either way, she didn't like him, or the fact that he'd been around Róisin in the run-up to her murder and was having an affair with her. Also, strangulation tended to point to a crime of passion. It was such a personal method of murder, the kind someone resorts to in moments of pure rage. Or desperation.

Had Róisin done something to drive Gore to kill her? And had Andrew Kent captured it on film?

But how had Gore covered it up? As far as Tina knew, he had no connection to the Night Creeper murder inquiry, and she couldn't imagine a man like Gore—a scholarly lawyer—getting his hands dirty by smashing in his lover's face with a hammer. Did he have friends who had such contacts? The same friends who'd persuaded the prostitute to change her story? And were they in turn capable of organizing Kent's breakout from police custody?

It made sense, and it fit the facts. But it was also hugely

tenuous. And Tina had absolutely no evidence to prove any of it. According to the radio that morning there was no further news on Andrew Kent's whereabouts, and she hadn't heard anything from DCI MacLeod. She needed to phone him, so she got to her feet and dialed his number, looking at her watch. It was six thirty, and the sun was shining through the blinds, throwing thin rods of light across her old sofa. He would probably be up. It would have been difficult for him to sleep well, given what had happened the previous night.

There was no answer. She thought about calling the big boss of Homicide and Serious Crime Command, DCS Frank Mendelson. He ran all the Met's murder investigation teams and was the man DCI MacLeod reported to. She'd only met him once, when he'd come in to discuss the case a few months earlier. He was a short, pugnacious, and fiercely ambitious man, and she remembered him as someone who liked to do things methodically, which meant he'd tell her to write up a report and then, almost certainly, given the lack of obvious evidence and the fact that Anthony Gore was so high-profile, nothing would happen. So she decided against it. She also decided against calling Mike, mainly because she was sure that he would tell her to tread carefully, when she knew that treading carefully wouldn't work. She had to shake things up, and the only way to do that was to confront Gore.

It was a high-risk strategy. In fact, it was probably madness, given the trouble it could land her in, but somehow, standing alone in her shitty little front room, the thought didn't bother her. It actually excited her. Risking her job, risking everything, in a dramatic and probably vain effort to get some justice sent her adrenaline surging.

Ignoring the voice that told her she was being foolish,

that this was definitely not the way forward, she strode into the kitchen, pulled a half-full bottle of vodka from the fridge, took a single, hard slug—relishing the burning hit—then picked up the phone and called Dan Grier.

"Wakey wakey," she said when he picked up. "It's time to go to work."

Forty-five

DCI Dougie MacLeod lived alone in a spacious corner terrace three or four miles from me in Hendon. His wife, Marion, a small, severe woman who'd always been a bundle of nervous energy, had died suddenly of a heart attack years earlier, and his son, Billy, was off at university somewhere, which made things a lot easier from my point of view, because I didn't want anyone else to hear what I had to say.

I hadn't had much to do with Dougie these past few years, and things had never been the same since I'd assaulted Jason Slade and he'd put a contract on my head, but now that my own family was gone, he was the only person on this planet I trusted completely. He'd always been a man of integrity, prepared to put himself on the line for the people who worked under him, and even though it had been many years since I had, I was still sure I could rely on him to tell me what I needed to do.

My career was finished, I was beginning to accept that now. Even if I got away with this in the short term, I'd always be looking over my shoulder, wondering when someone was going to find out the truth. More than that, though, I no longer had the stomach for undercover work. I'd come very close to death four times in the past twenty-four hours, and the shock of this was tearing me up inside. I needed a holiday. A long one. Six months, a year, somewhere far away from all the violence of the city. But I'd also done what I'd set out to do all those years ago when I started out in undercover. I'd brought down Tyrone Wolfe and Clarence Haddock, and I took grim satisfaction from the knowledge that they'd paid the price for what they did all those years ago. Wolfe's denial that it was he who murdered my brother had caught me out, since it was a reliable source who'd heard him bragging that he was the man who'd pulled the trigger. There were three armed robbers there that day, Wolfe, Haddock, and Tommy. But now, at least, they were all dead, even if they had taken the true identity of the shooter to their graves, and my brother and my parents could finally rest in peace.

I'd used my own car to get to Dougie's. As I drove past his house, I saw that there were lights on on the ground floor. I wasn't entirely surprised. Although it was seven o'clock on a Saturday morning, I knew he was an early riser, and he was going to have his hands full with the Kent manhunt, so there wouldn't have been a lot of time to sleep.

I found a spot fifty yards down the road, parked up, and walked back, feeling nervous about what I was going to have to do.

Taking a deep breath that made me wince, I rang his doorbell, pleased at least that I no longer looked like something out of a horror film.

There was no answer, even though his car was in the carport, so I rang again and then rapped hard on the door. It was possible he'd gone out somewhere on foot and would be back soon, but I didn't want to draw attention to myself out here. So after about a minute, when it became clear that he wasn't going to answer, I took a quick look around to check that no one was around, then clambered over the wooden fence that separated the front of the property from the back garden.

As I walked quietly around to the conservatory, something caught my eye. A light had gone out upstairs. So someone was here.

I tried the conservatory door, and it opened. I went inside and was about to call out Dougie's name when I experienced a sudden uneasy feeling. Maybe it was paranoia after my recent experiences, but my instincts told me to be careful. I crept through the conservatory and into the kitchen, beginning to get worryingly used to sneaking about in places where I didn't belong, and feeling more and more like some kind of fugitive.

The kitchen led through to a narrow hallway with the stairs on the left and another room off to the right. Although it was upstairs that the light had gone off, I couldn't hear any sound coming from up there, which was strange. Again resisting the urge to call out, and wondering what Dougie would say if he caught me sneaking around his house at seven in the morning, I crept over to the other door and opened it.

The sound of the TV drifted out, and as I stepped inside, closing the door behind me, I saw that it was a Sky News report. The room was empty but it smelled of smoke, and there was an overflowing ashtray on the antique coffee table that sat between two traditional leather sofas. That was another thing that was strange. I remembered Dougie smoking when I first joined CID, but I thought he'd given up years earlier.

I walked further inside the room, my eyes focused on the huge forty-inch TV as a tired-looking reporter spoke to the camera from just outside the scene-of-crime tape in Doughty Street where we'd snatched Kent. Behind him, a few SOCO moved about in their white coveralls, and a uniformed officer stood guard. There didn't seem to be any frenetic activity.

The reporter didn't have much of any importance to say and was just repeating what had happened the previous night. Thankfully, the police officer who'd been shot was stable in the hospital, and his injuries were not thought to be life-threatening. The big news from the reporter's view was the identity of the kidnap victim, and the fact that he'd been charged only hours before with the Night Creeper murders. Police, he said, were keeping an open mind regarding the motive for the snatch, and although he reiterated the usual stuff about a major manhunt being under way, with a number of leads being followed up, the subtext seemed to be that no one knew who'd done it, why, or where he was now. He finished by saying that a police press conference was set for ten that morning.

The camera then returned to the studio where an immaculately dressed female newsreader moved on to the next story, which was a fire at an abandoned hotel in Hertfordshire, from which two bodies had so far been recovered. There was a quick shot of the previous night's rendezvous, which was now little more than a heavily smoldering pile of ash and stone, with a number of fire engines in front of it. Parts of the outbuilding where I'd discovered Haddock's body were still standing, and I could make out the generator poking above what was left of a stone exterior wall. I assumed that one of the bodies they'd recovered must be his, but I doubted there would have been much left of it. The newsreader was stating that arson was suspected, and quoted Hertfordshire's chief fire officer as saying it was possible there were more bodies inside. So far, unsurprisingly, no connection had been made between the two stories, but sooner or later DNA or dental work would be used to ID the victims, and then they'd merge into a superstory that would catch the imagination of journalists and police alike as they, like me, hunted for answers. The difference was, at the moment I was several steps ahead of them.

I froze. The door was opening behind me. And then there was another sound that I knew well enough from my firearms training.

The metallic click of a gun being cocked.

Forty-six

It was seven A.M., and Tina felt a sudden rush of apprehension as she parked the rental car in a resident's bay across the road from Anthony Gore's grand four-story Notting Hill townhouse. All the way there Grier had been asking her if she was sure she was doing the right thing, and suggesting that it would be far better to get authorization before barging in on a government minister and effectively accusing him of murder. To his credit, though, he hadn't refused to come along. "If it all goes wrong, I'll say I forced you into it," she'd said in an attempt to mollify him.

As they got out of the car now, Grier looked pale. "He's the Minister of Home Affairs, for God's sake, ma'am," he said again, with something close to fear. "I don't like the idea of doing this at all."

But it was too late for that, and once again Tina told him she knew what she was doing. "Just leave me to do the talking," she said, walking up to the front door and rapping hard on the knocker. "You're just going to be back-up. Look stern."

He said something she didn't catch under his breath, but which she was sure wasn't complimentary, and then she heard footsteps coming from inside.

"Who is it?" came a voice from behind the door that she

recognized from the occasional TV program she'd seen him on as belonging to Gore himself.

"Police, Mr. Gore," she answered firmly, holding up her warrant card to the spyhole in the center of the imposing oak door. Grier did the same.

There was the sound of locks being turned on the other side, then the door opened on a thick chain and a very irritated-looking Anthony Gore looked out at them. He was wearing a gray silk dressing gown and his collar-length silver hair was a mess. Even so, he looked sleek, well fed, and prosperous, as if he'd never had to struggle for anything in life, and Tina's dislike for him immediately hardened.

"It's seven on a Saturday morning, this had better be bloody important," he said, examining the warrant cards before finally opening up to let them in.

"It is," Tina answered, determined not to be intimidated, even though there was a charisma about Gore that hinted at real power. In spite of herself, she could understand why an attractive woman like Róisin, more than twenty-five years younger, could fall for him.

They followed him as he stalked down the grand hallway to a room at the end. It was a large study, tastefully furnished in mahogany and leather, with floor-to-ceiling bookcases lining two walls and a view out onto a walled garden. Gore took a seat behind an imposing desk so that it looked like he was in charge, and motioned for them to take seats opposite.

As she sat down, Tina stole a glance at Grier, who seemed to be wilting under Gore's grim, lawyerly demeanor.

"My name's DI Tina Boyd, and this is—"

"I know who you are, Miss Boyd. You have a very high profile for a police officer, which isn't necessarily a good thing. What is it that I can do for you?"

"We're investigating the murder of Róisin O'Neill," she told him, trying to remain as unfazed as possible.

"I thought someone had been charged with her murder," he answered smoothly and without exhibiting any sign of concern. "The man who was broken free from police custody last night."

"New evidence has come to light that suggests he didn't kill Róisin," said Tina, and this time she was sure she caught the first flicker of nerves on his face.

"Really? That's interesting."

There was a short silence. Tina knew she was just going to have to go for it. There was no alternative. "You were seeing Róisin O'Neill, I believe, at about the time of her murder."

He made a great play of looking shocked by her comment. "How dare you accuse me of having an affair with someone I've never even met."

But this time Tina could tell he was acting. "Don't lie to us, Mr. Gore. We have phone records between her mobile and a mobile that was used from this address on a number of occasions in the run-up to the murder, including the previous day. Just because you got rid of the phone after her death and never registered it in your name doesn't mean we can't trace it back to you."

"I don't know what you're talking about. You've come in here and made some unfounded and totally untrue allegations, and I'm not prepared to stand for it. Perhaps all the adulation and high-profile successes have gone to your head, Miss Boyd, but because of your much-publicized trials and tribulations, I'm going to let it go and not take action against you, if you leave here now." He turned to Grier. "This is your opportunity to save your colleague's career."

"She's my boss, sir," Grier answered calmly. He might

have looked nervous, but Tina was pleased to see he was holding his own.

"You've also been positively identified by a witness as the man seen entering and leaving Róisín's flat on a number of occasions, including"—she paused for effect here—"the night of her murder." This last part was bullshit, but she needed something to put him on the back foot, and she was pleased that Grier didn't ruin things by looking surprised himself. Instead, he remained expressionless.

"Rubbish," said Gore with an angry finality.

Tina shook her head slowly. "No, Mr. Gore, I'm afraid it's not."

"Your alleged witness must have been mistaken."

"She wasn't. I showed her your photo less than an hour ago, and she swears it's you."

Gore didn't say anything for a moment. "I may have had a very short, uh, dalliance with her," he said at last, choosing his words very carefully, as lawyers tend to do, "but that was all. I shouldn't have done, and it shames me to admit that I did, and that I didn't come forward after her death, but I was afraid of becoming involved. Especially as that was all the relationship was. A dalliance. Nothing serious."

"That's not what her sister said. She said you two were very close." Tina was lying through her back teeth now, knowing that this was blatant entrapment, but her desire to force the truth out of Gore was making her desperate.

A worried look flitted across the minister's face, and Tina smelled blood.

"You didn't expect that, did you?" she continued. "That her sister knew all about it? She said Róisín had told her that she'd tried to get you to leave your wife on a number of occasions. We'd have talked to her father as well, but you, or whoever you were using, got to him first, didn't you?"

"I don't know what the hell you're talking about."

"Why did you kill Róisin O'Neill?"

"How dare you accuse me of murder!" he shouted, his face contorting with a rage so intense that Tina was taken aback. Then, seeing that he'd shown too much emotion, and with an eye toward the study door that suggested his wife was somewhere in the house, he took a deep breath, clearly forcing himself to remain calm. When he spoke again, he was quiet and controlled, but rippling with venom. "I'm the fucking Home Affairs minister, for Christ's sake. Not some common criminal you can talk to like dirt."

"We know that the Night Creeper, Andrew Kent, didn't kill Róisin, Mr. Gore," said Tina firmly, wanting to press her advantage before he could recover fully. "He has a cast-iron alibi for the time of her murder. Plus, the MO was different. Unlike Kent's other victims, she was strangled and the hammer injuries inflicted upon her after death."

"What's this got to do with me?"

"Because you did it. Or did you get someone to help you cover it up? The same person who murdered Kevin O'Neill and organized the kidnapping of Andrew Kent, perhaps?"

Gore stood up. "I've had enough of this conversation. You have absolutely no evidence against me whatsoever—"

"Sit down."

"No. Get out. Now."

There was a finality to his words, and Tina knew she'd lost him.

But she wasn't going to let it go that easily. Standing up herself, she faced him down. "We know you killed her, and

I'm not going to leave a single stone unturned proving it. I'll have you for this, even if it's the last thing I do."

Out of the corner of her eye, she saw Grier stand up and stare at her in total shock, as he saw his own career getting caught up in the constant car crash that was DI Tina Boyd.

"Ma'am," he said, "I think we'd better go."

"We'll go when I say."

"You'll go now. Right this minute."

"You're finished, Minister."

Gore strode around the desk, a confidence returning to his manner now. "You haven't got the power, you little bitch," he hissed, coming in close so that their faces were only inches apart. "It's time you realized who you're dealing with. I'm a government minister. I'm one of the handful of people who run this fucking country. You are just a . . ." He paused, before spitting out his final words. "A small-time copper who thinks she's Robocop. And who's not. Now get out of my house. I'll be speaking to your commanding officer about this. I don't care who you are, or what you've done. You're going to pay for this. Do you understand? I'll have your job, and I'll have your pension."

Tina felt the anger in her seething beneath the surface. She wanted to hit this smug bastard. She knew he'd done it. Would have bet her life on it. "But you won't stop me," she said, facing him down, her expression coldly determined, just so he'd know she'd never give up. "Not unless you have me killed, like the others, and I wouldn't advise that. Not when there's a witness present."

Gore's face darkened. He stared at her with an animal-like ferocity, and she could hear him grinding his teeth. He wanted to hurt her. She could feel his hatred as if it was a physical thing, and she willed him to lash out, to knock her down and give her a chance to turn this situation around and jail him.

Go on, you bastard, hit me. Hit me hard. Put your manicured hands around my neck, just like you did with Róisín that night. Give me the chance to twist your arm behind your back, slam you into that pricey antique desk of yours, and finish your career for good.

But Anthony Gore wasn't that foolish. Breathing hard, he stepped away from her and turned to Grier. "If you know what's good for you, officer, you'll take your colleague with you and leave right now, and don't worry about her being your boss. In fifteen minutes' time, she won't be. She's finished. I'm willing to ignore your part in this slanderous fiasco, as I'm sure you were coerced into coming here, but only if you leave this minute. Otherwise, I'll hold you jointly responsible."

Grier looked at Tina with a quiet desperation in his eyes. "Come on, ma'am," he said. "There's nothing more we can do here."

For a moment, Tina didn't move, knowing she'd overplayed her hand, and lost the battle. Grier put a hand on her arm, gently nudging her toward the door. This time she didn't resist, and as they walked out of the study, not looking at each other, Tina focused on maintaining her poise. She didn't think she managed it, though.

But as Grier opened the door and stepped aside to let Tina into the hallway, she stopped dead. Standing there, facing her, still in her nightgown, was a small woman in her fifties, her tear-stained face a mask of rigid shock. Mrs. Gore. And Tina felt a rush of hope, because one thing was absolutely clear.

She was terrified.

Forty-seven

"Don't move," said Dougie MacLeod. "Or you're dead."

I was so shocked to hear my old mentor and the boss of one of London's murder investigation teams threaten me with death that I disobeyed his instructions and turned around.

Dougie stood in the doorway pointing a black revolver at me. He was dressed casually in jeans and a sweatshirt, and his face was etched with a tension I'd never seen on him before.

Seeing that it was me, he lowered the weapon. "What the hell are you doing here, Sean?" he demanded.

"You weren't answering your door."

"So you thought you'd just walk in?"

"I need help, Dougie. Badly."

He sighed. "This is a bad time, Sean. We've got an emergency on."

"What kind of emergency?" I asked, feeling a terrible lurch of disappointment, followed by resentment. I'd expected a lot more from him.

"The kind you've been watching on the news. The Night Creeper abduction. He was our suspect, remember?" He replaced the safety on the revolver and put it in the back of his jeans, then pulled a half-crushed pack of Marlboro Reds from his pocket and lit one. "I'm sorry I can't be more help," he continued. "Perhaps we can talk later." He walked past me, picked up the remote control from the arm of the sofa, and switched off the TV. "Right now, I've got to go."

I noticed he was sweating, and that his movements were stiff and hurried. "Do you always carry a gun for police work these days?" I asked him. "I didn't think DCIs needed them."

"I wasn't going to take it with me. I only had it out because I thought you were an intruder."

"I didn't even know you owned a gun."

"And I'd rather you didn't tell anyone. It's an illegal one. There've been a lot of break-ins here," he added, as if this explained why he was walking around with an illegal weapon I knew he'd never fire. "I'm sorry I pointed it at you, but if you will come trespassing around here . . ."

I noticed he wasn't looking me in the eye as he spoke, which again wasn't like him. Something was definitely wrong.

"I wasn't trespassing. I came here looking for help, and I still need it. And it's to do with your case as well," I added, not sure how else I was going to get his attention.

"And I'll help later if I can, but right now, I've got to go. We've got a press conference." He started toward the door.

"The press conference is at ten—they announced it just now. That's three hours away."

"There are things to do before then."

But I wasn't moving. "It's strange," I said. "I sneak into your house, battered and bruised, telling you I've got important information on what's got to be the biggest case of your career, and you don't seem to give a shit. You know what that says to me?"

He stopped in front of me, the muscles in his jaw working, his eyes wide and alert with nervous tension. "We'll talk soon, OK?"

My punch caught him, and me, completely unaware. My strength and energy reserves might have been running on empty, but Dougie MacLeod went sprawling to the floor. Within a second I was on him, rolling him over onto his front and sticking my knee into his back before he could resist. I whipped the gun out from his jeans, then yanked him around and shoved the barrel against his forehead, cocking the weapon.

"Start talking, now. Tell me everything you know about this whole case because I know you know something. Do it or I'll kill you here and now. I swear it."

I wouldn't have. I couldn't have. Even doing this to the man who'd once been a good friend and had saved my career when it could easily have gone down the pan, even that hurt me. I hated it. But I had to find out what was bothering him and why he was wandering around his house with an illegal firearm, and the only way I was going to learn that was if he took my threats seriously. I glared down at him, pushing the gun even harder into his head.

"I don't know what you're talking about," he whispered, staring up at me in fear, his nose bleeding where I'd hit him, his face turning an unhealthy puce color.

"I've almost died tonight, Dougie. I was involved in the Night Creeper abduction."

"What?"

"It was an undercover op that went wrong. Kent's dead. So's everyone else who took him, and someone set us all up. And the thing is, I think it was you. Now you've got one chance. You talk or you die. Understand?"

And that's when I saw the tears running down his face.

"They've got Billy," he said desperately. "The bastards have got my boy."

Forty-eight

For a long moment, no one spoke, then Tina heard Gore let out a tiny, barely audible groan from his position behind her and Grier.

"I'm just seeing these two out, Jane," he said, recovering quickly. "Why don't you go back to bed? I'll be up in a moment."

Tina addressed Jane Gore directly. "You knew about this, didn't you." It was a statement, not a question, and it stayed hanging in the air for a good second after she'd said it.

Mrs. Gore's face crumpled. "Did you kill her, Anthony?" she whispered.

"Of course I didn't," he answered dismissively, as if such a question was frankly ridiculous.

He pushed between Tina and Grier and went over to comfort her, but she flinched away from his touch. "Don't try to fob me off. Tell me the truth. Is what she says true?"

He leaned down toward her, marshaling all the persuasive skills that had served him so well in the courtroom in days gone by. "No it's not. I swear it, darling. This is a big, big mistake." He turned to Tina and Grier. "What are you still doing here? This is a private matter. Get out."

Grier looked at Tina, but she didn't move. She could sense Mrs. Gore wavering.

"Your husband's lying, Mrs. Gore," she said, "and we can prove it."

"No, you can't," shouted Gore. "You can't prove anything."

Mrs. Gore grabbed his arm. "Is that what they were blackmailing you about, Anthony? Murder?"

"Who's been blackmailing you, Mr. Gore?"

"No one. Get out."

"If you cooperate now, there'll be a way out. If you don't, we'll find out everything."

"How could you do this, Anthony? Did you kill her? Did you kill that little hussy? I thought it was all over!"

"Shut up! Now!" Without warning, Gore slapped his wife hard across the face, knocking her backward.

Tina and Grier both took a step toward them.

Jane Gore put a hand to her cheek and backed slowly away from him, the fear in her expression there for all to see.

"Oh God, I'm sorry," said Gore. "I didn't mean to hurt you."

"Get away from me. Don't touch me."

"Please, Jane . . ." He turned to Tina. "See what you made me do, you heartless bitch."

"Is this what you did to Róisin, Minister? Hit her just that little bit too hard? That's what happened, isn't it? You lashed out. Was she threatening to tell your wife? Is that why you strangled her?"

Gore's face contorted with rage. "You lying whore!" he yelled, and threw a punch at Tina.

She'd been expecting it, had hoped it would come, and dodged out of the way, letting the momentum drive Gore forward. As he passed her, she grabbed him by the wrist and yanked his arm up behind his back, while Grier got hold of the collar of his dressing gown from the other side. Together, they pushed him hard into the wall.

The fight went out of him now. "Let me go," he whispered. "Please."

Tina ignored his plea, putting her mouth close to his ear as she spoke, although her words were loud enough for everyone in the hallway to hear. "Andrew Kent, the Night Creeper, used to like filming his victims. Not just when he killed them but in the days beforehand too. He'd break in and set up a camera so he could film them in an everyday setting. It was like stalking them before the kill. He filmed you killing Róisin, didn't he?"

Gore took a deep breath but didn't say anything.

"We'll find out, Mr. Gore. And we'll find the film that Kent took too, and when we do, you'll be absolutely finished, because you've done so much to hide it. But if you cooperate now, if you let us know where Andrew Kent is, and who you've been using to help you, then you may be able to salvage something. I know you didn't mean to kill Róisin," she added soothingly, knowing she had to give him a way out of his current predicament, otherwise there'd be no way he'd talk. And if he didn't, then they still had nothing. But he was weakening fast, Tina could feel it.

"It's too late," he said with a strangled sob.

"It's never too late," she reassured him. "Now, where's Kent?"

"I don't know. I honestly don't."

Mrs. Gore approached them, anger replacing her earlier fear. "What have you done, Anthony? What have you done, you bastard? You've destroyed everything! All of us!"

Tina motioned to Grier, and he intercepted her, gently moving her into an adjoining room. She then let go of Gore and they stood facing each other, except now the balance of power had changed, and they both knew it.

"Let me lighten the load," she said to him. "Tell me the truth."

For a long time he didn't speak. Then, finally, he closed his eyes and sighed. "All right," he said. "I'll talk."

Forty-nine

They went back inside the study, taking the same seats they'd taken earlier, Grier joining them a few moments later.

"How's my wife?" Gore asked him.

"Upset," he replied tersely, refusing to give him any crumb of comfort.

Tina was pleased with his answer. It was essential to keep Gore off balance so that he wouldn't regain his confidence.

"I think you need to start talking, Minister," she told him, surreptitiously turning on the digital recorder in her pocket.

Gore's bearing had changed completely. He was slumped in his seat, his skin an unhealthy gray. He cleared his throat and began speaking. "My affair with Róisin was very passionate. It lasted a number of months. We didn't see each other that often. Usually no more than once a week. I have to confess, I had strong feelings for her. She was a vivacious girl, with the kind of joie de vivre that has been missing in my life for some years. Unfortunately, as time passed, Róisin became increasingly possessive. She wanted me to leave Jane. I resisted. I knew the scandal a move like that would cause. I tried to persuade Róisin that, though my feelings for her were very strong, I could only give her a limited amount of my time, and that she would simply have to accept that.

"The problem was, she didn't. We began to argue, as she became more and more resentful. Then one night she threatened to expose our affair to Jane. As you can imagine, I begged her not to, and eventually she saw sense and relented. However, by that point I'd concluded that the only course of action available to me was to terminate our relationship. It took me some days to pluck up courage, and Róisin didn't help matters by phoning me constantly and leaving messages. Some of them were loving, stating how much she missed being with me. Others were more angry in tone, suggesting that I didn't care for her anymore, and that I couldn't simply reject her, she wouldn't tolerate it.

"Finally, one night I went around to her apartment, which was where most of our meetings occurred, and told her that it was over. I apologized for becoming involved with her when I was married and threw myself at her mercy for the sake of my wife. I genuinely believed she'd let me go. If not for me, then for Jane. But I was wrong. She became hysterical and slapped me 'round the face."

He stopped talking for a few moments, shaking his head slowly.

"We'd both been drinking, and I lost my temper. I hit her back, and she threatened to have me arrested. Then she went for me again, and . . ." He sighed, and ran a hand across his forehead. "We fought. It was like some kind of surreal blur, and then . . . Then the next thing I knew, she was lying on the bed, not moving." He raised his eyes skyward, as if seeking forgiveness. "I couldn't believe it. I felt for her pulse, tried to revive her, but it was too late. She was gone." He looked imploringly at Tina.

Tina didn't believe Gore's version of events. He might not have meant to kill Róisin but, having seen his flashes of temper and the way he'd struck his wife, she was pretty certain he'd been the aggressor. However, she knew better than to interrupt a suspect when he was in full flow. "What happened then?" she asked gently.

"At first I didn't know what to do. I thought about calling the police, or an ambulance, but I panicked. Even though I hadn't meant to hurt Róisin, I was afraid that I'd be charged with murder. I know that was wrong, but at the time I wasn't thinking straight. I knew our affair had been kept secret, and I thought about simply leaving and hoping for the best, but I was worried I'd leave evidence behind. So I called a business contact, a man who I felt would be able to help me in my time of need."

Tina exchanged glances with Grier. She'd never had too many illusions about the integrity of the politicians who ran the country, and was aware that some of them were corrupt. Even so, hearing such an admission from a high-ranking minister shocked her.

"And this business contact, who was he?"

"His name's Paul Wise."

If she'd been shocked before, she was almost speechless now. Her head swam with the news that the man who'd done so much to ruin her life had also had a hand in this. It didn't seem possible, yet there was a grim logic to it. Wise had always been suspected of having high-level contacts within the establishment, which was one of the main reasons he'd never been brought to justice. But now there was a chance that he would be—a thought that suddenly filled Tina with a wild hope.

"And what did Wise say he'd do, Mr. Gore?" asked Grier, intervening so that Tina had a chance to recover herself.

"He said he'd take care of things. He told me to remain

where I was and that I'd hear from someone shortly. That person would identify himself as Alpha, and he would let me know what to do.

"The next half an hour was the longest and worst of my life. I had to stay in the apartment with Róisin's body while I waited for the call, wondering if I'd be discovered. But then, finally, it came. This man, Alpha, asked me a lot of questions: the address; which rooms I'd been in; the security arrangements for the building. He was very calm and businesslike and he covered everything. He told me to leave the address with Róisin's keys, lock the door, and put them under the front passenger-side wheel of the nearest car to the front door of the building. Then I was told to leave the rest to him and just forget it ever happened." Gore sighed. "I did what I was told. I wish to God I hadn't, but I did."

"Did you ever meet Alpha?" asked Tina.

He shook his head firmly. "No, and I didn't want to, either. Anyway, the next thing I knew, Róisin had been added to the list of the Night Creeper's victims."

Tina was suddenly aware how tense she was. She forced herself to sit back in the seat and relaxed her shoulders, resisting the urge for a cigarette. "You had access to the Night Creeper file in your role as Home Office minister, so you would have been able to check his MO easily enough. Are you claiming that you didn't tell Alpha what to do to make Róisin look like one of his victims?"

"I am, yes. You must believe me. I had nothing to do with any of the . . . mutilations Alpha may have carried out."

Tina and Grier exchanged glances once again. Grier looked skeptical. Tina felt the same. If Gore was telling the truth, it meant that Alpha must have had some kind of inside knowledge of the police investigation, which just wasn't possible. Gore might have been trying to paint himself as as much of an innocent as he could under the circumstances, but it wasn't a true picture. However, that was for a jury to decide.

"When did you find out that you were on film?" Tina asked him.

"When I received a phone call at my constituency office two weeks later. The caller identified himself to my secretary as Mr. Róisín, which is why I took the call. I knew it had to be something to do with what had happened, and I was terrified. As I've already told you, I thought our affair was a secret. And I had good reason to be. The caller told me that he had film footage of Róisín's death, and if I wanted it destroyed, I would have to pay him fifty thousand pounds. He made me give him my email address, and said he would send a sample clip, which he did." Gore shuddered visibly. "It showed everything."

"Did you keep it?" asked Grier.

He shook his head. "No, of course not. I destroyed it immediately."

A thought occurred to Tina. "And the clip didn't show Alpha performing the cover-up?"

"I don't know. I didn't watch it the whole way through. I couldn't."

Tina thought how surprised Andrew Kent must have been when he discovered film footage of a government minister killing his own intended victim. Blackmailing him was a dangerous move, but one that would have been hard to resist.

"At the time, of course, I had no idea who could have taken the footage," continued Gore, "but fifty thousand pounds is a lot of money, and I knew that if I paid it, the blackmailer would come back for more. So I called Paul

Wise. I had no choice. Again he was calm. He told me to arrange the delivery of the money, and that he would use Alpha to find out who the blackmailer was, get back the money, and make sure that I wasn't bothered again."

"By killing him?"

"I don't know. I didn't ask."

But Tina wasn't going to let him off the hook that easily. "It must have occurred to you that Wise and his fixer were going to kill him."

"I was terrified. I knew it could destroy my whole life, and more importantly, the lives of my family. I was desperate to make it go away." He paused for a moment, shaking his head. "But it all went wrong. The blackmailer set up the delivery of the money in Epping Forest, and he managed to get away with it without Alpha managing to identify or catch him.

"For a while, I didn't hear from him, and I hoped and prayed that he'd let it go, but then a couple of weeks ago he made contact again, demanding another fifty thousand pounds, or he'd release the footage to the media. I was mortified. It was hard enough to come up with the first demand. Contrary to popular belief, we politicians aren't all filthy rich. Thankfully, Mr. Wise came to my aid and supplied the money. We set up a second delivery of the money, this time on Hampstead Heath. Once again the blackmailer got away with the money, but this time Alpha managed to get enough information to ID him, and find out where he lived."

Tina frowned. "What day was this delivery made?"

"Monday last week."

Only days before the team had identified Kent and put him under twenty-four-hour surveillance.

"But Alpha never got to him, did he?"

"No. Mr. Wise told me that my blackmailer was the Night

Creeper, which was a shock. I wasn't expecting it. I thought it might be some ex-boyfriend who'd been stalking Róisin. Mr. Wise also told me the suspect was close to being arrested."

Tina heard Grier exhale as he too realized that Wise had someone within the police investigating team reporting back to him.

"Why was Kent kidnapped?" she asked Gore.

"I was terrified that once in custody he would say something, and that my secret would be exposed. I know Mr. Wise tried to deal with him while he was under surveillance, but that proved impossible. I last spoke to him yesterday evening, and he told me that everything was under control, that no evidence had been found linking me to Róisin's murder, and that he and Alpha had a contingency plan to silence Kent and recover the missing footage." He looked Tina in the eye. "That was the last I heard. I didn't want to be responsible for another death but I felt I had no choice."

"There's always a choice, Mr. Gore," said Grier, with uncharacteristic venom in his voice.

"Paul Wise certainly put himself out to help you," Tina added, feeling nothing but contempt for the man seated opposite her, but trying not to show it.

"I've helped him in the past."

"You know the crimes he's been involved in?"

"Allegedly."

This time her contempt boiled over. "Fuck allegedly. You know what he's done."

"By the time I heard the rumors, it was too late. He already owned me. He owns a lot of people." Gore sighed and looked at them both in turn. "Is there anything you can do to help me?"

Tina was amazed that after a confession like the one he'd

just given, he could possibly think he was going to wriggle out of his crimes, but perhaps that was simply the hubris of the powerful. "The fact that you're cooperating will count in your favor," she told him. "And if you're prepared to testify against Paul Wise, that'll also help. Will you do that?"

"If it helps matters, then yes, of course I will," he answered, giving her an earnest look.

"It will," she said.

Tina got to her feet and read him his rights, thinking that it was a strangely liberating feeling, arresting a government minister on suspicion of murder, and that it demonstrated the fact that no one, whoever they were, was above the law.

Including Paul Wise.

Gore didn't resist as Tina and Grier each took an arm and ushered him out of the study and into the hallway.

Which was when they saw Jane Gore standing facing them, still in her nightgown, holding a double-barrel shotgun in her hands.

"I'm not going to let you destroy our family," she said shakily, pointing it toward Tina.

Tina flinched but forced herself to remain calm. "Put the gun down, Mrs. Gore. Please."

She shook her head, an expression of worrying determination on her tear-stained face. "No."

And then she pulled the trigger.

Fifty

"What the hell happened?" I asked when Dougie MacLeod had finally recovered himself enough to talk.

I'd let him up, and he was standing. The tension was still coming off him in waves, but he looked calmer and his face was less puce, although a bruise was forming on his left cheek where I'd hit him.

"I got a call last night when I was in the pub. A man with a disguised voice told me they'd got Billy, and that unless I did exactly what they said, they'd kill him. I didn't believe him at first—I mean, Billy's away at university in Leeds, for Christ's sake—but he told me to wait by the phone, and they'd send me something that proved it." He paused, taking a deep breath, clearly trying to steady himself. "Five minutes later I got a photo from an unregistered pay-as-you-go showing Billy tied to a chair and gagged. It was him, Sean. It was him. If you don't believe me, check the PC upstairs. They've been sending me footage of him ever since."

"What do they want?"

"They wanted Andrew Kent. I was told to put some tablets in his drink, so that he'd get sick."

"Where did you get the tablets from?"

"They were in an envelope under the wheel of a car on John Street."

So the client, or someone close to him, had been in the vicinity when I was in the pub.

"Believe me, I didn't want to do it. But it was him or Billy."

This was one of the things that didn't make sense to me. If the client had wanted Kent dead, then why not just use some strong poison and kill him outright, rather than whatever it was that Dougie had slipped into his drink, which hadn't even made him that sick? It was yet another unanswered question.

I looked around. "Well, you did what you were told. So why haven't they freed Billy?"

"Because the kidnapper phoned back and said I'd be needed for something else, and to wait by the phone. Then at about midnight I got another call. I was told to get into the evidence room at the station and check through Kent's possessions. Among them was a mini Swiss Army knife, only about an inch and a half long, attached to his key ring. The knife had a USB stick inside it, which the custody sergeant who booked him in must have missed. The kidnapper wanted the stick."

"And where's it now?"

"I was told to put it in an envelope and drop it in a Dumpster on an estate in King's Cross."

"Did you get a chance to take a look at what was on it first?"

He shook his head. "No. These people are professional criminals. They told me that if I did they'd kill Billy, and I couldn't take the chance. I followed their instructions to the letter and came straight back here. I was told that I'd get a call as soon as the stick had been collected safely, and then

I'd receive instructions about where to go to collect Billy. I dropped the bloody thing off hours ago and I still haven't heard from them. When I heard you moving around downstairs I didn't know what to think, so I came down here with the gun. I've had the thing for years, since my army days." He sighed. "What the hell am I going to do, Sean? He's my son. Since Marion's gone, he's all I've bloody got left." His face cracked with the tension and he took another deep breath, trying to steady himself.

I put a tentative hand on his arm. "Look, you've done what they ordered. There's no reason to hurt him."

"He might have seen their faces," he answered, moving away from my touch. "They could easily kill him. You know that as well as I do." He turned his back on me and started to pace the room. "You said you knew something about the Kent case. What is it?"

I told him exactly what had happened, starting with my infiltration of the Wolfe gang, and finishing with Dougie himself disturbing me in his lounge. "Kent must have been kidnapped because of whatever he had on that USB stick. But I still don't understand why he was free when I went down the cellar to find him. He could easily have escaped."

Dougie stopped and gave a frustrated shake of his head. "And now he's dead, so he can't help us."

"And so's everyone else involved in his abduction. Except the person who set the fire back at the rendezvous. But I've got no idea who he is, and I'm completely out of leads." I was feeling the frustration now myself. "Someone's set both of us up completely and neither of us has got a bloody clue who it is."

We stood there staring at each other for a few minutes, each of us lost in his own private thoughts, me still holding

Dougie's old army revolver, knowing that you couldn't fake the fear he was exhibiting.

And then we both heard it at the same time. A loud, incessant ringing. Coming from the pocket of Dougie's jeans. He pulled out his mobile and thrust it to his ear.

He didn't speak. Just listened. After a few seconds he rushed into the kitchen and wrote down some instructions on an open pad on the sideboard. Then he ran back into the lounge and put the phone back in his pocket.

"That was the kidnapper," he said quietly. "He's told me where to go to collect Billy. And he's told me to come alone."

Fifty-one

The sound of the shotgun blast was deafening, and for a second Tina thought she'd been hit. She was knocked backward, letting go of Gore's arm in the process, and as she landed on the carpet she saw Gore fly past her and crash through the open study door. Grier, meanwhile, was leaning back against the staircase, looking dazed. Smoke billowed through the air leaving a bitter stink in its wake, and as it cleared, Tina saw Jane Gore place the barrels of the shotgun underneath her own chin, her face a mask of bitter emotion.

Tina only had time to shout her name before Jane Gore pulled the trigger for a second time, blowing the top of her own head off in a cloud of smoke and blood spray. She remained standing perfectly upright for a long moment, then crumpled to the floor like a stringless marionette.

For several seconds, the house was silent. Neither Tina nor Grier moved, as the shock of what had just happened seeped in. Tina had been in situations where firearms had been discharged before. She'd been on the receiving end of them twice, remembered the pain all too well, but she'd never been able to get used to the speed with which they could snuff out a life.

Finally, she clambered to her feet. Mrs. Gore was beyond

help. Half her head was missing. But Tina wasn't sure of the severity of her husband's injuries, and they badly needed him alive, so she rushed into the study, already reaching for her mobile to call an ambulance.

But as soon as she saw him, she knew it was too late. Gore lay on his back in the middle of the floor, his eyes closed. Shotgun injuries at close range are usually far more serious than gunshot wounds as the shotgun pellets don't have the chance to disperse, and this was no exception. There was a huge, uneven hole in his chest, exposing internal organs, including his heart, which didn't appear to be beating.

"Oh Jesus," she whispered, frantically feeling for a pulse. She thought she found something faint, but even as she tried to measure it, it disappeared. "Come on, come on," she whispered, but there was nothing there. Nothing at all. Gore was dead, as was her chance of finally bringing Wise to justice.

She stood up and called the ambulance, telling the operator to hurry even though she knew it was too late, before walking back into the hallway, feeling shaky on her feet.

Grier was beside Mrs. Gore. As Tina approached him, he rose, shaking his head, blood on his clean shirt, and his hands too. "She's gone," he said, his face pale.

Tina steadied herself against the wall. "And so are our chances of getting Wise, because Gore is too."

A wave of nausea washed over her, and she staggered past Grier and the ruined body of Mrs. Gore, flung the door open, and gulped in the fresh early-morning air. The street was empty. There weren't even any curtains twitching. It was as if the terrible events that had just occurred had passed everyone else by.

The nausea subsided and Tina stood in the sunlight for a good minute, taking deep breaths. A milk truck passed by, the milkman giving her an odd look, and she suddenly wished she could have a job like that, where you never had to deal with the dregs of society, and see so clearly its open, gaping wounds, or the evil that seeped through it from the top all the way down to the gutter.

Her mobile was ringing. She pulled it from her jeans, and checked the number. Mike Bolt. She felt a sudden relief. If there was one person she could deal with speaking to now, it was him.

"Are you OK, Tina?" he asked when she answered.

"No," she replied, her voice cracking, and she told him what had just happened.

"And he's definitely dead?"

"They both are. It was a murder-suicide."

He exhaled, and didn't speak for a few seconds. "Well, the shit's going to hit the fan now," he said at last. "Make sure you've got a Federation representative present when they interview you, because this is going to be a major scandal, and they're going to be looking for scapegoats."

"I was just doing my job, Mike," Tina protested, knowing how defensive she sounded, but angry that she was so close to solving a major crime, and was now going to be held responsible for the death of a killer.

"I know that. You know that. But that may well not be enough. You've got too much of a habit of getting involved in messy cases, and that's going to make you vulnerable to accusations that you provoked things. Maybe even more."

"I recorded our interview with Gore, so his confession's on the record, but I'd stopped it before the shooting. Do you think it's going to be enough to go after Wise?"

Bolt sighed. "I don't know, but I'd hide the recording somewhere safe, because a case like this, involving a high-ranking government minister, is ripe for a cover-up. No one in the corridors of power's going to want a scandal this size out in the public domain."

Tina knew he was right, and that it was going to be hard for her to talk her way out of this one, even with the taped confession and Grier as a witness. "There are other people still involved. The fixer, Alpha, for one. If we can find him . . ."

"Well, I might be able to help you there. That license plate of the car you were asking about . . ."

"The one that was caught on CCTV on Kevin O'Neill's road just before he died?"

"That's the one. It's been picked up on the ANPR. I just got a call from Hendon. It's currently in central London, and they're keeping tabs on it for me."

"Can you get someone to arrest the occupants?"

"On what charges? It's hard enough getting the ANPR people to agree to follow it."

Tina looked at her watch. It was only half past seven, although it felt much later. "Can you keep me posted on where it goes?"

"Sure, but there's not going to be a lot you can do about it now, is there? The local CID are going to want to keep you at the crime scene until they get a statement."

"Let me worry about that," said Tina, and hung up. There was no way she was going to let the occupants of this car slip through her fingers.

Fifty-two

"I still think it's risky you coming, Sean," said Dougie MacLeod as he drove down the Marylebone Road in the direction of King's Cross, and the abandoned building just east of the station where he was supposed to pick up his son. "If you get spotted with me, it'll put Billy in danger, and I can't risk that."

I was sitting next to him in the passenger seat, resting the revolver I'd taken from him earlier on my lap, with the barrel pointed in his direction. It wasn't that I didn't trust Dougie. I knew he wasn't involved in this—at least not of his own free will—but I was worried he might do something stupid, like try to get rid of me.

"I won't get spotted," I assured him. "All you have to do is tell me when we're about to pass the rendezvous, I'll get down in the seat so no one sees me, and then you can park a bit further up, out of sight. You go in alone, and I'll provide back-up. That's all."

"I don't need back-up."

"Bullshit. You've got to ask yourself, why are they telling you to go to an abandoned building on the wrong side of King's Cross first thing on a Saturday morning when there's no one else around? And what did they tell you to do? Go up to the third floor as well, so you're out of sight of anyone.

Why make you do that? If they're that serious about releasing Billy, why don't they just untie him and let him walk out of there? It can't be that hard."

"What are you saying, Sean? That they're planning to kill both of us?"

I had to be careful here. Dougie looked bad enough as it was—his face flushed, his thinning gray hair plastered to his scalp with sweat—without me planting the seed of his only son's death. "No, I'm not saying that."

"Because you saw the footage on my PC. Billy's alive."

Which was true. At least he had been half an hour earlier when I saw the images of him strapped to a chair with a gag over his mouth, in an empty room, his eyes wide with fear and confusion, just as Andrew Kent's had been. They could have been faked, of course, but my guess was that they hadn't been. However, this still didn't mean they planned to release him.

"I'm going to watch you go in, make sure there's no one following you, then if it's safe, and there's no one watching out the window, I'll tail you up to the third floor, just to make sure it all goes smoothly."

"If you mess things up for me or Billy . . ."

"I won't. I know how to handle myself. And I've been on plenty of surveillance ops so I know how to stay anonymous."

He turned to me suddenly, his eyes full of anguish. "Why are you doing this, Sean?"

"Because I want you to stay alive. And I want to find the bastard who set this whole thing up because he's got one hell of a lot of blood on his hands. Plus he tried to kill me. That's why." I also thought there was a good chance he was responsible for my brother's death, though I didn't say this to Dougie.

We passed the almost deserted frontage of King's Cross

station, and Dougie took a left onto York Way, heading north in the direction of Kentish Town. About a quarter of a mile up he took a right, then an immediate left, and I noticed that his breathing was becoming hoarse.

"OK, it's up here. Get down in the seat."

I did as I was told, watching from my new, cramped position as we passed by a number of grimy-looking industrial units.

"It's this place," he hissed, keeping his eyes fixed straight ahead as a half-finished shell of a building, five or six stories high, loomed up above a high strip of chainlink fencing.

He continued driving for another two minutes before taking another right turn, and parking on a backstreet. He took a series of deep breaths, psyching himself up for what was going to be the most difficult few minutes of his life. I knew he'd be asking himself if Billy was still alive, knowing that one way or another he was going to be getting an answer.

"I need the gun, Sean," he said, putting out a hand.

"When was the last time you fired a gun, Dougie? It's twenty-five years since you were in the army. I'm trained, and my training's up to date. It'll be best if I keep it."

"No. This is my son we're talking about. I need that gun." He leaned forward and looked me right in the eye. "You owe me, Sean. From a long time back."

And he was right, I did. I would have far preferred to keep it, because I knew how to use the damn thing, but I had no choice. So I placed the gun in his outstretched hand and watched as he put it down the back of his jeans, out of sight.

"Be careful," I told him, wondering if I was letting him walk right into a trap, and knowing that if I was, there was nothing I could do about it.

"Thanks. I will." He took another deep breath, and ran a

hand through his hair. "I appreciate you want to help, Sean, but I don't want to see you come in behind me. In fact, I don't want to see you at all. At least not until afterward." He opened the driver's side door. "Count to a hundred before you follow me." And with that he was gone.

I didn't quite make a hundred but I gave him a good minute before getting out and starting off down the road back in the direction we'd come. The houses around me were silent, the traffic minimal, even though a watery sun was already rising well into the azure sky. It was going to be a beautiful day.

For some people, anyway.

The road crossed over the canal at Regent's Wharf. Barges dotted the waterside, and I remembered vaguely walking here with a girlfriend years ago, one glorious summer's afternoon, not long after I'd joined the police. Her name was Davina and for a few months at least we'd been serious. Then things had ground to a halt and she'd disappeared, like everyone else in my life seemed to do. I straightened my shoulders. If I got through today, I was going to sort myself out, find myself a girlfriend, and settle down. Maybe even start a family. I was sick of spending my life alone.

The rendezvous rose up on my left against the skyline, a concrete shell that dominated the deserted building site around it. A sign on the fence proudly announced, "Brand New Luxury Apartments for Waterside Living, Coming in 2010," although I figured they were going to have to buck up their ideas to get the place ready by then.

I forced myself to slow down. Dougie had disappeared, but I wanted to make sure that if there was someone in the building watching to see whether he'd been followed, they'd be gone now.

The main gate to the building site was slightly open, the

heavy-duty padlock on it cut. I pushed my way inside, moving slowly along the rutted track that led up to the building's main doorway, keeping close to the abandoned machinery on either side of it as I watched for, but failed to see, any sign of movement on the upper floors.

When I reached the doorway, I paused for a second before creeping inside, conscious that without the gun I was utterly defenseless if something did go down. Moving through the gloom, I came to a flight of concrete steps that led upstairs. I looked up and listened. Dougie could only have come in here a maximum of two minutes ago, but there were no sounds of a joyful reunion between father and son. Just an ominous silence. I thought of him somewhere in here alone, a sitting duck, and I knew I was going to have to be so careful not to mess this up. I'd made far too many mistakes in the past twenty-four hours.

I crept up the steps to the first level. To my left, a doorway led through to a cavernous, empty room that stretched all the way to the other side of the building. Nothing moved, and the air smelled of brick dust and the beginnings of decay. This place must have been one of the many luxury urban living developments the moneymen had stopped building mid-brick when the property crash appeared out of the blue like a financial tsunami. Now, unfinished and neglected, it looked like a multi-story parking garage, but without the places to hide.

I carried on climbing, moving with exaggerated care, every sense attuned to my surroundings.

And then, just as I reached the second level, I heard it. A small cry, followed by a shuffling movement coming from further up. That was followed by what sounded like a grunt of exertion.

Then nothing.

It sounded like Dougie, but I couldn't be sure.

I stopped, trying to quieten my breathing as it quickened in the gloom.

Then I heard the sound of someone else moving about, their actions unhurried, which meant it couldn't be Dougie. He'd been so stressed as to be incapable of casual movement.

I tensed, knowing that if this was Alpha I was taking a big risk carrying on up the stairs when I was unarmed, but even so, I hesitated only a couple of seconds before continuing.

The movement was coming from beyond the third-level doorway. It sounded as though whoever it was was trying to move something.

I was at the top of the stairs now, only a dividing wall separating us.

Slowly, very slowly, I peered around, and gritted my teeth when I saw Dougie's son, Billy, tied to the same chair I'd seen in the images on Dougie's computer. He was about fifteen feet inside the vast, empty room. His head was slumped forward, the back of it a bloody mess, and he wasn't moving.

Dougie, meanwhile, lay on the floor. At least I thought it was him, but from the angle I had I could only see a pair of twitching jeans-clad legs. Nor could I see any sign of his gun.

So I'd been right. This ruthless bastard, Alpha, had never had any intention of releasing Billy, or letting Dougie leave here alive. I fought down the mixture of shock and rage that rose up inside me and remained silent and focused, angry at myself for not coming up sooner, but fully prepared now to take a bloody revenge for the murder of two innocent men, one of whom had been my friend.

I inched around a little more and saw Dougie's revolver

lying beside his body, barely five feet away. If I could just grab hold of it . . .

And then a man came into view, wielding a pistol with a cigar-shaped silencer attached.

And this time I couldn't contain my shock.

Fifty-three

He didn't see me. He wasn't even looking my way as he walked over to the chair containing Billy's corpse and crouched down beside it to pick up an empty shell casing, his back to me.

I had one chance, and I seized it.

Taking two swift but near-silent steps across the floor, I scooped up Dougie's revolver and pointed it straight at his back. "Drop the gun."

Tommy stopped, then turned slowly in my direction, and I saw that the cut on his brow that he'd had in the cellar the previous night was now bandaged.

"I said drop it. Otherwise I'll shoot you dead. Right here. Right now."

We stood facing each other. He held the gun down by his side, and there was an expression of vague amusement on his face. "Well, well, well. I didn't expect to see you here. You look like you've seen a ghost."

"I'm only going to say it one more time," I stated calmly. "Then I'm going to shoot you."

"You won't. I could tell right from the minute I met you that you were no killer."

But he was wrong. I was now. I cocked the revolver and pointed it right between his eyes, holding it perfectly steady.

"One thing you ought to know about me. I've been trained how to use a gun, and I've had a lot of practice. I shot three people yesterday. And the one I meant to kill is dead. Now, I'm going to count to three. If you're still holding that thing then, it'll be the last thing you ever hold. Your choice."

There was still a glint of amusement in his eyes, but this time he cooperated, placing his weapon carefully on the floor.

"Put your hands in the air."

He did as he was told. "So, what are you going to do now? Put a bullet in my head while I stand here defenseless?"

"You deserve it, Tommy."

"I'm just doing my job."

"On behalf of who exactly? Who is it who wants that USB stick Dougie MacLeod delivered? And what's on it?"

"You're well informed, Sean. I'll give you that. And you know how to get out of a sticky situation too. I misjudged you last night. I didn't think you'd be capable of getting out of that burning building like that." He whistled with admiration. "I have to say, I was impressed."

"I'm still waiting for answers, Tommy," I said, tensing my finger on the trigger. "Don't make me impatient."

He shook his head. "I'm walking out of here, Sean, and I suggest you do the same. There's nothing you can do for your friends here, and you're as deep in all this shit as I am."

I moved the gun down so it was pointed at his knee. "I might find it difficult to kill you in cold blood, but I'm sure I could stretch to blowing a hole in your kneecap, especially as you've just murdered my old boss and his son."

He frowned, giving me a disbelieving look. "You're a cop? No way. I had you checked out. Thoroughly."

"Not thoroughly enough."

"So why did you shoot those two gun dealers yesterday? And hold up a police van at gunpoint? What sort of cop does that?"

It was a good question, but one I wasn't prepared to answer. "I'm the one holding the gun, Tommy, so I'm the one asking the questions. Who are you working for?"

"A man called Alpha. I don't know his real name."

"I thought he was Wolfe's client."

Tommy's look was contemptuous. "Tyrone Wolfe liked to think he was the big leader but he never ran shit. He just thought he did. He traded on the fact that he was this big armed robber and thug, but he was no organizer. And nor was that idiot Haddock. Wolfe might have thought Alpha was his client, and I was happy to let him believe it, but it was me Alpha approached to organize the Kent snatch."

"Why was he snatched?"

"Because he'd filmed something very sensitive—don't ask me what it was, I didn't ask—and Alpha needed to make sure all copies of the film were destroyed. He also wanted to make sure that there was no way the job could ever come back to him. That's why he wanted Wolfe and Haddock got rid of afterward. He thought they might blab."

"So, you killed your own friends."

"There was no love lost between us. They were always treating me like a junior, even though it was me who brought in most of the money. No, I was happy to get rid of them."

"And me as well?"

He smiled ruefully. "Sorry, Sean, that was just business. I always liked you."

"But last night when I found you in the cellar, you were bleeding . . . I thought you were dead. Was that all fake as well?"

He shook his head. "No, it wasn't. That slippery toerag Kent got free. While you were locked away, and Ty was off burying the guns, I got rid of Haddock, then went down to the cellar to find out what Kent had done with that film he was meant to have taken. As soon as I showed him the hammer and knife I was going to use on him, he started blabbing. He told me he'd only kept one copy, and that was on a USB stick that was attached to a bunch of keys he'd had on him when he was nicked. Fancy that, eh? It was in some store cupboard in the cop shop and no one had spotted it.

"Anyway, when I went over with a knife to finish Kent off—nice and quiet because I didn't want anyone hearing—I got a bit of a shock. The bastard wasn't as well taped to the chair as I'd thought. He'd managed to get an arm free, and as I bent down he lashed out and got it out of my hand. Just like that. He was so damn quick, by the time I knew what was happening he was out of the chair and on me. He would have killed me too, if it hadn't been for you turning up."

"So I saved your neck."

"Yeah," he said with a small smile. "You did."

"You didn't have to kill these two," I said, motioning toward Dougie and Billy, and feeling the anger build in me.

"I couldn't risk letting either of them go. The kid had seen me, and it wouldn't have taken the cops long to realize that the old man was the one who'd lifted the stick from the station and put stuff in Kent's drink in the cells. He was a loose end."

I swallowed hard. Dougie had been a good man and he'd done a lot for me over the years. I wasn't going to allow Tommy to get away with this.

"Where is the stick?"

"I destroyed it."

"And you didn't even want to know what was on it? I don't believe you, Tommy. I think you do."

"I'm a pro, Sean. I don't ask questions that don't concern me. Neither should you. That way you'll stay alive and live to a ripe old age. Now, I'm walking out of here, and I suggest you do too."

He took a step forward, his bearing confident.

"Stay where you are," I snapped, thinking of Tommy's brutal callousness, working myself up into the kind of rage that would allow me to pull the trigger and rid the world of him.

He dived into me fast, like a cat, knocking the revolver to one side and driving me back into the wall. The gun went off with a deafening retort, the bullet ricocheting uselessly through the room.

I felt a sharp stabbing pain in my ribs but I kept hold of the gun and dodged the headbutt he launched as a follow-up. His forehead bounced off my shoulder and caught the edge of the brickwork with an angry crack. Seizing my chance, I delivered two short rabbit punches to his kidneys, and twisted away from him.

He tried to hold on and we did a manic pirouette across the floor, struggling savagely with each other. As he concentrated on trying to get me to release my grip on the gun by twisting my wrist, I slipped a foot behind his and pushed with everything I had.

He stumbled and lost his footing completely, letting go of my gun hand as he danced backward across the floor, arms flailing in a vain effort to keep his balance. A desperate look crossed his face as I turned the gun in his direction. Behind him, I could see Dougie's corpse, the blood pooling around his head, and Billy lying motionless in the chair, and this time I didn't hesitate.

Tommy's mouth formed a screaming "No!" but any sound that passed his lips was drowned out by the noise of the bullets leaving the barrel as I pulled three times in rapid succession, watching as he was propelled across the room before landing in a flurry of arms and legs on top of Dougie, and lying still.

I stood for a good ten seconds surveying the bloody scene in front of me. Three more dead bodies to add to those from the previous night, and all for the sake of a piece of film that Andrew Kent had made. I knew now that I would never learn who'd wanted it so badly, but I was just going to have to accept that and move on. I needed to leave now. Even this early on a Saturday morning it was likely someone had heard the shots and would be calling the police.

But as I turned and headed for the door, the sound of movement made me stop dead.

Then a mocking voice spoke from behind me.

"Bad move, Seany boy."

I heard a series of popping sounds above the ringing in my ears, and then suddenly the revolver fell from my hands and I was pitched forward, colliding with the wall, before crumpling uselessly to the floor, my arms and legs no longer doing what they were meant to do. My vision blurred, and almost immediately I felt myself becoming terribly cold and shaky. I could feel the blood dripping down my stomach and leg, sticking to my clothes.

Slowly, I inclined my head and saw Tommy getting to his feet and brushing himself down, the pistol with silencer now back in his hand. The striped shirt he was wearing had big black holes in it where I'd shot him, yet he seemed to look none the worse for wear. I wondered if my eyes were playing tricks on me.

Seeing the expression on my face, Tommy tapped his shirt. "Bulletproof vest, Sean. Always useful in our line. I thought you'd have known that."

"My brother . . ."

"What?"

I took a breath, forcing the words out. "My brother, John . . . the one shot during that robbery in Highgate High Street. 1995. The Gulf War veteran. The one Wolfe was bragging about."

Tommy frowned. "He was your brother? Are you serious?"

"Wolfe said he never killed him. I asked him just before he died. You were there, Tommy. Who pulled the trigger?"

"Sorry, mate," he answered, not sounding sorry at all, "that would have been me. He just got in the way, you know?" He took a step forward, pointing the gun down at me. "Just like you."

That was when I slumped onto my side like a dying man, and with my last vestiges of strength grabbed the revolver from where it lay on the floor only a couple of feet away and swung it around in Tommy's direction, my finger already tensing on the trigger, unsure how many bullets I'd used, not caring because this was my final chance to avenge the brother I hadn't seen in fifteen years, since Tommy had ended his life on a street corner as if he was nothing, just an inconvenience, when in reality he was the most important person in my life.

I heard the silencer's champagne pop just before I pulled the trigger, and the room once again exploded in noise.

Fifty-four

"As far as the operator can see, the car hasn't moved for the past twenty minutes," said Bolt over the hands-free as Tina drove past King's Cross station. "So it's almost certainly going to be somewhere in the rough square between Pentonville Road, Caledonian Road, York Way, and Copenhagen Street."

"Thanks, Mike."

"Tell me you're not doing this alone, Tina. Aren't you meant to be giving a statement about what just happened at the Gore residence?"

"It's going to have to wait. I've got to find this car. I'm sure it belongs to the fixer."

"But you don't know that," said Bolt, sounding more worried than ever. "It might have nothing to do with it. You could be making a terrible mistake."

"I need leads," she snapped back, "and at the moment this is the only one I've got."

"Tina, you're going to be in real shit for this. They're going to have your warrant card and everything. You can't just go chasing round after leads when you're a witness, and maybe even a bloody suspect, in the murder of a government minister. You can't get so bloody obsessed."

Tina gritted her teeth. She knew all this. Knew that her

job was on the line. Yet there was nothing she could do to stop herself. She was too close to give up now. "Thanks for the help, Mike," she said. "I owe you one." And she hung up.

She ran a hand through her hair, trying to focus on the task at hand, knowing that when the local CID found out that she'd disappeared, they'd go berserk, which was why she hadn't brought Grier with her. After she'd organized the first uniforms on the scene and the ambulances, she'd told him to keep an eye on things, saying there was something she needed to do, and she'd be back shortly. Grier had demanded to know where she was going, and when no answer was forthcoming he'd asked to go with her, actually stating that he thought they were a team. But she'd got him in enough trouble already, and told him firmly, as his boss, to stay put. "It might be the last order I ever give you," she'd said. "So take notice of it."

She took the turning into York Way, then the first right into Caledonian Road, zigzagging her way through the back roads, desperately trying to hunt down a car she only had the most basic description of. She hadn't even had time to look at a photo. It was as if she couldn't even stop to think things through anymore. She simply had to keep moving, keep chasing leads, keep running, because the moment she stopped, that would be it. She'd be suspended, then fired, and the fixer, Alpha, would continue to walk free, as would Paul Wise, the man she now realized she'd do anything to bring down.

Mike was right. She was obsessed. Maybe even deranged. But she got results. It was she who'd come up with the lead that caught Kent; she who'd spotted the discrepancies in the Róisin O'Neill murder; she who'd found Gore. The bastards couldn't take that away from her.

Five minutes passed. She became frustrated. Unsure of

herself and her lead, knowing that every minute she stayed away from the Gore residence was another nail in her career coffin, the realization that she was finally finished as a police officer looming larger and larger in front of her.

She noticed that her hands were shaking, her breathing getting faster and faster, and she pulled over and got out of the car, lighting a cigarette and willing herself to calm down.

And that was when she heard it. Coming from the building site behind her.

The unmistakable sound of gunfire.

Fifty-five

There was no pain, just a thick, dull sense of shock. A numbness, from my thighs to my chest. I'd been hit twice that I could see, both times in the initial burst of fire. One round had struck me in the thigh, the second in the gut. The thigh wound was bleeding less which told me that it hadn't severed any of the major blood vessels, and there was an exit wound just above the back of my knee. The gut wound, though, was bad, the exit wound the size of a golf ball, and spilling a lot of blood onto the dusty concrete.

I'd managed to prop myself up against the wall and, amazingly, still had hold of the gun. Opposite me across the room, lying on his belly, was Tommy. I'd caught him in the face or head with my last shot, I wasn't entirely sure which, whereas he'd missed me with his, so we were even now. For a while he'd made weird rasping noises, coupled with low moans of pain, and had even tried and failed to get up, but he'd stopped moving completely now, and I could no longer hear his breathing.

So there I was, trapped in this cavernous hellhole that would very likely become my grave. I couldn't move properly and no one would have been able to hear my cries even if I'd had the strength to make them. There were no sirens, so it seemed no one had even heard the gunshots.

I had a terrible thirst and I was shivering like a wet dog, but incredibly I wasn't panicking. I was too exhausted for that, and, even after everything that had happened, I felt this weird sense of achievement. I'd gone out alone to avenge my brother's murder, and I'd managed it. The gang responsible for leaving him dead on that street were now dead themselves, and by ridding the world of Andrew Kent I felt I'd done humanity a favor. And if it was my parting gift, then so be it.

But as I sat there, wounded and helpless, wondering how I'd got myself into this terrible tomb-like place, I could hear death's steady, inevitable approach and knew there was no escape. That was the hardest thing to accept, the fact that my life was finally coming to an end, and I wondered briefly in those last few seconds, as the pain and the shock squeezed at my insides, whether there was anyone left to mourn my passing. Whether I'd even be remembered in ten years' time.

Then I heard it. A sound directly outside the door. The scrape of a foot on the floor.

Jesus. Was this nightmare still not over? Was there a final act to come?

I clenched my teeth and slowly raised my gun arm, just as a dark-haired woman in casual clothes appeared in the doorway, a warrant card in one outstretched hand and what looked like a can of pepper spray in the other.

"Police!" she shouted. And then, as she took in the chaotic scene before her and her eyes alighted on me, "Sean?"

"Hello, Tina."

"What the hell's happened?"

Which was the moment when, out of the corner of my eye, I saw Tommy lurch upward from his position, the pistol in his hand, his face and neck a mask of blood, and start shooting, his bullets pinging angrily round the room.

With a yelp of fear, Tina leaped out of the way, hitting the deck with a thud as she tried to belly-crawl out of the door.

Tommy swung the gun around in my direction, while I took aim, concentrating all my efforts on keeping my gun hand steady, knowing that I had only one bullet left and this time I had to finish the bastard, and allow my brother finally to rest in peace.

He fired first, but missed, the round chipping the wall beside my shoulder before ricocheting away in a cloud of brick dust. He fired again, but this time nothing happened. He'd run out of bullets, and I saw his eyes widen as he realized he'd failed.

And then I pulled the trigger and blew the top of his head off.

Fifty-six

Tina leaned against the bonnet of the rental car and lit a cigarette with shaking hands as another of the ambulances drove out of the building site through the open gates with an angry wail of sirens. Squad cars and SOCO vehicles were turning up at the scene in numbers now, and a perimeter had already been set up at both ends of the street, behind which the first of the onlookers had gathered.

She took a long drag, feeling completely detached from all the activity going on, as if none of it had anything to do with her. She'd seen three people die in front of her that morning, and had only narrowly missed being the fourth victim herself. It was the third time in her life she'd been shot at, yet she felt as if on this occasion she'd come the closest to death. She'd actually felt the warm draft of air as a bullet whistled past her ear. Six inches to one side and it would have killed her. Just like that. Alive and functioning one second, gone forever the next.

She couldn't keep risking her neck like this. It had been utter madness running into an abandoned building alone and unarmed, trying to locate the source of gunshots, yet she hadn't been able to stop herself. It was as if, deep down, she had some kind of death wish, and if it hadn't been for Egan killing the shooter with what turned out to be his last bullet, she would surely never have made it out of there alive. She wasn't sure how serious Egan's injuries were, but he'd been in a bad way when the ambulance had arrived a few minutes earlier. She'd held his hand the whole time as he'd slipped in and out of consciousness, thanking him for what he'd done, but she wasn't sure that he'd really heard her. She'd make sure she thanked him properly in person as soon as he was well enough. She also needed to find out from him what had happened in there, whether the man he'd shot had been the fixer, and what part her boss, Dougie MacLeod, had played in all this. When she'd seen MacLeod lying there dead on the floor she'd felt a pang of terrible sadness. He'd been a good man to her, but she couldn't help wondering whether he'd been involved in this whole thing. There were still a lot of questions, but before she went looking for the answers, she had her work cut out trying to save her career.

A car pulled up at the edge of the perimeter, and two men got out from the rear passenger seats. One of them was Dan Grier, but it took a couple of seconds to identify the shorter, older man with him as DCS Frank Mendelson, the famously pugnacious head of Homicide and Serious Crime Command, and Tina's ultimate boss.

Mendelson seemed to zone in on her straight away, and he marched over, his face like thunder, with Grier slowly bringing up the rear, dragging his heels like a naughty schoolboy.

"What the hell do you think you're doing?" he demanded, stopping in front of her, his eyes blazing with a barely suppressed rage.

"Solving a murder," she told him calmly, meeting his gaze.

"Well, you haven't solved it, have you? All we appear to have is a string of dead bodies, and you nowhere to be seen whenever you're needed. You're a witness to the murder of a government minister, for God's sake! You can't just leave the crime scene." He shook his head angrily. "The Met can't afford to have unstable mavericks on board, and that's exactly what you are."

Tina felt like reminding him that was not what he'd said when she joined Dougie MacLeod's CMIT. Then, he'd called her the type of go-getting officer the Met sorely needed. But she didn't bother, preferring to let him talk until he wore himself out, while trying to avoid looking at Grier, who stood further back staring at the ground.

"That's why I'm suspending you until further notice," continued Mendelson. "You're also required to go immediately to Notting Hill police station where you're to give a statement to CID about what happened at Anthony Gore's home. I understand you recorded his confession." He put undue emphasis on this last word, his tone skeptical, as if he thought there was something inherently false about it. "If that's the case, I need to have the tape now." He put out a hand.

"You're mistaken," she said, without looking at Grier. "There's no tape."

"Are you sure?" He frowned, then looked back over his shoulder. "DC Grier, I thought you said DI Boyd made a tape of your interview with Mr. Gore?"

"I said I wasn't sure, sir," he answered. "I thought she might have, but if she says she didn't . . ."

Mendelson didn't look convinced. "If you're lying to me . . ." he growled at Tina.

"I'm not."

"I could have you searched, you know. I'd be quite within my rights under the circumstances."

She gave him a look of utter contempt. "Go on, then."

"I don't like your attitude, Miss Boyd."

"I couldn't give a shit, Mr. Mendelson."

The DCS's face grew so red she thought he might explode. He was literally shaking with anger. Finally, he seemed to bring himself under control. "You're finished," he said at last, a thin smile forming on his lips. "I'll make sure of it."

"Fuck you," she answered, but her words were drowned out by the siren from another ambulance as it left the building site, and anyway, Mendelson had already turned on his heel and was marching away.

She watched him go, then stubbed the cigarette underfoot and, leaving the rental car where it was, walked off in the opposite direction without looking back, feeling a strange yet exhilarating sense of freedom.

PART III

Nine Days Later

Fifty-seven

Tina Boyd was surprised to see how healthy Sean Egan looked, given all he'd been through. He was propped up in his bed reading a book when she knocked and walked into his private hospital room, carrying a box of chocolates and a bottle of decent Scotch she'd picked up en route. She'd wanted to come before but for the first week of his stay he'd been effectively in police custody, and under armed guard, with visits strictly limited.

He grinned when he saw her and put down the book. "So, to what do I owe this pleasure?"

"I came to say thanks for saving my life," she said, putting the chocolates and booze on his bedside table, and taking a seat.

"Tommy wasn't much of a shot. I think you'd have been OK."

"He managed to hit you twice."

"He just got lucky," he said, giving her a weary smile. "Anyway, if you hadn't turned up, I'd have bled to death, so I guess we're quits. Maybe we should share the bottle."

Tina had deliberately chosen Scotch because she disliked it. "No, you keep it for when you're feeling better."

"Fair enough," he said, "but at least tell me how you ended up in that building at eight o'clock on a Saturday morning. I've been answering a lot of questions these past few days, but no one's been giving me any information."

"It's a long story."

"Long stories are what keep me going in this place."

So she told him everything.

"Jesus," he said when she'd finished. "After all you did, and they end up suspending you?"

"I didn't follow the rules, and they don't like that these days."

He laughed. "I know the feeling. And if it's any consolation, I've been suspended as well. But at the moment I'm just thankful I haven't been charged with anything."

"I think there'd have been a public outcry if they'd charged you with anything. You've read the papers. You must have seen the coverage you've been getting. The *Sun*'s even nicknamed you Robocop."

Not surprisingly, there'd been a media frenzy over the kidnapping of Andrew Kent and the revelations surrounding Anthony Gore and his connection to it, and the story had rarely been off the front pages. With the stock of mainstream politicians at one of its lowest ebbs in history thanks to the ongoing expenses scandal, the allegations of murder weren't considered as unbelievable as they might otherwise have been. In fact, they were treated as still more evidence of the corrupt nature of the ruling classes, who it now seemed were capable of almost anything.

Most people—if you believed the tabloid headlines, at least—thought that both Andrew Kent and Anthony Gore had got what they deserved, and although the full extent of Gore's involvement wasn't yet public knowledge, there was a groundswell of support for Sean Egan. In tabloid eyes, he was the brave undercover cop, eager to avenge the long-ago murder of his brother, whose only crime was getting in too deep, but who'd redeemed himself by ridding the world of a sadistic killer.

Nobody, therefore, wanted to be the person to charge him with anything, even though the CPS could probably have created a file against him longer than the Bible.

"Did they ever find the missing footage that Kent took of Gore killing Róisin O'Neill?" he asked.

Tina shook her head. "It sounds like Kent only kept the one copy, and that was the one that was destroyed."

"And you think Tommy killed her father as well?"

"He must have. The car he was using, the one that led me to him and you, was filmed in Róisin's father's cul-de-sac on the night he died. It's too much of a coincidence for it not to be related."

"But why kill him? Particularly then."

It was a question that Tina had been thinking about a lot. "Gore must have been concerned that Róisin had told her father about their relationship. That wasn't a problem while her murder was being treated as one of the Night Creeper's. But when Kent was arrested in possession of information that implicated Gore in her murder, they must have decided it was best to get her father out of the way." She shrugged. "I think it was just a case of damage limitation."

Egan sighed. "Jesus. He didn't care whom he killed, did he? But I still don't understand who was organizing all this. Tommy said he was working for someone called Alpha."

"We think he was referring to Paul Wise, a gangster and thug based out of Northern Cyprus. He initiated everything on behalf of Anthony Gore—not that he got anywhere near the action himself. He used Tommy and Wolfe's gang for that."

A number of newspapers had mentioned the possibility of a shadowy businessman linked to Anthony Gore who may have helped him in his cover-up, but no one had dared accuse Wise by name, because the evidence against him was still so scant. Tina knew he'd be feeling the heat of his involvement, now that things had blown up so spectacularly, but it wasn't enough for her. She still wanted justice.

Egan frowned. "And what's going to happen to him? Is he going to get off scot-free?"

"No," said Tina firmly. "Paul Wise's days are numbered, and I've got the evidence that's going to make sure of that. I taped our interview with Anthony Gore, the one in which he confesses his role in the whole thing, and it implicates Wise completely."

"I didn't read anything about that in the papers."

"The papers don't know about it. Yet. Neither do any of my colleagues. I wanted to make sure it didn't conveniently disappear. Paul Wise has got contacts everywhere, and if any-one's capable of getting rid of evidence, he is."

"Would it be admissible in court, with Anthony Gore dead?"

Tina shrugged. "I don't know, but I've got a meeting with a journalist from the *Guardian* tomorrow—someone I've checked out, who's squeaky clean—and I'm going to give him the tape on the proviso he publishes it. If that happens, I think the CPS, the police, the government, all of them, will have no choice but to push to get Wise back from Cyprus to face charges."

"Won't he sue?"

"On what grounds? It's a taped confession from a government minister. He could sue Gore's estate, I suppose, but I can't see that he'll take on the paper. My journalist source doesn't seem too worried about it anyway."

Egan gave her an admiring look. "Jesus, you don't mess around, do you? I'm glad I'm not on the wrong side of you."

"Paul Wise has done me a lot of harm over the years. I just hope I get a chance to tell him face to face about my part in his downfall."

"I get the feeling you will."

"We'll see," she said, and stood up. "I'd better get going. Enjoy the booze and the choccies."

There was an awkward moment when Tina wasn't sure whether she should shake his hand, peck his cheek, or simply keep a reserved distance. She finally settled for the peck on the cheek, but wasn't entirely surprised when one of his arms encircled her waist.

"Will I see you again, Tina Boyd?" he whispered in her ear.

Egan was a good-looking guy, the kind it would be far too easy to fall for. And perhaps she would have, too, but her attention was still focused on another man.

"You never know," she answered, and gently moved away.

When she was back outside the hospital, she lit a cigarette and walked down Gower Street in the direction of Tottenham Court Road. The sun was shining and it was a beautiful day. In truth, she didn't know if what she was about to do with Gore's confession tape would finally bring Wise down, and releasing it to the media when she'd previously denied knowledge of its existence would certainly scupper any chances of her resuming her career, but even so, she was smiling as she went down the steps into Tottenham Court Road tube station.

Because she knew that she was finally becoming a real thorn in Wise's side.

Fifty-eight

It was evening and I was lying in my hospital bed feeling sick, having eaten all the chocolates Tina Boyd brought me, and wondering if she'd say yes if I asked her out for a date, when there was a knock on the door. A second later, the bald, cadaverous figure of Captain Bob appeared. He was dressed in a V-neck angora sweater and sensible slacks, as if he'd just come back from a game of golf, which he probably had.

"My God, you look different," he said, approaching the bed and putting out a bony hand, which I shook reluctantly. "What have you done to your hair?"

The last time I'd seen him it was short and light brown, but for the Wolfe infiltration I'd dyed it black, grown it long, and added a pair of mutton-chop sideburns which if they'd been a couple of inches longer would have constituted an Amish beard. "A man should always be adventurous with his hair, although I guess you've probably forgotten that. Anyway, thanks for coming to check up on me, sir. I've only been here nine days."

"I've been trying to contain the fall-out from your shenanigans," he answered gruffly, taking a seat. I noticed that he hadn't brought a gift, or even a card, but then Captain Bob had never been known for his generosity of spirit. "What were you thinking about, Sean?" he asked, his cut-glass accent heavy with exasperation.

"You know what I was thinking about. I was trying to get justice for my brother."

"Revenge, you mean, because there was nothing just about what you did."

"If you've come here to lecture me, sir, then you're wasting your breath."

"I haven't. I came here to see how you were. And to tell you that I've spoken up on your behalf to the officers investigating this sorry affair. I'm hopeful that they're not going to press charges, but I have to be honest, Sean. Your career's over."

"I gathered that." I'd always known that this was inevitable, yet I was still taken aback by the finality of his announcement.

"I'm sorry," he said, trying hard to sound like he meant it. "There's something else as well. I've been asked to come here to request your resignation from the force. We'll accept it on the grounds of stress, and you'll keep your full pension rights. I can promise you it'll be a lot easier that way." His tone was polite, sympathetic even, but there was no mistaking the threat behind the words. They wanted to be rid of me, and would do whatever it took.

"What's the alternative?"

"That it could get messy."

Sections of the media might have been portraying me as a hero, but I didn't think that would stop the bosses in their quest. I was an embarrassment, and I had to go. I could have fought on, but the last few weeks had taken their toll on me, and I'd done what I'd set out to do. Now was the time to withdraw from the battlefield.

"OK, then," I said. "I resign, if that's what you want."

"I don't want," he answered, "but you've left us with no choice. You kidnapped a high-profile suspect from police custody, and killed him before he'd even got anywhere near a court."

"I also helped break open a major case that led to the unmasking of a corrupt politician," I snapped back, stung by his criticism. "And there's more to come as well. Paul Wise, the gangster who was behind all this, is going to get exposed as well."

Captain Bob narrowed his eyes. "How do you know?"

"Tina Boyd's got a tape of Anthony Gore's confession in which he mentions Wise."

As soon as I said this, I regretted it. The last person I needed to tell was an establishment man like Captain Bob.

"I thought there was no tape," he said. "That's what she told her boss."

I shrugged. "I don't know. Maybe I got it wrong."

He gave me a look that said he didn't believe that for one minute, but chose not to pursue it further. Instead, after a few seconds of tense silence, he got to his feet and said he had to go. "You were an excellent operative, Sean, and I enjoyed working with you. You'll be missed, but you're doing the right thing." He gave my hand a cursory shake, wished me luck, then hurried out of the room as if he was being pursued by a bad smell.

I wondered if I'd now landed Tina in a big pile of trouble. I had little doubt that he'd report what he'd found out to his superiors, and that they'd try to get her to hand over the footage. I needed to let her know that she might be getting a visit so that she could at least take appropriate action. Unfortunately, I didn't have a number for her.

I was still very tired, and, despite feeling guilty about not trying to make contact, I drifted off into a restless sleep.

Something jolted me awake. Something that was bothering me. But I couldn't put my finger on what it was.

The digital clock on the wall said it was 9:53 P.M., and I slowly clambered out of bed. I was feeling a lot better, and the consensus among the doctors was that I was making a remarkable recovery. My right leg felt very stiff where I'd taken the bullet, but I could walk on it. I put on my dressing gown, grabbed my crutches, and went hunting for a payphone. I owed Tina. She'd done as much to save my life as I had hers. If she hadn't turned up at the warehouse when she did, there was no doubt about it, I would have bled to death.

Halfway down the corridor, I stopped.

Dead.

I put a hand against the wall to steady myself, because I suddenly remembered something that Tommy had said in the warehouse during those few minutes I'd questioned him at gunpoint.

And in a sudden rush, I realized what it was that was bothering me.

And how much danger Tina Boyd was now in.

Fifty-nine

Alpha looked down at the Glock 34, with 9mm silencer attached, in his hand. It was a wicked-looking thing that had been supplied to him three years earlier for use in case of emergencies, and as far as he was aware it was untraceable. The current situation was definitely an emergency, but Alpha still had no desire to use the gun. He wasn't a killer, and never had been. He'd always considered his role within Paul Wise's secretive organization to be nothing more than an information resource, helping Wise to run his business more smoothly by providing details of police operations against the various illegal arms of his business. But increasingly he was being called upon to perform far more extreme tasks, including the mutilation of a dead woman with a hammer in order to cover up the crime of Wise's most senior establishment contact.

And now this.

Alpha's instructions, delivered by Wise himself in his phone call, were simple and uncompromising. Get the tape that Tina Boyd made of Anthony Gore's confession. Make sure there were no further copies. And then kill her. Wise's tone had been angry and vindictive when he gave this last instruction. It seemed her actions had clearly riled him, as was proved by the price he was willing to pay for her death: a hundred and fifty thousand pounds, paid into Alpha's Pana-manian bank account within the hour.

Alpha knew he had no choice. He'd wanted to get out of Wise's employ for a long time now, but it didn't work like that. Wise had made it known to him that he had enough evidence of Alpha's involvement in his operations to ruin him if he so chose.

The job had to be done, and it had to be done now.

Taking a deep breath, Robin Samuel-Smith, better known as Captain Bob to his colleagues in CO10, removed the silencer from the Glock, placed both items in the concealed shoulder holster beneath his raincoat, and walked out of the Pimlico apartment that Paul Wise's blood money had done so much to pay for.

Sixty

I phoned my old colleague at Holborn station, Simon Tilley, from one of a bank of payphones near the hospital reception, and got him to give me Tina's address and phone numbers. Tilley had already visited me twice in hospital, so thankfully he didn't want to talk about my experiences, having heard it all already, but he did seem very interested in knowing why I wanted to contact Tina, assuming it was for romantic reasons. I almost told him about my fears, but I had the feeling he'd think I was certifiable. Instead, I cut him short, telling him I'd call him back in the next couple of days.

I still wasn't entirely sure myself about my theory. It seemed inconceivable that Captain Bob, the man who'd been my boss for getting on for ten years, could be Alpha, the man who'd set this whole thing up.

Yet it fit. Tina thought that Alpha was Paul Wise, but he couldn't be. It had to be someone who knew enough about the police investigation into the Night Creeper to be able to make Róisin O'Neill's murder look like his work. Although Bob wasn't a part of the inquiry, he was senior enough to have been privy to the details if he'd chosen to look.

I'd always known that Captain Bob had good contacts in the London underworld. After all, he'd played a major part in getting the contract Jason Slade had taken out on me lifted. And then there was Tommy's shock in the warehouse when I told him I was an undercover cop. "No way," he'd said. "I had you checked out. Thoroughly."

Was that because the person checking me out wasn't Wolfe at all, or Haddock, but a senior handler of undercover officers in CO10, someone whose word could be relied upon—someone like Captain Bob?

The thing was, because the Wolfe infiltration had been an unofficial job, I'd done everything possible to make sure my bosses didn't find out about it. I'd used an old ID from when I was temporarily seconded to SOCA a couple of years earlier, and because SOCA was a wholly separate organization from the Met, Bob wouldn't have been able to tell that it was an undercover ID. Also, I'd changed my appearance hugely for the job. Not just by growing my hair and adding big sideburns, but also by putting on more than fifteen pounds in weight. It was possible that if Bob had been given a photo to look at, and it wasn't a particularly good shot, he wouldn't have recognized me.

Having someone like Bob looking out for them would explain why Wolfe and his crew had always remained several steps ahead of law enforcement. And I suspected that if the police dug deeper into their activities, they'd find that the man they bought their drugs from was Paul Wise, one of whose central activities was drug smuggling.

And then there was the way Bob had hurried out of the room when I mentioned the tape.

It all fit. But it was still just a theory, and one that was so vague and lacking in evidence that it would be laughed out of a police incident room, let alone a court. A part of me wondered whether I was reading too much into it, that everything that had happened over the past days had made me paranoid. It was difficult to believe that my boss was protecting the men he knew were my brother's killers. Yet there are many cases in this world of men doing terrible things in the pursuit of money, and perhaps Captain Bob, a man for whom the term "self-interest" might have been invented, was one of them.

I tried Tina's landline. There was no answer, so I left a message, asking her to meet me at my flat and telling her it was urgent. I then tried her mobile, with the same result, and left the same message.

I stepped away from the bank of phones. I had no idea if she was home or not, or whether she was in real and immediate danger, but I wasn't going to be able to rest until I'd got hold of her, and if I couldn't do it by phone, I was going to have to turn up in person.

And do what? Stand guard over her, an invalid with a bad leg who'd just discharged himself from hospital, until she handed over the tape to the journalist?

In truth, I wasn't sure what the hell I'd do, but I had to do something, so I limped back to my room, wincing against the continued stiffness in my leg. I had a clean set of clothes I'd got Simon Tilley to bring from home when he'd visited, and I changed into them, careful not to dislodge the bandages that still covered most of my stomach area. I was a long way from fighting strength but, incredibly, neither of the bullets I'd been hit with had damaged any vital organs, and my injuries were healing well, stiff leg aside. In fact, my ribs, two of which had been fractured, had been giving me far more pain, and they ached now as I moved around the room.

The clock on the wall said 10:14. An hour at least, probably more, since Captain Bob had left in such a hurry.

I hurried out the door, hoping I wasn't too late.

Sixty-one

Tina Boyd was allowing herself to float gently in a mildly drunken haze, largely ignoring the documentary on the TV.

She was bored and restless, wanting to get the meeting with Nick Penny, the *Guardian* journalist, over and done with so that she could wrap this whole thing up and finally put her nemesis in the spotlight.

It had taken her days of thinking to work out what was the best thing to do with the Anthony Gore confession tape. At one point she'd seriously considered handing it over to Mike Bolt to deal with, knowing that he would never cover anything up. But, though she trusted him totally, she'd decided against it. He'd already done her enough favors, and as a result had found himself in plenty of trouble of his own. Far better to give it to an experienced investigative journalist like Penny, who specialized in sniffing out big stories, and who had a strong anti-establishment background. She knew it would mean the end of her career, as there was no way she could avoid the tape being traced back to her, but frankly, at that moment in time, she was past caring.

Tina was currently suspended on full pay, but she wasn't going to be hanging around the flat for much longer. The days were too long and empty, the opportunities to drink too many. No, as soon as Penny made the contents of the tape public, she'd take a holiday—somewhere warm, exotic, and a long way away—and kick the booze for good.

She yawned and picked up the empty wine bottle, wondering whether to open another, just for a quick nightcap. It was crap stuff, but drinkable, at least. But when she got to her feet, her head spun and her vision blurred for a couple of seconds, which meant it was definitely time for bed.

She tottered off down the hallway in the direction of her bedroom before realizing she hadn't turned off the TV.

But as she turned back around, she heard the lock on the apartment's front door click loudly as it was turned. Then, as she watched, wondering if she was imagining things, the door slowly began to open.

For a moment, Tina froze, unsure what to do, her thought processes slowed by the booze. But the door kept opening inch by inch, and then a gloved hand appeared around it, finally jolting her into action.

Moving as silently as possible in her stockinged feet, she darted into her bedroom. The light was on from earlier and she looked around frantically for her mobile, but couldn't see it. Nor could she remember where the hell she'd had it last, though she thought it might be back in the lounge. She vaguely remembered hearing it ring earlier, and ignoring it, because she didn't want to be bothered.

She heard the living-room door being opened, the sound of the TV growing louder. Someone was searching her flat, looking for her. Even in her befuddled state, she knew it had to have something to do with the tape, although how Paul Wise had found out about it was anyone's guess.

There was no time to think about that now. The most important thing was self-preservation.

She crossed the bedroom floor and opened the old wooden wardrobe that had been here when she bought the apartment. It creaked loudly, and Tina had to resist the bizarre desire to laugh out loud, because as she stepped inside, pushing the coats and suits out of the way and shutting the door behind her, the whole thing reminded her of games of hide and seek at childhood parties.

And then, as she heard footfalls moving stealthily down the hall in the direction of the bedroom, the fear set in again. She pushed through the coats in front of her, burrowing as far back inside as she could, desperately trying to focus on not making a noise.

His footfalls came steadily closer, and the floorboard just inside her bedroom door creaked.

He was in the room.

She held her breath, feeling herself wobbling, trying not to lean too hard against the back of the wardrobe.

The room was silent as she waited, no longer able to hear the intruder. Had he gone?

Then her foot slipped, knocking into a pair of shoes with an audible clack, and Tina froze, clenching her teeth, cursing herself for letting her guard down like this.

The wardrobe door flew open and the coats were yanked aside in one angry movement.

For half a second, Tina stood there face to face with a man in an ill-fitting balaclava and a long raincoat who was holding a pistol with silencer in one gloved hand; then she leaped at him with an angry scream, going for his wrists in an effort to stop him from using the gun.

But the drink had made her movements awkward and uncoordinated and he stepped away easily, punching her in the back of the head as she stumbled past him. She put out a hand to head off a collision with the bedroom wall, before tumbling to the floor.

As she turned around, the gunman loomed over her. "The tape. Where is it? Tell me now." He hissed the words, clearly trying to disguise his voice. But the accent was educated, possibly upper class. There was an edge of fear in it, too, as if he genuinely didn't want to be in this position.

"I don't know what you're talking about," she said, enunciating her words carefully, strangely ashamed at having her private drunkenness exposed as she played for time.

"You know exactly what I'm talking about. We can do this the easy way or the hard way. If you tell me, I leave now. If you don't, I'll put a bullet in you and turn this place upside down until I find it. And I will find it."

Tina looked up at him, trying to work out whether he would actually let her go if she gave it to him. She was desperate not to hand it over and see her last chance of bringing Paul Wise to justice disappear, but she also knew that she didn't want to die.

He held the gun steady. "Last chance."

She swallowed, something stopping her from telling him, even though she knew she was taking a huge risk.

"Tell me," he snarled, and she thought she saw the first hint of doubt in his eyes.

But then he picked up a pillow from the bed, folded it in half, and pushed the end of the silencer against it, still pointing the gun at her. Now if he fired, the report would be close to inaudible. Not even the neighbors would hear through the paper-thin walls.

She was about to die in her own home, the last sanctuary she had from the violent world outside. Yet still she couldn't bring herself to speak.

The gunman took a step closer and leaned down toward her so that the pillow obscured her field of vision. "I'm not going to ask again," he whispered, a renewed determination in his voice. "Where is it?"

The buzzer to the apartment went as someone from outside the building called up, a long, uninterrupted noise, as if the caller was holding his hand down on it.

She had no idea who it was—she never had evening visitors—but it managed to distract the gunman, who momentarily looked away.

Which was when the drink took over and she launched herself upward at him with an angry yell, ignoring the way her head spun as she went for the gun.

Sixty-two

I was still pushing down on the buzzer to Tina's apartment on the fourth floor of the bland-looking apartment building when I heard a shot—a faint but unmistakable pop—and the sound of breaking glass.

Behind me, the taxi driver was already out of his cab. He'd been demanding that I pay the fourteen-pound fare—something I hadn't been able to do since I had no money—and he was getting steadily more irate as it became clear that the person I was visiting, and who I'd said would pay the bill, wasn't answering.

But now he stopped and looked up as pieces of glass landed on the ground. "What the hell was that?"

I hobbled back from the apartment entrance and looked where he was looking. The window that had been broken was on the fourth floor, confirming my worst fears.

Then I heard a second shot.

I rushed back to the entrance and began ringing the buzzers for the other apartments, desperate to get inside. "Help me get this door open," I shouted to the taxi driver, who was a big guy about my age. "The woman up there's in trouble."

He put up his hands. "Look, mate, I don't want to get involved."

"I'm a police officer, for Christ's sake! Sean Egan. You might have seen my name in the paper. The Creeper case. And up there is DI Tina Boyd, being attacked. Now help me get this bloody thing open! Now!"

"How?"

"Kick it!"

He looked worried, but to his credit came forward at a steady run and launched a kung fu kick at the door while I continued to press the other buzzers desperately.

The door shook but held. The taxi driver grunted in pain.

A woman came over the intercom. "Hello?"

"This is the police. Let me in."

"Show the warrant card to the camera."

"I haven't got time. Let me in."

"No."

The taxi driver did another flying kick and this time the door flew open and I hobbled inside on the crutches. I told him to dial 999 and pressed the button for the lift. It opened immediately, and I got inside and pressed for the fourth floor. The taxi driver made no move to follow me as the doors shut, the phone already to his ear.

I knew what I was doing was insane. I was unarmed, on crutches. I could offer Tina no protection whatsoever, and could easily get myself killed. But I owed her. This was my fault and I didn't know what the hell I'd do if I was too late and she was already dead.

The lift doors opened and I charged through them.

Apartment 4B was opposite me, and straight away I saw that the door was on the latch, but as I shoulder-barged it, with no obvious plan of action whatsoever, it only opened a few inches. The chain was across it. Somewhere further inside I could hear the sound of a struggle.

I cursed, hobbled backward, and charged it again. This time it flew open, and I stumbled inside, only just about keeping my balance, before starting off down the narrow hallway in the direction of the struggle.

Another shot rang out, followed by the loud bang of someone hitting the floor, and I heard Tina let out a short, sharp cry of pain.

I hobbled faster. "Police!" I screamed. "Drop your gun, Samuel-Smith! It's all over!"

As I reached the doorway, I saw him standing above Tina, who lay sprawled out on the floor, her eyes shut, moaning in pain. He was still wearing the same raincoat he'd had on earlier, except now he also had a balaclava covering his bald head, and a gun in his gloved hands.

He turned my way, lifting it up to fire, his eyes frowning behind the mask.

Without hesitating, I threw one of the crutches straight at him, and as he knocked it aside with his gun hand, I threw myself forward, ignoring the searing pain in my leg, and slammed into him.

My momentum and his lack of preparedness drove the two of us across the room and we slammed into the window frame. I grabbed his gun hand by the wrist so that the weapon was pointing away from us, and with my free hand punched him hard in the face. He fell backward so that he was half hanging out of the open window, forty feet above the street below. I could see the taxi driver staring up at us, a look of shock on his face, the phone still to his ear as I punched Bob in the face again and again, leaning all my weight into him, ignoring the agonizing pain in my leg, a pure and terrible rage surging through me as I thought of all the treacherous things this man had done: the way he'd protected the men who'd murdered my brother; the way he'd mutilated an innocent woman to protect a discredited politician; the way he'd come here to murder Tina. I wanted to kill him now, to tear him to pieces. To keep punching him until he finally fell sprawling and lifeless onto the concrete like the piece of dirt he was.

The gun fell from his hand and clattered to the ground, but still I couldn't stop myself, enjoying the hot pain in my knuckles as I kept up my assault.

"Stop it, Sean. You'll kill him!"

It was Tina. On her feet now, her nose bleeding, her words slightly slurred, her hands grabbing at my arm.

"We need him alive. He's our only link to Wise."

And in that moment, the anger seemed to flood out of me, and I let go of Captain Bob and stumbled backward, before falling to the floor under the dead weight of my bad leg.

The last thing I saw before I shut my eyes and lost consciousness was Tina ripping the balaclava off the man who'd been my boss for ten years, revealing a face that was a bloody, defeated mess.

It was over. All of it.

Epilogue

Tina settled into her seat on the plane as it waited for takeoff, and relaxed with an orange juice. She'd been off the booze for close to a month now, and wasn't even missing it anymore, although she knew it was far too early to claim success. Alcohol has a way of sneaking back, unnoticed, into a person's life, but for the moment she was doing a good job of forgetting about it. The cigarettes were a different story. She'd managed to cut down from twenty a day to ten, but that was the extent of it. Still, she figured any normal person had to have some vices.

It was six weeks now since Robin Samuel-Smith's arrest for attempted murder, and he was currently awaiting trial in the top-security wing of Belmarsh Prison. Tina's own suspension had been lifted at the same time, it having been decided by the powers-that-be that punishing the police officer who'd done so much to break the whole case wouldn't sit too well in the court of public opinion.

However, Sean Egan, the man who'd possibly saved her life twice, and who'd also done so much to bring justice to those involved, had resigned his position. She'd only seen him once since that night in her apartment, when they'd met for coffee in a local Starbucks, and he'd told her he was planning on leaving the country for a while and going out to spend some time with cousins of his in New Zealand. He'd tried to get her out for a drink before he left, but somehow she didn't think it would work. When it came down to it, they were too similar. Both opinionated and impulsive, they'd probably end up killing each other if they ever got together. She'd told him that and he'd laughed and replied that she was probably right.

In the end, Tina had taken a leaf out of Egan's book and applied for a leave of unpaid absence to recuperate—something which had been agreed to immediately. She imagined that her bosses were secretly pleased at the fact that she was out of their hair for a while.

So here she was, on the way to Central America for a month-long backpacking trip in Costa Rica and Panama. She'd even treated herself to a business-class ticket, and though the cost had been frankly enormous and taken a great chunk out of her savings, she felt that she deserved it.

The stewardess came by with newspapers and she picked a copy of the *Times,* allowing herself a small smile as she saw the photograph on the front cover. It showed a short, balding man in an unfashionable cream-colored suit, with flabby cheeks and a pinched, shrew-like face, holding a hand up to shield himself from the flash of a camera. Paul Wise looked like a man under a lot of pressure, but then that was because he was. The government might have survived the scandal that had hit them in the shape of Anthony Gore, taking turns to get on camera and vilify every aspect of his life and career, knowing that he couldn't fight back, but for Paul Wise, it was a different story. The crimes he'd committed over so many years were finally coming back to haunt him, now that he seemed to have lost all his backers within the establishment. He'd been named as the man behind the Kent conspiracy, and had been named too as the Mr. Big behind a number of other serious crimes. Although he'd so far escaped extradition, and was fervently denying everything through his lawyers, as well as threatening legal action against those who'd named him, these threats and denials were being drowned out by the huge tsunami of pressure being aimed at the Northern Cyprus government, and at Turkey, which effectively controlled much of Northern Cyprus's foreign policy, to deport him back to the UK to face trial.

Wise had become a hunted man, hounded by a press that wasn't going to let him go, and Tina was confident that the hunt would soon be over and justice would prevail.

She put the paper down, no longer feeling the need to read the article, and stretched in the seat, experiencing a sense of real peace as she looked forward to the opportunity to take a break from the stale, painful life she'd been leading, and reinvigorate herself.

Before she left, Mike Bolt had called and asked if she was planning on coming back, or whether this was it, the beginning of a new life. It was a good question, and one she'd been thinking about a lot in the past few weeks. But the answer was always the same, and always would be, because in the end, there could be no other way.

"Of course I bloody am."

Acknowledgments

With thanks to my agent, Amanda Preston,
and my editor, Selina Walker, for being such
a huge help to me over the years

More Heart-pounding Thrillers from #1 Internationally Bestselling Author
SIMON KERNICK

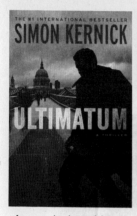

An explosion blasts through a café. Minutes later, a call from an unknown terror group warns that a far greater attack will be launched. In twelve hours.

A carefully orchestrated hostage takeover led by an ex-soldier going by the name of Fox brings chaos to a prominent London hotel. Who will survive?

A man is on the run with his two children from the police—who think he has murdered his missing wife—and the far more dangerous organization that probably did.